Talion Rule

Whitney Hill

Benu Media

6409 Fayetteville Rd

Ste 120 #155

Durham, NC 27713

(984) 244-0250

benumedia.com

ISBN (ebook): 979-8-9873785-1-9

ISBN (pbook): 979-8-9873785-2-6

Library of Congress Control Number: 2023903182

Cover Designer: Pintado (99Designs)

Editor: Jeni Chappelle (Jeni Chappelle Editorial)

Content Warnings

This book contains strong physical violence and gore, on-page death, swearing, slurs (not toward any real racial or ethnic group/identity), alcohol use, knife violence, the threat of sexual violence, mention of past abuse by a guardian, deadnaming, state-sanctioned violence, blood-drinking, and consensual on-page sex scenes.

For everyone who's enjoyed the love story I've been building in this series, and for everyone who's still looking for one of their own.

Chapter 1

Duke was avoiding me.

I wasn't sure at first. He'd visited readily enough when I'd asked him to look at the blood-magic ring the witches had gifted me for my birthday. Magical trinkets generally caught a djinni's attention. But after that? Crickets.

To be fair, it'd only been ten days or so since we'd last spoken, but that'd thrown his earlier absence into greater relief. I'd been busy trying to pretend my life could go back to normal after the Wild Hunt. Now it was apparent that was neither good nor desired, so I was picking up all the threads I'd dropped. Duke's bizarre, extended absence over the last few months and the walled-off callstone connection was one of those threads. It was long overdue, given how tenuous my link to the djinn was, which was why I was at the boathouse at Jordan Lake on a balmy March afternoon, working up the courage to break a promise to Duke and use our family tie to summon him here.

If I didn't need his head on straight to basically be a Watcher for me, I'd keep giving him space to work out whatever it was on his own. Or at least not be so invasive as to invoke a blood summoning. But Duke had become one of my more solid allies—when he was around—and I needed answers. Not as his little cousin, but as Arbiter of the Triangle and the Carolinas. And aside from all that, strengthening my connection with the djinn faction would get me a step closer to what I really wanted now that I'd decided I was going to rule the Carolinas and Virginia: to see my parents' vision of the Atlantis War truly ended and reconciled come to fruition.

Maybe if I achieved that, the Elemental Collective would actually talk to me.

A nudge in the bond from Troy preceded his mental whisper, cranky with the nearly full moon even in my head. *Dragging it out isn't going to make him less mad when he gets here.*

I turned and scowled at the tree line, where Troy was checking the security measures we'd set up here and renewing Aetheric protections.

You know I'm right.

That didn't mean I had to like it.

Duke and I had a rocky history. His fault, mostly. He'd been the one to pluck me from my dead mother's arms on the banks of the Cape Fear River. But he'd been an abusive guardian, and not all of it could be laid at Callista's feet, even if she'd been holding him with a geas. I was still navigating how I felt about our slowly evolving relationship, which I had thought was on the upswing after freeing Iaret and stopping the Wild Hunt. I got the feeling there were things he wasn't telling me though, and I hated being ignorant.

More than that, I was afraid those things might be about my parents and their forbidden djinni-elf love affair. Or maybe about the djinn at large, given they were still holding themselves apart and Duke had complained they were breaking his balls.

Part of me wanted to just let it rest. My parents were twenty-eight years dead now. I'd killed the people responsible, and with Troy, I was rebuilding my father's elven House. But every time I thought about them or fiddled with the gold-and-onyx prince's pendant hanging alongside the hematite callstone around my neck, I got a nudge.

The Sight. A djinn talent that was growing in me of late.

I had questions for Duke.

More to the point, I needed to know what Duke had needed to talk to Iaret about when he'd spoken about Dreamwalking and my mother having the talent. Maybe he'd been referring to the tricksters though?

Quit stalling, Arden. I have to get back home for more negotiations with Samarre and the Lyon elves.

I blew out a breath. "Fine."

Just to be fair—and safe—I tried one last time with the callstone. I hit the same wall I had nearly every other time I'd tried to reach Duke for the last few days.

Okay then.

From the leather backpack at my feet, I drew out a hand-sized box of carved black walnut and a bottle of Shiraz. The wine, I set on the ground, hoping Duke would either be happy to drink from the bottle or would take it with him rather than bitching about not having a glass. Opening the box, I plucked an old iron railroad nail out and scratched the eight-pointed star of the Goddess in one of the bare patches of dirt, then placed a cuneiform-etched bone in the center.

While I technically didn't need to draw blood to summon Duke—being cousins was enough of a blood tie—I had a feeling he was going to be pissed about my using a binding summoning ritual. Using my blood as an anchor to tighten the call would piss him off even more, but I was tired of playing hide-and-seek with him at such a critical time. And as Troy had pointed out, we didn't have the luxury of waiting and letting him decide when he wanted to show up.

I drew the elf-killer I'd taken to carrying again from its sheath on my thigh. The enchanted lead-and-silver blade was overkill for the little bit of blood I'd need to compel Duke, but it was my best option for defense if someone—an elven someone—tracked down this property and ambushed us here. The slice the knife made in the heel of my palm was so clean I didn't even feel its bite until my heartbeat throbbed.

Grimacing, I squeezed out a drop on each line of the star before carefully stepping out of it. "Nebuchadnezzar, come to me."

The bright scent of lemon zest suffused the clearing. The wind chose that moment to pick up, sending a cloud scudding across the sun and making Duke's entrance extra dramatic.

"What, by Ishtar's flaming tits, do you think you're doing?" Duke roared even before he was fully materialized.

"Hey, Duke. Sorry about the—"

"You're not sorry yet, but you bloody well will be when I'm through with you." The djinni finished materializing in the star, all smoke and lightning with carnelian eyes. "I was in the middle of something, you little bitch."

"Keep shouting at me and calling me names, and I'll leave you trapped in there until I can find a Goddess-damned bottle," I snapped.

"You dare threaten me with that? I swear, I—"

"Swear all you want. If you hadn't been *avoiding me* I could have spoken to you in a more civilized fashion. But you wanted to act like—"

"Avoiding you?" Duke spluttered, and his cloudy form expanded like a cat going fluffy. "I have no fucking need—"

"Then where have you been? I told you—"

A hand on my shoulder made me jump and whirl, already moving to free myself and punch the attacker.

Troy blocked me easily, despite keeping his attention on Duke. "Hello, Duke. I don't have time for the two of you to squabble. Let's get to the point."

Duke shifted to his human shape, the lithe, young Black man in a fancy suit. A hint of malicious amusement flashed in his dravite-colored eyes at my being snuck up on by my own bondmate.

"*You* don't have time," he drawled.

"That's right. I don't. We've all but declared war on the Richmond Houses." Troy bent to scoop up the bottle of wine. "Stick around and have a drink. I'll fill you in on the plans."

That caught Duke's attention more than anything else had. "War? Between elven Houses?" He chuckled. All his earlier outrage fled. "Little bird, why didn't you lead with that?"

I glared at him. "I was getting there."

"You were making threats about bottling."

"Enough," Troy snapped. "Duke, stay long enough to hear us out. Take this when you go. No harm or mischief on us or this place. Do you accept the terms?"

The djinni rolled his eyes. "Fine. You lot are so boring sometimes. You're lucky it's war, or I'd tell you to hang yourselves."

I sighed and crossed my arms, trying not to remember the bad old days of being under Callista's guardianship. Duke—and my other cousin, the now-dead Grimm—had had a big role in the bad times. Things had gotten better, but not always and not as much as I might like.

Troy nudged me and tilted his head toward the summoning star.

"Be free in this place," I muttered. For good measure, I reached out with a toe and scuffed one of my lines.

"That's more like it." Duke stepped quickly out of the star and accepted the bottle of wine from Troy. "Now. When last we spoke, little bird, you were simply dealing with that pompous ass Santiago and this Bureau for Supernatural Investigation—delightful assignment, by the way. Plum job."

"Glad you're enjoying yourself. I need an update on that situation as well, if you please."

Duke waved a hand like it wasn't important. "How much more trouble could you possibly have gotten into between then and now? It hasn't even been a fortnight."

I tightened my shields as another gust of wind buffeted us. Spring was on its way, and if last year was any indication, my Air powers would get a boost. Having to maintain so much control and focus was making me as cranky as Troy was at full moons, when his power ebbed. It hadn't been like this before I started practicing. Well, before I'd reached my greater potential as a primordial elemental.

I refocused on the topic at hand. "House Ead is working with the Sinners." For an elven High House to work with the mundanes was outrageous, and a sign of how much they hated me as an elemental and feared Troy as a king. They'd risk giving up Otherside's secrets to bring us down.

Frowning, Duke tilted his head. "So you declared war."

"We need a buffer between the Carolinas and Washington, DC."

"Again—so you declared war?" He grinned. "I'm not complaining. I'm just surprised at you. You're not usually quite *that* delightfully chaotic."

I couldn't help the defensive note in my voice. "We haven't officially declared it, and either way, it's not like I wanted it. What I want is to keep people safe. The feds went on live TV and basically said they want to hunt us down. I can't let that happen. I'm trying to protect my people as best I can."

"So you'll hunt Othersiders yourself."

Troy huffed an annoyed sigh. "Enough, Duke. Quit picking at her. We have an offer for you. And the rest of the djinn."

Duke's brows lifted. "Oh, now, this should be rich."

"Help us against the Richmond elves."

"Help you." Duke narrowed his eyes. "Ninlil got involved with House Solari, and look where it got her."

Troy met his gaze with a level one of his own—he had his mission, and it supported me in the end—but I grimaced at the mention of my mom.

Duke pounced on my uncertainty. "And now you want us as—what? Mercenaries?"

I hugged myself tighter at the reminder of my mother's choice and the fate it'd sealed for her. The muscles in my jaw hurt from how hard I was clenching it. Technically, the djinn and the elves were still at war over Atlantis, even if it was more of a cold war at this point. But the steps I'd taken to secure the Triangle from the Chapel Hill Conclave and stop their bounty hunts and attacks on me had dramatically reduced the number of local elves. Even with Omar Monteague bringing us the Darkwatch, between deaths and desertion, we had a fraction of the elven population we once had. I was working with Troy on reforming elven society to make it more appealing for our recruiters, but truth be told, I was still iffy on how many elves I felt comfortable having in the territory. Especially *new* elves, background checks be damned.

"The capacity is up to you," Troy said. "This is just the opener. I fully expect there to be counteroffers."

"Interesting." Duke's grin showed sharp black teeth. "You know the Djinn Council is going to put you over a barrel."

"I know." The grim note in Troy's voice carried through in the bond as well. "We're working on other alternatives."

Duke turned to me. "You're awfully quiet, little bird. Don't like this plan?"

"I don't like a lot of what I've had to do in the last two years. But I'm here, and the people who tried to hurt me are not." I gave him a pointed look. "I'm gonna keep doing what I have to do. I told you. I will keep the people who look to me safe."

"So I see." He gave me a peculiar look, one I couldn't read. "Very well. I will take your opener back to the Council."

"Thank you," Troy said.

Glad to have that part done, I said, "What's going on with the Bureau?"

"Much less than there would be without Iaret and me interfering." Duke grinned. "What did you do to Senator Wright, Arden?"

I glanced at Troy. "Um. We broke into his house and told him to back off."

Duke *tsk*ed. "Heavy-handed play. Absolutely no subtlety to you. Never has been."

"It was my play," Troy said.

"*That* surprises me." Duke studied Troy with eyes gone back to djinn carnelian. "Reckless. Messy. That's not like you. Did Arden finally find the stick up your ass? Or was it her hand there, guiding your actions?"

"It was a necessary risk," Troy snapped back. "I can't spend all my time looking over my shoulder for the US government's next attempt to kidnap my bondmate."

"Hmm." Again the strange look flashed across Duke's face.

I was tired of it. "What is going on, Duke? What aren't you saying?"

He stiffened. "Nothing. I'm just worried about this path you two seem to be heading down. Be careful. Both of you." Raising the bottle of wine, he offered a quick fist-to-heart salute. "Now if you'll excuse me—"

"Send a report, Duke. Please," I said. "Or check in more often. We need to know what this Bureau is doing."

"For now, not much of anything. You scared them to Erșetu and back, so they're re-evaluating their plans and doing research."

I didn't like the sound of that, but it was better than making plans to attack. "What kind of research?"

"Mostly hassling other agencies or organizations for all their weird cases that have anything to do with what looks like vampire, werewolf, or elf involvement. Not that they've quite figured out what elves are." He glanced at Troy. "Lucky for you, little king."

"Good," I said. "See that they don't, please. We're working on disrupting their communications with House Ead, and so far, they've been reluctant to share information about elves with the feds, but that could change."

"Understood. Now, if that's everything?"

I nodded. I still wanted to ask about Dreamwalking, but he and Troy were both anxious to get back to what they'd been doing. "Thank you, Duke. And whatever's going on...I need to know you'd tell me if it would impact the alliance. I can trust you that far, right?"

The flicker of what might have been a wince crossed Duke's face before he softened slightly.

"Yes, little bird." With a quick, unexpected chuck under my chin, he offered a lopsided, almost paternal smile before changing planes with a shimmer of Aether.

Drained by the whole exchange and the mental whiplash it gave me, I dropped to sit down on the ground right where I was then kept going and went all the way onto my back. Fortunately, it'd been dry lately.

Troy eased down to sit cross-legged beside me and took my hand, raising it to kiss my knuckles. "Thank you, my love. I know you were dreading that."

"Yeah." I stared up at the sky, alternating patches of blue and grey, wondering if we'd finally get spring rains. I could make it happen, of course, but I tried not to interfere with nature too much. "But hey. We need to explore all our options."

"Agreed. Even if I never thought the djinn would be an option for me as an elf."

"Desperate times," I murmured.

Troy gave me a few more minutes to settle before rising. "Come on. I know you like when I drive like hell, but we're pushing it to get home in time for this video call with Samarre."

I held back a sigh as I pushed myself to my feet. The only person I really had to blame for where I was now was myself. I'd chosen to keep my titles rather than abdicate and live the simple life I'd thought I'd wanted. That meant now I had to figure out how to fight—how to win—a war currently being fought on three fronts.

I just prayed the vampires, humans, and elves were all I had to worry about. But with the trickster gods potentially in the picture, I had a feeling those prayers wouldn't be answered in the way I hoped.

Chapter 2

While Troy negotiated with Samarre, the leader of a contingent of rogue European elves, for sanctuary in my territory, I threw myself into research in the bedroom.

I had three problems at the moment. First, a vampire turf war between the Master of New York and the Master of Miami, briefly centered on Raleigh but now shifted to Jacksonville, Florida. Less of a problem now than it had been a week ago, given Matthias was making progress against his former ally, but still something to keep an eye on.

Second, a betrayal of House Solari by House Ead, with the latter selling Otherside secrets to the new mundane federal agency that'd kidnapped me less than two weeks ago.

Third, the mundanes, in the guise of that new agency, local law enforcement, and ongoing tensions with anti-Otherside groups amidst waning support and "allyship fatigue" from pro-Otherside activists. Raleigh PD was still sore about Troy and me allegedly resisting arrest when they tried to take us in for defending Claret, and it was only the ongoing sabotage enacted by an allied gremlin that was giving us breathing room right now.

Those were just the external problems.

For myself, I had the additional challenge of figuring out what the hell a Dreamwalker was. Duke had changed the subject and refused to tell me more when he'd said I might have the talent. My Chancellor, former royal archivist Iago Luna, had turned up a grand total of two resources in the elven archives on the topic, and one of those was a single scroll fragment the size of my hand. Neither was very helpful. Maria's people had found nothing in her extensive library.

Whatever it meant to be a Dreamwalker, I was on my own figuring it out, until and unless I could get Duke to talk to me.

The bedroom door swung open.

I jumped as Troy filled the doorway, not having heard him end his call in the other room, and a smile flickered on his lips before it died.

"Didn't mean to startle you," he said. "We've reached an impasse. One I want to run past you."

"You're fine. I'm just trying to figure out this Dreamwalker shit. I have a feeling Duke knows something."

"Oh?" Troy came to the bed and slid into the space I made for him between me and the headboard. "Tell me."

I settled back against him, soothed by his nearness and physical touch in a way that still baffled me sometimes, even as I enjoyed the hell out of it. "You first. Either I lost track of time, or that was an unusually quick call."

"Bit of both, probably."

Schooling myself to patience was easier with him massaging my shoulders with slow, even movements while he ordered his thoughts. As tempting as it was to try following their path in the bond, I kept myself out of his head.

"They're making some pretty bold asks," he finally said. "Some, like positions of leadership in House Solari, are unreasonable."

I twisted out of his grip to stare at him. "Excuse me? They hid their true purpose for being here and asked for what?"

"Like I said. Bold but clearly unreasonable."

Somewhat mollified by our being on the same page, I turned back around and let him restart both the massage and the report.

He kissed the nape of my neck before continuing. "Other demands...I don't like them, but they make sense."

"Like?"

"Guaranteed employment."

"As what?"

"Anything that suits their skills. Likely Darkwatch or Ebon Guard. It adds to our defensive numbers, and having a job waiting helps with visas in the mundane system."

I turned that idea over in my mind, trying to set aside my bad past experiences with most unknown elves and see both the individuals and what they could bring to the table. "We need the people, but you don't like bringing them in from outside the territory. Especially not when they've already tried playing games with us."

Another kiss signaled his agreement. "That and I don't want to put you in a position where you don't completely trust your security."

Because I tended to go off on my own whims anyway, which was hard enough on people who knew me and who I trusted. I sighed. "I told you. I'm working on getting over it."

"I know, my love. I know."

I filled in the part he was holding back. "But our timeline is faster than my healing."

The bond twisted with the mental and metaphysical equivalent of a grimace.

Taking his hands in both of mine, I drew them from their massage work and kissed the knuckles before pulling his arms around me in an embrace. "Put the House first on this."

"You're sure?"

"I'm sure deciding to remain as High Queen means I need to make more decisions for the good of the House that I may not personally like. I have to move forward eventually. If it has to be now, then it's now. I won't stand in your way on this."

Troy's embrace tightened. "Thank you. That gives me more room to maneuver."

I leaned to kiss his arm and was rewarded with a nibble on my neck that sent shivers over me, even though he'd only used the blunt, humanoid primary teeth and not the sharp secondary set hidden in his gums.

"Before you get too distracted," he said, "talk me through your research."

"There isn't much of anything." I flicked the cover on the one book Iago had couriered over. "Dreamwalking seems to be purely a djinn talent. I'd been hoping the Lunas would have something on it—it seems most aligned with auratic Aether—but Iago had next to nothing."

"That had to frustrate him. Both as a Luna and as an archivist."

"Probably." I didn't see Iago as much as I'd like these days. My Chancellor was busy making sure I had everything I could possibly need resource-wise and busied himself working on the theoretical implications of the bond between me and Troy out of personal interest on the few days he took off. "But Troy, Duke knows something. I know he does."

He hummed, a considering sound. "That doesn't sound like the Sight talking."

"It's not. It's being raised by the asshole from the age of seven to twenty-five."

Troy held his tongue.

Which was fine because I had plenty more to say. "He's been dodging me for *months*. And it's not over stupid shit like the Council. Or not all that anyway. It can't be."

"Cariñamí, you might be the only one who considers the business of the Djinn Council 'stupid shit.' They don't meet often, as far as we know. If they're bothering to stir themselves now, it's a big deal."

"It's irrelevant," I insisted. "Because this is *personal*. Duke knows something, and given that we're cousins, it has to be about my mom."

Troy's arms tightened around me again. "Your mom." He made the same connection I had. "And your dad?"

"Yes." I hesitated, wrestling with whether I should speak aloud what I'd been thinking about for the last few days. Fuck it. Brutal honesty was our policy. "You remember what you said about Fate converging on me?"

"Mm-hm."

"You're part of it. You have to be."

Troy froze.

"Think about it. The Lyon elves just happen to know *your* dad's whereabouts right as I start learning about Dreamwalking? And there are no elven sources for Dreamwalking, just broken copies of djinn texts? A year and a half after two mortal fucking enemies fall in love for the second time in a few decades and right as I get hints that the trickster gods are going to have their turn at reshaping the world?"

I'd thought Troy had been still before, but now he was utterly motionless. In the bond, thoughts raced too quickly for me to track.

"Damn." The bond wrenched as he forced his mind out of whatever track it'd gone down, and he shifted to start kneading my shoulders again. "Fine. So what do you want to do?"

"I don't know. We don't have enough information. About Dreamwalking, the tricksters, any of it."

He sighed, an annoyed huff that stirred the curls that'd come loose from the hair piled in a bun on top of my head. "Which means focusing on what we do know how to handle. Lyon and Richmond. And wooing the djinn. Even if Duke doesn't really want to clue us in."

"Exactly."

"Okay."

I groaned as his thumb pushed into a knot under my shoulder blade. That was always the spot.

He barely noticed. The bond flickered with the speed of his thoughts. "On that front, the scouts we left in Virginia have reported in. House Bedoe is still minding their own business and pulling their people in from external assignments. But House Hilith has joined Ead in making trips to Washington, DC."

I snarled. "What, as special consultants?"

"Seems that way."

Troy and I had anticipated that as a possible outcome when we'd planned the mission to the home of Senator Wright, the head of the Committee for Supernatural Affairs and the political sponsor for the Bureau for Supernatural Investigation. Given the captain of House Ead's guard, Sixtus, had flat-out told the senator's aide that "Solari" meant "terrorist" and that both Troy and I were Solaris, it was going to be difficult to get them to see our little visit in any positive light.

Even if they'd kidnapped me first and, in my opinion, had it coming. And even if I had body cam footage of the entire event, proving all we'd done was talk. I supposedly had security clearance to hear about updates from the Supernatural Affairs committee, but I had yet to be informed of anything or hear a response to my polite inquiry.

"Fuck," I muttered.

"Agreed."

"Where are we with Raleigh PD?"

"I need to check in with Rice on the final details for the press conference announcing the alliance's role in finding Santiago's rogues and bringing them to justice."

The master vampire of Miami had allied with Matthias, Master of New York City, to attack the mundane population of Raleigh in an effort to undermine Maria. We'd outmaneuvered Santiago by getting Matthias to switch sides, but getting the space to do that had meant allowing law enforcement and government officials in Raleigh to declare a curfew due to a supernatural threat. Which put us in a really shitty position, given the increasing activity and hostility of the Sinners and the local chapter of the human supremacist Sons of Seth.

"Hmm." I rapped my fingers on my thigh. "I don't like how long it's taking. That was wrapped up a week ago."

Malicious delight rolled through the bond. "I'd be happy to express your displeasure to Detective Rice. In person."

I couldn't help grinning at the mismatch between the bond and Troy's neutral tone. I'd never understood how the man managed to control the external expression of his internal landscape so thoroughly. "Let's try a call first, cariñomí. We've been the aggressors kind of a lot lately."

Troy's low, stubborn growl said they had it coming, but he didn't argue with me.

Hopefully, Rice would follow his example, but I doubted he would.

I indulged in allowing Troy to work the last few knots out of my shoulders as I tried to figure out what our best next move was. There wasn't much we could do about the vampires just now. Troy had spoken to the Lyon elves trying to break away from their High Queen and find sanctuary here in the Triangle. We'd spoken to Duke.

That left figuring out what to do about my territory expansion needs and how to get the Richmond elves to play nice. Dealing with them might help with the feds, but this arrangement with Raleigh PD was the nearer and more urgent concern.

I twisted to kiss Troy's jawline with a languid brush of my lips. "Let's go figure out next steps. We need this follow-up press conference to happen sooner rather than later, or the feds are going to have too much leverage on us. Senator Wright was acting like the curfew was damning evidence that Othersiders are all out of control, rather than trying to help with a few opportunistic assholes."

We moved to the kitchen. Easier to focus on work when the bed wasn't calling.

My phone rang as I was making a quick cup of chamomile tea for me and a coffee for Troy, thinking we could both use something fortifying to deal with Detective Rice. The ringtone wasn't the Bad Boys song I'd set for all the local police stations, but the Imperial March I'd picked for calls from blocked numbers. Which, lately, were all from a certain US Senator.

Troy snorted and looked up from the pocket-sized device he was fiddling with. "Seriously?"

I shrugged as I poured his black coffee into the black mug that read, "I'm smiling on the inside" with a frowny face on the reverse and brought it to him.

The flat look he gave me on seeing which mug I'd given him made the point as he took it before waking up his laptop.

I managed to keep a serious face for all of a second before I cracked. "You can always throw it next time you're mad."

"I have the jamming program running. Answer your damn phone." His face slipped into a hint of a smile though, which he hid behind the mug as he blew on the coffee.

Tempting as it was to ignore the call and focus on Detective Rice, I answered it as I slid into the chair beside Troy, where he could hear without me putting the call on speaker. "Finch."

"Ms. Finch. Or should I say Solari?"

"Senator Wright." My heart thudded, and I wasn't sure if it was apprehension for who I was dealing with or hunger for the hunt. "It's been a minute. I trust your wife and children are well?"

The senator hesitated. Then, in a hard-bitten tone, he said, "Don't you ever bring up my family again."

I glanced at Troy to find his brows lifted and his mouth pursed, his expression indicating his opinion that the senator was overreacting as much as the bond did.

Nice to see him emoting rather than just getting it through the bond. I cupped his cheek affectionately as I answered the senator. "Of course. Simple courtesies aside, what can I do for you?"

After a long pause, Wright sighed. "As much as I hate to say this, I think we got off on the wrong foot, Ms. Finch. Or Solari. Or whatever your name is."

"Finch will do," I said.

"And your...partner?"

I glanced at Troy to find his expression gone blank again. "Don't worry about him. I'm your contact."

"Be that as it may, I have my concerns about Mr. Monteague. Part of why I'm calling, Ms. Finch."

Chapter 3

That drew a superior sneer from Troy, rather than the usual stiffening at the use of his birth House rather than mine. Curious. He'd been growing out of the beaten-down box he'd been shoved into under the old queens and had surprised me recently with his proposal to hunt down the senator and deliver a firm message. But even two weeks ago, he'd been triggered by the use of his birth House. Maybe he'd decided he'd had enough?

"Oh?" I said to keep Wright talking.

"We spoke to the Raleigh police. They didn't sound happy about it, but they did confirm that you orchestrated the...let's call it firm resolution to the vampire situation there and, in the process, demonstrated authority over both the vampire Maria and Mr. Monteague."

Outright amusement flashed over Troy's face before he tamped it down to neutrality with just the hint of smugness to it.

Very curious. Despite his little vendetta with Detective Rice, he hadn't liked the idea of being someone's monster before. On the contrary. It'd sent him to a negative headspace previously. Allegra had mentioned something similar once over drinks: be mindful of how I used him because what he'd allow from me might stray into territory he otherwise wanted nothing to do with.

His reactions might just be the nearly full moon; elves preferred new moons, and the opposite phase sometimes had him in a weird mood. I made a mental note to suss out whether this was something good—a role he was stepping into because he saw a benefit to it—or something bad, like a backslide into something the queens had beaten into him. If it was simply that Troy was embracing everything that came with being King to my High Queen, fine. But he was too powerful for me not to have some idea of where his head was at.

He was also looking at me funny, and I realized I'd let the pause go on too long.

"Look, Senator, I played it straight with you. Influential people look to me to coordinate and resolve matters. Consider me a supernatural fixer." I hesitated before plowing forward. "Good card to have up your sleeve in an election year."

Troy straightened, blinking fast at the new consideration. *Take it slow,* he sent. *I don't have the resources to send with you chasing all over the Goddess-burning country.*

I squeezed his thigh in acknowledgment. "Consulting only, of course. From my home territory."

"That's right," Senator Wright said. "Turf wars."

"Times are changing," I said, tone neutral. "There's lots of opportunity there. For those who know how to leverage it and have the resources to do so."

Troy smirked. *And if I ever doubted you were raised by the djinn...*

I rolled my eyes. *Shut up. You think the same way.*

Fair. He gently pulled the hair tie free from my bun and set his fingers to massaging my scalp, a peace offering, given he knew I didn't like when elves snarked about djinn or vice versa.

I rested my head on his shoulder, accepting it.

The senator sat with what I'd said for a few more heartbeats. "This does open new considerations, Ms. Finch."

Something about that felt squicky and gross. Grimacing at what I might have gotten myself into, I said, "Great. Why don't you tell me what you called for now, and we can discuss the changing times at a later date."

"Certainly. We'd previously discussed security clearance for you to be read into confidential matters."

"Yes, I recall."

"I've secured that clearance, under certain conditions."

I sat up straight and pulled free of Troy, already seeing where this was going and annoyed as hell about it. "If those conditions involve snitching on Othersiders, you can forget it. All of it."

"Ms. Finch—"

"If the next words outta your mouth are 'be reasonable,' I'm afraid I'm gonna have to remind you what happened the last time you tried playing that hand with me. That is a hard no."

Another long silence. "I see. That's disappointing."

"I'm sure it is, but I've had to learn to live with other folks' disappointment. Yours is just another small drop in a very large bucket."

The senator wasn't easily deterred. "Ms. Finch, I need some way to trust you."

"You've already gotten it."

He spluttered. "You think threatening my home and family builds trust?"

"I think all of that still being intact after you had me drugged and kidnapped off the street builds trust. Certainly in my restraint and good intentions."

"And you wonder why more than half of America polls at some level of concern about supernaturals."

"Barely more than half." At Troy's urging, I'd started paying attention to the damn things. Measures of pro- and anti-Otherside sentiment were now part of standard political polls, alongside the president's approval ratings. "The ones who consider themselves the quiet majority are in fact rather fucking loud and probably not as numerous as they think themselves to be. And we're not gonna ignore the fact that a government agency attempted to *kidnap me*. You want to talk about trust? You start there."

"I can neither confirm nor deny—"

My frustration boiled over. "Oh, cut the shit."

The bond simmered with Troy's anger, and I was glad that at least this time he wasn't going to tell me to take it easy or be diplomatic. I was starting to hate that word.

I squeezed his thigh again, trying to ground myself. "I have it on very good authority that it was your Bureau for Supernatural Investigation who ordered the action. Might've been some contractors who carried it out, but I know the source. For someone who claims to want to have me as an ally, you are doing a shit-poor job of being one yourself. It's a two-way street."

Good authority being the cell phones I'd stolen when I broke free of the kidnappers' van. Not that I was going to tell the senator that. Let him wonder.

"Now, Ms. Finch—"

"No. The only words I want to hear from you are a sincere apology and your plan to make amends. *Then* we can talk about what you want from me. Other than snitching, of course."

Dark amusement bubbled up in the bond, and a smile flickered at the corner of Troy's mouth. Not a nice one. He knew all about making amends to me.

Wright spluttered. "Amends? Be serious."

"I am. Very." And I was also mentally noting that he was no longer denying the Sinners' involvement. "Call this a cultural crash course. When there is a trespass in Otherside, a debt is owed. Usually three times over. Treat others with respect and courtesy, or pay the price."

Or be strong enough that you could do whatever the hell you wanted, or clever enough not to get caught, but I wasn't going to say that. I didn't need the National Guard deployed to my house in a misguided and futile attempt to show strength or anything else.

Troy's mood sobered, presumably at the memory of his own past debts to me. I gave him a quick peck on the cheek, a reminder that it was over and done with.

"You came to my *home*," the senator said.

"After you came to mine and committed several egregious acts of violence against me and someone I was with. And, of course, after you practically commanded my appearance." I let my tone chill. "Queens are not commanded, Senator. Come correct next time. Or don't come at all. I do not have time for these political games."

I nearly put the phone down then, but decided to *try* being diplomatic.

After a pause long enough for me to get annoyed, Wright said. "Very well, Ms. Finch. I hear you."

"You hear me? Or you're listening?"

"I will take on board what you've said."

"I hope so. Because the way things are going, neither of us can afford this bullshit." Time to quit while I was ahead. "Now, if you'll excuse me, I have a territory to manage. I look forward to our next conversation."

"Of course. God bless."

I rolled my eyes and hung up, recognizing sarcasm when I heard it and out of patience to play the game. "Fucking shitshow. This is going to be a mess, Troy."

"Agreed. You don't fit the mold of power for him. And he thinks it's his game to win to begin with." He leaned in and nibbled on my neck in a thoroughly distracting fashion. "But it's hot when you assert yourself."

"I thought I was supposed to be diplomatic."

"You were. Perfect balance."

Warmth spread through me even as I snorted. "What I'm hearing is I'm gonna get ravished much more often then, because I'm fucking over being disrespected."

His teeth pinched as heat flickered through the bond.

I gasped. "We have shit to do today."

With a frustrated growl, he pulled away. "The one part of power I don't enjoy. When playing politics gets in the way of seducing you."

I very nearly gave in, but we still had to call Detective Rice. Or rather, Troy did. Etain was due shortly as well to discuss restarting Callista's Watcher network, which I'd been part of until negotiating for my release.

The wards pinged against my aura, and the sound of a car coming up the drive pulled both my and Troy's attention.

His tension eased almost immediately, apparently recognizing the sound of the engine. "Let me know what happens with Etain."

"Will do." I got up and ducked outside. Etain and I had started doing walking meetings. As Captain of the Ebon Guard, she'd increasingly found herself behind a desk, and I simply didn't have Troy's dedication to an exercise routine beyond our combat practice.

Outside, the temperature was plunging and the wind was picking up. As Etain parked, I closed my eyes and reached for the coming storm, shivering with pleasure at its wildness. This was gonna be a bad one. I might worry about how the arrival of spring would boost my natal Air powers—and my control over them, never quite as strong as my raw power—but deep down, I reveled in the taste of the wind and rain and lightning.

I could be the storm as easily as tame it. Part of me wanted to let go.

"Ma'am?"

With a sharp inhale, I came back to myself to find Etain standing at a parade rest and Troy shielding and walled like his life depended on it. Whoops.

Etain's eyes were more slate than their usual pewter in the porch light but still sharp as they flicked over me.

"I'm good," I said. "Storm coming. A bad one. An hour, maybe two."

She nodded and relaxed, which amused me. My acting like an elemental was fine with her, no matter how strange it looked to anyone who couldn't read the elements or how unsettling my power signature was when I stopped bothering to tamp it down. It was one of the reasons I liked Etain. Some of the elf-blooded accepted me as queen because I offered a better choice than life under the other queens, but they still smelled of fear if I did anything with elemental power. Etain just took it as natural and normal. Always had, even if she hadn't been one of the original Ebon Guard.

I tipped my head toward the track forming at the edge of my yard, outside my fence. "Shall we?"

She fell in alongside me. "We're definitely spread too thin with the Ebon Guard to use elves or half-elves as Watchers, ma'am."

"Understandable. What are your recommendations for alternatives?"

As always when asked for input, Etain didn't quite puff up, but she definitely stood straighter. Pride in what she'd earned but not ego. "The fae, if we can get them. Their wild magic makes it difficult for anyone trying to keep tabs on us to establish patterns. But given how hard it's been to reach King Rí since the Wild Hunt, we might need to ask the weres."

I mulled that over as a whiff of sulfur announced the presence of Bás and Marú, the fae black dogs gifted to me. Gifted was a weird way to think about it—like all fae they were fully sentient, and they could shift to a secondary human form if pressed—but apparently they'd agreed to the arrangement and were loyal to me, not Rí.

Struck by insight, or maybe the Sight, I called to them. Both gytrash trotted out of the darkness under the trees, the inky blackness of their fur seeming to drink in the rest of the night and accentuating the glow of their eyes.

"How do y'all feel about taking on more responsibility?" I asked.

They tilted their shaggy heads.

"We need Watchers," I said. "People who can keep watch, investigate, or disrupt as needed. It'd take you away from here sometimes, but there might be more of a hunt in it for you."

Green-eyed Bás dipped her head and yipped. Marú was even more enthusiastic, his golden gaze bright as he barked. About as strong a confirmation as I'd get without them shifting to human form, which they hated and hadn't yet seen the need to do.

"Awesome. I appreciate it," I said. "Etain will evaluate where we can send you and come back. Sound good?"

They both yipped in what I took to be an affirmative before melting playfully back into the brush that preceded the tree-lined borders of my property, if pony-sized dogs with massive teeth and glowing eyes could look playful.

"First recruits," I said, turning back to Etain. "That work?"

"Yes, ma'am. I have a few situations I wouldn't mind having them sniff out."

"Good. See what Terrence, Ximena, and Vikki say for the rest. Make it clear their people don't have to out themselves. I stayed hidden as a Watcher for seven years before having to pull Callista's sway on Maria."

"That works."

We kept walking the edges of my property, debating who we could trust to take on a Watcher's responsibilities and spare from other work. The list was frustratingly short.

I blew out an annoyed breath. "We're going to have to recruit from the newcomers."

"I was afraid of that."

"Nothing for it. Matthias might have people in Jacksonville now, but who knows how long it'll take to end Santiago's threat? If we're at war with Santiago, the Richmond Houses, and various mundane government and law enforcement agencies, we can't afford not to ask. Carefully."

"Understood."

Despite my annoyance, I grinned at her tone. "Why do I feel like you already have a starter list?"

She smiled back. "Because I do."

"That's why you're Captain. Thanks, Etain. Anything else?"

Her lips pressed together, and she toyed with the end of the long auburn braid hanging over her shoulder.

"Etain?"

She sighed. "I haven't figured out if it's legit yet."

"But?"

"But it's big news if it is. House Bedoe might want to talk. *Might.*"

"Bedoe? In Richmond?"

Her tight nod was full of reluctance.

"Talk about what?"

"According to what we intercepted, a non-compete agreement."

I frowned. "The hell does that mean?"

"In House Sequoyah, it basically meant they wouldn't fuck with you if you didn't fuck with them. In other words, they're recognizing that Houses Ead and Hilith are heading down a road they don't agree with, but they're all still part of a conclave. That makes maneuvering difficult."

That confirmed my initial thought about Etain—that she'd been born to a scion of House Sequoyah before first Callista and then I had battered it into the ground. I briefly wondered how she'd been treated there, given what I'd learned about Leith Sequoyah and Lydia Desmarais, and if that was why she'd been so quick to accept an elemental queen.

Focus. This was big.

"Okay," I said. "So it's...a vote of no confidence?"

Her head bobbed. "Effectively, yes. They're still part of local government, just not aligned with the agenda of House Ead's High Queen. Enough so to possibly—very possibly—take action. Or at least prevent a consensus by refusing to take action against us, which should hypothetically block outright hostile action against us since the conclave would have to use House Guard contingents rather than locally loyal Darkwatch triads."

"Got it. Who knows?"

"Zadie Monteague. Her passive monitoring program flagged the comm, and she passed it directly to me after reviewing it."

"That's it?"

"Tight ship, ma'am."

Excitement thrilled through me, and I nodded. This might be the break I'd been hoping for. "Good work, Etain. You wanna come in and tell Troy?"

"I'll leave that to you, ma'am. I need to get back and see if we have any supporting intel."

Translation: Troy intimidated the shit outta her, even if she respected and generally trusted him as King, and she wanted an ironclad case before she presented it to him personally.

I was beginning to wonder how much more of his Darkwatch reputation I was unaware of and whether I needed to ask about it. I didn't push Etain though. Most of the local Otherside community was either intimidated by or politely wary of Troy, me, or both of us. We were the only ones left in the territory with power signatures, gained at an unusually young age, and we could join our magic in a way the rest had never seen before and didn't understand to become far more powerful than most could have imagined.

"All good. I'll talk to him. Let me know what you find out, okay?"

"Yes ma'am. Thank you."

I smiled as I clapped her on the shoulder then mounted the stairs to the house. At the top, I turned my face to the wind, dropped my shields, and indulged in a last taste of uncomplicated power as Etain left.

I had a feeling it'd be the last thing that wasn't complicated for a while.

Chapter 4

A hand cupped my jaw.

Gasping, I pulled away from the raging elements woven into the chord of the coming storm even as I pulled on Air and Fire.

Something stopped me from casting lightning.

Troy.

His nearness in the bond. His touch. His love and concern.

I blinked fast, panting as I came back to myself and swallowed down the surge of elemental magic. The earth rumbled to my senses as I poured power into it rather than into Troy.

"Toro ben?" he said softly.

The elvish words flowed over me like the wind, and I squeezed my eyes shut, trying to find my own words as I realized too late that, in opening myself to the storm, I'd sunk myself into its maelstrom pull. Power surged in me and kept growing, like I was a living battery.

"No." Words were hard while I was trying to contain the surge in power, but I forced myself to find more. "Not good. Storm."

"Okay, cariñamí. Okay. Come on inside."

If I moved now, half the Triangle might move with me, starting with the sky and going straight through to the ground and waters.

I shuddered, trying to find myself. "No."

Rather than fight me, Troy hesitated then shifted to stand beside me and lean on the porch rail.

The wind picked up again. Calling to me. Pulling at me. I could be the wind. I could ride it. Direct it. It could be mine like little else was.

"Not true," Troy murmured. "I'm yours."

I shook my head. Not denying him. Trying to clear my thoughts and pull in his. What he'd said was a truth. A safe one. A proven one.

But so was my magic. It'd kept me safe. Defeated my enemies.

The trees whipped and the wind howled as Air responded to my instincts. The big oak in the front yard creaked, and the poor little fig tree thrashed.

I shuddered as the weather front moved in fully and the initial strength of the storm crested and broke, dropping ice-cold rain dotted with hail on us.

Troy didn't move. Didn't try to force me to listen to him or go inside or anything at all. Just stayed at my side, crossing his arms and hunching a little against the freezing wetness, while I squeezed my eyes shut and tried to find my center.

This was so much worse than last year. That first spring after becoming a primordial had been distracting.

This was a full-on war with myself and my magic.

Help. I needed help.

I wrenched my arm away from its clench around my body and extended a hand.

Troy gripped it immediately, despite the crackle of lightning dancing over it. Trusting that our link would ground him against it. "I've got you. Breathe, cariñamí. Breathe."

I tried.

Tearing inhale. Exhale. Inhale again.

"Channel it. Disperse the storm."

I grabbed Troy's words like they were flotsam atop waves. Read the ebbs and flows of the storm front. Countered them.

Calmed the winds. Sent the energy to the eight compass points, an equal amount to each, rather than a crushing force where we were.

When I was done, I breathed in so hard it hurt deep in my lungs. My knees ached; I must have dropped to them. Hard. A piercing pain bit into my finger as my hand curled against the wood of the porch. A burst of Troy's Aether barely stopped me from throwing up from the greater pain thundering through my head, like the storm had relocated inside me rather than dispersing.

I let go of the elements, hoping it'd help.

It didn't. But it did signal to Troy that he could pick me up and get me out of the rain.

He might have damaged the door bulling through it the way he did and back-kicking it shut behind him. I caught a flicker of indecision as he glanced from the fireplace to the bathroom before he carried me to the bathroom and set me carefully on the floor next to the bathtub.

I sat shaking, teeth clattering, as he turned the taps. Water thundered into the tub, too loud, and I groaned, hunching tightly into myself and covering my ears.

The brush of his fingers on my forehead presaged another cool wash of Aether that soothed the jagged edges of my nerves.

"Oh, thank fuck." I slumped and finally caught the edges of controlled fear in the bond. "I'm okay."

"You're not," Troy snapped. Rough jerks shook me as he worked to strip wet clothes from me. "You're hypothermic. I'm using Aether to tell your nerves and brain that you're warm so you don't go into shock."

"Oh."

More Aether curling over me. I forced down the urge to resist it and dropped my shields and walls completely, letting him in.

"Good." He tugged my jeans off as I lifted my hips to help as much as I could, given shakes had set in. "Up we go."

Upward movement then down. Warm water. More like tepid, probably, but warmer than I was. Heaven, as far as I was concerned.

"At least you're conscious this time," he muttered as he rubbed my arms. "It's a pain in the ass getting wet clothes off deadweight."

I probably knew what he was referring to, but I was wiped out from riding—or maybe more accurately, being ridden by—a major storm, sitting in the freezing rain, and not killing my fiancé with the backwashed power. The specifics evaded me for the moment.

He stepped away long enough to dig through one of the bathroom drawers then returned to kneel at the side of the bath. "Let's see your hand."

I let him take the one he was tugging on then jerked upright with a hiss a few moments later at a jolt of pain.

"Splinter. From the porch." He held up the tweezers with the offending piece of bloodied wood. "Can you stay above the surface for a few minutes? I want to get some towels in the dryer."

"'Kay." The adrenaline from the pain had already worn off. I was crashing. Fast.

"Arden. Look at me."

With an effort, I met his gaze. Gold flecks shone against shadowed labradorite. I smiled and reached for his cheek and the muscle twitching in it. He really was a gorgeous man. All over. Even if he didn't always believe it, with the scars or whatever. "Pretty eyes."

He caught my hand and pressed a kiss to my palm. "Stay awake."

"I will."

With a last stern look, he was up and out of the bathroom elven fast.

I let myself slip a little deeper into the water. My shivers grew more violent then slowly eased. As they did, I came back to myself, which told me how cold I was all of a sudden.

"Don't," Troy said when he ghosted back in right as I reached for the knob for the hot water.

"But—"

"I know you're cold. That's what the towels are for." He held one up and shook it out. Beguiling warmth wafted from it, agitating the air molecules between us.

I wanted it.

He let me get myself out of the tub, slow and stumbling as my efforts were, his jaw clenched and muscles tight as he stopped himself from trying to help me. Knowing I'd be stubborn about needing help when I'd managed power hangovers on my own for years.

I relented, turning and tucking myself into the open towel, pressing my back to his front as I shivered with pleasure at the heat kissing my skin and his arms wrapping tightly around me.

"Come on." He kissed my temple. "There's more in the bed."

He let me go long enough for me to dry off and get under the covers, and for him to strip out of his damp clothes, then rounded the bed and tucked in behind me.

When I'd warmed up enough to stop shaking and just lay in his arms and a nest of towels in relieved comfort, he asked, "What happened?"

"It's almost spring."

His lack of response indicated his confusion as much as a question would have.

"Duke told me once that spring is when sylph powers are stronger. Last year, I was still growing into my full strength. Before that I was hiding. I didn't know it'd be like this, so I wasn't ready for it when I sensed the storm."

This time, the lack of an answer was more strategic consideration.

"I'll be more careful next time," I said. "And, um. Thanks. For pulling me back. It'd suck to trash Durham again."

"Mm."

"What's wrong?"

"We might be able to spin this."

"That doesn't sound too wrong?"

"Aside from the impact to you, there was a tornado warning when I came out to find you." The warmth lessened as he leaned away, and there was a scrape on the nightstand on his side of the bed. When he came back and curled his arm over me, his phone was in hand, unlocked to show the weather app radar. A virulent red line of storms tracked along the entire Southeast...except for a sharp break across the North Carolina Piedmont, the Sandhills, and southern Virginia.

Centered on the Triangle.

"Oh," I whispered.

He'd said to disperse the storm, and I had. In sending the elemental energy to the winds in every direction, I'd broken the storm front over Durham and the surrounding area. Even as I stared at the weather map, the alert blipped, downgrading from a severe thunderstorm and tornado warning to a canceled status for Durham county.

"Yeah." Conflict raged in the bond. "You're out as an Othersider but not formally as an elemental." He hesitated then plowed forward. "We can use this to make elementals valued. At best, anyway."

"And hunted all over again at worst. That's a fucking massive working, Troy. Dissipating a storm that size? You know better than I do how much of a threat that looks like, *especially* to the Houses."

Shit. What would the other elementals think? I'd promised to protect them, not expose the full extent of elemental magic.

The tightening of Troy's arms said more than words. *I* wouldn't be hunted. He'd kill anyone who tried. But I knew we were both thinking about Laurel and Val and Sofia, elementals who wouldn't have been able to manage what I had but would still be targeted if what we were became public knowledge.

This might be a way to save us. Or it might make us targets all over again.

I didn't like it, and I worried about the reaction of the elemental Collective. But I needed leverage. And that made me feel gross. "I need to sleep on it."

"Yeah."

"Before I do—Etain had news. She's not sure of it though."

"Oh?"

"Zadie intercepted comms from within House Bedoe. There might be a non-compete coming."

Troy stiffened against me. "What? Are you sure?"

"Etain's not, which is why she left it with me while she investigates further. Can we use that if it's true?"

"Absolutely." The distant note in his voice said he was already plotting how. "It might be enough to get the Richmond Conclave to agree to a summit. Especially if we can tie this storm to it somehow. Get them to see it's in their best interest not to come against us."

Exhaustion dragged at me. Troy might have washed away the pain of the power hangover, but the energy drain was still there.

"Okay. Tell me in the morning." I was out before he could respond.

△▽△▽

Troy was gone when I woke to the slanting intensity of morning light cutting through the blinds. Late morning. Better than sunrise. But still not my favorite time of day. Even when the smells reaching me from the kitchen said Troy was cooking a full English breakfast, which the elves preferred for the higher protein content compared to a big American breakfast.

"Food's on the table," Troy called. "Don't make me come get you."

I was half tempted to do just that, but an Aether sting made me set the temptation aside with a grumble for touchy elves. Dragging myself out of bed, I snagged my robe and hauled the bedroom door open to lean against the door jamb and watch him.

His gaze flicked to me, taking me in head to toe before turning back to the sausage. Bowls and plates on the dining table held baked beans, bacon, fried eggs, toast, sauteed mushrooms, and sliced tomato. "You're going to eat all of that."

"Okay."

That earned me a suspicious look. I didn't usually want to eat breakfast and did so as much to humor him as to stave off a power hangover. Having just had one of the damn things for the first time in months made me more inclined to be grateful for his protective caretaking tendencies.

"Good." The feeling of ruffled feathers settling came through the bond. "Then if you're feeling up to it, next on the agenda is a summit."

"Summit."

Another look, concerned this time. "Getting ahead of House Bedoe and proposing we go to Richmond. To negotiate."

I frowned, trying to find the thread of what we'd been talking about last night before I crashed. Right. "We use the leverage of Bedoe's effective vote of no confidence and last night's weather event to secure a deal. Rather than to declare war."

"With war as the implied alternative, yes."

I went to the table and sat down, piling a plate with what was ready to eat so the sharp feeling of a watchful hunter would stop stinging me in the bond. Mother bears had nothing on

Troy trying to take care of me. I smiled at my plate full of food, overcome with sudden emotion.

"What's wrong?" Alarm threaded both Troy's voice and the bond.

"Nothing. Nothing's wrong." I twisted in my chair so he could see my face. "I'm just grateful. For you. For this. I really might have hurt a lot of people last night. You stopped me. You took care of me, even though I was literally sparking lightning. And now you make sure I have what I need to stop the damn power hangovers. Thank you."

"Oh." He flushed slightly then tilted his head to crack a bone in his neck and turned back to the stove. "I— Thank *you*. For saying so." Sausage popped as he stabbed it and piled the links on a plate before bringing them to the table and sitting across from me. "Honestly, Arden...I do it out of instinct. And because that instinct was further honed by training. But you make me *want* to do it. You make it a reward. Not a burden or an obligation."

That might be the sweetest thing anyone had ever said to me, after growing up with Duke and Grimm making me feel like a burden and Callista actively disliking me. I reached across the table with the hand not busy stacking my fork with meat and eggs.

He put his hand in mine, and we had a moment of contentment before getting back to figuring out how to avoid outright war. I was anxious about what it would require—me at the heart of elven power—but it would be another step closer to what my mom had been trying to do when she sought out my dad.

"We're agreed then?" I asked after I'd gotten some food into me. I'd missed dinner passing out last night and was hungrier than I'd thought, given I could never be bothered with breakfast and had been known to forget meals on a regular basis. "Negotiate with House Bedoe and see if we can get a summit?"

Troy nodded and grunted an affirmative around a mouthful of food. "But you need to understand something first. They might agree to a summit with us. But they will not consider either of us legitimate."

"Excuse me?"

"You're High Queen, affirmed in battle. But you're the elemental daughter of a dead and disgraced prince. I'm King—"

"But I should have put you down like a rabid dog the minute it was apparent you'd become one. Right." I let him feel the fullness of my disgust and anger. Fuck the elven death cult. It had killed my father, and then it'd nearly killed my bondmate. I might not trust all elves, but I hadn't missed that all of those who'd sided with me were people who would have been put to death by the old queens for one reason or another or loved someone who would have been.

"It will be ugly, Arden."

"I figured."

"You figured. But you haven't faced it."

I looked up, angry and ready to fight. I knew exactly how ugly people could be. But then I saw how blank his expression was and caught the echo of deep pain, swiftly submerged, in the bond.

"Okay," I said instead, forcing myself to back down. "Ugly how?"

Troy relaxed a little at my acceptance of his assessment and his own pain. "They'll need to find a way to do two things. First, discredit us. Word's gotten out about your decree ending the death penalty for most so-called offenses."

I nodded. I'd expected that. It'd solidified the Ebon Guard around me further and even just in the last ten days, drawn in a handful of new elves. Not enough to replace all those who'd died when I secured the Triangle, but some.

"Second, they'll aim to break us up."

Chapter 5

"What?" I put my fork down. "Break us up?"

Troy nodded, looking grim.

"Do we need to push forward with a marriage or what?"

A spark lit the bond, quickly pushed down as he tilted his head and considered it. "I don't think that would be enough."

"Why?"

He leveled a flat, blank stare at me. "My father was married to my mother."

Oh. *Oh.* Because elven males were treated more like property than people. Troy's father had been useful and promising enough to secure long-term rights to him through marriage, but Keithia had broken those vows on her daughter's behalf quickly enough when her son-in-law had tried to make a political arrangement into a love match.

She couldn't have people getting above themselves, after all.

I'd had enough of my own difficulties in my life. My own battles to fight and prejudices to face. And because the elves had been the root of most of them, I kept forgetting that Troy—despite having more power than me in some ways—had had his own share to deal with, despite being one of those elves.

"I'm sorry," I said.

He shrugged and went back to eating. "Don't be. You weren't responsible. But I'm saying it to make the point that we can't count on your claim to…"

As he trailed off, I frowned then figured out what the problem was.

"To protect you," I said gently.

Troy nodded sharply and kept eating, keeping his focus on his plate.

This sucked. His life practically revolved around protecting me, largely from his people, when it wasn't the mundanes. He was strong and smart and ruthless. He had made choices I prayed I'd never have to and would do again because he was that dedicated. But if we were going into the heart of an elven seat of power, a *foreign* elven seat of power, then I would truly have to be High Queen.

And I had a pretty shitty track record at it thus far for anything that wasn't outright destruction.

"I trust you," Troy said, breaking me out of my thoughts. "I have faith in you. I know you wouldn't do the things Keithia threatened my father with. Or did. So I'm okay with playing this traditionally."

"But it's time for me to step up. Especially if we're going traditional." Appetite fled, I leaned away from my empty plate without refilling it. "I need to be the queen I've resisted being."

"The queen you didn't realize you had to be until recently," he corrected. Reaching across the table, he squeezed my hand. "You don't have to turn into Keithia."

"No. But I do need to stop being the bully Omar called me and start being more…strategic."

Troy tilted his head, and a smirk flickered before he stifled it, giving me the sense of *You said it, not me* more than saying it would have.

Crossing my arms, I slouched in my chair and looked out the window. Spring was clearly on the way. The fresh, green buds on every plant proclaimed it as much as the birds' songs and the smell of the air. A fresh start.

"I don't want it to come to fighting a war," I said. "I know that's effectively what I've defaulted to, with getting rid of the queens in the Triangle. But Troy…"

"I know. It's never what you wanted. And it kills a piece of you every time. You've started to wonder how many you can kill before you're no longer you."

Of course he understood. I nodded, hugging myself tighter and following the path of a pair of squirrels as they chased each other around the yard, chittering madly.

"Hey," he said.

I resisted turning back to him for a minute. When I did, he'd let his mask drop.

Compassion shone in his eyes, and a rueful half-smile quirked his lips. "You're doing fine as High Queen. You're finding a path that's authentic to you. Helping all of us follow it. The Richmond Houses will hate it. But that just means you're doing it right."

That made me choke up. I ate a little more straight from the serving bowls just to save myself from having to find words but let him read my emotions in the bond.

"I'll talk to Etain," he said. "See what we need to do to get this moving. Even if the intel isn't a hundred percent accurate or complete, I can do something with it."

"Thanks." I needed to change the subject before I got too wrapped up in it. "Where'd you get with Rice last night?"

"He's reluctantly agreed to hold a press conference in three days."

I eyed Troy at the spark of pleasure in the bond. "How much did you help him arrive at that particular destination?"

My suspicion was confirmed when he glanced at me, smirked, and said, "Only a little."

"You're enjoying this."

"I am. And I will continue to do so as long as the mundanes continue to be a personal pain in my ass."

I snorted at hearing one of my phrases coming out of his mouth then sobered, eyeing him. "Troy, you know I don't expect you to be my monster, right?"

The sharp look he gave me and the flash of gold in his eyes said that somehow he hadn't expected that.

"I'm not saying you are or have been. But I am saying that if at any point you start to feel like you're having to go further than you'd like, tell me. Please. We're both having to step to some shitty lines, but we'll figure something out."

He studied me for a long few heartbeats. "Thank you. I'll remember that."

I gave him a small smile, glad he was taking it seriously but not taking offense. "Good. Okay. We're getting somewhere with Raleigh PD. Negotiations with the Lyon splinter group are ongoing. You'll talk to Etain about the Richmond Conclave. We're waiting for the Sinners to get their heads out of their asses while Duke and Iaret keep an eye on them and negotiate with the Djinn Council for their assistance in any conflict with other conclaves." I frowned. "And Duke is still hiding something from me, the bastard."

Troy just nodded, agreeing with everything and staying out of my personal quarrels with my djinni cousin. We finished our breakfasts and cleaned up, moving in the easy companionship I'd never dared to dream of having for myself before now.

At the edge of my awareness, the wards jangled against my aura.

I froze, having forgotten the sensation of someone breaking through.

"What?" Troy snapped. "What's wrong?"

"Wards."

He didn't answer as he went for the longknife resting on the divider between the front door and the dining area. He rounded on me as I darted after him. "Stay here."

"No." I raised a hand as his brows drew down and his mouth tightened. "*Think.* The last time someone got through, it was Neith."

My patroness among the hunter gods had given me a cursed godblade on one visit, and nearly killed me in a "test" on another. Without Troy, I might not have survived either the blade or the test.

The deadly sense in the bond sharpened. "I told you, they can't have you."

"Let's just find out what they want first, okay?"

He glared at me so long I thought I was gonna have to fight him. Then he relented, staying in front of me as he got the door and led the way out onto the porch.

We discovered our visitor when we got to my car. A person leaned against one of the trees edging the yard, seeming sort of masculine but completely average in every way: medium build, brownish skin, medium-length brown hair, brown eyes, neutral clothing, neither young nor old. It was almost impossible to put any determination to them, or more like it shifted when I tried. I got the strong impression this wasn't the only form they wore, just the one that was convenient for now.

More than their appearance, their scent made me stop dead. The static nothing of the In-Between.

I grabbed Troy's arm to stop him when he moved to stand in front of me, longknife in a guard position.

"You've finally come to this plane then?" I said quietly.

Troy bristled as he realized our visitor was a celestial, if not a god. Then his eyes darted around the yard, like he was determined to figure out how they'd gotten through the wards.

The newcomer tilted their head, seeming amused. "You've done a number of interesting and tricksy things these last few weeks. The rest of us hadn't quite believed Eshu-Elegba when he said you were one of ours given the claim the hunters had on you, but I can almost see it now."

"Who do we have the honor of addressing?" I asked.

"Call me Harqil." They grinned and offered half a bow. "A simple messenger."

"Celestial?" I asked.

They nodded. "The pronouns you've settled on will do, before you tie yourself up in knots over it."

I flushed with embarrassment. The idea that they could see into my head was intensely unsettling, and I pulled my shields up tighter. Celestials had all kinds of powers, and the tricksters were...well, predictably unpredictable in what they could do.

In any case, it looked like Troy had been right—everything happened all at once around me. "What message do you have for us?"

"For you, really, primordial. But I suppose you and your elf are a package deal." Their grin widened. "That was a delightful twist. But hmm, no djinn this time?"

"They're occupied. With tricks."

"Of course they are. Delightful beings, djinn." Harqil cut a mischievous glance at Troy. "The elves were created to be the orderly side to Aether. You might be one of ours though, boy, taking up with an elemental and trying to change the world. Such a mess you're creating." A pause drew into a long, considering silence. Then their eyes flickered as they rested on Troy, like they'd just remembered something at the sight of him. "Yes, the message can be for you too."

Troy frowned, like he heard a slight that might or might not have been there. Or maybe it was about this message that was supposed to be for me but might also be for him or the supposed mess he was creating that was interesting enough to draw the interest of a trickster. If I was betting though, I'd say it flustered him that he, as Mr. Law and Order, had strayed from that enough to be embraced by the tricksters.

A headache blossomed between my eyes and started to throb. "Is this about a gift?"

"Ha! You do remember. I told them you would, even if we used the In-Between instead of the Crossroads. Too much traffic through there. Too many nosy souls."

My head was spinning. "What is the gift?"

"You'll see. But first we want to...let's say, evaluate you. Now that you have our full attention and we aren't just relying on what Elegba brings us."

My mouth dried. Neith's evaluations had nearly killed me—possibly would have if Troy hadn't arrived in time to do some field medicking. I wasn't keen on more godly tests, even if this Harqil was only a celestial and not a full god. Callista had been a celestial. I might well become one, as the Eternal Huntress, if some god decided I'd served well enough to throw me into the stars rather than letting me die. Maybe I'd take Orion's old place in that constellation.

It wasn't a fate I was interested in. Not if Troy couldn't come with me.

Harqil must have caught my sudden fear because they chuckled. "Don't worry, little primordial. Evaluate, as in, observe. Nothing more." The toothy grin reappeared. "Not yet."

"How comforting." I stood up straighter, reminding myself that I was the damn Arbiter and had already survived the gods of the hunt. "What are the terms?"

"Be yourself. It's what we do best." They winked. "We'll be watching. And primordial? I'm rooting for you."

With a folding of magic, Harqil was gone.

"Fuck." I turned to look up at Troy.

He glanced down at me, lips in a firm line as the muscle in his cheek twitched. "I assume you'll refuse to increase security."

"Correct. In fact, I don't want anyone to know about this."

His expression tightened. "Etain?"

"No."

"The Guard is going to take it personally if something happens and they weren't told."

"I know, Troy, but if the Guard knows, Allegra knows. And if she knows, Maria knows, and it ripples out from there. Everyone will tell everyone else, while telling them not to tell anyone else, and it'll be an open secret. We just need to get through this press conference and whatever the fuck the senator wants. Then I promise I will tell everyone that the trickster gods are evaluating their leader for something to do with a gift that none of us remember receiving."

"You know this is probably playing into their hands, right? The not telling?"

"I know. But what is anyone here really going to be able to do against a celestial?" The elves couldn't even cross planes. *I* could barely manage it, and not without help. But if the gods were stirring again, this was definitely going to be on me to handle.

Chapter 6

I went to my office at the bar that had once been Callista's seat of power and was now mine while Troy headed over to Ebon Guard HQ to talk to Etain about House Bedoe. I had reports to stay on top of and needed to be at least somewhat available to any Othersiders who needed the Arbiter.

I'd been there an hour before a rap on the door pulled me out of a report about what I'd been drugged with the other week, right when I finally managed to get my mind off of Harqil's message.

"Yeah?" I called.

Haroun leaned in. "Val is here for you, ma'am."

"Send her in."

Odd that she'd be here now. I hadn't heard from the other elementals since my birthday and had assumed the presence of the Lyon observers had spooked them. Val in particular rarely came to the bar, keen to maintain her cover as a mundane so that she could both continue her work as a firefighter and protect her younger sister, who didn't want to be known to anyone.

Val's short, choppy hair was messy when she stepped in, and her tan skin was flushed. For all she was a dea, she kept the fiery side of her nature banked and well under control. I'd seen her at two emergency situations, and she'd never looked this flustered.

I waved her to a seat and took my own, forgoing a hug. "Hey, Val. Everything okay?"

She studied me with a hard expression I'd never seen directed at me before. "No. Everything is really not okay. What the fuck happened last night?"

Cold stole over me. "The storm."

"Yes, the storm. Goddess! Are you insane?"

"Are you asking literally or figuratively?"

The hard look somehow got harder, and a flash of heat burst from behind her shields. "This is not funny."

"I didn't think it was." I held up a hand to stop her next comment as she opened her mouth. "No, I'm not insane. And I didn't lose control of my magic." A grimace slipped before I could stop it. "Not exactly."

"What in the nine hells does that mean?"

I had to fight to keep a lid on my magic. My grasp of Air always got chancy when I was stressed, and it didn't help that I usually relieved stress by creating little zephyrs and spinning them through a room. But if Val was here with concerns about my control, I had to be rock solid.

Leaning forward on the desk, I met her gaze. "It means that it's almost spring, I'm a sylph, and I'm stronger than I've been in twenty-eight years. Things are getting complicated and—"

"Complicated? Are you shitting me? Otherside has never been more at risk and you're falling to seasonal madness?"

I stiffened as though she'd slapped me. "I'm not—"

"Apparently you are, if a major storm is suddenly dissipated and you 'didn't exactly' lose control of your magic. That means you didn't exactly have control of it, either!"

My phone buzzed with a text message. Probably Troy, reacting to my rising agitation. I ignored the text and walled off the bond.

"Why are you coming at me like this, Val?" I asked as softly as I could. We were friends, or at least I'd thought we were. This attack was completely unexpected, and it had my head spinning. I scrabbled to give her the benefit of the doubt, even as anger flared to life and the heat of my own grasp of Fire flickered. "Is it the Collective?"

At the reminder of my greater strength with Fire, she went very still then took a deep breath, settling. "Yes. Granddad in particular. I didn't mean to come at you like that. But the entire elemental community is in an uproar, and the brunt of it is falling on me for the crime of being the person who told you about the rest of us."

That hurt even more than her initial attack. Both that she was taking hits on my behalf and that the Collective still refused to talk to me, preferring to heap shit on one of my few friends. I couldn't help feeling like it was intentional; I'd learned that like the elves, elementals also used ostracism as punishment. Val might not see it, but I'd spent enough time in elven politics lately to see the early moves here. The Collective was going to punish her, threaten her with the risk of being cast out of the elemental community to make her fall into line—which would mean breaking off her friendship with me.

As hot as Val's temper had burned coming in, it went out. She slumped and scrubbed her hands through her hair, ruffling it worse than ever. "I'm sorry, Arden. It's just a lot of pressure. I hadn't heard any warning that you were doing a weather working, let alone one of that size, and now some of the older members of the Collective are stirring everyone up with tales of the elven bounty hunts again because there's no way in hell anyone could have missed that."

"And all the elves will probably know the signs."

She nodded tiredly.

"I get it," I said. "And I'm sorry. I just needed a break, so I opened myself to the storm. I didn't expect to get hit that hard. Troy pulled me out as soon as it was safe."

"Troy?" She frowned. "How?"

I hesitated, trying to remember how much she knew about us already. The bond was the result of magical trespass, and though

I'd forgiven Troy, I didn't need to give the rest of Otherside an excuse to put him on trial and break up our power base. "Our Aetheric connection lets him calm me somewhat."

She eyed me, like she heard that I wasn't telling her everything, but let it go, even as she scowled. "I don't know if that helps or hurts the situation, to have an elven king with at least partial control over a primordial elemental."

"Does the Collective need to know?"

That got me a glare. "I have to tell them something."

My temper finally went. "Then tell them I prevented a tornado from hitting the Triangle. It's my territory to protect," I snapped. "I'm not gonna go out of my way to shift weather patterns just for the hell of it, and I am trying my damnedest to keep knowledge of elementals from getting out. But, Val, we all fucking know that it *is* going to get out sooner or later. I've bent over backward to make special arrangements for us all. I've tried over and over again to reach out to the Collective. I've offered to hold a summit at my house, which the weres took as an honor but *my own people* seemed to think was an insult."

"I know—"

"So what the hell am I supposed to do? I'm fucking *tired* of this! I get why the djinn are assholes. I get why the elves are assholes. So why are both of those factions more willing to talk to me than any of the Collective?"

"Maybe because you *are* talking to those two factions above your own people."

The coldness in her voice caught my next comment in my throat. "Excuse me?"

"Everyone has a place in your alliance except the elementals."

"No. Nuh-uh. I am not owning their refusal to step out of the shadows. Not after everything I did to destroy the local elven conclave and not after staining my own soul with killing or exiling anyone who wouldn't swear to protect the elementals. I've tried reaching out. I did my part."

"And yet we still don't feel safe." She shrugged and rose. "I hate to say it, but I don't blame the Collective. Something's gotta budge, Arden."

"Agreed. But it can't be all on me."

With a slow, sad nod, she left without another word, leaving me and my overactive mind spinning on the situation and wondering if our friendship was just strained or truly broken. Guilt slithered in, coiling in my stomach as I reviewed and second-guessed everything in the last two years. Had I tried hard enough to create a safe space for the other elementals? Or had I been too busy chasing my own power and security?

As I stared at the ceiling trying to make sense of it all, a knock on the door scattered my thoughts.

I sat up. "Yeah?"

Haroun stuck his head in. "Omar and Allegra Monteague."

"Both of them? Here?" That was unusual, and not the best timing, given what'd just happened with Val. I sighed, resigning myself to getting nothing done today. "Send them in."

"My queen," they said together when they'd stepped in.

I nodded and gestured them to the chairs on the other side of the desk, hoping my apprehension wasn't showing. "What brings both of you here together?"

Omar smiled faintly, like he could scent what I was trying to hide and was just polite enough not to poke me about it. "I can't catch up with my only daughter?"

"I'm just surprised you're doing it here and not in Chapel Hill."

Allegra toyed idly with one of her locs. "Dad thinks we need to remind people that we're still allied with you." She glanced at him guiltily then back at me. "That *I'm* still allied with you."

Rather than completely won over by Maria.

I rearranged my mind from elemental politics to elven as quickly as I could. "Gotcha. I appreciate that. Things are still a little antsy after everything that happened in Raleigh."

Omar nodded, pleased to be proven right. "On that note, my queen, we have news. The Charleston Conclave has reached out to me with a marriage offer for Allegra."

I crossed my arms. "Excuse me? Aside from the whole 'reaching out to a woman's father' thing, she's her own person and *my* heir."

He nodded. "And as such, they should have spoken to you first, Troy second."

I glanced at Allegra and lifted my brows.

"I didn't know anything about this," she said. "And I have no interest in it."

With a shrug, I leaned back in my chair. "Then we tell them no. I told y'all. No more forced marriages."

Omar sighed. "It's not that simple. If we don't handle this delicately, that will set Charleston against us. We need them."

"That can't be the only option, given some Ebon Guard intel that says House Bedoe is debating offering a non-compete agreement."

Omar's sudden grin was not what I'd expected. "I wondered when that op would bear fruit."

"Excuse me?" I asked. "Have we been running ops against them before this year?"

"Of course. The Darkwatch has anyway. I have had ops running in every House on the East Coast and some on the West since the day you toppled the Chapel Hill Conclave." He tilted his head. "Apparently, I underestimated your Ebon Guard, if they heard about results before me."

"Apparently," I said. Etain would be over the moon to hear it, as long as it was confirmed. "In any case, Troy and I have agreed to push for a summit."

"Bold play," Allegra said. "I like it. Surprised T would go for it, given it forces him to both put you in potential danger and put himself up on the block, but I like it."

Omar looked at the far wall, eyes distant. "I don't see a way around it without looking weak or fearful. We can't afford either, which Troy knows. It also means you'll need an entourage. Taking some of the Darkwatch will make a point." He turned to his daughter. "And you will need to stay in elven territory while they're gone."

Allegra's brows drew down, and for a moment, I thought she'd argue him on it. But all she did was incline her head. "As you say."

A flicker of pride warmed Omar's expression at his daughter's acceptance of her duty before he buried it. "Good. If nothing else, it gives us room to stall on a response to this request from Charleston." He turned back to me. "Is there anything else, my queen?"

I started to say no then figured I should tell them about the conversation with Duke the other day, the one about the Djinn Council potentially being willing to help—at a price. When I finished, Allegra looked grim and Omar, tired.

"This could be the Atlantis debacle all over again," he said.

"It could," I agreed, glad I'd kept my conversation with Val out of it. "Or it could be the beginning of a new era."

Omar was looking thoughtful again. "Get the Charleston Conclave in on this summit as well, if you can. We need to move aggressively to secure our borders, and I won't push Allegra into a marriage she doesn't want. Even if it would be politically expedient."

Allegra scowled. "Gee, thanks."

He gave her a stern look. "Richmond should buy in, if only because it's been a good decade since there's been a meet and they have a few royals who will have reached their majority in that time. I'll plant some seeds with my West Coast teams about sending observers this way. Even if a summit falls through, Lyon's precedence might give the Seattle Houses in particular the excuse they need to move."

My head spun at all of this. Being Arbiter was one thing. I just had to make sure everyone in my territory played nice with each other and the mundanes. Being High Queen? I was wondering all over again if I was the right person for the job. Allegra was nodding along like this was all par for the course, and I was still figuring out what it meant just to think about pushing a summit at all, let alone who should go and what needed doing there.

Someone smarter than me had once said, "Fake it til you make it" though, so I focused on looking confident and tried to think of something clever. "Omar, would you compile a list of possible targets we could work on swaying if this all comes together? Maybe we could help some of your ops along."

He narrowed his eyes. "I wasn't expecting you to be willing to participate that deeply in elven politics, my queen."

Ouch. I deserved that, but it still pinched. "I can't be High Queen in name only. Troy does an excellent job as King, but if we're going in together, we need to be a proper team. I can't leave him to carry everything."

"I'm very glad to hear that." Omar rose. After a short hesitation, he offered a fist-to-heart salute and a small bow. "If there's nothing else, my queen, I'll get on that for you."

"That's all. Thank you," I said.

"Daughter. We'll continue our conversation later."

"Bye, Dad."

Allegra watched her father leave with the usual conflicted bitterness half-hidden in her expression. When the door closed behind him, she muttered, "He'll always love T more."

I held back a sigh. Troy wasn't the only one who got the full moon crankies. I pushed past my usual reticence about hugging people and rose to pull Allegra into a side hug. "Troy's who he was allowed to love. And that's on Keithia."

"Keithia's dead," she said bluntly. "His choices are his own now."

"Allegra, I'm not making excuses for him. But he's, what? Eighty? Older? Even if that's barely midlife, it's a long time spent schooling himself to be what he needed to be to keep y'all safe. He definitely needs to do better by you. But don't forget other people love you. Troy most of all, I think. But Maria and me too."

"Yeah." She sighed. "I don't like any of this, Arden."

"Me neither. But we've got a solid chance at avoiding war with Richmond. That's gotta be worth something."

"It is." She half turned to glance down at me. "Just watch the eligible princesses if this summit goes through. Troy was the most eligible bachelor in North America until you claimed him, and some of those bitches are sore losers. Especially if it's to an elemental."

"Noted." Something not at all nice curled through me, a smaller echo of what I sometimes got from Troy when the hormonal bond was spiking. "But frankly, they'd better watch themselves."

She chuckled. "Oh, now I really wish I was going. Because I would pay good money to see what you did to someone who tried to lure him from you."

I'd never had a jealous bone in my body and Troy was far too head-over-heels for me to be tempted into pursuing anyone else. But at that comment, I decided that didn't mean I had to play the fool either.

I was High Queen after all. And as I'd told Matthias, I protected what was mine.

Right now, that needed to include Allegra as well. After she left, I checked my phone—I'd been right that Troy had texted earlier—and called him to relay that I was fine but stressed over elemental business, the conversation with Omar and Allegra, and Omar's recommendation that Charleston be included in the summit.

"Makes sense." Troy sounded annoyed. "Fine. We need to be in town for the next three to four days to handle this damned press conference with Rice. It'll take at least that long to hammer out terms for a summit between Richmond, Chapel Hill, and Charleston."

Which meant I had a few days to one, figure out how to deal with Senator Wright and his damnable requests; two, help Troy deal with whatever prep was needed for the presser; and three, figure out how the hell to be the kind of queen I was expected to be at a summit of at least seven major Houses.

And that didn't even count these new wrinkles with the tricksters and the other elementals.

Chapter 7

T he first day flew past.

With Senator Wright unreachable and Troy more experienced than me at dealing with the politics of hammering out a press conference, I spent the time in a home crash course in elven court etiquette, much to Allegra's intense amusement and frustration. If nothing else, it distracted me from the argument with Val.

"And I thought Troy was a stubborn ass." Allegra leaned against the wall separating the kitchen from the bathroom. "You just might have him beat. And you know what? He deserves it. You deserve each other. You are each singularly the most aggravating people I know, no matter how much I love you both, and you absolutely deserve to spend the rest of your lives together with your heads up your asses bickering like djinn."

I gave her a stern look as much for the snark at the djinn as for making this an issue. "I just don't see what it matters if he enters on my left or my right. He's righthanded. The draw of his blade from over his shoulder works better if he's on my right."

"Yeah. *Tactically*, that makes sense if you're going into battle. *Strategically*, we need to communicate that you don't need him to fight for you. He's there to be *pretty*, Arden, and he knows it. It's what he was trained for."

"He was trained to be an assassin, a commando, and a consort. To fight and to fuck," I snapped. "But what he *is* is a king. I want them to know he's an equal. Not a toy."

"It lowers your own status."

"So be it."

She tilted her head and gave me a look that said I was being ridiculous.

"I thought you'd be happy about this. Aren't you the one who wanted him to have options?"

That got me a wince that felt like a victory. "There's options, and then there's strategy, Arden. You two aren't going to change elven society overnight or in a single appearance."

The front door opening made me jump and whirl to find Troy on the threshold. I'd been so caught up in my argument I'd missed his presence drawing closer in the bond.

His eyebrows lifted as he scented the room. "I'm assuming the argument is about me?"

Allegra snorted. "I'd call you a self-centered ass—"

"But you know that's not in my nature, or if it was, Keithia had it beaten out of me," Troy said. At Allegra's grimace, his gaze flicked to me, and he tilted his head, inviting an explanation.

"I want you to come in on my right," I said. "And at my side. Not behind me."

He came the rest of the way in and shut the door behind him, taking his time in getting his boots and socks off and setting them neatly at the end of the half wall before crossing to where I stood in the living room. "Alli's explained what message that will send?"

"Yes," I said.

"Okay. You're High Queen." A smile flickered before he buried it and turned to Allegra. "We serve at her command."

"Oh *come on*, T. I just got finished reminding her how fucking stubborn you are, and you roll over on basic etiquette?"

"I'm picking my battles."

Allegra snorted. "You want a chance to throw your new title around."

"So what if I do?" Troy's demeanor chilled. "Alli, I've earned it."

"More than," I muttered.

I sent a little pulse of approving pride to him in the bond as well. That was big for him, admitting that he wanted something for himself and not just seeing that he'd earned it, but speaking up about it. Old Troy would have clung to self-sacrificing duty and insisted on lowering himself regardless of what I said, on my bringing him in behind my left shoulder, being the consort or the bodyguard he played to throw off the mundanes, rather than the king and equal I considered him in Otherside. This whole argument might seem like little shit, insignificant points of detail, but just like I personally needed to step up and embrace my new role, I needed to make space for him to embrace his.

Troy curled an arm over my shoulder and pulled me in to kiss the crown of my head, the bond radiating with the quiet satisfaction of a cat getting exactly what he wanted.

Allegra threw her hands up. "Okay! Fine. Next point of order. The welcome ball."

"Ball," I said flatly. Maria had tried to make the vampire Reveal a ball. I didn't do formal anything. Definitely not a ball, no matter how good Troy looked in a tux or how hot the memory of the first time he kissed me was.

My future sister-in-law was smirking like she knew where my thoughts were going, and even Troy felt smug in the bond.

"Fuck off, both of you." I pulled away from Troy, only to have him catch my hand and pull me back to him in an unexpected spin that pressed my front against his as his other hand slipped around my waist.

"It could be fun. If you let it," he said.

The heat in his eyes stole my breath.

"Here we go again," Allegra muttered. "Y'all gonna need me anymore tonight?"

"Yes," Troy said.

I frowned. "You can't do dance lessons?"

"I can," he said. "But there's a variable. Elven gatherings, especially summits, typically involve lots of alcohol. Toasts, oaths, general social lubrication..."

"Fuck," I muttered.

Allegra's gaze darted between us. "What am I missing? Why— Oh, for the love of the Goddess. She's half-elven."

Troy nodded, still looking at me.

"I thought that was just a human low-blood concern. Definitely a maenad?" Allegra asked.

I sighed. "Yes. I don't feel like telling the whole story now. But that's why I'm a one-and-done gal."

"Which you could do at a summit," Troy said.

"But you want to know what you're in for if, for whatever reason, I have more."

Allegra rolled the end of one of her locs between her fingers, not quite looking at me. "Or how to use it to your advantage."

Troy's hands fell away as I twisted to glare at her.

"What?" Was she serious? I couldn't believe it. "It's a curse. Even Val said so. What advantage is there?"

She glanced at Troy then shrugged. "In a word? Enchantment. It's the one way you or a half-human low-blood could magically influence one of us like you were a full-blood Monteague or Luna."

I stared at her as my world rearranged itself. I was terrified of one day drinking too much in trying to balance a power hangover and waking up to find Troy dead next to me, which was a large part of why I followed his instructions on eating breakfast and getting a proper protein balance to prevent the power hangovers.

"What the hell do you mean, 'influence'?" I said. "I almost killed a boy the last and only time I activated that magic. Callista beat me bloody for the riot it caused at the bar and the coverup she had to do downtown after."

Troy snarled at hearing of me being hurt, but all he said was, "There are ways to focus it. Dance is one of them. A hunt is another. Or an orgy. But the more people the influence is spread over, the less likely you are to kill an individual. Half-elves with maenad tendencies usually become actors or rock stars and channel the influence over a mundane crowd."

I stared at him, letting my mental *what the fuck* come through clearly in both the bond and my expression.

He winced. "You didn't want to talk about it. I wouldn't push, except—"

"Yeah. Fine. Fair." I didn't like it, but it was fair. And if I was honest, I was intrigued and relieved to hear that there were ways to manage what the other elementals simply called "the curse."

Allegra pushed off from the wall. "Okay. A drink then? For you two, anyway."

Looking up at Troy, I sent, *You trust me with this?*

The gold flecks in his eyes seemed to spark. *You love me too much to kill me. And I love you too much to let you kill me knowing you'd likely follow.*

Tears sprang to my eyes at the certainty in him, and I turned away, going to the back door and looking outside. Twilight was falling. His magic would still be at a low ebb with the moon just past full, but I did love him that much. I wouldn't hurt him. I had to have faith in that. In myself. More than that, I had to assume that if Allegra could figure out an implication of being half-elven, so would one of the Richmond or Charleston Houses. And if they did, they could use it to outmaneuver me, leaving both Troy and House Solari vulnerable. I couldn't let my weakness bring greater downfall.

"Red wine, please," I said.

Troy embraced me from behind while Allegra got glasses and opened a bottle. "It'll be okay. I promise. We've got you. And if you want to stop at any point, we stop."

I couldn't answer. I'd run from this part of myself and my power for over a decade, and I had so much more to lose now than I ever had. I trusted Troy. I trusted Allegra. But after losing control to the storm the other night, I didn't trust myself. Especially not with the argument with Val still festering in my heart.

"Cheers," Allegra said as she offered us our glasses.

I downed mine, barely tasting the burst of tobacco and spice before going to the counter to refill it. I drank the second glass more slowly, eyes on Troy's worried face the whole time. There was no power hangover to divert the energy to.

Magic flickered as I finished it, and I shuddered.

"That fast?" Allegra murmured.

"She doesn't drink more than a single serving at a time," Troy replied. "Not in my company. We control the power hangovers with diet. And she has fewer of them now that she practices regularly, eats better, and sleeps more."

I didn't bother reminding them that I was right here. My nose told me they were just as nervous as I was, odd as it was to have improved senses that could pick it up and to think that either of these two battle-hardened elven warriors would be worried about little ol' me.

Except I wasn't little anymore. I hadn't been for two years. And it was time to get that through my damn head and start embracing all of what I was.

As I poured and sipped a third glass, magic crested a notch higher. Tension ratcheted up. I shivered as anxiety slipped away. Good. This was good. I'd held it off for far too long.

"Do we need Thana?" Allegra asked.

Alcohol and magic blended through me in a warm, smooth curl. "You might. If she doesn't want to kill or fuck me."

Both Troy and Allegra stiffened at the shift in my voice to a lower register than usual, one that was harder yet more sultry.

"Call Thana," Troy said. "Just in case. Etain and Haroun as well. If we need to dissipate the effects, they won't mind having an excuse to work them out on each other."

"So I'll have to fight Thana while you and Arden go at it again. Great. Thanks, T."

Troy approached me rather than answering Allegra. "Toro ben?"

The smile spilling across my lips made his pupils dilate. "With you here? Always. Always and forever."

He caught my chin as I reached him. "Focus, Arden. We have a dance lesson."

I squeezed my eyes shut then blinked them open, trying to find a thread of my usual self. "Air."

Without a word, Troy led me to the back door then outside and down the deck steps to the backyard. His grip on my hand was warm and comforting, sending a zing of heat through me.

"Better," I said. The cold air sobered me a little, and I drank more of my wine.

"Can I have some?" he asked.

I grinned and gave him the glass.

He took a sip and set it on the bottom step then turned back to me with his hands positioned for a formal dance.

Laughing, I stepped to him and pressed myself tight against his body, leaning in to scent the corner of his jaw and breathe deep before nipping his neck. I really did love dancing. When I allowed myself to do it, anyway. I used to get shitfaced and dance in the woods, far away from anyone who would be affected, but I hadn't since Troy had moved in. I'd been too afraid of my own magic.

"Arden," he said. "Focus."

Fuck. Right. Dance *lesson*, not just shits and giggles under the moonlight. And the bigger issue. Practicing control for the summit. But the strain in his voice sparked a fire in me. I didn't want to focus. I wanted to consume him.

A thought skated across his consciousness as he grew hard between us. *This is going to be harder than I thought.*

I laughed. I couldn't help it. "We could just fuck."

"Not helping," he said.

The deep growl of his voice turned me on even more, but before I could do anything about it, music split the night. Sultry strings, something with classical guitar and piano.

"Go on then," Allegra called. "I thought you were having a dance lesson."

Dance. Dance was good.

"Show me?" I asked.

"I have an idea. Let me in."

I dropped my shields and walls completely.

Troy slipped into my mind with a light touch, even as he gathered me up again with his hands. "Like this."

And then we moved.

I gasped, stumbling once at the unexpected effects of having him threaded through my mind while completely open to him. But then every step made perfect sense. I knew where he was leading. What he needed my feet and hips and hands to do, when he was going to spin me out and draw me back in.

Power rose. A beguiling threat laced with sweet command, overlaying a demand for blood and sex. I gloried in it.

Exclamations from somewhere else nearly broke the spell, but Troy said, "Stay with me."

I fell into his voice, strained though it was. Followed his direction. I didn't know how long we'd been dancing and I didn't care as long as the energy kept building with our steps.

"Can you sense the others?" he asked, breaking through the surface of my thoughts.

I reached with Chaos. "Yes."

"Can you influence them?"

I couldn't see how at first. But then with a twist, I saw what they each wanted.

"Gently, cariñamí," he reminded me. "Don't break them. They're our friends."

And with gentle taps, I poured the energy that wanted to rage and rend and fuck and kill into the auras around us. Enchanted them.

"Don't force them," Troy said. "Back to me."

I followed Troy's voice back to us. Back to our steps. But there was still more in me. And I wanted more. Ignoring the music and Troy's direction, I used his closeness to leverage free of him and trip him to the ground, riding him down to straddle him.

Mistake. The ground was Troy's domain.

He went down easily enough, taking my weight with a grunt, and flipped our positions even more easily. His hand closing around my throat just made me laugh.

Perfect. The thrill of creating life or welcoming death in the squeeze of a hand.

"Control it, Arden. Now." The low growl in his voice spoke to the strain he was under to resist me.

I didn't want to listen. I'd been controlling so Goddess-damned much lately. I wanted to *let go*. Like with the storm, Val and the Collective be damned.

"Control it. Or I'll use the bond."

A kiss of pain accompanied the threat, and I hissed. For a moment, I considered hunting him. Tasting his blood and flesh.

Then my mind recoiled in horror.

What the fuck?

This wasn't me. I didn't want his blood. This was the curse.

I reeled it in, gasping as Chaos snapped back into me.

"Good," he said. "See? You control it. You're in charge."

In charge. Me.

I blinked then squeezed my eyes shut, trying to sort out all the conflicting pieces of myself. The maenad magic roared, cresting against my shields as I tried to keep it contained. I'd kept it under control for so very long, and it wanted blood now. It wanted chaos and deviltry and all the sexual promise Troy had teased forth in our dance.

"You've got this, Arden." Troy's grip tightened around my throat as I involuntarily tried to buck him off. "Lock it down."

"T, I'ma need you to wrap this up," Allegra said. "Super fucking fast."

The strain in her voice pulled my attention to the deck. She was hunched over the railing, breathing hard. Thana was in a similar position on the opposite end, lips curled in a snarl as she pointedly avoided Allegra's eye. Etain was in the yard at the foot of the stairs, hugging herself as she stared hungrily at Haroun, and Haroun was in the far corner nearer the woods looking at her the same way.

Fuck. The last thing I wanted was to hurt my people.

I fought the burn of the wine in my veins to wrench back control of the magic it'd awakened. Shoved it back into its box. And let go of Chaos.

As I did, everyone present gasped like they'd been drowning and then relaxed.

"Fuck," Thana said.

As Troy backed off of me I sat up and said, "Sorry."

"All good, my queen." Thana shook herself. "I just wasn't expecting to get hit that hard."

"Me neither," Etain said. "I've been around a maenad before, but it was nothing compared to that. Usually, it's just a suggestion of a good time but this? Goddess save me."

Troy studied me. "Are you okay?"

I took a minute to check myself before answering. "I think so. I'm tipsy as hell and Chaos is fighting me, but I'm in control."

"Just tipsy?"

I just looked at him. He was linked into my neural network. He knew exactly what my state was and was probably being affected by it.

Allegra saved me from having to answer. "She's too strong to use this at a summit, Troy. That was a few glasses of wine on an empty stomach with no power hangover to shunt the power to, and she nearly wiped out five of us who knew what was going on. It'd be discovered and taken as an act of aggression at a gathering."

"Agreed," Troy said. "Arden, that means we continue controlling your alcohol intake. Maybe hint that you're a maenad so they don't test it and risk being pulled in, although that would run the risk that they try pushing it to put you in breach of the peace."

"Fine by me." I was relieved, but even so, my heart fell.

Once upon a time, I'd asked Troy to help me learn to control Chaos in the hope that I could eventually turn the maenad magic into a gift rather than a curse. Now, we needed some kind of advantage going into any kind of negotiation or summit with the other elven Houses. But I couldn't help but feel like rather than finding one, all I'd done was prove that once again—as with the storm—I was too much for everyone to deal with. Too dangerous.

And in trying to embrace all of myself, all I was doing was setting myself further away from everyone around me.

Chapter 8

I fled to the bathroom to take a shower while Troy talked to the other elves, then took myself to bed.

Problem was, the unspent magic kept building. I hadn't worked it up to that level since the first disaster, and that time, I'd unknowingly loosed it on an entire population downtown. The energy had dissipated, so I was fine.

This time, it was trapped within me, raging like a rabid were.

By the time Troy got to me after seeing the others off, I was clenched into a tight little ball in bed, my face buried against the pillow, trying to swallow my pain and need as I desperately walled myself away from him and tried to ride the power until it burned out.

"What— Goddess, Arden." He leaned over the bed. "What do you need?"

"Don't know. More." It was all I could say about the pit in my core.

If anyone other than Troy was with me, it might have ended badly. But he knew.

First came the sounds of him stripping then the opening and shutting of the nightstand where I kept a small silver knife.

"I'm going to give you a little blood, okay?"

"I'm not—"

"Stop. Smell."

The scent of his blood burst through my senses, rosemary and sage and power. I uncurled enough to reach for it. The maenad magic wanted two things above all: blood and sex. Chaos and destruction as well, but those were at the root.

"Thought so." He climbed into bed behind me and wrapped his arm over me, offering his wrist.

I managed to hold off for all of a single heartbeat before taking it. Hot, herby liquid hit my tongue, more like ambrosia than anything I'd ever tasted. I pulled harder on his wrist and fell into sensation.

The next time I was aware of anything, he was gently pulling free. The warmth of his naked body ran the length of mine behind me. I was safe. More importantly, I was sated.

Or almost sated. Turning in his arms, I kissed him.

He rolled to his back and pulled me on top. Heat and desire reached me through the bond, echoing my own, but I hesitated to give myself over to it.

Troy's grip on my waist rocked me against him as he arched his hips. "I want it, Arden. You're not using me. Don't worry."

That was all I needed.

I kissed him again, allowing the remnants of the maenad hunger to pour into it. Claiming every inch of his body, starting at his lips, making my way down his neck, his scarred chest, the flat planes of his abs. His deep groan of pleasure when I took the length of him into my mouth redoubled my own.

I wasn't working him long before he dragged me back up and guided himself into me. Then I rode him. Hard. Fast. Taking pleasure even as I gave it, chasing my climax until I toppled over the edge of it.

He came right along with me.

I stayed where I was, leaning against his chest and spiraling back down into myself. Really myself, not the maenad's madness.

"Better?" Troy asked.

I nodded, still not moving off of him.

"Good. I'm sorry."

That got me to lift my head and frown blearily at him. "For what?"

"Pushing you into that."

"Don't be." My voice was my own again, if hoarser than usual. "You didn't push me. We had to find out, and I could have said no." Either way, it was better than the time Roman had tried to startle me into showing more of myself, without asking or talking about it first.

Troy pulled me back down for a kiss before carefully rolling us to our sides and resting his forehead against mine. A flash of fear, quickly buried, hit me from him.

Words tried to stick in my throat, but I got them out. "Are you afraid of me now?"

"No! No, cariñamí. I love your strength and your power. All of it. No matter how far beyond me it is. Hell, I'm honored you chose me. But I'm afraid *for* you." His arms tightened around me. "People resent and fear strength. You can't hide forever. Nor should you have to. But that means there will be attempts. And I don't ever want to go through what I felt when I thought you'd died on the freeway again. Not when I love you this much."

I cuddled tighter against him, relieved. I needed someone not to be scared of me. Someone who would hold my hand as the world burned and walk alongside me every step of the way. Someone who didn't think I was too much, when even other elementals were threatened by my strength.

I needed *him*.

"I'll be there," he said in reply to whatever he picked up from the bond or maybe an unintentional sending of those thoughts. "And you will never be too much for me. All your power does is inspire me to step up into my own, so I can be worthy of you." He kissed my forehead. "Now go to sleep. We need to be sharp for the press conference tomorrow evening."

I did as he said, allowing the dregs of all the magic I'd used to pull me under.

△▽△▽

I slept in the next day, well into the afternoon. When I got up, I felt lighter than I had in a while. Like a pressure valve had been released. Maybe I needed to tap into the maenad more often. Carefully. But I'd learned with my elemental powers that practicing with them and working the energy was a must.

Maybe accepting all of my magic was long overdue.

Troy smiled at me from the dining table when I emerged. He had his laptop out and a fresh cup of coffee steaming next to it. A light bandage wrapped his wrist. "There you are."

The last knot of worry in me loosened, and I went to make a cup of tea.

"You're okay?" I asked. The bond said he was feeling good, relaxed and satisfied, but I never wanted to take it for granted or assume I knew the reason. Besides, silver didn't hit elves as bad as it did weres, but he'd heal a little slower than usual. I couldn't help but worry about the bandage.

"Better than okay. You trusted me to help you make a personal decision that impacted the House last night." His smile broadened and got a little smug on the edges. "And you claimed me in as close to the old elven fashion as you can."

Ah. That was what drove the satisfaction. Last night had triggered something feel-good in the hormonal bond tying him to me.

I brought my tea to the table then went back to dig in the fridge for some cold cuts and cheese before he could remind me to eat something. "I was thinking I should practice with it, when I have some breathing room. Maybe it could be useful to the House if I got better with it." I brought the charcuterie and some crackers to the table and sat opposite him. "And...maybe it could be fun for our hunts. Once I have better control."

That perked him right up. The bond tightened as his focus zeroed in on me and his pupils dilated, his expression hungry. "I would like that. Very much."

I smiled at the drop in the pitch of his voice and the banked heat in it, reaching across the table to squeeze his hand. "Okay. Priorities though. Press conference."

He squeezed his eyes shut then blinked rapidly, the sure sign that wrestling his brain back on track was an effort. "Right. Let's see if I can get through that without thinking of a hunt now. Um. The weather thing."

I winced. "You think it'll come up?"

"You know it will. Someone is bound to remember you throwing lightning at the Wild Hunt and connect the dots."

"Shit." I ate a little and drank some tea then filled him in on the relevant parts of the conversation with Val while he listened grimly. "So, with all that, I guess we have three options. Deflect, truth, or lie. And as much as I don't mind lying to mundanes, I have a feeling it'd be a bad idea this time. It will come back to bite me in the ass later, now that we're out, and it might hurt the other elementals even more." My face heated. "I also have a tendency to get mad at people who lie to me so...can't be a hypocrite."

Troy just sipped his coffee, letting me think it through aloud.

I sighed. "It's a policy decision, isn't it."

He nodded.

Which meant I couldn't just avoid the presser and let Troy handle it. I had to step up as Arbiter of the Carolinas demesne.

What path would best protect my people? What would help me navigate the situation with the other elementals?

Truth. It would have to be the truth, no matter how much deeper in the shit it got me with the local elemental collective. Deflection would be seen as a form of lying. Hell, the whole point of the Reveals had been telling the truth. That we existed. And as I'd told Val, I couldn't keep owning everything for everybody else. I was doing everything I could. At some point, someone other than Troy needed to step the fuck up and help me help them.

I sighed and ground the heels of my palms into my forehead. "I hate this."

"I know. It's the right thing to do though."

"I didn't even say what I chose."

"You don't have to." Troy swatted my hands away and tipped my chin to look at him. "You don't take the easy road. You take the right one. It's why we work together, in spite of everything."

"I'm not gonna be stupid about it though. I need to spin it somehow. And protect the other elementals, as much as I can and as much as they'll probably hate me for it."

"Start as you mean to go on."

I finished my tea as I thought that through. "Acknowledge it. But don't explain it."

"Exactly." He toasted me with his mug before finishing it. "You're a queen. You don't owe anyone an explanation, and your time is a gift."

That thought stayed with me as we spent the rest of the afternoon honing our talking points for any questions that might come up in the press conference and signing off on various things to push negotiations for the elven summit forward.

Two years ago, even one year ago, I would have been overwhelmed.

Now? Yeah, it was a lot. But I finally felt like I was growing into my role.

I tried to hold onto that feeling as we arrived at the Raleigh Police Department's press room. The space was packed, wall to wall, with a few people standing. It smelled overwhelmingly like too many mundane bodies and all their excitement and fear. I'd never noticed it so strongly before my power boost amplified my physical senses.

Steady, Troy sent. A forbidding expression combined with a minor Aetheric suggestion to get anyone inclined to approach us to think again as his hand at a professional height on my back steered me toward our places to one side of the stage. Maria already waited there in a surprisingly modest and understated long-sleeved gown in a grey that made her Tyrian purple hair pop.

"Good to see you, Arbiter." Her voice was an all-business tone, low enough that mundanes would struggle to hear, even with mics.

"Likewise." I stood between her and Troy, with Troy on the side closest to the stairs—and anyone who might try to reach us.

He was in working mode, walled off except for the barest crack that would let him know if I noticed something and didn't have time to verbalize it. We had the Ebon Guard scattered throughout the area, but he never took chances. Not with me.

Maria glanced at him. The desire to tease flicked across her features so quickly I nearly missed it before she resumed a seemingly bored scan of the room.

"Thank you," I murmured.

That got me a quick smile. She knew exactly why I was thanking her. "We're all in this together, and you didn't leave me hanging."

"I wouldn't."

The look she gave me said as clearly as words that she'd learned people would do the contrary, and I resisted the urge to give her a side hug.

It was good to be on better terms with her again. Even if it was here.

The buzz of conversation in the room hushed as Detective Rice and his captain entered. Rice stood before the podium.

Apparently, they were going to let him take the fall if this turned into a clusterfuck.

For half a minute, I felt bad for him. Then I remembered how he'd been acting lately and shoved it down.

"All right, folks, let's simmer down," Rice said. "There we go. Thank you. Now, we're here to address and clarify the recent situation of the vampire-related deaths here in Raleigh and the subsequent curfew. You can see here we've got some representatives from the supernatural community. That's because this investigation is being carried out jointly. Today, we're sharing the results."

The room erupted.

At my side, Troy tensed. A bare tightening of his form most people might have missed. But not me.

I barely resisted the urge to soothe him. I had my job. He had his.

Rice raised a hand and waited for silence. "We implemented a curfew not because of the local supernaturals but because these acts of aggression were being carried out by out-of-state vampires. I have Maria, who's in charge of Raleigh's vampire community, here to explain."

Well, I'd be damned. He was actually telling the truth. Part of it anyway. I noted he left out the part where some of the bodies were *faked* vampire deaths committed by humans. Bastard.

Maria stepped forward when Rice moved to the side. Her usually flirtatious expression was grim. "First, we deeply regret that members of the supernatural community behaved in this manner and extend our condolences to the grieving families. Murder is against our code and—"

A white woman wearing the badge of a conservative news channel shot to her feet from among the reporters. "You expect us to believe that? Vampires aren't out for blood?"

Maria tilted her head. "I said nothing of blood. I was speaking of murder. We have laws against it, same as you, and strict rules around consent. Keep up, dear."

A few people in the room tittered as I wrestled to keep a straight face. If a man had said that, it'd be taken as sexist and condescending, but Maria leveraged her tiny stature and flirtatious femininity to make it charming. Even the reporter sat down. Huffily, but she sat rather than fight the double-standard.

I made a mental note to have a word with Maria about it at some point though.

"Now," she continued, "we're not interested in murdering humans. If you won't believe it's because we're good people, then believe that it's bad for business, bad for our reputation, and bad for everyone's long-term survival." Her voice hardened. "Those who crossed that line two weeks ago have been found guilty and put to death, as per our laws. Justice has been served."

Stunned silence held the room.

With more gravitas, Maria said, "We do not mess around. Those vampires who committed this grave crime were based out of state. They thought the work we're doing here, to cement better relations between the vampires and the people of Raleigh, would distract us. That it would make us weak." She paused, shaking her head. "But my friends, it takes strength to build bridges and strength to maintain them. Your fight is ours. We will not let interlopers take advantage of this city or murder its people. We are with you. We *are* you. And when we work together toward peace and prosperity for all, we are Raleigh strong."

With a small, courtly incline of her head, she stepped back to allow Rice to take the stand again. I watched the crowd of reporters, noting a few of them with the startled or bemused expressions suggesting they heard what Maria hadn't said outright: that she and her coterie were needed as protection against these outsiders.

"There you have it," Rice said. "Raleigh PD will continue to work in concert with law-abiding members of the supernatural community. *Our* laws, not theirs, and we will continue to keep Raleigh safe as we navigate these troubled times. We will briefly take some questions now."

A different reporter from before stood, an East Asian man. "Is that Arden Finch?"

Rice glanced over his shoulder at me. "It is."

"I have a question for Ms. Finch."

Of course they did. Sensational vampire murders were nothing on the woman who'd stopped the Wild Hunt, apparently. The elves had done a pretty good job of scrubbing me from digital records, but it'd taken time. If the world didn't know my name and face before, they would now.

No more quiet work behind the scenes or in private rooms. I was stepping into the spotlight.

Chapter 9

I steeled myself and stepped to the microphone Rice had just vacated.

"Ms. Finch," the reporter said, "you seem to be in the midst of a number of supernatural situations."

"Is that a statement or a question?"

He gave me an annoyed look. "There was a strange weather disruption centered over the Piedmont the other night. Do you know anything about that?"

Here it was. The question I'd been praying not to get. If the Elemental Collective was pissed now, they'd be furious at having elemental magic be openly admitted to. But I couldn't make policy decisions based solely on who would be angry with them, or there would be no decisions made at all.

I reminded myself to be the Arbiter and schooled my face to something vaguely disinterested, even as my stomach knotted, as much for my own safety as theirs and their inevitable outrage. "I do."

The room exploded as seemingly every reporter in it shouted a question at once. It took every ounce of my self-control and Troy's Darkwatch training to maintain my composure as the air molecules in the room assaulted my sixth sense as much as my ears and the scent of fear spiked. To give them an unimpressed look and keep my mouth shut until they quieted.

"Do any of y'all wanna try speaking one at a time?" I asked in a forced drawl.

The same reporter as before spoke again. "Was it something you did?"

"Yes."

The reporters practically quivered with the desire to shout more questions but, somehow, kept themselves in check this time.

"Would you elaborate?" the reporter asked.

"No."

"No?"

I offered as bland a smile as I could. "As I've told others, it's a full sentence, and I'm not in the habit of repeating myself."

"Surely, you can understand the magnitude of what you've just said."

"Again, is there a question in there?"

"People have a right to know what's going on."

"People have rights to all manner of things." I forced myself to smile more warmly this time to take the sting out of it. "Privacy, for one. And I'm sure *you* can understand that, until the people of Otherside are secured in our full and equal rights with humans, privacy and safety are two sides of the same coin. Right here in Raleigh, we had to worry about disruptive human elements seeking to take the law into their own hands the other week."

Another reporter, a white man, stood. "That sounds like you're hiding things."

"That didn't sound like a question."

He sneered. "Fine, Ms. Finch. What are you hiding?"

"No more or less than anyone else. Unless you want to tell us what goes on when you're alone?"

"I'm not a public figure."

"That's debatable if you're a journalist, but neither am I. Merely a local person willing to assist in local matters."

Hopefully that would communicate to any Othersiders watching that I wasn't trying to step on toes, only manage my own backyard. For now.

"But you can wield magic."

I just arched an eyebrow.

The reporter barely managed not to roll his eyes. "Don't you think the ability to wield magic means you have some kind of responsibility to people who don't?"

"Would you really like to discuss responsibilities and what's owed by those who have power because of their heritage or features they were born with? That'd be an interesting conversation in this country. Perhaps you'd like to start with LandBack or reparations to the descendants of the enslaved? Or maybe reproductive rights and gender-affirming care." I fixed him with a steady stare, letting a hint of my frustration with both the elementals and this press conference peek out. "Yes, I have power. And I try to use it to do what I can for those who do not. Usually at significant personal cost to myself and those who support me, but shit cannot continue as it's gone up to now."

The reporter's pale skin flushed a very deep red, and the energetic equivalent of "oh shit" rippled through the room as people abruptly made connections they might rather not have.

Yeah, it was a bunch of what-aboutism and deflection, which I'd meant to avoid.

But I was not going to own responsibilities for a human populace that'd voted for the politicians who had spent the last year gleefully and maliciously rolling back every hard-won piece of legislation I, Maria, and others had negotiated after the Reveals and tearing down their own people along the way.

I didn't owe them any piece of myself. And yet, I was still stood up here, with these hot lights glaring into my eyes and the scrape of all their agitation in every bump of an air molecule against my skin, answering their questions.

I was tired of this. Abruptly, I decided that was enough of a reason to be done with it.

I didn't owe anything to anybody here, and I'd given more than enough. Troy had the bond completely walled off, giving me space to think without his influence, but I knew he had to be feeling some kind of way. Every moment I stood at this podium, I was exposed to sniper fire, either literal or metaphysical. We were here to talk about the actions we were taking to secure Raleigh and reassure that the local vampires weren't a threat, not to talk about me.

Yeah. Time to wrap it up. Steer it back to what this whole mess had been called to talk about in the first place.

With a last small smile, I said, "Given that we're here to support our friends and allies in the vampire community, let's keep this focused where it's important. No more questions for me. Thank you."

Of course, the room exploded again.

Detective Rice waved it down as I resumed my place between Troy and Maria while Rice wrapped up. I tried to pay attention, but the questions started repeating themselves, and my mind wandered to what the elemental reaction would be. Or rather, how bad it would be.

When it was done, I let Troy do his bodyguard thing to get me through the crowd and to the back door, where Allegra was waiting.

Her eyes brightened and her features relaxed to see Maria following us, but they didn't give any other outward sign of being together. We were careful to stay out of the line of sight of the windowpane in the door, but none of us wanted to take any risks in betraying how close we were.

"That little mention of LandBack and reparations and all that was well-played," Allegra said. "Polls are already creeping up among Black female respondents in particular. Small, but you sent a message."

I sighed, annoyed that doing the right thing was treated like points in a game. "But let me guess. I'm losing the white male segment by much more."

She shrugged. "For what it's worth, the majority of that segment wasn't with you to begin with. They're still hung up on that batshit conspiracy theory about the president feeding babies to the vampires so they'd rig the vote."

"Yeah." I scrubbed my hands over my face as Maria growled low in her chest but blessedly kept her mouth shut. That was a disgusting bit of nonsense that somehow wouldn't go away, no matter what we did to counter it.

Reassurance curled through the bond from Troy, grounding me.

"I know it's a numbers game," I said. "I know they have the numbers. But I can't chase people who are never going to come around to my side. I have to keep speaking my truth and painting an alternative for those who need me. Need *us*. We have to come together."

"Agreed," Troy and Allegra said together.

Allegra squeezed my arm. "Stay strong, Arbiter. Thanks for taking lead."

Because if I hadn't, Maria would have been forced to. "It's my job."

"I'm just glad to see you doing it. Callista wouldn't have. She would have found a scapegoat." She looked at her brother. "T, keep her safe."

"Always."

With a nod, Allegra gestured Maria to stay behind her and left.

I frowned as Troy and I waited to follow them out. *Is Allegra playing bodyguard to Maria?*

Seems so.

Omar's not going to be happy.

Not my problem.

I glanced at him, surprised at the sharp edge to his thoughts.

Sorry. I don't like having you on display like that. Queens move in the shadows of Otherside. Not in public. Certainly not on stage.

It's fine. I get it.

He swiped a text, and the phone buzzed almost immediately with a response. "Pickup in five minutes."

"You mind if we wait outside?" I glanced back toward the room where the press conference had been. "I need some air."

The scent of burnt marshmallow flooded the small hallway as Troy murmured a spell in elvish. He must have been worried. English worked just as well, but he tended to use elvish when he wanted to put more intention behind it. If I understood correctly, it went beyond "don't see us" and into flat-out "fuck off."

When we stepped outside, Harqil was lounging against the wall.

I jumped, looking around to see if anyone else noticed them. Troy's hand twitched as he stopped a reflexive move to grab his longknife from its spine sheath.

"Nobody else can see me. Or hear me," the celestial messenger said in response to my reaction. "One of the perks of the job. So maybe you two want to stand so it looks like you're talking to each other?" They grinned. "Unless you're happy to appear quite mad."

I gritted my teeth and did as they said, shifting to face Troy and leaning to look like the two of us were having a conversation. His spell should cover us, but no use taking risks.

"So good at subterfuge," Harqil said approvingly.

"What's this about?" I asked. "We need to make it quick before the press finds us."

"A congratulations on the conference. And a gift. A clue."

"What kind of clue?" After Neith's gift—the dagger that'd briefly stolen my will—I was extremely wary of things given by the gods or their emissaries.

They narrowed their eyes and glanced between Troy and me. "I can't say I've ever seen auras mingle like the two of yours. It's more now than it was the last time we spoke. So much the better."

"For what?" Troy asked.

"Our clue. This...situation"—they waved their hand between us—"with the aura will insulate you somewhat."

I stiffened. "What exactly is this clue?"

"As I said. A gift."

"I'm not sure I want gifts from the gods," I said as alarm spiked in the bond. Neith had used the knife I now kept locked in a lead-lined box at home to bind me to the gods of the hunt. I'd nearly killed Troy with it, twice. And apparently the reason the tricksters were interested in me to begin with was because of a gift.

"Nevertheless, a gift is to be given." Harqil's expression became dangerous. "Don't be rude. It's unwise to refuse the gods."

I looked at Troy.

If you take it, I'll catch you if you fall, he sent.

Unless it pulls you down too.

"Now that is a very good trick." Harqil straightened. "Mind-to-mind communication? Between an elf and an elemental? Superb. Completely unexpected."

I froze, and Troy shifted into a ready posture. I put a restraining hand on his arm, not wanting him to throw himself at a celestial as much as reminding him that nobody else in the area would be able to see why he was ready to attack. The Guard listened to him but were fanatically loyal to me, which was why I generally stayed out of it when he gave them orders. If they arrived with our ride and thought their king had "gone feral," as they called it, or was any kind of threat to me, they'd do their best to kill him, and then all of them would die.

Harqil watched as Troy relaxed, a mischievous smile curling their lips.

A burst of lemon zest-scented Aether pulled all of us around.

"Arden," Iaret said, "I have— Oh bloody hell, what are you doing here?"

"I could ask you the same," Harqil said. Again the narrow-eyed scrutiny, this time at Duke's djinni life partner. "You shouldn't be able to see me."

Iaret rolled her eyes and sneered. "Celestials are hard to miss. Especially those I have a particular grievance with."

"Hang on," I interrupted, too surprised by the exchange to scold her for manifesting in public like that. The Détente might be in tatters, but it still wasn't smart to even hint that an Othersider could do that. "Y'all know each other?"

Harqil's tone became mocking. "We're acquainted. It happens."

"Acquainted," Iaret snarled. "You—"

"Just the messenger. As ever. Don't shoot me." They arched an eyebrow. "And don't forget the terms."

With a sharp-toothed snarl, Iaret subsided.

I really, really wanted to know what the hell this was all about. My private investigator's instincts and curiosity were tingling. Iaret had been caged in a crystal of her own soul for thirty years, so this had to go back before the events that'd led to my birth. It could have nothing to do with anything.

On the other hand, it could be another piece in a puzzle I'd only thought was completed.

I sighed as the Sight prickled. There was something here. And I didn't have time for it right now.

"Can we please wrap this up?" I glanced around, relieved to find us oddly alone. Troy's spell in action, maybe, because we should have been followed out. Somehow, that put me more on edge.

I turned to study Harqil, wondering if they were a shapeshifter like many of the tricksters and their allies were or if their gift lay in defying categorization. My eye kept trying to slip away from them. Useful, for a celestial messenger. Would I see them if they didn't want me to know they were there?

Not the important question just now. I refocused. "I will accept the gift on the terms that you tell me what I owe in exchange."

"Silly girl. It's a gift." Despite the pronouncement, something dark sparked in Harqil's eyes, like I'd seen something I wasn't supposed to.

All of a sudden, I remembered the ring I wore on the middle finger of my right hand. To see the unseen, Janae's note had said. Blood magic. Activated blood magic now. Duke had said it was to see the true nature of a thing, like the lie in a truth or the soul in a body.

Seeing the unseen. And the Sight.

Goddess, but I was slow sometimes. Whatever the ring was supposed to do, it was boosting my connection to the Sight.

"That doesn't mean you're not expecting an exchange," I said carefully. "A gift for a gift." I didn't remind them I'd already been told something was expected in exchange for whatever the original gift of the tricksters was. "It's only polite, of course. Reciprocity is sacred."

"So it is. But it wouldn't be a trick if I told you." Harqil reached within their jacket and withdrew something small. "Take it or leave it. But you may find yourself wishing you had this clue later."

They pressed whatever it was into my hands before I could object, twisted reality, and disappeared. A gem rested in my palm—a huge, princess-cut ruby. It glinted in the faint light from the parking lot.

"Fuck. I really don't want this," I said.

Iaret snorted. "You're smarter than you look."

"Thanks? What's your story with Harqil anyway?"

"Nothing worth talking about." Iaret's tone was too light for that to be true.

"Mm-hmm. You wanna give this gift a check before I blow us all to the ninth circle of hell?"

Despite her implication that it'd be wiser not to mess with the thing, Iaret perked up. Like Duke and most djinn, shiny objects—especially magical ones—were like catnip. She flitted over, and I held very still as she passed a hand over it. The scent of lemon zest spiked as she made a similar evaluation to when Duke had looked at the ring the witches had given me.

"That is interesting." A frown creased her brow. "Magic won't touch it."

Chapter 10

"What?" I glanced at Troy. "Like the soul gem that canceled my magic out? The one you used to reconnect Troy and me?"

"No, that was attuned to elemental magic and modified to layer Aether. This is like a black hole. Every time I reach toward it, it sucks magic in but does nothing else."

Troy shook his head. "This cannot be good."

I was inclined to agree. A gift that was also a trick. The implication being that the trick was on me. Or was it?

"Is it safe?" I asked.

"Arden." Troy's expression was hard. "I will do my best to catch you. But if eats magic, if I can't—"

"I know. It didn't end well last time. But we can't leave it here, and it's not bothering me any to hold it. Maybe as long as I don't try to do magic?"

He closed his eyes in a long blink and sighed. "I'll see if we have any neutrality boxes in the car."

"Thank you."

The lead-lined boxes weren't common, especially in elven spaces, given the harm lead caused elves. But knowing Troy, we'd have at least one handy, just in case. Especially after that last godly gift.

"If anyone asks, Iaret found something," I said.

"Fine." He pulled out his phone then put it away again when Thana arrived with his car. When she pulled to a stop, Troy opened the door to the back seat for me.

Iaret grabbed my arm. "Wait. I need a minute. A private minute."

Troy's lips pressed into a thin line. "Make it fast, before the press finds us."

"Moody thing, isn't he?" Iaret said in a low voice when the door shut behind him.

I elbowed her, amused in spite of myself when she jumped at the physical contact. "He's just trying to take care of me."

"He's being an elf and trying to impose order on a world that is inherently disordered. It's why they're all such pains in the ass. They're dedicated to a futile task, and they don't even live long enough to see it. It's boring." She glared at the car, missing my dirty look at the commentary on elves. "He's usually more fun. For an elf anyway."

I shook my head. Only a djinni, with a lifespan of thousands of years, would think the centuries a healthy, powerful elf could live were short. "Be that as it may. What did you come to talk about?"

For all her usual bluster and snark, Iaret's sudden stillness put me on guard.

"Iaret?"

"Duke's hiding something," she murmured.

"I thought he might be. He's been avoiding me. Do you know what?"

"No. But something is off. We were supposed to be handling Council business together, but he kept disappearing."

I frowned, weighing her body language, tone, and words. She was seriously worried. "Off how?"

"I can't put my finger on it."

"Do I need to step in?"

"No. But I..." She trailed off and turned away. For a minute, I thought she was going to disappear again. "I want you to trust me, Arden. I know sometimes you don't. Maybe I deserve that. But I liked the power we shared during the Wild Hunt, and if Harqil is walking again, something is coming." Her expression became fierce. "Duke is all I had for millennia. I will protect him from himself. I would normally find a way to use you to do it. But..."

"But you want trust," I finished softly when she didn't.

She nodded once, sharply, her jaw clenched. She might want trust, but she hated that she did. Maybe especially that she wanted it from me.

"Iaret, I get it." I looked pointedly at the car. I couldn't see Troy, but she knew I'd do anything to protect him from anyone, including himself. "Keep an eye on Duke. I'll see if I can get him to talk to me. If whatever this is looks like it'll cause trouble with your work though, part of that trust is going to come from knowing that you'll tell me before it causes the kind of chaos you might enjoy but I don't have time to clean up. You got me?"

"Yes. Thank you, Arden."

Without another word, she disappeared, leaving me to contemplate what the hell might be wrong with the one tie I had left to my childhood—and my one remaining blood family member.

Sighing, I joined Troy in the back seat. He handed me a lead-lined wooden box without comment, and I dropped the stone in, snapping it shut and wiping my hands on my pants.

Thana twisted to look at us. "Toro ben?"

"Fine," I said.

"Je. Par nu. Iro," Troy said. Good for now, but let's go.

Thana did as he said, getting us out of Raleigh in record time.

I noted two of our other cars tailing us on the freeway and took a deep breath to calm myself. All of this was still weird to me. The public awareness, the protection details.

Get used to it, Troy sent. *This is nothing compared to what we'll deal with at a summit.*

I don't want to get used to it. That means I've given up.

That got me a look, a considering frown. *I hadn't thought of it that way.*

I reached for his hand and held it as we raced home, letting him brood. Usually, we were very much on the same page. Other times, something that seemed obvious to me smacked him hard and vice versa.

Sometimes he needed me to pull him out of his moods. This wasn't one of them. He was still alert to threats, almost running his own thoughts in the background as he kept an eye on the surroundings.

My phone buzzing interrupted both our thoughts.

"Blocked number." I scowled at it. "I really don't want to take this."

"I'd say don't, but if House Ead is going to be part of this summit, we need an idea of what the senator's been told."

My lip twisted. He was right, even if I hated it.

I stabbed the answer button harder than strictly necessary. "Finch."

"Ms. Finch. This is Acting Director Lara Sinclaire with the Bureau for Supernatural Investigation. I hope this is a good time."

She was being polite, so I could at least try and get off on the right foot with a new person. "Ms. Sinclaire. What can I do for you?"

"Your case file just landed on my desk. That was a rather spectacular statement you made at the press conference. If it was true."

I closed my eyes and took a long breath. Would none of these people learn to simply ask a Goddess-damned question? "Maybe it's also in my file that leading statements from authority figures or all-around nosy people irritate the hell outta me, largely because I am a licensed private investigator with extensive experience working with law enforcement and know how the game works."

Troy squeezed my hand. *Diplomacy.*

Sinclaire didn't answer for a moment. "Duly noted. Senator Wright apparently did not pass everything along like he said he would."

Heat flared in my cheeks for snapping. I pushed it down. "I appreciate that. Now. What can I do for you?"

"Is it true that you are responsible for the weather phenomena three nights ago?"

"Yes. But you watched the press conference, didn't you?"

"I did, ma'am, yes."

I frowned. She'd ma'am-ed me. I couldn't recall Senator Wright offering that. Still, irritation flickered at being asked to repeat myself. "There you have it."

"You weren't bluffing for the cameras to keep your people safe?"

"No, I took a risk on telling the truth."

"A risk?"

"Of course it's a risk. I'm assuming it's why you're calling. Senator Wright ghosted me after telling me he got me security clearance for the proceedings of the Supernatural Committee, and the minute I suggest I can do something interesting, here you are."

"I can neither confirm nor deny anything about security clearance, Ms. Finch, but I did want to talk to you about your...powers."

I looked at Troy, knowing my expression mirrored the sneer on his. That meant they'd lied. We kept playing it straight, and they kept lying. If I wasn't careful, I'd turn us into the Otherside version of the humans' Democratic Party—always on the back foot because they expected the other party to play by the rules and keep their promises.

Yeah. Not having that.

"My powers aren't up for discussion," I said curtly. "Was there anything else I could help you with? Maybe a conversation about getting the Sons of Seth listed as a terrorist organization, given how many individuals, homes, and businesses they've attacked and terrorized in the last year, both supernatural and mundane? I'm also quite interested to know what Verve Health's relationship with your agency is, given some concerning information that's crossed my desk."

"Now, Ms. Finch—"

"Sinclaire, I'm gonna tell you the same thing I told Wright. You come correct, or you don't come to me at all. I keep trying to work with y'all, and y'all keep demonstrating you can't be trusted. So here's the ground rules."

She tried to get a word in, and I raised my voice and kept talking.

"I will not talk about my powers. I will not share information about Otherside or any individuals who are suspected or confirmed to be supernatural. And so long as groups like the Sons of Seth are allowed to operate with impunity, especially while any suspected Othersiders are unfairly treated whether as victims or as perpetrators, I will reserve the right to take whatever actions I deem necessary to protect my people in the absence of fair and equitable treatment under the law from your people. Oh—and y'all got the one kidnapping attempt for free. I'm calling it a cultural misunderstanding. Best pray you don't find out what happens if you try it again. Are we clear?"

"Kidnapping attempt?"

"Bless your heart. Looks like Senator Wright hid an awful lot from you. If he does anything other than admit it, he's lying. If you don't want to trust my word, I have the records, and I have video."

"You seem incredibly well informed and well connected for a simple private investigator, Ms. Finch."

"That's right. I am. Think on that. Now, you know what I want and what I expect if we're going to have a working relationship. Given that *you* called *me*, you also know I'm the best shot you have at achieving whatever your objectives are. Was there anything else?"

Sinclaire sighed, an irritated huff of air. "Yes. You may not want to talk about your powers, but we need to talk about limits. And since you brought up Verve, we also need to talk about registration and what the United States Government is going to require from Otherside."

I couldn't help it. I busted out laughing. It was either that or cry as she echoed my thoughts—my fears—from the other night, that I was too much, and added another layer of danger for all of Otherside.

"That's funny, Ms. Finch?"

"It's fucking hilarious, that you think I will help with any of that."

"We know about bronze."

All amusement fled, and Troy stiffened as in the bond his mind slammed down into the cold, empty zone that said he'd kill without a second thought and without a shred of regret. He freed his hand from mine to grab his own phone and started swiping out text messages.

I let my voice get as icy as his did sometimes. "That sounds like a threat."

"It doesn't have to be."

"But it's intended as one. And Director Sinclaire, I truly do not take kindly to threats. Nor do I take them lightly. Too many people have followed through on them for me to assume they're idle or empty bluffs, and the US government has already invoked the Patriot Act when speaking about Othersiders in the context of terrorism."

Maybe that got through to her. She paused. A silence stretched long, and I let it.

"You're not what I expected based on your profile, Ms. Finch."

"Something to reckon with, should you continue working with the Eads. They have an agenda. Maybe think about where it doesn't coincide with yours or with what's best for most people."

We hit the offramp for Durham. Troy was still swiping texts, and Thana's expression was grim in the rearview mirror.

"I'll take that under advisement," Sinclaire said. "Well, I can see we got started on the wrong foot. Let me go think about our conversation and see if we can't try again in a few days."

Get a real number, Troy sent. *No more blocked calls. Not if they're making threats.*

"I could be amenable to that," I said. "So long as someone calls me off a real number. I won't answer blocked calls anymore."

"Understood. Thank you for your time, Ms. Finch. God bless."

The call ended, and I scowled as I shoved my phone into my backpack. What the hell was it with these government types and their god? Wasn't separation of church and state supposed to be a thing?

As we navigated the streets toward home, I used my callstone to fill Duke in. For once, he answered. Maybe offering a deal was helping with whatever Iaret thought he had going on.

"I don't like it, little bird," he said in my head.

"I don't like it either. Fuck some shit up, will you? Keep them busy. And keep your end of the callstone unblocked. We're pushing hard for this elven summit, and I need to know how much trouble House Ead is making for us."

"Make trouble? I thought you'd never ask."

The connection ended before I could ask about any updates from the Djinn Council on Troy's offer for greater djinn involvement. Something was still going on with Duke, and I had a sinking suspicion it was to do with the tricksters.

Worse, I suspected it was to do with me too.

Chapter 11

I shelved the strange stone Harqil had given me in the hiding place in my closet. I'd figure out what it was and dig into the connection between Iaret and Harqil when I wasn't dog tired. Given how late we were working these days, I was starting to consider flipping to a nocturnal schedule. I still had to deal with mundanes, but maybe it was time to shift to a schedule that allowed more overlap with most of Otherside so I wasn't pulling these eighteen-hour working days. I'd had time to shower and inhale some leftovers when we got home, only to get a flood of calls and texts from the other factions about the press conference, an angry voicemail from Val, and an urgent request from Lyon right as I was ready to wind down for the night.

Troy nudged me under the table, having caught my mind wandering as he tried to focus on Samarre. "We can arrange for work for those who resettle," he said in response to something she'd asked. "But leadership in the House is out of the question."

I nodded to the screen as Samarre glanced at me, hoping she'd think I'd been paying attention the whole time. "Perhaps it can be revisited later," I said to back Troy up. "But not now."

Samarre mulled that over. "Very well. And the matter of King Troy's father?"

Troy leaned back in his chair, the picture of casual disinterest even as the bond tightened. "What of him?"

"A charter flight will need to be arranged. No records. We'll also need funds in advance."

"The funds, I get," Troy said. "It's not cheap arranging transfers or buying documents. Charter flights offer more flexibility. But no records? What aren't you telling us, Samarre?"

The elfess glanced to the side, like she was conferring with someone. "Let's just call it a precaution."

Troy frowned. "For who?"

"All of us."

Something wasn't right here. I half-closed my eyes, willing the Sight to tell me something as I rubbed the ring Janae had given me, to see the unseen. A fraction of a thought came to mind, and I let it slip past my lips. "Political prisoner."

The bond tightened even further as Troy held himself back from demanding I explain.

"He wasn't just exiled," I said, feeling my way. "And you don't know where he is by happenstance. You know where he is because he's being held prisoner somewhere, for something more than what Keithia publicly charged him with."

Samarre stiffened. "You're very well informed, my queen. Better than we were led to believe. That will be good for our partnership."

"It will if you stop treating all of this like a game that's yours to lose," I said. "See, I'm not impressed by how tricky y'all can be. Withholding information doesn't make me more inclined to offer those leadership positions you asked for."

She nodded slowly, her expression carefully blank. "Noted."

Troy's voice was cold as he asked, "What's our window for extraction?"

"We have a three-day window each month. The next one is in nine days."

"Understood." Troy glanced at me.

Summit first, I sent.

He turned back to the screen. "We'll be in touch in the next week with our answer. And Samarre? If you really want this, stop fucking around."

With an uncharacteristic but satisfying lack of diplomacy, he ended the call and shut the laptop. I kept my mouth shut as he leaned back in his chair, closed his eyes, and tilted his head back.

"That sounded like the Sight," he said.

"It was."

"Good. Because I didn't want to have to ask you how long you've known."

"I would have told you."

He cracked an eyelid open and looked at me sideways.

"I would have. I told you, when it comes to him, all of this needs to be your choice. If you don't want to deal with this, we can call it off. It's entirely up to you."

"No. Let's see it through. You just answered a question I've had for years."

"What question?"

His hand turned over, and I took the invitation to lace my fingers through his. He pulled my hand up to kiss it before answering. "Bonding to my mother might have been enough to merit exile, since—according to Keithia and Omar—he didn't tell anyone when he must have realized it was happening. But torture?" Troy shook his head. "That was too much. Far too much. It's a biological response. It happens even when we try to defend against it, especially if they were matched well enough to have me. And Keithia would have had them trying for a daughter after I was born, upping the odds of a bond. There had to have been something else."

I didn't say anything. He might be right. Or he might be a thirty-one-year-old man trying to parse a ten-year-old boy's blood-soaked memories.

With a heavy sigh, Troy dropped my hand and stood. "I don't know, Arden. I can't make sense of any of this. You were right.

About me not being able to see through the thorns, let alone move through them."

I rose and slipped my arms around him from behind, kissing him between the shoulder blades. "We'll figure it out."

"We can't—"

His phone went off.

When I moved to let him go, he tightened one hand around my arms and pulled me after him to the table to grab it. That made my heart swell, that he'd let me be there for him physically while he was in a muddle. Sometimes, he punished himself by insisting on space when he needed touch more.

Wariness darted through the bond, and his tone was hard when he answered the phone. "Solari."

"Troy?"

"Who is this?"

"Sonia Bedoe. Long time no see, my dear."

I couldn't help stiffening. House Bedoe was the one Etain thought might bring a non-compete agreement. But this Sonia's tone edged toward flirtation.

"Sonia." Troy turned in my arms and sat on the table, pulling me between his knees and kissing my forehead. "I'd say it's a pleasure, but the Richmond Houses haven't been that friendly lately."

"I know. But first, apparently congratulations are in order? You've been claimed?"

"Very much so. And happily."

That made me relax.

"Well then. Congratulations to you and the lucky woman."

"Come on. You know exactly who she is. And what she is."

I leaned back to raise my brows at him.

We have to play the game, he sent.

Sonia laughed. "Busted. Yes, we'd heard House Solari had been resurrected by an elemental queen claiming Feliciana's bloodline via Quinlan." She paused. "And that the oyëoro held their promise, and she's made you an equal king because of it."

I frowned, not liking the word "claiming" in this context. That sounded like it might be in question.

"All true." Troy cupped my jaw with his free hand and ran a thumb over my lips. "But you didn't call after fifteen years to confirm things your intelligence assets already knew."

"Mm. Also true." She let a silence drag out, during which Troy kissed me. "Very well. I'm calling on behalf of my mother."

"And what can House Solari do for Queen Esi?"

"She wants a non-compete agreement."

Troy smiled against my lips then leaned away. The gold flecks in his gaze—the oyëoro Sonia had mentioned—seemed to dance. "That so?"

"House Ead has made some...interesting choices, let's say."

"I'm aware."

"Let's cut the shit then. What's the price?"

"A summit."

"Of course it is." Sonia sighed. "That's a big ask. Especially from you."

I had no idea what that was supposed to mean, but apparently Troy did.

"The oyëoro don't make us more violent." Carefully leashed rage was under his tone. "The way we're treated because of them does its part though."

"I know, Troy. I know. But a king on equal footing with an elemental High Queen—where is she, by the way?"

Troy handed the phone over without hesitation.

"Hi," I said. "Sonia, is it?"

"Oh. Oh dear. I suppose you do treat each other as equals."

"In everything."

"How novel. Well, I'm sure you can forgive me calling your...mate. We had his number. Not yours."

"Of course. But what he said stands." With an effort, I moderated my tone. "I think we have some mutually beneficial things to discuss. Not just with Richmond but with Charleston as well."

Sonia whistled. "A true summit then. That might be interesting enough for Mom to agree."

"What, and the chance to meet a primordial elemental wasn't? I'm a little offended."

She laughed. "I really don't want to like you."

"It's mutual. But I promised Troy I'd try to start building bridges rather than simply eliminating potential threats."

Troy watched me with the narrowed eyes that said he was trying to read what I might do next.

I raised my eyebrows right back. If I started weak, they'd treat me that way. I didn't have time for it.

"I see," Sonia said. "Maybe you are trueborn after all. You certainly sound like one of our queens."

Despite the backhanded compliment or implied doubt or whatever it was, that actually reassured me. I'd been feeling like an imposter. And yet this stranger thought I sounded like a queen. Maybe that wasn't necessarily a good thing, given how the queens acted, but it was weirdly validating.

When I didn't respond, she said, "Fine. I will inform my mother that a summit is requested. Getting Charleston to the table is on you and Troy though. We'll have enough on our hands getting Ead and Hilith to play along. *If* Mom agrees to it, of course."

"Of course."

"What number can I reach you on?"

"This one is fine."

Troy smirked, knowing exactly what I was doing in staking a claim on him and liking it.

"Got it," Sonia said. "Well, I'll be in touch."

"You have one day," I said. "The last time I tried getting elves to the bargaining table, I lost an entire summer and ended up burning three Houses to the ground. I try not to let history repeat itself."

This time, Sonia's voice was much colder. "I'll be in touch."

Troy took his phone back and set it on the table behind him when the call ended. "You are going to hit them like one of your lightning bolts. I can't wait to see it."

I leaned back when he tried to kiss me again. "What the hell happened to being diplomatic? I thought you'd be pissed."

"That *was* diplomatic. For elves anyway. You kept your cool. Claimed what's yours. Didn't shout or snap or let her petty play for my attention land. And you reminded her of the consequences without making an outright threat."

"Oh."

He clasped my jaw with both hands and pulled me to him.

This time, I let him, the thrill running through me equally for his approval and the skill in his kiss. Maybe I could do this. If Troy was going to kiss me like this every time I did something right, I was certainly more incentivized to try.

Lemon zest burst through the room right as I was dragging him off the table and toward the bedroom.

"Goddess damn—" Troy cut off and turned to scowl at Duke, who was slouching against the bookcase next to the fireplace. "Your timing sucks."

Duke chuckled. "And you've gotten mouthy, little king. You never used to use such language. Our little bird is a bad influence."

I scowled at him and fished the polished hematite sphere hanging around my neck out of my shirt. "Callstones, Duke."

"Yes, yes, but this is too important."

"You locked me out for months, and suddenly something is important enough to turn up at my house at" —I checked the clock— "almost midnight? When we've already spoken today?"

"Arden." Troy arched an eyebrow.

Fine, so we were squabbling. Like djinn. Again. I took a breath. "Let's hear it."

"The Djinn Council has agreed to treat with House Solari."

"Oh." That was good news.

First House Bedoe coming through before I had to have Etain push, then the Djinn Council coming round? What was next, the Sinners finding sense and the Sons of Seth packing it in and going home?

My good mood wilted when I remembered the elementals would be pissed either way. Not like they needed more of an excuse.

"'Oh'?" Duke echoed. "Arden, this might be the biggest thing since the Atlantis Accords." He frowned and wrinkled his nose. "Or since Ninlil broke them to have you anyway."

I blinked. Started to ask what he meant about my mother. Swallowed that question in favor of the more urgent one. "What do they want?"

"For now, to be on equal terms with the elves."

"So...territory in the Triangle, advisors...what?" I held up a hand. "Troy's the only partner I'm taking, so a second royal bondmate better not be an ask."

Duke smirked. "That was on the table, but I told them you wouldn't go for it. They've also accepted that Iaret and I are suitable advisors." The grin widened. "Mostly because I can get past the wards here, and nobody else living can, at least among the Council's favorites."

That answered a question I'd had after Grimm's death—if I had any other family or blood ties among the djinn, given Keithia Monteague had killed all of those I had among the elves. Apparently not.

"What else?" Troy asked.

"Secrets, little king. They want secrets."

Troy crossed his arms. "What kind of secrets?"

"The archives."

"That is an enormous demand."

Enormous or not, I couldn't close the door on any options. "Let us think about it. And Duke? There are going to be guardrails on any agreement. This is not going to be free rein."

"Bo-ring," he sing-songed. "But fine. The Council expected as much."

"Good." I started to mention Iaret's visit then bit my tongue. If she'd wanted Troy to know, she'd have said something in front of him. I didn't like keeping secrets from Troy, and I didn't like being the third wheel with Iaret and Duke. But I hadn't figured out what to do with this new wrinkle yet. "We'll be in touch when we have news from the elven summit."

Duke grinned maliciously. "Mind your head, little bird."

With a twist of Aether, he was gone.

Chapter 12

Tired as I was, I didn't sleep until I convinced Troy to knock me out with a wallop of Aether that cut off my higher-level neural functioning and effectively forced me unconscious. He didn't like it, because if we were attacked, it'd take some doing to wake me up. But with another spring storm on its way, I couldn't take the risk of being physically exhausted. Not with Val's follow-up text confirming that the Collective was still arguing over how to "handle" me.

Storms. Tricksters. Elven summits. Overbearing reporters and federal agencies telling me to give more and yet be less. My head spun.

Maybe what I needed to take away from all this was that I wasn't too much, in terms of who and what I was. What I could offer. And I wasn't too inexperienced or too ignorant in terms of the role I was playing or the job I was doing.

I was at the confluence of all of it. I was exactly what I needed to be to deal with all of this, the Collective be damned. The elves weren't the only ones who needed to be dragged into the future.

Troy and I spent the next day negotiating with the Charleston Conclave. From the grimly accommodating conversation, I got the feeling they'd been waiting for us to turn their way. Callista had claimed all of the Carolinas after all, and I'd been wise enough to know I couldn't enforce that claim as things stood up to February this year.

But Santiago's vampires had attacked on my birthday, and I couldn't afford to neglect my southern border any longer. Matthias might have pushed the Miami coterie back home to defend their nest when he staked a claim on Jacksonville, but I'd been caught off guard too many times now.

It couldn't happen again. And that was where imposter syndrome kept creeping in. Telling me I should be better than this by now. I should anticipate my enemies. I *should*.

Should. Should. Should.

Should-ing would literally be the death of me if I didn't get it under control and focus on what was actually in my ability to influence and to action.

Troy and I took a break from negotiating with Charleston in the early evening, catching a breath over a late lunch/early dinner of grilled steak kebabs and rice. We ate much faster than was probably healthy and left the dirty plates on my deck table to take advantage of a balmy spell and lounge in the double hammock he'd gotten me. It groaned under our combined weight, but it'd hold.

I was just starting to doze, lulled by the contrast between Troy's warmth and the cool breeze, when his phone rang.

The hammock swayed as he shifted to fish it out with a grumbled elvish curse. "It's Sonia."

Sighing, I disentangled myself from him and the hammock and sat on the ground. Partly because I was going to nod off if I stayed tucked against Troy while swinging in the breeze like that and partly because I'd need the grounding of solid earth to face more elven politics tonight.

He followed me, and I leaned against him as he answered the call and put it on speaker. "Sonia."

"Troy. I can't believe I'm saying this, but you have a deal."

"Excellent. Charleston is working out a few last details before confirming their attendance. Terms?"

"All of y'all come to Virginia. Not far, don't worry. We have a facility where we hold retreats and such, near the Great Dismal Swamp outside Chesapeake. Very scenic. Very private. Close enough to the border that your elemental queen should feel safe."

Troy frowned. "My queen fought off the gods of the hunt. She can make herself safe regardless. You're selling it too hard. What's the catch?"

A heavy sigh echoed. "That's our Troy. Always digging deeper." She hesitated, and even not knowing much about her, I got the feeling she didn't want to say more. "Fine. We need this. House Bedoe does, I mean. Maybe as much as you do. Ead and Hilith are talking about giving up elven secrets to that Goddess-burning mundane agency now, if it means ruining Solari. They're positively obsessed with destroying you."

The bond flared with Troy's alarm. "They'd put themselves—put our entire faction—at risk to bring Solari down?"

"Yes. We need a firebreak. You and your queen are it, elemental bounty or not."

"There will be no fucking bounties on Arden." Troy's power signature slithered free of shields burst in his anger, chilling me as much as his tone. "I'm telling you here and now, Sonia. If there is a threat to her at this summit, I will invoke Talion Rule. And I will carry it out, Goddess save us all."

I kept very still. Aside from Troy dropping f-bombs, I had no idea what Talion Rule meant.

From the long silence, Sonia did. "We can't guarantee her safety. You know how—"

"I don't give a flying fuck. We can negotiate in summit, and all of us can get a little more than we lose. Or we can have war, and I will take everything in her name. I might be a king. But I was trained to be a general. And Sonia? You do not want the two of us—my queen and me—coming in violence."

Another long pause. "You're that committed to her."

"Till death." The grim, hard-bitten note in his voice was utterly implacable. "And beyond, given we've both already seen the other side of life."

I scooched closer to Troy and ran a hand along his spine.

Whatever this was, it was scaring me. Truly scaring me, in a way I hadn't felt in over a year, back when he'd been reacclimating to elven social hormones reactivated by constantly being around me and occasionally behaving erratically as a result.

I walled the bond off so he couldn't sense it. He'd spent enough of his life being used as a monster. Feeling like one. Having me scared of where he was going would break something in him that we were only just starting to repair. And it was making me wonder how much this summit would set us back in terms of his healing the wounds of his past. Coming to terms with the abuse, neglect, and harm he'd faced over the course of his life wasn't easy, but he was safe here. I knew he felt safe here, and especially *here* at home, with me, no matter how long it'd taken him to recognize my house as *our home*, a place he was loved and wanted for himself and not just somewhere he was, in his mind, tolerated for what he could offer.

"I'll take it back to Mom and see what we can do," Sonia finally said.

"Good." Troy dug a small stone out of the dirt of the yard and hurled it over the fence with a force that would probably crack a skull if it connected. "When?"

"Two days."

"Charleston will balk."

Sonia's exasperated sigh spoke volumes. "Then they can be left out. Mom truly does not give a shit. She wants this unholy alliance between Ead, Hilith, and this Supernatural Bureau over yesterday."

"Fair. Fine. If nothing else, Bedoe and Solari can meet."

"Agreed."

"See you in two days then." Troy ended the call and promptly got up to pace, bending to gather more stones and hurl them into the woods with bone-shattering strength. Not as bad as the one time he'd thrown shit in the house but not good.

I stayed where I was, too tense now to be tired. "What's Talion Rule?"

He answered without looking at me, continuing to throw his stones. "An eye for an eye and blood for blood. But the entire conclave is held culpable for the acts of an individual member or vassal. It's an extreme measure, invoked when a sworn truce is broken or something of similar gravity. Hasn't been used in my lifetime. Even you didn't use it when you took down the queens. You judged them on individual crimes and offered leniency to anyone who would take it."

My stomach twisted at yet a new iteration of the elven death cult.

He turned back and stared down at me. "You disagree?"

"More like I wish it could be any other way." I rose and snagged his hand before he could find more rocks. "Come on. Let's get Charleston to the table."

Beyond protecting my people and all of Otherside, I couldn't let Troy backslide into a space where he'd hate himself. He'd worked too hard to drag himself out of that pit, and I'd burn the world to ash before I let him fall back into it.

That meant finding a way to protect myself or, at the very least, making damn sure I filled the boots I'd claimed as mine.

△▽△▽

Two days passed in a blur, as did the drive up to Chesapeake. We got all three Charleston Houses in the end: Averill, Tossavi, and Quet. And House Bedoe got Ead and Hilith on board, making it the first full summit of three conclaves in decades.

Omar's Seattle op fell through, so there would be no observers, but I was glad of that. We'd have enough to deal with as it was.

Troy and I each had an honor guard. I brought the Ebon Guard, the traditional protectors of elementals way back when. Troy had the Darkwatch in lieu of a currently non-existent Solari House Guard. Allegra and Etain stayed behind to protect the territory, much to their undying frustration, and we had Haroun and Thana heading up our respective guards. Thana was technically Ebon Guard, but everyone at the summit knew her as Darkwatch, so that was what she came as—head of Troy's honor guard.

I had time on the drive up to review the list of names Omar had sent for us to try swaying and then read some info on the history of the Houses Iago had pulled for me. We were just turning onto the road leading to the facility when I read the key part though.

"Holy shit," I muttered.

Troy's hands tightened on the steering wheel. "What."

"If this scan is correct..." I reread it, just to be sure. "The Houses? They started with elementals. That's where the tradition of associating a House with a gem came from." I toyed with my father's prince's pendant, the nickel-sized onyx disk wrapped in gold. "The gem was chosen based on its correspondence with an element."

"What?" Troy's question was more confused than flat this time.

"Yeah. The queens? Might also have been kings but were always elementals. Until the elves adopted the system and adapted it to elven society and goals."

"That's in the material Iago sent over?"

"Yep."

Troy stayed silent until he'd found a place to park and turned off the engine. "We'll need to find a way to use that. Not directly. But an implication."

"Yeah."

We waited until the rest of our party had parked up alongside and behind us to get out.

Troy moved to my right, as we'd agreed, and held an arm out to me, crooked at the elbow. *You're a true queen. Diplomacy here means oblique threats. But you're allowed to use me to defend what's yours.*

What if I want to defend what's mine by myself? I took his arm, reminding myself to lean into the old-fashioned gesture even if I was wearing a ridiculously expensive pair of black designer jeans and a sinfully comfortable gold-trimmed black sweater he'd picked out rather than some kind of medieval gown.

Remember this: the more power you have, the less you do for yourself.

I barely stopped myself from frowning. I didn't like that. I was used to doing things for and by myself. But everything about this summit went against my nature and my instincts. I had to trust Troy and our honor guard to steer me through.

Okay, I agreed.

Chin up. Big attitude.

I let my power signature spill out as I lifted my chin.

That's my queen.

The curl of approval in his thoughts made me flush as our honor guard fell in around us.

Haroun and Thana got the doors, handing them off to the elves coming after us and falling in at bodyguard positions to create a diamond.

The space was laid out like a hotel lobby: a front desk close by the entrance, a lounge space, a bar. Large windows with doors you only knew were doors by the metal bars set in them made up the back wall, leading to a large room overlooking a view of the Great Dismal Swamp. It was haunting, with tall pines and gnarled bald cypress rising out of murky water just past a wooden boardwalk. Something about it called to me.

Arden.

At Troy's mental prompt, I pulled back from my instinctive elemental reach. He'd brought us to the desk.

"House Solari," Troy said to the wide-eyed elf behind it.

"My queen. My king." He stank of fear, and his voice shook. "You and your House are, uh, welcome to this summit."

I bit my tongue to stop from saying that we'd better be, given that it was thanks to me and Troy that most of it was happening at all.

"How many total?" Desk Elf asked.

"Twenty," Troy said.

Two triple triads as honor guard, Troy, and me.

When the elf—Josiah, according to his name tag—looked at me with big eyes, I smiled. "As is proper for a High Queen and Arbiter accompanied by a King."

"Of course, my queen." A flurry of typing. "We have rooms to accommodate you all on the third level, which has been mostly set aside for House Solari."

From the furious churn of the bond, Troy wasn't best pleased by that.

Do I need to protest?

Don't bother, he sent back. *It's irritating from a security perspective but not worth the battle.*

I smiled at Josiah, making it nice rather than a snarl. "Thank you."

The next hour was a flurry of busyness, picking rooms and getting settled. Troy and I ended up in the best room, a huge suite on the northeast side with an entire corner turned into a window.

I loved it. The swamp and the land around it stretched for miles. I was sure Troy hated it for the possibility of snipers or whatever, but I stared hungrily out at the view.

"Will there be time to go out there?" I asked.

"Maybe. Here." He handed a thick sheet of paper to me.

I took it, still distracted, and glanced down to find an agenda. "Oh. That's helpful."

"It's a ploy."

At the snap in his voice, I turned from the window to give him a questioning look.

"Don't trust any of this, Arden. Not a schedule. Not a word. Not an action. Everyone will have their own personal agendas." He flapped another copy of the agenda against his hand. "This is a guideline. At best. A ruse, at worst."

In the bond, he was already spiraling into the headspace he used to live in all the time. A place where there were only a few options, most of them deadly and all of them harmful, to himself as much as anyone else. The place that used to make my stomach cramp and set my teeth on edge with paranoia every time he was within a few blocks of me, even if I didn't know it was because of him at the time.

I went to him and slid my arms around his waist. "Then it's a good thing we have our own agenda."

"Mm."

Shit. We were down to monosyllabic noises. I'd been afraid this would happen but hadn't fully anticipated how much being in a situation like this would set him back into old habits and patterns, or how quickly.

"Troy." I snaked my hands up his body, over his chest and shoulders and around his neck, going for soothing rather than sexual when he stayed in distant thought. "Cariñomí."

"Je?"

"Look at me."

With a few blinks, he brought his eyes down.

"Talk to me."

He just stared at me with empty eyes for a long handful of heartbeats.

I reached for him in the bond. Not invading his thoughts, just letting him know that whatever it was, I was here.

With a grimace, he inhaled sharply and shook himself. "I— There were marriage offers from half the attending Houses. Before I met you."

Allegra had said as much.

"From what I've heard," I said, "you were North America's most eligible bachelor. Maybe beyond as well."

His gaze met mine with startling speed as blood drained from his face. "You know about that?"

I shrugged. "Even if I didn't, it'd take a fool not to see that you're a catch." Slowly, in case he startled, I drew my hands back over his shoulders and cradled his face. "If I said I'm not worried and you don't have to worry because you're mine, does that make it better or worse?"

"Better." Relief flooded the bond.

"Okay. Make me the bitch in this. Whatever you don't want to do, you can't because I'm so fucking possessive."

"But—"

"If this but is because that's not true rather than because it'll work, maybe don't go there."

"You'd be the monster." He looked down at me like he was trying to anchor himself in my soul. "For me."

My heart broke a little. That said as much as anything that nobody had ever really gone to any lengths necessary to be on his side, at least not in a long time, and I let him feel it in the bond. He needed to know how much I valued him.

"Troy, I will always be the monster if it keeps you safe. If I have to weave a net of Fire over you to burn whoever tries to touch you, I will do it. Just say the word. I don't care what it takes. We might not be married yet, but you. Are. Mine. For life."

While that statement would have terrified me a year or two ago, for Troy, it was the anchor he'd been seeking. He shuddered, closing his eyes and leaning forward just enough to rest his forehead against mine. "I love you."

"I love you too. And I'll make you a deal. We keep each other safe. Like we have for the last year and a half. You watch my back. I watch yours. We're *partners*, not just royals. Not just you serving me. I'm yours too."

And with that, my Hunter and King was back. Savage certainty lanced through the bond as he drew me into a bruising kiss.

"Mine," he said when he pulled away.

"Yours. And together, we conquer all."

For once, that wasn't an empty promise or a bluff. That was my intention, down to my soul. I had to take Richmond and Charleston both. If they didn't want to play ball, there'd be hell to pay, both for myself and for the elementals.

And it wasn't gonna be me who was paying.

Not this time.

Chapter 13

We went over our game plan with Thana and Haroun. An hour from sunset, they left, and we all got changed. The agenda had a welcome ball as the first item, which made me grumpy as much for my failure to control Chaos and my maenad nature a few days ago as for having to get gussied up.

I couldn't complain about the dress in the end though.

It was a sleek black number that was somehow softer than my sweater earlier and flashed gold in the right light, even nicer than the one Noah had found for my birthday. The graceful drape from my left shoulder bared my right to show the Lichtenberg-line scar on the front and parts of my kestrel tattoo on my back. From my hips, it fell in loose folds to my ankles, a slim silhouette that would let me run if I had to.

I looked like a damn goddess. Strong. Powerful. Un-fuck-with-able.

I fingered my scar as I stared at myself in the mirror. I never showed it off. Not because I was ashamed of it but...well, hell. I didn't know why. But I'd always covered it up. In this dress though, it felt like a true battle scar for the first time, rather than a wound inflicted upon a lost little girl.

My gaze found Troy's in the mirror. He was in a tux with the same black-and-gold effect, watching me with critical eyes.

"This dress has to be custom," I said.

The first smile I'd seen on him in hours flickered as he approached, resting his hands on my hips as he leaned to kiss my bare shoulder. "It is."

"Where the hell did it come from?"

"Doesn't matter. You have people for this now."

"But—"

"Arden, you are a high queen. No more department store dresses. Not for something this important."

I leaned back into him, trying to find the stability I needed to be comfortable with this. A few years ago, I'd been worrying about getting enough cases for my private investigation firm to cover all my expenses. Now, I had a born prince—a king—telling me fairytale dresses were simply mine to have without my knowledge and without any discernible impact to my finances.

Troy kissed my neck and pulled away. "Missing a few things."

I spun to watch him go for one of the suitcases, which he'd insisted on packing alone. Apparently, I was too chaotic in my start at getting ready for this trip, which had grated on his deeply ingrained sense of order and need for control in the face of an uncertain and dangerous situation. He knew what I'd need better than I did, so I'd left him to it and headed to the bar to do some last-minute work. I had a feeling the dress was only the first surprise.

After a little digging, he came up with a velvet bag, from which he pulled a classy, understated gold circlet set with tiny onyx spheres and a small, gold-and-onyx brooch in the shape of a stooping raptor.

My jaw dropped. "What…"

"Allow me." With gentle fingers, he pinned the brooch to my dress then set the circlet amidst the curls I'd left to their full abundance. "There."

While I stared at myself in the mirror all over again, he went back to the suitcase, returning with a similar brooch pinned to his jacket.

I fingered mine. "Is this a Solari thing?"

"The colors and materials are. I had it made as a kestrel for you though." This time, his kiss fell on my right shoulder blade, atop the hovering bird tattooed there. "Seemed like a good personal symbol."

"Personal symbol?"

"All royals get one. And whatever your doubts, you are a royal. By birth and by conquest." His gaze heated as it flicked up to meet mine. "Eventually by marriage. Even if our situation is a little backward."

"So what's yours?"

"You've heard it hinted at."

I thought back to various conversations. "A bull."

"Mm-hm. Technically, I should wear something of it here, since we haven't formally exchanged vows. But I wanted to make a point." Concern pinched his eyes. "Is that okay?"

Turning, I went on my toes—only a little, given my black heels—and kissed him. "Of course it is. I told you. Whatever keeps you safe." I sent a playful little sting through the bond. "Besides, I don't need these bitches getting funny ideas. You're mine, Troy Solari."

That settled him, as I'd hoped, and I held back a comment that, for all his stubbornness, he'd always seemed more cat-like to me. He was already on edge, and I had no idea what all this of personal symbols was about or how they were selected.

He extended his arm again. "Shall we?"

I took it and tried to still the sudden racing of my heart. I was a queen in the Triangle. That was easy enough. But this was my debut as a queen on the larger stage of elven politics. This fancy dress, the mini-crown, even a king on my arm...despite my best efforts, it only drove impostor syndrome higher.

I wrestled it down. I could do this. I'd fought and killed to be here. To have these responsibilities and this man and this birthright. This was all mine in every way it could be, and I'd face it with the same courage I'd had in facing the gods of the hunt.

"Wait." Troy pulled me to a sudden halt as I reached for the doorknob. "I need you to understand something before we go down."

Dread snaked through me, adding to what was already sitting heavy in my chest. I turned back and gave him my full attention. "Okay."

"Remember how I said they might try to split us up?"

I nodded, my mood souring.

"Things are going to be said. Things neither of us will like."

"About...you?"

"About me. And you. And us together. There will be speculation about everything from our legitimacy to my training to whether or when we'd have heirs. They'll try to drive a wedge between any cracks they think we might have."

Outrage flared, boiling from my gut to my throat. None of that was anyone's fucking business.

Before I could speak though, Troy rested fingers lightly over my lips. "No. None of that."

"But—"

"No, Arden. Remember. They will expect both of us to behave like brutes. And if we don't, they will try to instigate it. Either as a petty game or to make a point that one or both of us can't be trusted to stay civilized. Do not give them that."

"Aside from the insult of 'civilized,' I can't defend myself? Defend you?"

The ghost of a smile flickered before he sobered again. "You can. But with cleverness. Not temper." He rested a hand over my heart. "Keep your rage and hurt locked in. For now. I managed for twenty years, and you know what my temper looks like when it goes. You can do it for three nights. Okay?"

"No," I snapped. "It's not okay. But I understand."

Troy leaned forward to kiss my forehead. "That'll do. Ready?"

I took a deep breath. Reminded myself that attitude could carry the day and that I was a fucking high queen. That I could level this entire building and probably not even have a power hangover anymore.

That Troy, always my shield and my Hunter, needed my strength now as he faced his own demons.

I'd said I was a protector. That had to start with the person I cared for the most, or the word meant nothing.

"Let's go." I pulled the door open.

Haroun and Thana waited outside at the head of a triad each. All of them were dressed in black with onyx-and-gold accents: scarves, jewelry, pins, accessories.

"Toro ben?" Troy murmured.

"Je. Teams two and four are resting. Team six is doing recon," Haroun replied in the same soft tones. He was in a trim, black tuxedo with a white shirt that had the same shimmery gold effect as my dress, with a gold cravat. "The other three triads will be with us. Team three is already downstairs."

Thana grinned, a tight curl of her lips that was equal parts amusement and threat. "And we're ready to party."

Didn't take a genius to see the different ways "party" could play out. Her gold dress was overlaid with black crepe-y material and slit high on one thigh. With her bright red lipstick and heavy eye makeup, she looked like a classic femme fatale.

"Final orders?" Haroun asked.

Troy glanced at me and, at my small nod, slipped a hand in his pocket as he muttered a spell in elvish under his breath. My guess was a jammer in his pocket and something to stop casual eavesdropping.

So it was going to be that kind of night.

"Mingle," he said. "I want intel reported by dawn. Not just likely threats. Pinch points. Who's sleeping with whom, who hates whom." He glanced at Haroun. "Who harbors prejudices against those of mixed heritage. I'm sorry, Haroun. I wouldn't ask if we didn't need the intel."

I'd spent enough time around Haroun to see the tension in him ease at Troy's acknowledgment of the extra emotional labor on his part, as a half-elf.

"Of course, my king," Haroun said. "I'll get what we need to keep the House and our queen safe."

I squeezed his arm and gave him an appreciative smile that made him blush. An acknowledgment that we were both in this as half-elves, technically, even if his human heritage gave him less privilege than I had. Or different, I guess. Half-elves weren't hunted as bounties like elementals, but most high-bloods were still assholes to them, and they had less power to push back.

Troy nodded. "Last thing. There will be everything from crude comments to outright insults and veiled threats directed at Arden and me or to you about us. Let them go. First, they're beneath all of us. Second, they tell us who's threatened and by how much. You're not expected to defend our honor. We have nothing to defend. We're above that."

Thana's expression darkened. "As you say, my king."

"Good. Let's go."

Stepping into the elevator gave me a flashback to the vampire Reveal all over again. I'd been on Troy's arm then as well, but he'd had the power, not me, and he'd been an almighty ass about escorting me.

From the quirk in the bond and his lips as he met my gaze in the mirrored surface of the doors, he was thinking of the same thing.

I could push you into a doorway again, I sent.

Don't threaten me with a good time.

I couldn't help a choked-off laugh.

None of that, Troy sent as Haroun and Thana glanced at me with a hint of concern.

I cleared my throat. "Sorry. Danger giggles."

"Get them out now," Troy murmured.

A tickling dart danced through my nerves in the bond, and another round of giggles burst free before I could catch them. This time, I pressed my lips shut and glared at him.

He just stared back impassively even as the bond bubbled with his amusement. Our bodyguards, aware of both Troy's quietly savage sense of humor and the Aetheric bond—even if they didn't know we could use it to talk to each other—relaxed at the exchange.

Then the elevator doors were opening, and I was scrambling to find an appropriately arrogant expression as air molecules charged by elegant live music and body heat and the movement of dozens of elves crashed into me.

Breathe, Troy sent.

I did, opening myself more fully to him than I had on the night we'd tried maenad dancing. He slipped into my neural network, seamlessly fitting alongside my own thoughts.

Yes. That made life much easier.

We moved so smoothly that nobody could tell he was guiding our movements around the room, and letting my body move on autopilot freed my mind up to focus on introductions and barbed pleasantries delivered with shudders and sneers.

An older woman approached, all haughty blue eyes and narrow chin.

Queen Merle of House Averill, Troy sent.

The queen stared at me, anger flickering when I only stared back rather than quailing or submitting or whatever the fuck she thought I oughta do. Then she shifted to face Troy. "I suppose you'll do in the absence of Omar Monteague. What word on our offer of marriage for your sister?"

All yours, I sent to Troy.

He lifted his chin to give the effect of looking down his nose at Merle, a level of arrogance I hadn't seen from him since we'd met. "Merle. May the Goddess bless you and yours with what you've earned."

I had to hold in a snort; from that phrasing and the bite in the bond, he was fully wishing the Goddess to beat Merle's ass.

From her expression, the queen heard it too. But the words were polite, even if Troy's tone conveyed a hint of disrespect, and she couldn't snap at him for that. They were technically equals now. "You've grown rather bold since we saw you last."

"My sister isn't inclined to join our Houses," Troy said, not bothering to grace that with a response. "I'm sure you understand."

"I'm not sure I do. This marriage—"

"Is out of the question." Troy tilted his head and offered a predator's smile to match his suddenly dead eyes. No sharp teeth but every deadly intention.

Ishtar, but he gave "terrifyingly polite" a whole new spin, and I was finding it sexy as fuck now that it wasn't directed at me.

Merle stiffened, and the faintest tang of fear spiked from her. "That's rather—"

I cleared my throat as I matched the arrogant tilt of Troy's chin. "My king said it's out of the question. Was there anything else, Merle?"

"How dare you. Elemental bitch. Who in the nine hells do you think you are?"

"She's High Queen and Arbiter. That's more than enough." Troy's voice dropped into the quiet, dangerous octave that even I paid attention to. "Off you go, Merle. Before I need to be offended on my queen's behalf."

For a moment, I thought Merle would argue with us. Then her gaze darted between us and something calculating slithered into it before she turned and fucked off without another word, the scent of her fear trailing her like a fart.

After that, it went as well as it could, given the veiled insults and outright rudeness, until we finally met Sonia Bedoe.

She was, in a word, statuesque. Flawless dark skin, full lips, intelligent brown eyes, goddess braids tumbling nearly to her hips. Her understated makeup was set off by a sleeveless, ruby red dress that screamed royalty as much as her casual confidence. A pin that I took to be a running fox sparkled ruby and gold on her shoulder.

I wasn't generally given to envy, but she was what I wanted people to see me as: royal, confident, effortlessly powerful. And that—as much as her evaluating look first at me, then longer at Troy—made me jealous. Made me want to dislike her.

To fight, even.

It was so incredibly unlike me to have that kind of reaction that I froze, trying to sort out what was me and what I'd just realized was a belatedly awakened sensitivity to elven pheromones. I'd had a reaction like this once before, to Allegra of all people, when she was trying to save me from crashing after the Wild Hunt and had gotten too close to Troy while I was outta my mind with him threaded too close in it.

It wasn't me. I was better than this. I was responsible for myself and my reactions.

"We finally meet," Sonia said into the awkward silence. With a small incline of her head, she added, "My queen. My king."

"Princess," Troy said in tones so neutral they were almost rude as he sent a soothing wave through the bond. "It's been a while."

"It has." She looked me up and down, eyes tight, and sniffed. "So this is an elemental? You don't look like much under that power signature."

I dragged my brain back under my control and ignored the barbs, offering as much of a smile as I could. "Thank you for arranging all this."

Her brows shot up. "Either this is a sham partnership, or you're very good."

That set alarm bells ringing. I stiffened, squaring to face her fully. "Excuse me?"

"Sonia," Troy said, a snap in his tone.

She ignored him completely as she studied me and scented the air between us again. "No, not a sham. You're both too irritated, and your scents intertwine deeply enough that you've fucked and probably enjoyed it. Shit. That good then. I'm flattered, I think. Definitely more scared than I was a few minutes ago."

With an effort, I wrestled down the impulse to strangle her or to admit that I had no fucking clue what she was talking about.

The flick of her gaze to Troy said they both knew.

Sonia leaned closer, not looking the least bit ashamed, although the tightening of her hands on the purse she held in front of her gave away her anxiety at getting closer to me. "Your secret's safe with me, my queen, and I have no designs on your mate. He's clearly yours." She smirked. "Congratulations. The Bull was quite the prize."

I clenched my jaw to stop from snapping at her that he wasn't an object. Troy had said there would be comments and told me to watch my responses. This was far from the worst a comment could be.

I could do this. For him.

That only seemed to impress her more. Her gaze darted down to my brooch before meeting mine again. "A raptor indeed. Rising above petty bait. Excellent choice." She smiled. "I hope we get a chance for a more private conversation. Woman to woman, seeing as you are one and not the bogeyman I was raised to look for."

Forcing a smile, I said, "Maybe later."

With a last incline of her head, Sonia moved on.

Air? Troy asked.

Yes. Please. Now.

As one, we moved toward the patio and, once outside, leaned on the railing overlooking a decent-sized lawn.

I couldn't stifle the irritation as I asked, *What the fuck was that?*

He shifted closer to me so it would look like we were talking and not just standing here. *You reacted to her like she's a worthy queen. A potential competitor. Which is why she was flattered. The fact that you reacted that way at all says you're not a pretender to the title or your blood. And your control was excellent, cariñami. Even if she was being extremely rude in calling attention to it. Keithia slapped a princess in the same situation once.*

I flushed with embarrassment at his having to explain. The djinn side of my heritage—the Sight, the dreams, the blood-tie summonings—I was used to, thanks to being raised largely by Duke and Grimm. The elven side? A mess and one I was struggling to accept. The Chapel Hill Conclave had been set on removing me, and I'd killed almost everyone who might have been able to trigger this reaction in me at home.

I was in the deep end, and I hadn't even realized how deep until just now. From the disquiet in the bond, Troy hadn't either.

Closing my eyes, I breathed deep of the late-winter air, irritated with myself. *I forgot about the physiological responses.*

So did I. Troy's hand was warm where it rested against the small of my back. *At least that you haven't been dealing with them as long. I'm sorry. I should have thought to warn you.*

Don't be. I gritted my teeth. *I have to be better than this either way. I'm the only elemental here. I'm representing all of us, not just me. Fuck, I'm betting I'm the first and only elemental they've ever met. Alive, anyway.*

Troy stiffened and didn't respond to that immediately. *This is one of those things you couldn't have known until you were in it.*

It doesn't matter. Elementals get no grace. There are no do-overs, Troy. No second chances. There's strength and excellence, or there's isolation and death.

His hand tightened on my back. *I won't let anyone hurt you.*

I wanted to tell him that it wasn't up to him. That in a group of his peers, he might be my ally, but that only meant he was someone who would raise their voice or their blade if it came to it. Not that I'd be safe to begin with. Not that I could avoid harm. Not that I'd leave this event unscathed, with my body and pride and dignity all intact. We could have everything go right, and I could still leave ruined by it.

Arden. We have this.

Yeah. I sighed. *Best go back in then, before they start to get ideas to the contrary.*

As we swept back indoors, I hardened my resolve.

I had to be better. For the House. For Troy. For my territory. And for me.

So I would be. I just had to try not to burn it all down this time.

Chapter 14

It turned out to be a good thing we'd encountered Sonia when we did, because it only got worse from there as the alcohol Troy warned me about flowed. Sniping comments, blatant flirtation with Troy, and naked threats on both our lives filled the rest of the early evening. I didn't give them my pain or my outrage, but I also didn't bother trying to smile through it. They got cold courtesy, arrogant boredom, or amused disdain.

For all it exhausted me, my reaction—or lack thereof—also seemed to cement, in their minds, that I was one of them. Especially after some royal or other in House Ead tried calling me a Solari terrorist to my face and I just busted out laughing.

It was that or call lightning, and I couldn't afford to kill elves tonight. Not when I needed to build my own base. Not when I needed to sway those of their Houses who might be thinking of jumping and show them an alternative.

The next time Troy and I got a break, we found a quiet corner to sip sparkling water and eat some offensively tiny hors d'oeuvres. I got a few looks—apparently you weren't supposed to eat a dozen of the things at once—but I ignored them. I was hungry for once, dammit, and there was only so much I could be bothered to worry about tonight. Not burning the building down or falling under the sway of the weather shift I could sense to the west was a bigger priority than high-blood royals sneering at my lack of decorum.

I set my empty plate on the tray of a passing server with a murmured thanks then tilted Troy's face toward mine with two light fingers for a kiss. He accepted eagerly, hungry for the emotional respite and the public show that he was mine even if it undercut his position as king. We were both running on big balls and banked outrage at that point.

I owe you an apology, he whispered mentally when I let him go.

For what?

Not seeing how much harder it is to claim what's yours by rights when you're not among your own people.

I rolled that around in my head. *Being king is hard enough when the people in your territory accept you. Here, you're not accepted so much as tolerated as a dangerous novelty.*

Irritation spiked. *Yes.*

Fair. I gave him another kiss. *Thank you.*

Having him acknowledge that I had even more of a struggle in fitting into the role I'd claimed eased a longstanding frustration I'd been carrying. Even knowing what I faced as an elemental, he'd always acted like all I had to do was stand up and fill the boots—because that's what it had taken for him up to now. Here, we were both in new depths with sharks nearly our size, who were wary of our achievements and our power signatures but had too much experience and too much to lose to be impressed by them.

From the ballroom, the first notes of a stirring and surprisingly sexy song rang out.

Troy took my hand and kissed it. "Come on. We need to join this dance."

I sighed and caught up so that we were walking side by side, not bothering to ask why. *Guide me?*

Of course. It's the one we practiced in the yard the other night.

When we reached the floor, the partnered couples we'd briefly met earlier in the evening were already whirling to the music. I let go as Troy slipped in, and we were off. My feet flowed along with his, even as he pulled me through what I distantly realized must be a more difficult variation of the dance from what I was peripherally aware of. Everything just cascaded past me though. It could only have been a few minutes, but in my connection with Troy, I briefly had the peace of ages.

The music ended on a crescendo. Troy spun me fast enough that the room blurred then caught me and whipped me into a backbend. When the room fell silent, my teeth were at his throat, but his hand gripped mine. Two top predators fighting to a standstill.

I clenched my jaws before I could stop myself, and he gently drew us upright. A surrender, of sorts.

Take a bow, he whispered.

Gathering the skirts of my dress, I made a small curtsy to him as he bowed more deeply to me.

Perfect. He extended a hand.

I took it and let him guide us off the floor as the room burst into scattered applause amidst a cresting undercurrent of whispers. *What statement did you just make?*

A darkly amused grin tugged the corners of his lips. *That we're powerful equals, with you first between us. And that you might be an elemental, but you know the old ways. Something for them to gossip over other than personal matters that aren't their business.*

I had a feeling it was as much for that as to keep any possible attacks at bay but kept that thought to myself. *Divide and conquer?*

Yes.

Good, because I need the ladies'.

Troy leaned down to kiss my cheek and whisper in my ear. "Be careful. We can't be joined at the hip for all of this without looking afraid, but they'll be waiting for a misstep. Don't give it to them."

"I won't." With a last squeeze of his hand, I let him go and headed for the bathrooms.

Thana fell in beside me. "Quite the show you two are putting on."

"What are you hearing?"

"Some sneering comments about the half-elves in the Ebon Guard. A few comments that you and the king should both be beheaded, and damn summit truce." Her expression flickered to something darker before she smoothed it. "Those are Hilith and Ead of course. Bedoe and the Charleston Houses seem to be on the fence. Neither of you are what anyone expected. It's giving them pause. Especially you. It's pretty obvious they thought you'd try to take the building down the way the elementals of old were said to have torn down Atlantis, but you haven't so much as yelled at or slapped anyone. They're frustrated that you won't react."

I fought to keep my face smooth at the mention of both death threats and defying expectations. "I need them to fall in line, Thana. All of them."

"I know, my queen. For what it's worth, it's the royals who are feeling threatened. Some of the House vassals and extended family are cautiously interested in what kind of alternative you might offer."

The people who wouldn't get a voice and who would have to be assured of their safety before committing themselves to leaving their current situations and moving to my territory. I might think people should stand up and fight, but some had either too much to lose or hadn't lost enough yet. Everyone's breaking point was different, and some who reached it would hide or run before fighting.

"They're saying it?" I asked. "That they're interested?"

"No. It's in what they're not saying."

"I see. Thank you. I'll think on it."

The bathroom was blessedly empty when I got inside after Thana swept it. After taking care of business, I leaned on the counter and looked at myself in the mirror. Closed the bond and gave myself ten seconds to have a small freakout about feeling in over my head, lost, endangered, and insulted. Crammed it all back down and reopened the bond before Troy could start to worry.

I could do this. I repeated it to myself a few more times just for good measure. I didn't look anything like my usual self in this dress, with the little queen's circlet. I was surrounded by enemies. But I'd worn a lot of disguises as a private investigator, and I'd always been surrounded by enemies.

As that thought clicked into place, I calmed.

I could do this. I'd done it all my life.

Footsteps warned me someone was coming the moment before Sonia Bedoe swept in, ignoring Thana's exclamation.

I held up a hand to have Thana wait outside, which she obeyed with clear reluctance.

Sonia's dark eyes took me in head to toe, another examination that made me stiffen. "Having a good night?"

"Are you?"

She wrinkled her nose and snorted. "Fuck no. I hate this shit."

I kept my expression as neutral as I could. "Really."

"Really." She sighed as she took in my expression and stance. Burnt marshmallow filled the small bathroom, and she muttered a spell of silence.

Immediately, I went on high alert.

Arden? Troy sent.

"Look, I don't want to play games with you," Sonia said. "I really don't. So I'm going to ignore my mother's orders and deal with you straight."

That made me even more suspicious, but I told Troy to stand down even as I reached for Chaos. "What's with the spell?"

"Soundproofing. You have no reason to trust me. But I have one job at this summit, and it's to convince you and Troy to ally with Bedoe. The US government is an unknown quantity. You? Personally destroyed Keithia Monteague's family mansion and killed three queens with your own hands. That little dance just now showed everyone you have Troy wrapped around your little finger, and he's always been most dangerous when he has a cause he believes in. Clearly, that's yours now."

"And?"

"And I'm telling you, Bedoe will throw in with Solari."

Nope, still didn't trust things being this easy. Not on this, anyway. "In exchange for what?"

"Assurances. Troy was willing to declare Talion Rule. Somebody *will* make an attempt on you while you're here. House Bedoe will support you. If we're excluded from the repercussions."

I gave her a flat look. "For all I know, you're orchestrating all of this to get close to us for more nefarious purposes."

"Which would be a clever plan, definitely. But nothing in our dossier on you suggests you appreciate that kind of cleverness or that it works. And you're djinn-blooded as much as elf, so for all we know that involves the Sight. House Bedoe is the smallest of the Richmond Houses, but we're the oldest, the only one that has maintained our membership in the conclave since the beginning of the elven presence in this country. We don't play stupid power games. We don't need to."

At Sonia's mention of the Sight, I wrestled myself back into focus and tried to tap it through the ring while studying her. I got a little nudge but nothing conclusive.

"There's something you're not telling me," I said. "Best hope I don't find out what it is before this attempt happens, or I won't hold Troy back from whatever he determines would be justice. Excuse me." I slipped past her, but not before catching a flash of frustration on her face.

Thana was waiting with the tense air of a bodyguard who was on the verge of kicking someone's ass. "Toro ben?"

"Fine. Sonia just wanted to talk. This time." I paused as we passed the stairs to the upper level overlooking the floor. "Come on up and show me who she's been talking to."

She followed me up and did her best to point out various royals. Sonia had been busy. Where most of the royals had stayed within a few set networks, she'd spoken to someone from each House—and not just the royals. Captains and spouses were also in the mix. Even a few vassals.

"Be careful, my queen. We're keeping an eye out, but you're your own first line of defense here."

"Understood." I stayed leaning on the railing and looked over the floor below as she slipped away.

Troy was politely paying attention to a light-skinned elfess. He was still doing the political thing with a pleasant expression, despite the thrum of irritation in the bond. The royal he was talking to had him in a fit over something...and with our dance fresh in my mind, I couldn't help but imagine what that might inspire in him in bed.

As soon as the thought crossed my mind, undefended by walls, he turned his head. Unerringly met my gaze and, for the barest second, let me see what he might unleash on me, his one real outlet while we were out of our own territory, in his frustration.

I shivered.

He liked it. He recovered quickly, of course, returning to his conversation as though his glance at me was coincidental rather than reactional. But in a heartbeat, Aether snaked through the bond and bit into my nervous system, a brief sting of pleasure I barely managed not to react to.

Goddess. I was in trouble when he finally got me alone.

All that did was make me want to tease him. *Something* about this evening had to be fun if I was going to keep my temper, and I was tired of the effort.

I made my way down the curving staircase, dress held in one hand like I'd seen Maria do countless times. Back straight. Chin up. Eyes cold. Exactly what was to be expected from an elven queen, taken to the nth degree to command respect for myself as an elemental amidst my ancestral enemies.

Troy felt me drawing nearer in the bond and waited until I was nearly at his side to half-turn and lift a hand for me to rest mine on. "My queen."

I barely managed to hold off a physical reaction this time as I set my hand atop his. "King consort."

"This is Princess Bel Hilith," he said. "She was telling me about House Hilith's population replacement program."

So probably something to do with trading family members like stud horses. Or, worse, an attempt to pique Troy or break us up. Either would explain the undercurrent of fury he was carefully keeping from his face despite the heat of it in the bond. From the nasty little smile and the wine-flush in her cheeks, this Bel knew exactly what she was doing and thought it was funny.

I only just managed to stop my expression from twisting.

She looked at me with barely concealed disdain. "How unique to have an elemental as...queen. Positively barbaric, really." She gave a delicate shudder and sipped her wine. "How *do* you manage, Troy?"

I gave her a cold smile. "I think you'll find it's rather traditional. If you go back far enough of course."

She paled, her expression blanking at the suggestion that elemental queens were the correct way of things and that I might have information she didn't.

My smile widened at her discomfort. Time to move on. I needed to get Troy away from her and resettle him before he sank too far into the headspace I could sense him falling into. "If you'll excuse us."

She nodded with a stiffness that screamed reluctance, although I caught her eyeing Troy as I drew him away.

What's wrong? he sent.

I waited until we were in a quiet corridor before pushing him against the wall and kissing him, flashing back to the vampire Reveal at The Umstead as I did. I was both the instigator and the pursuer now though.

The heat that'd been fury earlier became pure lust as he forgot himself and caught my jaw in his hands, pouring himself into returning my kiss with all his skill.

It was all I could do not to press my hips against the growing evidence of his desire for me. Not to grab him, to untuck his shirt and skim my hands over the lines of his body. To pull on the flesh of his throat until he'd go back to the ball with a hickey.

To limit myself to just kissing him so I didn't hit any of his triggers around being used for sex, triggers that might be heightened among present company. I'd seen some of the elfesses staring at him with hot eyes and the way he carefully ignored them—not just to respect me but with a curl of apprehension that spoke to something that might have happened while he was still effectively owned by Keithia.

Somehow, he caught the conflict in me and pulled back just enough to speak.

"Don't worry. It's good when it's you," he whispered. "I needed this. I love what's going through your head. How much you want me. But I love you most for worrying."

"Your needs as a person come first," I whispered back. "No matter how much I want you or need your political brilliance with these people."

That earned me another kiss and his fingers tight on my hips, pulling me flush against him and grinding me against his hard-on so that I barely managed not to groan aloud with suppressed need.

Footsteps coming toward us made us both loosen our grips and shift our positions to appear as though we'd only been talking even if the scents we had to be throwing off would say otherwise. When the elf passed, Troy smiled wickedly and leaned down to speak into my ear.

"My new goal tonight is to make you scream."

Chapter 15

I stiffened and flushed hot, my whole body on fire even as my core clenched. My breath came so short it hurt. I knew fifty different things he could do to pull a scream from me. All of them would feel good, if he wanted them to. And he would.

"Nothing to say? My queen." Troy's smirk felt like a victory after how tense he'd been earlier, even if it was at my expense.

I tried to say something. But my imagination was busy projecting hopes, wishes, inspirations. All that came out was an embarrassing gulp.

"Good. Then I'm on the right track."

Aether curled through the bond, and I didn't quite manage to swallow a whimper.

Troy gathered me to him, drawing a single finger in a tingling line up my spine to make me arch my chest against his and tip my head back for his kiss.

I definitely didn't manage to hold back a sound this time, and when he freed me, I was glad for his arm around my back and his grip on the back of my neck.

The lips he pressed to my forehead were shockingly sweet after the sex teased in his kiss. "Thank you. I was ready to kill someone a few minutes ago. This helped."

"Good." I swallowed and tried to sound less breathless. "I mean. That's what I wanted. You. Feeling better."

"That's not all you wanted. But there'll be time later for the rest. And now I'll have something to think about other than dismembering all of them." Another small, pleased smile, which could be as much for his fantasies of me as for those of dismembering people he hated. "Now let's get back to the party before we're missed too much."

I let him lead the way so I could pull myself together, aching to hold his hand but keeping mine at my side. Queens were supposed to use their consorts as studs, not fall in love with and bond to them. My attachment to Troy would be seen as a weakness to exploit if the depth of or reason for it was discovered, even as his plans for later would simply underscore his perceived value in our enemies' eyes by letting them think he was a well-used toy.

I fucking hated elven politics.

As Troy and I drifted apart to mingle separately a little longer, I was determined to find a way to solve the case Sonia had inadvertently dropped into my lap: figuring out who was going to make an attempt on me, how to use it to win all the Houses present to my side, and what it was she hadn't told me.

The ball dragged deep into the night. It seemed we were going on the elves' natural nocturnal clocks for this. Fortunately, there was more substantial food—and an insult along with it, as I was served chicken while the elves got pork or beef. I managed to send it back and get something that wasn't a bird without creating too much of an incident, but it was a relief when Troy signaled we'd indulged their curiosity and meanness long enough and could go back upstairs. I filled him in on what Sonia had said on our way up, keeping it to our mental communications, and he just shook his head and sighed tiredly like he'd been expecting worse.

Despite that, as soon as the door shut behind Troy, he gripped my arm and swung me around against it with a thud, trapping me with his body.

"Now. I made you a promise," he said.

"No." I licked my lips, knowing exactly what I was about to start. "You set me a challenge."

He almost got me right then, drawing a gasp from me as he caught my chin and turned my head to nip my neck. "Is that so?"

"Yes."

"You're sure you want to walk this path?" He pulled away and smiled a hunter's smile, a full one this time, all teeth and threat. "We'll both enjoy it, but some of the rooms down the hall are Bedoe. You'll have questions to answer in the morning."

"Not if I don't feel like answering them," I snapped. My skin felt too tight, and my temper was frayed. I needed this distraction. We both did.

Troy unzipped my dress and let it drop in a careless pool of fabric at my feet then nibbled his way down my neck, stinging me with the smallest pricks from his sharp teeth without actually biting. "Of course, my queen."

Somehow, he turned the honorific into a reminder that, while everyone outside this room might traditionally consider me the one in charge, in this room, I was under his power. A point he underscored by skimming his hands up my body before pinching my nipples.

Hissing with the struggle to stay quiet, I arched against him.

"Good effort," he murmured before swapping his fingers with his mouth, alternating until I was panting with need. "Let's see what I can do about that."

I shuddered as he kissed his way down my body until he was kneeling in front of me. When he dragged my panties off and looked up, wickedness in his gaze, I realized what he was planning.

"Troy," I hissed.

His eyes didn't leave mine as he lazily licked me, his tongue skillfully tracing along my folds. "Mm?"

I shook my head, eyes wide. He was *not* going to do this with me right against the Goddess-damned—

He slipped two fingers into me, curling them as he pumped them in concert with the movements of his mouth and tongue.

I groaned before I could stop myself then slapped a hand over my mouth and tried to stay still so people passing by outside wouldn't hear me or the door rattling and stop to investigate.

"They'll hear you at some point," Troy pointed out as he continued to stroke with his fingers. "What does it matter if it's against the door or in bed?"

"They won't hear anything because I won't—"

I yelped in surprise as he bit my inner thigh. Not the sharp teeth. Those probably wouldn't come out for real, lest our hosts think Troy feral.

But he could do plenty with his primary teeth.

He grinned as I glared at him then kissed where he'd bitten me before turning his attention back to the main objective.

I tried to hold off my climax, if only because I'd made such a point about him not doing this here. But he kept working me then fell into just the right rhythm in just the right spot. My fingers laced through his hair of their own accord as my mouth ran off on its own. "There, right there, I—"

Promptly forgot all of my earlier protests as I came, crying out something that might have been his name.

Troy kept going until I'd finished then rose and pulled me away from the door, marching me to the bed with a hand on the back of my neck. My thighs hit the edge, and he kept pushing while the other hand gripped my hip to make me hinge forward.

"Look at yourself, Arden. Already coming apart on me after telling me you wanted a challenge." His whisper against my ear sent shivers over me as much as his fingers restarting their work between my thighs. "I didn't even have to use Aether to get you to come all over my face, right there against the door where anybody could hear you. Were you that worked up earlier?"

I put up a token struggle, but he had me pinned and I didn't really want to escape.

The sound of his zipper opening and his pants dropping seemed louder than it should.

He positioned himself and pressed into me so slowly I almost shouted at him to get on with it and just fuck me.

But no, resistance was the game.

I lasted maybe a minute before I groaned and gave in, struggling to move against him and get him to go faster.

"Did you know claimings used to be public?" he asked.

The casual question made me clench around him as I envisioned it. "No."

"Mm-hmm. It had me thinking about fucking you like this on the dining table, where everyone could see how hot and wet you are for me. And how unavailable I am for their plans."

Troy wasn't usually such a talker in bed, but the picture he was painting, forbidden and explicit, combined with his relentless thrusts against me to build another climax. I tried to hide my face against the duvet, but he wouldn't let me.

"Oh no. They might not see us. But they'll hear you." He pulled my hair to draw my head up.

He got what he wanted in the end, when I couldn't keep quiet any longer.

"That's right," he growled against my ear. "Let them all know exactly what they're missing."

A sting of Aether drew out my climax even further, and only when I'd surrendered entirely did he finish with silent, aggressive thrusts.

When Troy caught his breath and came down a little, he pulled away. "Stay here."

I was happy to oblige, dragging myself into a boneless sprawl on the bed after tugging off my shoes and coronet. My eyes dragged shut, and I floated in a cloud of elven pheromones.

After a quick rummage in one of the suitcases, water started running in the bathroom. Then the familiar snicking sound and sulfur scent of a match followed by...was that sandalwood incense? What was he doing in there?

After a few minutes, the water shut off, and Troy came back out. Before I could ask, he scooped me up, carried me to the bathroom, and set me back on my feet.

I gasped at the sight that greeted me. Not just the huge, luxurious jacuzzi bath with rose petals swirling lazily on the surface but also gently flickering candles and smoky curls of incense.

"Earth is a little hard to manage in a hotel," he said when I spun to look up at him. "But I was hoping covering the other three elements would be enough." He glanced down then back up, looking almost embarrassed. "I thought it could help. With being away from home and your land. And all the fuckery I knew we'd have to deal with."

Tears pricked my eyes at the thoughtfulness of it, and I launched myself into his arms. He grunted in surprise as he caught me and hugged me close.

"I love you," I said. "I love you so much."

He leaned away enough to search my face and winced. "Even if I was an asshole and potentially undermined you by staking a claim on you with loud sex?"

I started to answer with a quip then paused to give his unusual behavior tonight some thought. "Were you being an asshole? Or were you reclaiming something you were always told wasn't yours to give where you wanted?"

The bond wrenched, and he stared at me, pure shock blanking his features. "What?"

"My understanding of what you've said before is, the only way you were able to own your body and who you shared yourself with was to have nothing at all. And that Keithia was probably going to kill you for it. Now she's dead, and you have a choice."

I kissed his jaw. "Seems more like it was defiance in the face of all the people here who believe the same as her and want to use you in the same way. Plus, I'm sure someone said something to that effect at least once tonight, despite who and what you are now. It's not assholery. Not intentionally anyway."

The bond flipped through too many emotions for me to track as Troy processed that.

I kissed him again and wiggled to get down, partly to give him space but also because I wanted to try the jets in the tub. I really did need the elemental grounding after the overwhelm of this first evening. "Besides, you know I care more about keeping you safe and healthy than a damn title. If all that accomplished something more than a few solid orgasms, great." I dipped a toe in and found it perfectly hot. "As long as our people are safe, stake all the claims you want."

With a sigh of pleasure, I slipped into the water, hissing as the heat kissed tender parts and then sighing again when Troy reflexively soothed the nerve endings with a brush of Aether. When I looked up and held out a hand for him to join me, he was rubbing the back of his neck and looking at me in consternation.

"I didn't realize what I was doing until I came in here," he said. "I didn't mean to use you like that. Me dealing with shit isn't a reason to use you."

"I know." I tapped the back of my own head, where my sense of the Aetheric bond was strongest. "But there was nothing calculating in your head. You just really, really wanted me, and you wanted people to know it was mutual." I gave him a reassuring smile. "There's nothing wrong with that. You wanted to be king, and you are. But you're not in the Triangle where people accept it. We're both disconnected from our sense of place. We're both overwhelmed and trying to take back control. Now I want you to stop feeling guilty for wanting what you want and fucking who you wanted the way you wanted to fuck. Get in here and soak with me."

Relief eased his features. He stripped the rest of the way, leaving his fancy clothes in an uncharacteristically messy heap.

I shifted over so we could sit side by side in the massive tub and dropped my head to rest on his shoulder when he was in. "This really is lovely, Troy. Thank you."

"My pleasure." He kissed the crown of my head. "And thank you for seeing me. Always. Even when I can't see myself, you're there." His voice dropped, and the bond wavered. "It's good not to be alone anymore."

I tilted my head to breathe in his scent and kiss his neck.

We drove each other up the wall with bad habits and trauma responses. We butted heads a lot. We had competing needs sometimes, and being an elemental high queen mated to the only elven king in the world was far from easy. But moments like this, when we got our broken pieces to line up, made it all worth it.

Moments like this were what I fought for.

Chapter 16

I woke early the next morning, too warm and feeling trapped, to find Troy half-sprawled on top of me with his hand heavy atop my heart. Usually, we slept the other way around—me on him or as the little spoon—but I wasn't surprised being here had him more insecure, protective, or both.

Slowly, to avoid waking him, I shifted so I could wrap my arms around him. Me waking up first almost never happened, so while I occasionally played with his hair while he catnapped with his head in my lap during a slow day, holding him like this was rare. It felt good, like I was someone he could be vulnerable with. Someone he could be safe with. I wasn't a bully; I was the protector I wanted to be.

I swallowed hard against a burst of emotion, not realizing how much I needed that feeling. I tried so hard to stand alone. But sometimes I forgot that meant pushing other people away. Even Troy sometimes. We'd be dealing with more bullshit like last night—worse, maybe, now that they'd seen us and gauged our initial reactions—so I needed the connection between us to be strong.

Rather than ruin the moment by worrying about the day, I kept myself focused on him. Grounding myself in the present for once but also feeding him love, affection, and as much peace and faith as I could draw from this dawn moment.

He made a sleepy noise of pleasure and nuzzled closer before relaxing deeper into sleep.

For a moment, I thought my heart would burst at how adorable it was. This was a side of him I rarely saw, even when we were relaxing at home. With a light touch, I ran my fingers down his spine then back up over the faint scars left where Fi Sequoyah hadn't managed to heal the wounds from his torture completely. Scars he'd gotten as punishment from his grandmother for choosing me.

We might be in another nest of snakes, but I'd protect him from them better now than I had then.

He stirred, and I shoved the fierceness back down, not wanting him to wake thinking something was wrong. After another few minutes though, his internal clock brought him awake anyway. Nocturnal preferences or not, he'd been living on a human clock most of his adult life.

"This might be one of the best wake-ups I've had in my life," he mumbled against my neck.

"Maybe you should sleep in more," I said.

Troy kissed my jaw. "I'm not late. You're up early. I'd ask what's wrong, but I wouldn't feel this good if something was wrong."

"Nothing's wrong. I just found myself awake."

"Mmm." He rose to kiss me on the lips this time, though his eyes were still heavy-lidded with sleepy pleasure. "Well. Thank you for that. I needed it." Another shift brought him between my thighs. "As much as I want to take advantage of this, there's a packed schedule today."

"And you need to get your workout in before the politics start."

He grunted an affirmative, pressing more kisses along my jaw. "It'll make the day more tolerable."

"Does sparring with me count as a workout?"

He pulled away, his attention suddenly sharp. "Yes. What's on your mind, cariñamí?"

"What Sonia said last night. That thing about an attempt on me or us, and Bedoe doesn't want to be caught up in Talion Rule."

"Where does that tie into sparring?"

I gave myself another few heartbeats to think. "Everything we do here is watched. And everyone knows you were the Captain's second, top ranked alongside Allegra, right?"

He nodded.

"Okay. So we put on a show. A real one. If I win, they'll know I'm not easy meat. If you win, they'll see elven power can keep the elemental queen in check. Maybe slip up around me. Maybe we can draw out this attempt before they're ready. On our terms."

Troy narrowed his eyes. "I don't like that it makes you bait. But that's devious. And well-played." He thought about it, his gaze distant and hard. "All right."

This time of morning was effectively the elven equivalent of a human night shift, but there were a handful of elves already in the gym when we got there. From what I could tell, they were all wearing a House color. Troy and I were both in all black, which could have been as much for the Darkwatch as for the House of Onyx, I supposed.

The room quietened as we made our way to the side of the room with sparring mats.

When I set my elf-killer and the shorter duplicate of the godblade Neith had gifted me alongside his black longknife, the weapons brought murmurs from the other elves.

Thana made her way over. "Spotter?"

Troy and I both nodded, and she took up a position lounging against the wall with our weapons where she could keep them safe from being messed with. I was surprised she was already up after the late night, but maybe I wasn't the only one who couldn't sleep.

I closed off the bond on my side and smiled at Troy. The thrill of this little show was sending adrenaline singing through me. It'd be dangerous as hell, but I was eager to show off my hard-earned skills. "Best two out of three? Live tiebreaker?"

His answering smile was all predator. "Agreed. No magic."

"Agreed. Wouldn't want to bring the building down. Thana?"

"Square up," she said.

Troy and I faced each other and bowed. Voices rose as elves made hushed calls at our signal of a formal bout.

"Go," Thana said.

I shut the other voices out. Troy was fast and brutal. There was no room for dist—

He moved, surprising me. Usually he was the patient hunter, relying on my need for action to make the first move. I barely blocked his first flurry of attacks before clearing him and sending him dodging back with a solid kick.

"Almost," he taunted.

Oh it was definitely a show. He never talked when we sparred except to give instruction. Definitely not trash talk. And that meant this was another side of him I'd never seen.

I didn't have time to worry or wonder. He attacked again. Terrifyingly fast, trying to get me to the ground where I was weakest and he was strongest.

I sank into my training. There was nothing but block, strike, block. Defend and attack.

Nothing until he managed to fake me out, sweep my feet from under me, and get me to the floor.

I almost managed to wriggle free, but my strength was in keeping it moving. Quick strikes, staying out of his longer range. On the ground, I had none of it. I froze as he got a hand under my lifted chin and a thumb across my throat.

"Hold!" Thana said. "Bout one to King Troy."

Applause broke out.

Troy eased away much more slowly than he did at home, probably making a point to the spectators, given he dragged his thumb across my throat as he pulled back.

I blinked as I rose to find elves ringing the sparring area two deep. Some looked on with savage glee, to see an elemental bested and symbolically beheaded, as they no doubt thought should happen for real. But some wore expressions of calculation or concern. Troy was one of their best, and I'd held him off without a hint of magic, locked down so tight I might be a magical null.

As we squared up again, I was determined to do more than just hold my own. Troy was way better than me. But I'd been fighting him, learning his tricks, for years now.

Thana had barely finished the word "go" when I launched at him.

He smirked, having expected my lunge.

He hadn't expected me not to attack though.

Rather than strike, I ducked, whirled under his pre-emptive block, and got behind him. As he spun to face me, I captured his wrist, twisted, and locked his arm while kicking the back of his knee to drop him. A little hapkido, a little Darkwatch training, and a little luck.

He nearly broke free, hooking an arm behind my knee, but I hauled up on his wrist and laid my thumb across his throat.

"Hold! Bout two to High Queen Arden," Thana said. "Tie breaker with live weapons."

Given the show Troy had already put on, I gave one of my own. Before releasing him, I leaned over to bite his earlobe hard enough to pull a grunt from him.

This time, the room was silent. Heavy with the weight of calculation or shock at how quickly the bout had ended.

The look Troy gave me when he stood might have looked murderous to anyone else, but I could read the flush on his neck and the drop of his eyes to my lips. He was thinking about a public claiming again.

Thana approached slowly with our weapons in hand and scented the air. "Are you two good to continue?"

Troy nodded, his gaze not leaving me.

"Yes," I said.

"You still want live weapons for the tiebreaker?"

"Yes," Troy and I said together.

"Goddess protect you both," she muttered as she handed them to us.

Despite her standing over the blades, we both checked first our own, then each other's, knives. Couldn't be too careful.

Satisfied that neither had been physically or magically tampered with, we backed away from each other and took guard positions.

Wickedly sharp secondary teeth flickered in Troy's smile this time, drawing a few mutters from the crowd. Those mutters grew louder as I grasped Air briefly to make my eyes flash gold in response.

He might be a Hunter, but I was the damn Eternal Huntress.

The word "go" had barely left Thana's lips when Troy moved. With live weapons, his enchanted longknife of meteoric steel would beat either my lead-and-steel elf-killer or the silver-edged steel dagger both in reach and in material. The only way to beat him was to be flat-out better: disarm him or get inside his guard before he could do something tricky.

He was real fucking stubborn about holding onto that weapon though, and he moved like it was part of his arm.

No room for thought. No room for fear. I twisted more than dodged, letting the blade clear me by bare inches, and slammed the butt of my dagger down on his wrist. He grunted in pain but kept his hold on the longknife.

I ducked as he turned his backswing into an attempt to elbow me in the face.

Troy blocked my attempt to sweep his feet, adding force to throw me off mine.

I rolled away, pushing to my feet and turning it into a backflip. Clipped him in the jaw with a foot to make the scent of rosemary and sage and iron blossom.

He didn't bother to do more than lick the blood from his lip before lunging again, trying to force me against the wall as the crowd scattered out of our way.

A dart of Aether flashed toward Troy.

I dropped to a knee to duck a slash from him, opened the bond wide, and made a scythe of Chaos to slice through the chord of Aether targeting him. "Troy!"

Someone at the back of the room cried out as whatever they'd tried to cast at Troy snapped back on them.

Without words, the bond flew open, and Troy's back was to mine when I rose, our sparring shifting to immediate defense, weapons held ready to block.

The room was in an uproar.

"You okay?" he asked.

"Yes. You?"

"Fine. Let's hunt."

Side by side, power signatures throbbing through the room, we made our way to where an elf writhed on the floor, held down by Haroun and Pascale with blades out.

"Apologies, Majesties," Haroun said.

I shook my head. "It was a friendly sparring session. You shouldn't have had to be on defense."

"Gerard Ead," Troy said. Glaciers had nothing on his tone. "Taking advantage of that opportunity is going to cost you. And your House." He turned to me. "Who was the spell aimed at?"

"You." Where Troy was ice, the banked heat of a volcano was in my voice.

"She's lying!" Gerard said. "She attacked me without cause!"

"If that's true, then why is your aura tinged with untruth while you deal with the physical effects of a backwashed spell?" Troy said in a dangerously soft tone.

Gerard paled.

Troy shifted his jaw to drop his secondary teeth and gave a sharp smile. "I suppose Keithia kept it well-hidden that I could read auras for truth. And you didn't know my queen could read both halves of Aether, even if she can't wield them." He shook his head. "Unprovoked magical trespass is a killing offense. At a summit, under a truce? It's a painful death."

The doors swung open, and a triple triad of Ead House Guard poured in. They froze to see both Troy and me on our feet though, with the crowd being held back by the Darkwatch and the Ebon Guard.

"There's the rest of the plot," Troy said.

Sixtus Ead pushed through the crowd. "What is the meaning of this, Solari?"

He might have been addressing Troy, but I answered him. "My king and I were having a friendly match. Your man here decided to try taking advantage of that."

"We're all under truce here." Sixtus sneered, giving me an ugly up-and-down look. "But the Solaris are the only ones with bared blades and teeth."

"Truce isn't broken if we're just getting our morning exercise between ourselves," I said. "It is if I have to counter a spell cast by one of your House against my king."

Sixtus stiffened. "Are you making an accusation?"

Troy nodded. "We are. Attempted magical trespass."

A dark-skinned elfess pushed forward, and I nodded at Thana to let her pass, recognizing Sonia Bedoe in some fancy yoga get-up. "I second the accusation, in case Queen Onora won't take the word of an elemental high queen and a claimed king consort. That was sloppily done, Sixtus." She shook her head, lip curling. "What was the plan? Push the Bull into killing his queen in a tragic but incredibly fortunate training accident?"

House Ead's Captain glared down at the elf now laying with the stillness of terror before blanking his expression. "I don't know what you're talking about."

Troy's voice was a caress as he squinted and read the man's aura. "Lie."

If looks could kill, Troy might have been in trouble. Sixtus dropped his secondary teeth and reached for something at the small of his back.

"Sixtus! You will stand down," Sonia snapped. She met the eye of another dark-skinned elfess with a cloud of curly hair dyed a vibrant orange. "Keeya, get the rest of the Bedoe House Guard. We remember honor, even if House Ead has forgotten it climbing into bed with the mundanes."

Sixtus flushed a deep, furious red. "Better than fucking a filthy elemental."

"It has its perks," Troy drawled before I could reply. He dropped his shields almost completely, allowing his power signature to slash through the room with an even deeper chill. "But the next time you want to make a comment about my queen, Sixtus, it'd better be a civil one, or you will answer for it with blood."

I barely kept my surprise under wraps. Not the drily snarky comment about perks; that was part of his humor. The implication that his power was due to being with me though—that I wasn't expecting. It was sort of true. He'd always had the potential, but the bond with me had unlocked it early. Maybe this was his way of balancing his guilt for "using" me last night.

Sixtus held his ground, chin up. "If you think you're going to change anything, Solari, you're dead wrong."

The bond carried Troy's quiet, savage certainty as he stepped forward and into Sixtus's face. "If you're not careful, Sixtus, you'll just be dead."

The Ead House Captain twitched a hand toward the small of his back again, but Troy tapped his flank with the longknife he still held bared.

Shaking his head, Troy said, "You've been foolish enough for one day. Try to live to see the trial." His smile widened. "Or don't. I'm within my rights, with witnesses."

Sonia hustled forward, pulling hard enough on Aether that I snatched Air in response. She glanced at me, raising her hands, as my power signature flared. "Everyone calm down. Sixtus, whatever you came here to do, it failed. Troy, your queen is still living and unharmed. This has to go before a joint conclave now."

Tension stretched as neither man backed down.

The word "diplomacy" rattled around in my head. We couldn't make progress, not like this. Troy had been the one to remind me that they'd try to make us brutes. There was a time to fight, and this wasn't it.

I hated it. I wanted to fight. But I couldn't burn this place and everyone in it to the ground. Not this time. Not when we needed to recruit at least a few of these people to our side or watch the slow decline of the elves accelerate until they wiped themselves out and left Otherside unbalanced.

They might have committed genocide against elementals. *I* would be better than that.

I would put the world on a new track. It wasn't like the other elementals were going to support me either way. They'd made that clear, and I had to deal with the danger in front of me, even if it all broke my heart.

"Troy," I called gently but firmly with a nudge in the bond, putting my knives in the sheathes Haroun handed me. "With me, please. We'll deal with this at trial."

It took a few seconds, but with a deep, shuddering breath, Troy obeyed, cracking his neck and hiding his secondary teeth as he backed off. "Stay the fuck away from my queen."

"Your so-called queen should be dead." Sixtus spat on the floor then turned on his heel and left. The Ead House Guard followed him out.

That was almost enough to set Troy off again, but I caught his arm and squeezed. *Cariñomí. Long game.*

The words got through, and Troy settled, putting his blade away even if he left his power signature at full ebb.

I turned to Thana and Haroun, both of them grim-faced. "Let's go," I said. "Pull everyone in until we can be assured our people will be safe, since we're apparently among oathbreakers."

Angry comments sputtered through the remaining observers. They might have been in favor of me or against me, but either way, I didn't give a fuck. Sonia had been right about an attack. Which meant it was time to find out what else she wanted and what she'd give us to avoid Talion Rule.

Because for all I wanted to be better, at this point, it was just my damn good manners stopping me from opening a sinkhole and dropping the building into the swamp. And I was not above stacking this trial for my own benefit.

There was doing better, and there was being foolish. I was done being the latter in pursuit of the former.

Chapter 17

After arranging with Sonia to meet in one of the venue's smaller conference rooms in an hour, I tamped down my power signature, gathered my people, and left the gym with my chin up.

That wasn't the goal we were trying for, Troy whispered in my mind as we made our way back up to our rooms. *But I think it worked out better.*

Definitely. But Troy…we need to figure out our response to the death sentence for magical trespass.

The burst of frustration I got back seared through my mind, enough that I barely stopped myself from reacting. I was equally frustrated. Otherside justice was clear: an eye for an eye and blood for blood. This wasn't just a killing offense for the elves either. But it would be easy for someone to score political points by making us out as hypocrites, while undercutting us as potentially weak or leaving us open to a repeat attack if we did nothing.

No good—or at least easy—roads forward.

We'll figure it out, I sent. *We treat with Sonia first though. And then I either need to go home or make a land tie here.* The itch of separation was starting, digging deep now that I wasn't distracted with sparring or attempts on my life, and it was adding to the social stress to make me cranky as fuck.

Troy sent an affirmative nudge, and we all kept quiet until we'd reached our floor.

"Everybody do what you need to do for an hour. Nap, eat, whatever will help you get through what might be a very long day," I said.

Haroun and Thana nodded, turning to those of the Guard and Darkwatch who'd followed us up or popped out of their rooms.

I didn't wait to see how they divvied up responsibilities. I needed a closed door so I could let off some steam in peace.

While Troy swept the room for bugs again, I showered, making it quick. Then we swapped. As the shower came on again, I dressed in another of the understated but expensive outfits I found in my suitcase. A tight-fitting gold silk blouse with billowy sleeves and onyx buttons at my wrists went over tapered black slacks that fit me like they'd been painted on. The silk probably wouldn't hold up well under the heavy kestrel brooch, so I strung my father's pendant and my hematite callstone around my neck. Looking at myself in the mirror made me think I was missing something though.

The gold-and-onyx circlet I'd worn last night sat on the bedside table. Feeling silly, I put it on, tentatively settling it among my curls.

"I'm a queen," I whispered. "A *high* queen. I *earned* this." Goddess-damned Keithia had worn her coronet around her home. I could stand to make a point wearing mine in a place where I was surrounded by enemies who didn't believe in my legitimacy and openly attacked me.

To work off the tension that added atop what I'd already been carrying, I drew on all four elements and created two balls of primordial energy.

"Arden?" Troy called from the bathroom.

"Just relaxing!"

"Okay. Be careful."

That he said the last part out loud hinted at how frustrated and paranoid he was feeling. I let it go, focusing on making the balls swoop through the air in figure eights. Maybe working this much magic would be enough to make a tie and I wouldn't actually have to go down into the swamp. As much as I wanted to, even I could see the strategic mess it'd make when House Ead had already made an attempt.

When Troy came out, he'd dressed as a king consort: designer slacks and button-down shirt in black, the cuffs embroidered in gold with a pattern vaguely reminiscent of gusts of wind and the first two gold buttons undone to tease his chest. Hands in his pockets, his gaze swept over me from head to toe and back up before he nodded at the circlet. "Good choice. You look great. Maybe add one of the knives. The elf-killer."

I blinked. "That's not exactly diplomatic."

"Neither is trying to get me with an Aether sting. I want you safe."

I considered that. I wanted to be safe as well. But if I acted scared and insecure, that was how I'd be seen. "No. If someone comes for me, I have my powers."

Troy's expression hardened. "And if they have bronze?"

That made me hesitate.

"I know why you don't want to carry it. But don't let ego and optics get in the way of safety."

That stung. I didn't have an ego. Did I?

He stepped closer and ran his hands down my arms, answering my unspoken and unsent thought. "You don't. Much. But if you overcompensate on optics in response to the attack, it potentially boils down to the same result. You, hurt." His gaze was shadowed labradorite as he peered into my eyes. "And while you might be okay with my burning the world to save you, I'd rather neither of us was in the position to need it."

I winced. "That's fair."

"Thank you." Troy kissed my forehead. "Let's get downstairs. I want time to sweep the room before Sonia arrives."

The venue was as abandoned as an old cemetery when we got downstairs. Word of this morning's show and the fallout had certainly spread, and for all their nasty little games, the elves were apparently not too keen on finding out what I'd do about the attack. I doubted anyone was still asleep, nocturnal or not.

Part of me was satisfied. The Richmond Conclave could only be powerful if I wasn't. And I was. *We* were, Troy and me, together. We'd proven it. So now they fell back. Charleston as well. With the exception of Queen Merle, they'd been better-behaved last night than Houses Ead or Hilith, icily neutral rather than bitingly provocative, but in this situation, neutrality was as good as declaring for the other side.

People who wouldn't fight for equity and justice stood against it, as far as I was concerned. So it'd be interesting to see what happened in this trial because there *would* be a trial at this summit. Like I'd told Sonia, I was no longer inclined to allow the elves to drag their feet on anything at all. Especially not this.

Justice delayed meant there would be no justice at all.

We had just enough time alone in the conference room for Troy and Pascale, the Darkwatch agent who'd accompanied us down, to sweep the room for bugs while Uri Luna and Vern Monteague, two of the newer members of the Ebon Guard, stood watch outside the door.

"Got something." Pascale held up a small, round device that looked like a fancier version of one of the bugs I'd used at Verve Health. The ponytail she'd pulled her long, blond hair into tightened her features and made her expression look even harder than Troy's. She was one of my more dedicated supporters; like Thana, she'd hesitated to start a family in House Sequoyah because of the policies of the former queens. Pascale had taken the extra step of seeking formal adoption into House Solari, something few of the other elves had done.

Troy nodded. "Me too. Arden?"

I took the chair he gestured to, at the head of the table with my back to the wall farthest from the door. He sat at my right, and both elves dropped what they'd found in my palm. I fried the devices with a burst of blended Air and Fire.

Moments later, Sonia swept in, shutting the door behind her when it became clear Pascale was going nowhere. Her nostrils flared at the scent of burnt electronics, and her grim expression cleared a moment too late for us not to see it. "Majesties."

Troy gestured for her to come all the way in and sit down. "Princess."

She sat, not opposite me at the foot of the table as I was expecting, but opposite Troy, at my left. Her nearness put me on guard, but I tried to keep my reaction under control.

An awkward silence hung before she broke it. "I suppose I owe you both apologies, as the primary organizer of this summit."

"You do," Troy said bluntly. "And then some."

A wince flickered on Sonia's lips, quickly suppressed. "I did warn Queen Arden there would be an attempt."

Troy didn't bother to hide his disgust. "That's very convenient."

"Are you saying I knew what would happen?"

"Are you saying you didn't?" he threw back.

Sonia started to answer then stopped and glanced between me and Troy. "How serious are you about Talion Rule?"

I reached for Troy's hand, running a thumb over the swordsman's calluses on it. "He speaks with my voice. And I with his."

She grimaced. "That's problematic."

My laugh startled her. "No. What's problematic is House Ead working with the Sinners and then thinking they could take a shot at me. Priorities, Sonia."

"You wouldn't—" She paused at whatever she saw in my expression. "You really would let him destroy the royals of the Richmond Conclave."

"And those of the Charleston Conclave, if they want to fuck around too," I said. "Personally, I'm hoping they see what I plan for Richmond and make smarter choices. Troy's an excellent general, but I need him for more important tasks than fighting an elven war. And I really do mean what I say when I talk about ending the elven death cult. At this point, y'all's biggest worry should be your own damn selves. Not me."

Sonia stiffened, blinking fast. "Wait. I— What are you planning for Richmond?"

The fear scent rising from her sparked the new instincts in me, the ones that tasted fear as prey, and I couldn't help the widening of my smile. "I don't leave enemies at my back. Keithia taught me the foolishness of that."

Troy shifted to lean forward and rest his forearm on the table. "The problem with our society, Sonia, is that the queens have stifled all imagination." He smiled, a sneering twist of his lips. "If an elven Darkwatch agent is fucking an elemental queen, he's just getting close enough to strike. And if he's fighting her, they can't just be sparring. It must be that he wants her dead, right? Easy enough to push a latent desire like that to the fore with a little Aether."

Sonia leaned back in her chair, studying Troy like she'd never seen him before. "You have no intention of usurping her. That little sparring session was a setup."

I smiled like a mean girl. "Thanks for the tip."

"I didn't think you'd action it like *that*." She looked at Troy again. "And *you* might need a new sigil. I'm not sure a bull fits anymore."

He glanced at me, satisfaction flickering across his face. "I have one."

"I suppose you do." She shook her head, tired enough to let a dazed look settle. "You really had everyone fooled. For *decades*. The perfectly trained prize. Keithia's bait. We all knew it, even if the payoff seemed worth it. But all this time you were...what? A sleeper agent? An assassin?"

I shifted, ready to snap at her, but Troy brought my knuckles to his lips and kissed them.

"I was what I had to be," he said. "And now I'm whatever I want to be."

Sonia returned her evaluating stare to me. "And you allow it."

I couldn't help snorting. "I know better than to get in his way."

Her dark gaze flicked between us a few times more. Then she shuddered. "I underestimated you both. I won't make that mistake again."

"Mistake or not, what else do you want?" I asked Sonia bluntly. "You've told me what you don't want. Bedoe implicated in this attack. But what do you want?"

"I told you—"

"Stop. You have your dossier on me. Think very carefully about what games you want to play next and how you want to play them." I didn't need the nudge of the Sight to tell me she was still trying to spin this in her favor.

She stared at me expressionlessly. For a moment, I thought she'd tell me to go to hell. Then she wilted, slumping back in her chair and crossing her arms. "Darius Monteague."

Troy scowled. "What do you want with my brother?"

"To marry him. Like it or not, Solari is the rising power. I want ties. Call it first dibs on whatever comes next."

Shock bounced so hard between me and Troy in the bond I had to close it.

"First," I said, "it's up to him who he marries."

Sonia looked at me like I was speaking in tongues. "But you're High Queen. You can just—"

"No." I sent a curl of reassurance to Troy as outrage spiked in his scent, strong enough for me to recognize it. "My people are free to make their own personal choices, no matter their gender or their rank. *Especially* when it comes to who they share their lives and bodies with and in what ways."

Sonia's confusion was painted clearly across her face. "But I thought that was just propaganda. Infowar bullshit."

It took an effort not to roll my eyes. "Nope."

"Well, we've always done it to the contrary," she said. "The queens make the choice for the good of the House."

I shook my head. "We are no longer doing things the way they've 'always' been done. And if you want to marry into my House—into my family—that is the first thing you're gonna get through your head. That's the choice I'm making for the good of the House."

She looked at Troy, bafflement painting her features as she followed that thought to the logical conclusion. "You chose her? Freely?"

"Yes." He tugged his shirt open enough to show the burn scar where his Monteague House tattoo had been. "And Keithia and my sister tried their best to kill me for it."

Sonia paled. "We—we understood that Queen Arden had claimed you. By force, blood for blood as payment for Prince Quinlan, and that Keithia took you back to challenge her."

Troy sneered and shook his head disgustedly. "You understood what you wanted, based on the idea that I had no agency or any desire for it. *I* chose and bonded to Arden. She accepted it. Accepted me. And as King, I will not allow otherwise for any of my House. Not after what Keithia put me and Darius through as royal marriage bait."

She leaned back in her chair, studying us. "It's not just that you've made a commitment to support her. It's love, isn't it?"

Troy nodded solemnly.

"Well then," she said. "All of that changes a great deal in a way I'm not sure I like."

I rolled my eyes. "Fortunately, I don't require you to like it. But I do require you to accept and respect it."

She stiffened, glaring. "Giving up power—"

"Is required," I interrupted, "for us, by which I mean both the elves and the more powerful in Otherside as a whole, to do our part for a more equitable society. There are a whole bunch of people who don't want to see that. They're gonna be real pissed about it when they realize lip service and performative allyship does not fly in my House, my territory, or my demesne. And you know what? I'm okay with that. If you want Darius, if you want to join *our family*" —I gestured between me and Troy with my free hand— "then the first thing you're gonna do is demonstrate *publicly*, with actions, that you're on board with that." I shrugged. "Or you can cut us out of the picture and win Darius's affection on your own merits. If you can find him, which you will not have our help in doing unless you agree here and now to our terms."

Sonia sat there looking flabbergasted, like the idea of merit had never occurred to her.

I decided to try a different tack. "Lemme put it this way. You're an elf. But mundanes see you as Black. Right?"

She wrinkled her nose. "They see money. When they see me at all. I don't have much to do with mundanes."

My mistake for thinking someone who looked vaguely like me might have had similar experiences. Allegra had, but apparently being Darkwatch took her into closer contact with humans and their societal fuckery than being a princess had brought Sonia. Social class and money bought a hell of a bubble.

"Fine," I said. "The point is, those who have, and have had for a long fucking time, are going to need to give some shit up now. Those whose invisible knapsacks have carried less weight are going to have to take some on. And those who've had easy paths are going to have to help build some roads for those who've had to cross more difficult terrain. You get me?"

Sonia glared like she wanted to disagree. Then looked away, out the window, as her scent curled into something small and sour. "I get you. But I don't like it. Not at all."

"That's a you problem," I said curtly. I had no more patience for diplomacy, and for once, Troy didn't try to rein me in. "Here's another thing that's a you problem: I want all the queens and their seconds or heirs, or both, in council. And I want it by this evening."

Her gaze snapped to me. "The agenda—"

"Doesn't mean a Goddess-burning thing," Troy said. "And we both know it. House Ead's actions would demand blood for an elven queen, and it would be happening a hell of a lot faster. My queen is being generous." He leaned forward, pulling Sonia's attention, and flashed his secondary teeth. "You know I don't make empty threats. Get it done. Now. Or Talion Rule will be the least of your concerns."

Chapter 18

After Sonia left, Troy slouched in his chair and closed his eyes, tipping his head back. "What's this plan for the Richmond Conclave?"

"Severing."

Troy snapped upright, and in the corner, Pascale gasped.

I just gave them both a resigned look. "I know the goal is to show people a better way, but I can't have these queens alive and at my back. Killing them negates everything I've tried to undo about the elven death cult. And given how things have been going lately, I'm starting to wonder how much longer the elven population is viable and sustainable." I flicked the hematite callstone around my neck. "So I call one of the djinn. Throw them a bone with both the presence here and the action, given they haven't fucked me over in a summit yet."

With a grimace, Troy bowed his head. "So be it."

"I don't like it either. It feels cruel, and I never want to be Callista. But I keep getting pushed into impossible choices." I slumped in my chair, miserable with the idea of what I was planning to do and hoping it wouldn't be too big a setback in my goal to reunite the elves and the djinn somehow. "Maybe setting a second example will finally make the point."

From Troy's expression, that was pretty damn unlikely, but I had to hope. Not just that the elves would quit their bullshit, but also that taking this action might win me some support with the

Elemental Collective. I was always demanding actions, and now it was my turn to show that I'd act to protect one of Otherside's most threatened factions.

Either way, we could do better by not only the elves but Otherside as a whole. We had to do something to balance out the factions.

That sparked a thought. "Troy, how do the queens expect to maintain their position as the primary faction in Otherside if they keep killing their own people? Samarre mentioned her high queen doing it in Lyon. Keithia slaughtered my father's entire House. They have this chokehold on who gets to have kids with whom and when. What is the end game?"

He frowned. "Power."

"Okay but to what end? Who the hell do they rule over if they've killed everyone?" I looked between him and Pascale, who were frowning at each other.

She shook her head. "If I may, my queen, all of this only started happening in the last couple of generations, at least in House Sequoyah. I always thought it was a territory thing."

"Explain, please," I said.

Crossing her arms, she took a minute to think, half her attention on the door and windows. "Humans are reproducing exponentially. Way faster than elves ever could. There's no more space for all of us—at least, that's what I think they're thinking—and once, I overheard Queen Catrionne say they'd rather we die out than blend with humanity."

My stomach twisted. So it was back to blood and purity ideals and species supremacy. Again. I'd hoped Leith Sequoyah and his Redcap conspiracy to overthrow the queens was an extreme reaction to what they were doing. But maybe it was the same track on a parallel course.

Troy rapped his fingers on the table. "That's part of it. Now that I'm thinking about it, I think the other part is that the impending decline we can all see drove them to look at short-term measures. It doesn't matter how long we live. There's no need for long-term planning when the environment is degrading to the point that fertility rates have plummeted and your species is headed for a tipping point. But at the same time, consolidating power among your chosen increases in its allure. They probably told themselves they were securing their own chances."

This was a mess. A disgusting mess.

I rubbed my temples, trying to hold off the headache thundering to the fore. "So if we need to be diplomatic, what's my leverage? What gets them to stop? The most powerful leaders of the most powerful faction in Otherside have given up. They either can't see a better way, or they don't think mine is better. What's the incentive?"

Troy shook his head and closed his eyes. "I need to think on it, cariñamí. You're asking the right questions. I just don't have the answers yet."

That was a relief, in a shitty kind of way. It wasn't that I was undiplomatic or unskilled at politics.

It was that I was finally asking the questions that needed asking.

Maybe I could make it as queen if I remembered my beginnings as a private investigator. Get to the root of the problem. Figure out the motivations. And make a case with the evidence.

Yeah, I could do that. If the elves didn't force me to do shit I couldn't reverse first.

"Let's take a walk and make a plan," I said. "I need some air, and this will need to be flawless."

△▽△▽

I didn't know what Sonia had promised or traded to get the gathering I demanded, but by sunset, we were all together in a much bigger conference room, seated around an honest-to-Goddess round table like we were some kind of fairytale council. Sixteen people—the queens and their seconds or heirs, counting me and Troy—sat around the table. An honor guard for each House stood behind their charges. Thana had relieved Pascale and was standing behind me and Troy.

Tension held the room hostage, everyone in it seeming afraid to make the wrong move. The other queens weren't even bothering to hide their ugly expressions of disgust, fear, anger, or in the case of Sixtus Ead, outright hatred.

Troy watched him where he stood behind Onora, expression neutral even as the temperature in the room seemed to drop from the icy cold of his power signature.

"Why isn't he cuffed?" Troy asked the room at large. "I made an accusation of attempted magical trespass against Gerard Ead, witnessed and affirmed by Princess Sonia. I want Sixtus on trial for complicity."

Onora Ead, a light-skinned older elfess in an aubergine dress with ornate gold embroidery, her hair the silver grey of age, rolled dark eyes. "The Carolinas demesne might recognize kings as valid, but that's not how the Dominion demesne works. My House won't be accused by a pair of animals." She looked around the room. "I'm here to call for the rest of you to join in putting them down. We've entertained this sham of a summit long enough. It was meant to be information gathering and a trap, not a legitimate humoring of their ridiculous claims."

My heart thundered and my skin felt too tight, too clammy. So that was how this was going to go—and she was pretty damned confident if she was spilling everything now. And yet, not confident enough if she was trying to get a committee together. Either way, I supposed she was a contemporary of Keithia, if not older, and that old bitch had held similar sentiments.

We might have been outnumbered, but I could take them.

With Troy, we might even make it bloodless.

Hopefully.

I wrenched my mind away from what other plans they must have had given Gerard's failure and rose, slowly enough that they couldn't take it as an attack, keeping my voice low and level. "My king and I have put up with quite enough slights, insults, and threats." I met the eyes of every person around the table who'd look at me. Not all of them would, some avoiding my gaze out of disgust, some in fear. "I'm only going to say this once. You will treat us with the respect we're owed as equal members of this group. Or you will wish you had."

On the far side of the room, Sixtus snarled. "*That* was a threat."

"Yeah, it was." I raised my voice to be heard above the outraged mutters. "See, I learned something in trying to be civil and courteous with the Chapel Hill Conclave. The more I bowed, the harder their feet pressed on my neck, trying to press me lower. I won't have it. So, you can accept that times are changing, and we can work together to the benefit of all. Your only other choice is that I will change them for you. I have the power to do it, and you don't have the power to stop me. If you did, I'd already be dead and this conference wouldn't be happening."

Throwing that in their faces so baldly was like throwing a match into a gas leak.

I sat back down as the room erupted, letting them speak over each other. Watching to see who fell where. This was the dangerous part of the plan: giving them enough time to either show their asses or indicate who I might be able to work with. I genuinely didn't want to have to sever everybody or kill anybody.

Sonia looked sick where she sat next to her mother. Queen Esi had better control over her expression, but her dark features were tight and her eyes hard as she too read the room.

Across from the Bedoes, the royals and captains for the Charleston Houses seemed split. High Queen Merle of House Averill was hollering something in my general direction that I didn't bother trying to make out, given that her blue eyes would be shooting flame if they could. House Tossavi's Queen Idia was arguing with Richmond's other queen, Leta Hilith, while the Queen of House Quet, Yna, stared at me with narrowed, suspicious eyes. The captains and knights looked like they wanted to reach for weapons.

Underneath it all ran an undercurrent, the scent of gut-twisting fear that sharpened my senses. This was a hunt. My hunt. And they were mine for the taking.

I focused on Troy. *Last chance to find another way.*

There is no other way. I'd hoped you were wrong, but I've never seen a council of royals this chaotic. They can be cruel and nasty, but this? A sick feeling slithered through the bond, even as his expression stayed haughtily neutral. *This is worse than I'd thought. There's no salvaging it. And I won't have enemies at your back.*

So be it. I casually took hold of my callstone and pushed for Duke.

Sixtus's attention snapped to me as I did. That was interesting. Most elves couldn't sense the blip of Chaos it took for me to make the connection with a djinni. Damn inconvenient for that asshole to have a special talent of some sort, but he wouldn't be able to do anything about it.

"Duke," I murmured when he accepted the connection. "You know how the Djinn Council was asking for intel?"

"Mm-hm. And you seem to be surrounded by the most distressing energies, little bird."

"If you or Iaret fancy popping by, I'd like to make a rather firm point to an elven council of royals."

I'd barely finished before Duke pulled himself through in a burst of lemony Aether, anchored by our blood tie, manifesting to stand behind my chair in his preferred human-looking form.

"My, my, I don't think I've ever seen such a chaotic gathering of elves," he said, echoing Troy's sentiment. "You do have an interesting effect on people, Arden. I thought Ninlil was good at stirring up trouble, but you make it an art."

The rich amusement in his deep voice cut through where the scent of his magic and his sudden appearance hadn't, and the room dropped into silence before exploding to a level even louder than before. An impressive array of knives and guns almost cleared their sheaths and holsters before I pulled hard on Air and, rather than trying to manage multiple chords with precision, simply blew everyone's chair back against the wall and tied off the chord to keep them there.

Thana murmured a soundproofing spell. Troy muttered into his wrist mic as I blocked the door with Air to prevent the many guards and members of entourages outside the room from coming in.

Onora was right. This was a trap.

But it wasn't hers. It was mine.

I was not the naïve, lost little girl anymore, walking into situations thinking everyone would play by the rules of decency. Here, we played by the rules of power.

I had it. So I had to use it. Even if it made me sick to my stomach.

With a much more careful burst of Air and Fire, I slagged all the electronic devices I could sense at the edges of the room then focused on the table. Elves jumped and swore as phones and earpieces popped, and smoke rose from a few points under the table where bugs or recording devices had been hidden. Another burst caught a few more in the wall vents.

If I'd thought the royals were loud before, it was nothing on now.

The smell of burnt marshmallow, rotted herbs, and fear swamped the room as various elves recovered from the shock of being trapped by elemental power and grabbed for Aether.

I reached for Troy's hand. We didn't need to be touching to boost our power, but it was part of the show—misdirection in case of future betrayal, to make those who walked away from this think we had to be close or touching to tie our magic together.

With his power amplifying mine even further, I sliced through all the spells coming at us with a scythe of Chaos. Then we flipped the current so my magic powered Troy's.

He snarled a monarch-level spell in elvish that dampened all elven Aether in the room except his own, followed by a "don't speak" spell to prevent any further interruption.

The scene had Duke roaring with laughter. "I know we need to keep an eye on your Sinners, Arden, but Iaret can't miss this."

"By all means," I said. "Couldn't hurt to have more witnesses."

Again, I rose to stalk around the room with my hand on my elf-killer, channeling the predatory sense that'd awakened recently. While Duke connected with Iaret, I addressed our captive audience. "This is what consequences look like. I'm taking a page outta the fae's book. Y'all had a chance to treat a traveler kindly and with respect. But instead, some of you—*most of you*—behaved abominably, even murderously."

Another burst of lemon zest from behind me announced Iaret's arrival, followed quickly by her squeal of glee. "Oh, this is *delightful*, Arden. A party!"

"Hey, Iaret. Thank you for joining my little conclave meeting."

She grinned as I made another circuit of the room, giving each person trapped behind my walls an evaluating look in turn.

"The djinn's presence is just the first of the changes we'll be seeing," I said. "Some of y'all may remember that, once upon a time, the djinn and the elves were partners in keeping the world in balance. I'm bringing that back. Starting now. The djinn are and will be equal players in things going on around here, and all of you *will* leave elementals the fuck alone, even if you can't respect us as people."

Onora Ead sneered as she acted like there was no wall of Air keeping her from me. When she tried to speak, nothing came out.

Smiling, I shook my head. "You've had your say. More than enough of it, especially given how many of those words have been falling into the ears of the mundanes' Supernatural Investigators. And now it's my turn."

Onora went so deep a red with rage that I wondered if she was going to have an aneurysm and save me the trouble of dealing with her.

"Now. I called these conclaves together because there are some things I want to address. First and foremost, the attack by Gerard Ead upon my king this morning. That was attempted magical trespass with ill intent, no matter which faction you hail from in Otherside. I won't stand for it." I glared at Sixtus as I passed him again. "Second, Houses Ead and Hilith have been sharing Otherside secrets with the mundanes. This endangers all of us and directly undermines my efforts to keep those very secrets out of their hands for all our safety. I won't have that either. Finally, we are going to revisit the Atlantis Accords. Because this bullshit cold war between the djinn and the elves is leaving my fellow elementals stuck in the middle with bounties on their heads. It's not right or fair. And it's going to stop, if I have to claim the entire continent as mine to enforce it."

I returned to my place at the table, where Troy remained seated in an arrogant slouch that definitely had more cat in it than bull. Iaret was perched on the edge of the table, practically vibrating with excitement in a long, flowing black dress, and Duke leaned on the back of Troy's chair in an unusual display of camaraderie from both of them, given how much baggage Duke carried about elves and how much Troy hated having people at his back. They all exuded a dangerous beauty, and it made a hell of a point, even if the itch of paranoia ran in an undercurrent in the bond.

But I liked the message it sent. Unity in the face of prejudice, hatred, and abuses of power.

Yeah. It was time for a new beginning. A real one this time.

Chapter 19

I cupped Troy's chin, tilting it up and brushing a kiss on his lips. Even the quick gesture sparked heat in his eyes when I pulled away, and I couldn't help a smile. Everything was going to hell on a handcart, but at least he was along for the ride. Let our captive audience see what Sonia had figured out—that we were a team and he wanted to be here.

I unblocked the door with a thought. "Have Gerard Ead brought in please, cariñomí."

"With pleasure, my queen."

As he managed that, I turned to Duke. "Do you remember how we dealt with the queens and their Houses at Jordan Lake?"

He grinned to show sharp, black teeth, unsettling in his otherwise human face, and his eyes flashed carnelian. "I'm so glad you're finding your way to a suitable use of your power, Arden. This is much better than I'd hoped."

From Iaret's brilliant smile, I guessed he'd told her about that. Of course she was happy. The Chapel Hill Conclave had effectively bottled her in a crystal of her own soul, and she wasn't particularly bothered about who she took her frustration out on.

Still, I firmed my expression and made sure everyone could hear me. "This is not a step I take lightly, at all. And it's not going to be the default choice going forward. Appeasement didn't work, and they didn't stop at insults."

Duke sobered, studying me. "You really want things to work out with the Houses."

Hmm. Let the queens hear this as well. I raised my voice. "I want things to work out with the Houses. Between Houses. These attacks on each other have to stop. They have to. Or there won't be a faction left, just a few ultra-rich and powerful individuals for a hundred more years. But I also want things worked out between the elves and the rest of Otherside. Especially between the elves, the djinn, and the elementals."

I paused as the door opened, bringing the rumbling sound of conversation from outside.

Troy allowed Haroun and a handcuffed and lead-cuffed Gerard Ead into the room before peeking back outside.

Only speculative commentary and a lot of tension. For now. We need to make this quick, he sent as he shut the door.

Got it. I blocked the door again and turned back to meet Sonia Bedoe's frustrated gaze. "Troy?"

With a burst of Aether, he muttered the counterspell stopping the elves from speaking, adding Sonia's name.

Coolly, I said, "Sonia. As thanks for your forthright candidness, I'm granting you a boon."

She stared, smart enough to see the trap I was laying and looking sick. "But you don't even like me."

I shrugged, allowing the verbal dodge to make another point of my own. "You're right. I think you're arrogant, insultingly ignorant, and entitled as fuck. Fortunately for you, liking folks isn't a requirement for me to work with them." Smiling wryly, I gestured over my shoulder at Troy. "I didn't like him much either, to start with."

"Understatement," Troy said under his breath.

Sonia's attention darted between the two of us. When I just waited rather than calling him out for backtalk or whatever, she lifted her chin. "I want House Bedoe protected from whatever is about to go down here. My queen, my captain, me, and all our people."

"Smart choice. Granted. For what happens now as a result of what occurred this morning. No free passes for later." With a firm look and a thought, I shifted the chord of Air keeping her and her mother in their chairs and against the wall. Keeya, I left where she was for the moment, not wanting to give Haroun and Thana too much more to keep track of.

Queen Esi shuddered as the elemental magic lifted from her but held her tongue and inclined her head, despite the hardness of her eyes—a hardness that sparked into shock when I inclined mine in turn, if to a lesser degree.

I could be polite. Even if I didn't want to be.

"Right. Time for a trial." I pushed aside the guilt at the partiality of it. None of these queens would feel guilty when elementals were hunted down and killed without even the semblance of one.

At my nod, Troy spoke the counterspell to the one keeping Onora silent.

"You can't do this." Horrified rage tainted her voice, turning the musical arrogance to jangling discordance. "You have no right."

"I have every right," I said. "By conquest, if nothing else. But I'm an Arbiter. Does the Dominion demesne have an Arbiter, Onora?"

She stared at me, mouth agape.

"Apparently not. What a shame. Between the Richmond Conclave and the Farkas werewolf pack out west, you really should." I gave her a savage smile. "So I'm stepping into the role, effective immediately. First order of business: attacking other elven Houses while everyone is under truce."

With that established, I flicked a hand to Troy to signal him to shut her up again. When I turned to Gerard, he was staring around the room with wide, brown eyes, his pale skin gone paler and sweat visible on his brow.

"Please," he whispered. "Don't hurt me."

That sparked rage in me. I closed my eyes and breathed as Fire flickered, pushing it all down into a box before it could set flames flickering over me or race through the bond to Troy. Control. I had to have control. "You attempted magical trespass against the King of House Solari. You brought the consequences on yourself."

He wobbled on his feet, shaking his head.

I studied him. "Let me guess. Orders."

"Yes! Yes, my—my queen, I was ordered."

I glanced at Troy, who was squinting at the man.

"Truth," Troy said. "Entire."

Which meant not just the orders but the acceptance that I was a queen. Shit just got interesting. I'd been ready to sever Gerard as well, but this gave me pause.

Gerard blinked rapidly and swallowed hard. "You really are a Truthreader?"

Troy nodded.

"But you're a Monteague! That's an auratic skill."

"I'm a Solari," Troy said coldly. "And my father was a Veisi."

By now, Gerard looked like he was going to jitter to pieces. I'd never seen an elf so visibly anxious and wondered how he'd drawn the task of trying this. Magical ability, maybe. That had been a pretty strong whip of Aether he'd thrown at Troy. The size of the backwash matched the size of the power behind the initial casting, and Gerard had landed on his ass.

I nudged Troy in the bond. *If we can draw him into exposing the plot, would you take him in?*

Yes.

"Gerard," I said aloud. "Who was the ultimate target of your attack?"

"You were, my queen." He swallowed hard.

"And what was the intent?"

"I—I was to use a talent of mine. To influence King Troy." Gerard's eyes darted between me and Troy. His voice dropped. "To get the king to kill you so we could kill him in turn."

Hearing it confirmed hurt all over again. Nobody here would acknowledge me a queen. But they'd tried to have Troy kill me so they could claim a feral king had killed a queen, put him down, and hold it all up as an example in a tidy package of fuckery.

I took a breath as quietly as I could, trying to keep my temper under control. "What's the penalty for your actions today?"

Haroun swore as Gerard dropped to his knees and slipped from his grasp. "Please. I don't want to die," Gerard said. "They were going to exile me away from my daughter if I didn't, and then she'd always be tainted by my treason. She's only a baby. She's done nothing wrong, and her mother is blameless. Please."

I closed my eyes, heartbroken and sick. That's what'd happened to Troy. He'd been older but still a child, and the cruelty was the same.

Arden, he sent. The urgency behind it bordered on desperation.

I know. We'll take them all if they want to come.

Grimly, Troy said, "Truth. Entire. All of it. The plot, the target, the intent, and the threat."

I crouched in front of Gerard. "I will offer sanctuary to you and your family."

His gasping pleas cut off. "What?"

"You were given a choice that wasn't one. That's not fair."

"But I—I did it. I did what they—" He cut off as I raised a hand. Fearful hope shone in tear-laden eyes.

"Name the person or persons who gave the order. I'll deal with the rest."

Fear overbalanced hope then, but I didn't miss the glance behind me.

I turned to see Onora Ead glaring with a murderous rage, mouth moving without sound. That seemed guilty enough to me, but Gerard hadn't accused her.

"A name, Gerard," I said. "I have this entire room under my control."

"I want my family safe first."

I looked up at Troy. "Make the call."

He gave an order in elvish via his wrist mic.

Returning my attention to Gerard, I said, "That's the best we can do for now. If this council goes too long, someone's gonna try to find out what's going on. That will force me to hurt people who don't deserve it in order to defend myself. I need a name."

With a shudder, he closed his eyes, panting like he'd run a mile. "I can't give it."

Troy said, "Truth. Tinged though. Probably his House oath."

That presented a problem. I needed a clear culprit before carrying out justice, but Onora had made it impossible. Those oaths would hold until the queen who held them was dead.

I sighed. "Fine."

Rising, I took in the room, leaning on my years as a PI to try reading everyone again. The Eads were entirely unrepentant, furious and hateful. The queen and princess of Hilith were about as bad, although the guard captain's expression was blank. He might be smart enough to work with.

At the table, Sonia and Queen Esi sat with their jaws locked so tight I wondered if they'd be able to open them again.

I looked at Sonia. "The King of Solari made you a promise when this was arranged."

"I understand," she said in a taut whisper.

At her side, her mother nodded once.

"Very well," I said. "As Arbiter of the Carolinas and the Dominion demesnes, I render justice. King Troy of House Solari, the attack was against you." Best to keep myself out of it. Not only would they not accept it as valid, given the elemental bounties, but it was as impartial as I could make this bullshit trial. "What recompense are you asking?"

He let some of his inner monster slither into his expression even as he kept a haughty tilt of his chin. "I told Sonia I would invoke Talion Rule if an attempt was made on my queen. I do so now."

Before answering, I took in the room.

Nobody was trying to speak now. Everyone had gone pale, jaws dropped, postures stiff, eyes darting where they weren't closed as chests rose and fell too fast. Apparently, Talion Rule was as big a deal as Troy and Sonia had made me think.

"Granted," I said, just to make the point that I had the final say as High Queen and Arbiter, even if it made all of this look like a kangaroo court. The alternative would have been the same or worse in the other direction. I couldn't have it. I had to stop all this. It wasn't revenge—it was justice.

I had to believe that. Or I was just another Callista.

The pronouncement sent fear into the expressions of everyone in the room except the Bedoes, and a shameful part of me enjoyed that they were experiencing what I'd been made to feel for so long.

"Oh, what fun!" Iaret said, bursting up from her perch. "Where do we begin?"

"The Eads," I said. "Troy? Allow Onora to answer for herself, please."

He spoke the counterspell again, focusing on Onora only.

Slurs and threats spouted from her the moment she could give them voice.

I crossed my arms and waited for her to run out of breath, letting them slide past me. I'd heard them all before. They meant nothing here and now, even if the familiar old rage that she thought she could talk to me like that flickered and smoldered in my heart.

When she wound down, panting, I said, "That didn't sound like a defense or a denial of what's been suggested by your vassal."

"I don't need to defend myself against beasts! Filthy elemental whore! You should be *dead*, and damn Keithia to the ninth circle of hell for failing to do it herself."

I closed my eyes, praying for strength, then held out my hands. "Talion Rule is granted. But not death."

If the room was tense before, it was on the verge of shattering now. Troy and Duke slipped their hands into mine, and Iaret calmed down and focused. She hadn't seen this done before and no doubt wanted to learn.

Troy's power slipped into me so easily it might as well have been my own. Duke funneled his in more slowly, which was good because I hadn't blended the two halves of Aether in almost a year and a half.

As it had before, icy shadow froze my metaphysical senses as fiery sunlight heated them.

I gritted my teeth, trying to find the balance. Troy had gotten a lot stronger and overbalanced Duke. Onora's threats were distracting, so I muzzled her with Air and refocused on what I was doing.

There.

When I lifted my head, lightning crackled over me, and Sonia gasped.

"Today, Arden," Duke muttered.

Rather than bothering with grand pronouncements, I simply shaped Chaos into a knife. With three quick metaphysical cuts, Onora, Isla, and Sixtus were severed from Aether. It went much smoother than it had the first time, for which I was grateful.

Behind us, there was a thud as Gerard toppled over, freed from his House oath. A good thing, since it meant I wouldn't actually have to kill anyone, but it meant all of the Ead retainers and vassals waiting outside would do the same.

Shit. We were out of time. The rest of my agenda—Ead and Hilith working with the Bureau for Supernatural Investigation, revisiting the Atlantis Accords—would have to wait.

Troy had the same realization. *Wrap it up. Now. We can't leave our people alone.*

I retained control of the magic flowing through me as I met their horrified expressions. "There's too much death in the elven Houses to throw lives away carelessly, even when the law allows it. Be grateful I want justice, not revenge." I looked around the room. "I'm going to free the rest of you on your own recognizance. House Hilith, consider yourself warned. Talion Rule was invoked. It can still be carried out in full. Nobody speaks to the mundanes or their governments or any combination thereof about Otherside. Or I will consider you a threat to my demesnes and deal with you accordingly. Likewise for anyone crossing the state border into North Carolina unannounced."

When I released the chords of Air holding the other House royals in place, nobody moved except the three severed elves, who dropped to their knees with lost expressions.

I tried not to feel so damn satisfied.

Go, I sent to Troy, releasing him and Duke before unblocking the door again.

To the royals, I said, "Get your people under control. There will be no bloodshed between elven Houses or between the Houses and the rest of Otherside. If there is, I will hold this entire room responsible."

When we stepped out of the room, elves I recognized as belonging to Ead were on the floor. Angry, scared, dangerous expressions were on the faces turned our way from the other side of a half circle of Ebon Guard and Darkwatch elves facing the rest of the room.

I eased through to stand in front of them, unwilling to hide behind my people. "Queen Onora still lives," I said softly into the silence. "But she, the princess, and their House Guard captain have been severed from Aether."

Those kneeling next to the fallen elves sprang to their feet. Voices rose to shouts.

I compressed the air into a thunderclap, sending them all crouching with their hands over their ears, waiting for them to recover before I spoke again. "There will be no more elemental bounties. There will be no more senseless killings or exiles in the elven Houses. No more families torn apart by the whims of the queens. No more trading *people* as studs and broodmares."

Shocked silence met my proclamation. Fine. I had one last thing to say.

"Change is coming for us all. As Arbiter of the Carolinas and the Dominion demesnes, you are free to contact me for resolution and justice. But there will be no more attacks against House Solari. King Troy has invoked Talion Rule. In my role as Arbiter, I have commuted death to severing in special consideration for the plummeting elven population and the effects of the House oaths on what actions a vassal elf is or is not able to take." I softened my tone as much as I could, willing them to see we could do better. "Help me preserve our people and bring Otherside back into balance. Because with House Ead's help, the mundanes have the upper hand, not only in numbers but now in information as well. That's a danger to all of us. One I cannot and will not allow to stand."

And with that, I marched to my room as quickly as I could without looking like I was running away, before I threw up.

Chapter 20

Back in our room, I asked Duke and Iaret to be ready to ride home with us in an hour. I had to get to the bottom of Duke's avoidance and Iaret's concern. I'd drop-kicked the hornet's nest with the elves. We had to have the djinn behind us.

They grumbled about sticking around but drifted off to watch what the rest of the elves here were doing in the meantime, mollified by the permission to spy on the Houses. The Council had demanded information as part of their price. I needed to make sure we'd leave Virginia alive. Two birds with a single handful of seed. The rest of our people were focused on packing, securing vehicles, and planning an exit, because I refused to stay here and put us in any further danger away from our own territory.

When the djinn left me alone with Troy, the shakes started.

"Hey, hey, easy, Arden." Troy stepped to me quickly, clasping my shoulders and peering into my eyes. "What's wrong?"

I couldn't answer him. I was too sick at heart, too overwhelmed by the territory and responsibilities I'd just claimed, and coming down too hard on the adrenaline I'd ridden to power through what I'd just done. I couldn't help feeling like no matter how justified I thought all of it had been, no matter how careful I'd tried to make it justice and not revenge, I'd done something wrong. That I'd overstepped.

Or, worst of all, become Callista.

Absolute power corrupted absolutely, didn't it? I'd felt *satisfied* by what I'd done.

Had I finally lost myself?

Troy shifted his hands to pull me against him, squeezing me tight against his chest. Then he sidestepped, tugging me along with him to a nearby armchair, sitting in it, and pulling me into his lap. "I'm here. I've got you. You're okay. We're both safe."

Safe. Were we though? We were surrounded by hostile elves. Even with House Bedoe supposedly on our side, that left Hilith likely against and Ead fully against with all three Charleston Houses in question. Solari was outnumbered.

"Talk to me, Arden. You're scaring me."

"Sorry," I whispered. I didn't want to do that. And we didn't have time for it. Taking a deep breath, I held it for a few beats until exhaling. "I didn't want to have to do that. I just wanted us to be left alone. And now I'm—"

I cut off. I couldn't say it.

Troy understood anyway. "No, cariñamí. You're not Callista. Or Keithia. I would tell you. Believe that I would tell you. I swore I would. Remember?"

"Yes. But..."

He waited for me to find the words.

"No matter what I do, I'm somebody's monster. I'm exactly what they said elementals are. Destroyers."

He was silent for a few breaths. When he spoke next, his voice was carefully empty. "That's a feeling I understand very well."

I flinched. Of course he did. Embarrassed now on top of everything else, I tried to pull free of him.

"Stop."

The command in his tone froze me.

"Arden..." He sighed. "We're in too much of a hurry for me to say this nicely. But if you want this role, if you want to be a protector, you need to learn to be okay with not being liked. And with making hard choices."

"I *know* that."

"You *thought* you knew that. When it was just about you and me and the people at home who do like you. And when the people who didn't like you had all moved to hurt you in some way. You could hurt them back and feel justified about it." His hand moved along my spine. "You hurt people today who made no move against you when you severed Onora. When *we* severed her. And there are a lot of people who will go home tonight afraid. Some will hurt others because of it. Others will be hurt by it."

I flinched again. That was why I felt like I'd done something wrong. "I should have done better."

The first hints of frustration crept into Troy's tone. "How?"

Frustration of my own burst through, and he let me go this time when I pushed against him. "I don't know how, or I would have done it! But I have to be better than this."

"Why are you the only one who has to be better in all of this?"

"Because I'm the only one like me in the room! Yes, you're a king, and you're the only one, but everyone else there was still an elf. Duke had Iaret. It's—"

"Not just you, and don't you dare say it." The coldness in Troy's voice broke through the emotion clouding my mind. "If I thought there was a better way, I would have told you. I'm on *your* side, Arden."

I shut my mouth, clenching my jaw so hard I thought my teeth would crack. I hadn't meant to imply Troy wouldn't be there for me. He would be.

But I stood by what I'd said. My feelings were legitimate too. My truth was valid—that no matter how much he loved and supported me, I was still alone in that room as an elemental. And I'd been doing so fucking much with and for the elves, while the other elementals were still exactly where they'd been since Atlantis: isolated, hunted, and prevented from living the life I'd had the power to claim for myself.

Worse, everything I did just pushed them further from me. Until I fixed that, I'd continue being alone in every room we entered because I hadn't managed to add seats at the table for the other elementals to sit at safely, let alone build a new table.

It pissed me off.

From the tautness of the bond, Troy caught my feeling. There was a swirl of annoyance as he held back whatever else he was going to say, which only set a new dagger in my heart, slicing through my anger to add a layer of sadness. I never wanted him to feel like he couldn't speak his mind to me.

But I also wasn't in a place right now where I could guarantee I'd be receptive to whatever he was going to say. I was running on feelings too deeply rooted and too tightly strung. Even if I had enough self-awareness to understand that, I didn't have enough to know what to do about it. Or what to say to fix the wedge I'd just smashed between us.

"Let's just get packed and get home," I whispered. "We can finish this conversation later."

He didn't answer, just moved to start packing.

Shit.

Was I going to fuck everything up today?

I put the walls up in the bond, hopefully before he could catch the feeling, not wanting to guilt trip him. This was on me. I kept breaking the things I was trying to fix and hurting the people I was trying to protect.

We had everything packed and in the cars in record time. Duke and Iaret caught the mood, sitting quietly—for once—in the backseat. It sent me plummeting further downward, to have the discord so obvious.

With an effort, I shook it off as Troy got us on the road. "Duke, you've been avoiding me."

"Have I?"

I twisted in the passenger seat to glare at him. "No games. Not today. We came to you with an opening offer to have the djinn work with House Solari. You came back with a counter. Other than that, I've seen barely a hint of hide or hair unless I summon you directly. What the fuck is going on?"

He grimaced, glancing at a suddenly serious Iaret. "Ah. Hm. Since you're asking, there may have been some developments in the Old City."

"Developments," I said flatly.

His lips pressed into a thin line. "Yes."

I drew on Air to make my eyes flash gold in warning. "Enlighten me."

This time, his gaze flicked to Troy in the driver's seat, unimpressed with me as ever. "Seems like your hands are full at the moment."

I was so frustrated I could cry. I didn't want to be a bitch. It made people call me bully or worse. But if I was meek and accommodating, they walked all over me.

I couldn't win.

And suddenly I was too tired to care anymore.

I turned back around and slumped, looking out the passenger window. Virginia flew by in the dark, but I wished Troy would drive even faster. I'd worked enough magic at the council of royals to claim the land the summit facility sat on, but I ached for my own land. My space.

To be let alone for just a little while so I could be in my feelings without judgment or explanation.

From her seat behind Troy, Iaret said, "Duke, talk to her. Talk to *us*. Something's not right, and we can't fix it if you don't say something. We're meant to be advising them."

"Et tu?" Duke muttered. "Fine. The Djinn Council thinks Arden is favoring the elves too much. They want me to bring her in line. Or there will be no deal."

"That can't be everything," Iaret said. "You would simply have goaded her into doing what she's just done."

Silence stretched. Then Duke said, "She's a bloody Dreamwalker, okay?"

Iaret's gasp sent ice through me. "She can't be."

"She is, and the less I fucking know about it and about her, the better. What I don't know, I can't reveal. I'm trying to *protect* her, Ishtar save me."

Dreamwalking again. But what was so wrong about it? Duke had mentioned it before—and promptly ignored my efforts to learn more, which hadn't seemed all that unusual, given our history.

Apparently, I should have pressed harder.

I closed my eyes, already numbed by the evening's events and the discord with Troy. Tired of defending myself, my actions, and my reputation. My very being. Against the humans was bad enough. Against elves was worse, and the elementals worse still. But the djinn had raised me. With the other elementals rejecting association with me, if I didn't have the djinn, I had no people at all.

It hurt more than it had a right to after twenty-eight years of it.

Iaret sighed. "And you didn't say anything?"

"I was trying to keep you free of it. Arden is my responsibility."

"Ninlil might have asked you to look after her, but that doesn't mean you alone."

And then they were bickering. I ignored it, used to it from growing up with Duke and Grimm. The concern with me was the same I'd already had with myself: too much and not enough, all at the same time, only with some new power now, one that threatened the djinn. My earlier confidence that maybe I was just right for what I needed to be seemed painfully out of reach.

"Enough," Troy snapped.

"Are you going to pull the car over?" Duke taunted.

After the earlier unity between them showing a hint of my parents' vision finally coming to fruition through my efforts, that was too much dissonance.

I whirled to face him again. "Let's go, Duke. Right now. Take me through the Veil and let the Council tell me to my face what they think."

"Arden, no!" The car slowed as Troy refocused his attention away from the road. "Duke, if you take her—"

"There is fuck all you'll be able to do about it, little king." Duke rolled his eyes at Troy's threatening flash of his secondary teeth in the rearview mirror and settled back against the seat. "Don't get your panties in a wad. I promised her mother I'd keep her out of trouble as Ninlil lay dying. Taking Arden to the Council would be more than trouble. Ishtar save me, she'd probably pull the entire Citadel down in a fit of pique."

And just like that, hurt lanced through me again, dragging me lower. "Gee, thanks for the vote of confidence."

"Get over yourself, Arden," Duke said. "You had to do a hard thing today. Boo hoo. That is the bare minimum of what I needed to take back to the Council to prove you will give us equal consideration without my taking more drastic measures to ensure it. Ishtar blow me but this is exactly why I didn't say anything. You were always such a dramatic little wench."

Again, the car slowed as Troy looked in the rearview mirror. "You would regret trying to take her. And you *will* regret it if you continue speaking to her like that."

I didn't know how to feel about Troy's defense of me. He was clearly still upset with me, but apparently that didn't mean he would leave me hanging with the djinn. But was it *for* me or *against* the djinn? The walls were still up between us in the bond, and while normally I wouldn't have questioned, my mind and confidence were in tatters.

Duke didn't bother replying.

Nobody spoke as I counted two mile markers. Then a third.

Iaret cleared her throat. "What happens now that this summit has fallen through?"

I waited for Troy to answer. When he didn't, I said, "We see who comes around to our way of thinking and who tries to attack. Either way, I still want to work with the djinn."

There was also the sanctuary and settlement request from the Lyon elves, but if the Djinn Council was pissed about us appearing to favor the elves and afraid of Dreamwalkers, that wouldn't help. It wasn't any of their business anyway. The former was between me and Troy, and the latter wasn't on me.

I glanced at Troy, aching to touch him but afraid he'd pull away.

His hands tightened on the wheel as he felt my attention, but he kept his eyes on the road.

Fuck. I'd really hurt him.

Misery made me short. "Is that good enough, Duke?"

"For now. I'll carry the good news to the Council." He shimmered and disappeared, making Troy crack his window to clear the scent of lemon zest.

Iaret stayed where she was. "Thank you, Arden." Tentatively, she reached forward and squeezed my arm. "Keep your chin up. Like I said, things will get worse before they get better if Harqil is walking."

I slumped in my seat, completely depleted, as she too disappeared.

Harqil. The tricksters. I'd been so wrapped up in dealing with the summit—with surviving—that I hadn't given any further thought to the gem Harqil had left, still hidden away in my closet.

My brain started spinning on it, but I pushed it away. I couldn't. Not right now. If Troy wasn't in the mood to talk, I just wanted to sleep.

Maybe it would help me figure out what to say to fix things.

△▽△▽

I startled awake when the car stopped, not really having expected to fall asleep.

"Can you get the gate?" Troy asked quietly.

We were home. I got out and opened the gate, shutting it behind his car but making no move to get back in. He took the hint and kept going up the road.

I just needed a few minutes to clear my head and reconnect with my land. Or, more honestly, to find the courage to finish our conversation when we got up to the house. We'd gone to bed angry once, and the space between us on the bed had hurt me like a physical pain, even if I was the one who'd pushed him away. I didn't want to do it again.

Reluctance and misery overpowered the night's chill in getting me to the house faster though. I wasn't wrong to have the feelings I had, and I hated that speaking my truth had hurt Troy. Feeling punished by his silence wasn't fair though. He'd felt genuinely hurt in the bond before we'd closed each other out. Because, objectively, he had given a lot. Some would say too much.

I didn't know how to fix it. But my traitorous feet brought me to the front door anyway, and there was no more time for stalling.

Chapter 21

The luggage was already inside when I stepped in. Troy was standing at the back window, arms crossed, looking out over the yard. He was standing right there, but he'd never felt so far away.

As much as I wanted to hide, I stayed where I was, heart racing and mouth dry as I took him in. I loved him. I loved him so much, and as before, he'd had to get hurt for me to see it. Only this time, it was me who'd hurt him. How did I fix this?

He turned around and took two steps closer, even as his expression stayed shuttered. "We need to finish our conversation."

"I know." The words came out in a choked whisper.

"Come here," Troy said. When I hesitated, hurt flickered across his expression before he shut it down again except for the twitch of a cheek muscle. The wall came down on his side of the bond though, letting me in. "Arden, I'm not mad at you."

I could tell. He'd opened up completely. Not angry. But there was a deep well of the hurt he was keeping off his face hiding in his heart.

I wanted to be better. Maybe I had to start with him.

But I owed it to myself to stand strong for my own heart too. I had to find a compromise.

"I'm sorry," I said. Heat filled my eyes as I held back tears, but I hugged myself and stayed where I was. I had to say this. I needed him to get it. Words spilled out of me like wind forcing its way through a crack in a wall. "I didn't mean to hurt you or suggest that you haven't done enough. Goddess knows you have. But a year and a half with you is a fraction of a lifetime hiding from elves. And the first time I go to a summit, the first time I really try to work in their system, they attack. Not just words. They wanted us *dead*. I'm past scared, Troy. I'm fucking—" My voice caught. I inhaled deeply, trying to keep the tears in and open my throat. "I'm terrified. And not just for me. For you too. For us. And for the elementals, even if they won't have me. I need you to get that."

He nodded, sadness making the movement slow. "I get it."

"Do you?"

"You remember when I said I could never understand how alone you've been for you to look for comfort from me?"

That made one of the threatening tears fall. It'd been in Callista's—my—office. He'd sworn himself to me, but we hadn't yet acknowledged the feelings between us.

I nodded, my throat too thick with emotion to speak.

"I was thinking. On the drive home. That's still true. I have my struggles. They're rooted in what I was born with." He flicked a hand in the direction of his eyes and the gold flecks in them. "Just like you. But unlike you, I still had people growing up. I had a place, even if it was on sufferance. So while it hurts like hell to feel like everything I've given you, or given up for you, *still* isn't enough...it's not fair for me to want it to be magically fixed now. Both things—both feelings—can be true. And you're clearly justified in being scared. I grew up with all that, so it just felt normal. Even if I was furious they threatened you. It was *normal*. And this might have been the first time I saw exactly how fucked up it all is."

That sent the rest of the tears cascading down my face.

His expression cracked, but he just looked at me like I was breaking his heart, hands fisting and posture tightening as he resisted the wave of feeling the bond told me was pushing him to come to me.

Everything wasn't magically fixed, but enough was mended in my heart with his understanding. Even with the bond, we were two very damaged people. His people, and the system they'd built, had caused so much harm to mine that I wouldn't always be able to overlook it just because I loved him as an individual.

Things would never be perfect. But as long as we loved each other enough to try, I had to trust we'd work it out in the end.

Besides. I needed him. I needed his strength and his faith that I could find a way forward, for me and for the elves and all of Otherside. And while sometimes I wished I could be *let* alone, that didn't mean I wanted to *be* alone.

But I might be if I pushed him away.

I broke, dropped my walls, and threw myself into his arms.

He caught me with a grunt as I hit his chest hard enough to send him a step backward, into the wall. A shuddering breath escaped him, and relief washed through the bond. "I'm sorry."

"Me too. I'm trying, Troy."

"I know. I am too. And there's a lot at stake." He cupped my jaw and made me look up at him. "But I will fight for you—fight *with* you—as long as I'm alive to do so. Okay?"

"Okay. And same." I leaned against his hands until he let me go up on my toes and kiss him.

My lips meeting his was the balm I needed to soothe the pain of the last day. He might not understand how I'd come to choose him for comfort, but I couldn't imagine finding it anywhere else. I pressed my body against the full length of his, wanting more.

His hands skimmed down my sides before landing on my hips and gently easing me away. "I want this, Arden. But we need to get ahead of the fallout of today."

And now that I was paying attention to his body, under the lust was bone-dead tiredness. With an effort, I stopped myself from trying to rile him with a nip to the earlobe or throat. I couldn't set boundaries and then not respect his.

"Okay," I said. "If you wanna sit a spell, I'll take care of dinner."

He kissed my forehead. "Thank you. Shower first." He hesitated, the gold flecks in his eyes seeming to spark. "Then I need to contact Samarre and tell her we can move forward with the extraction."

That meant more elves. Fast. Everything was moving too fast. But it was what had to happen. And what I'd already agreed to.

"Sounds good," I said, unable to help the faint rasp in my voice.

A strange expression, half amusement, half disbelief, flashed across his face. "Does it?"

I tried to make the most of it. "It does if it means the Ebon Guard and the Darkwatch can stop pulling double shifts." I rested a hand on his heart. "And if you have at least a shot at finding the truth. Keithia was hiding something."

His expression firmed, and he nodded before kissing me again and slipping into the bathroom.

While I got some burgers, fries, and salad going, I let my mind wander over the question of Harqil's damn gem. Something was bugging me.

Magic.

Iaret said the gem ate her magic. I'd sensed it, distantly, when she tried a spell to ascertain what it was and what it did.

But I hadn't felt anything like what I had when holding the soul gem Darius had carried. That gem stripped elemental magic, making me feel dead and empty. But Harqil's gem had been just another shiny bauble.

Otherside abhorred a vacuum. So, what if the first soul gem was just half of a pair? It had only eaten elemental magic. What if this new gem ate everything *but* elemental magic? And if that was the case, what the hell did it mean as a clue about what the tricksters wanted?

I needed to ask Troy to hold it. Then someone from every other faction.

The bathroom door creaked, and steam rolled out. Troy stood in the doorway, toweling his hair. "What has you thinking so hard now?"

With an effort, I brought my eyes up to his face as he finished drying his hair. From his smirk, he knew exactly what I'd been looking at, but he let it go as he made a tease out of wrapping the towel around his hips, tight enough for it to bulge in the front.

Flushing, I cleared my throat and turned back to the oven, hoping I could pretend the heat from getting the fries out was what made me hot. "Um. The gem. Harqil's gift."

"And?"

"Iaret said it ate her magic, as soon as she touched it." I got the fries on plates and dumped the baking tray in the sink then dropped buttered burger buns in a hot pan to caramelize. "It didn't eat mine though, even though I was holding it."

"What? How do you know?"

"The soul gem Darius had. That definitely ate my magic. I felt it the minute it was in my hands. The one Harqil gave me didn't do anything." I reached for the chord of Air walling off all the things I didn't want to leave laying around the house and undid it. "Go look. It's in the closet with everything else."

Troy must've gone straight for the gem because the bond disappeared for a heartbeat and a vicious elven curse filtered out of the bedroom. Then he was back in my head. By the time he came back into the kitchen, wearing grey sweatpants, a fitted black T-shirt, and a scowl, I had the food plated and on the table.

He joined me. "It ate my magic."

I wrenched my mind away from the sight of him in grey sweatpants and back to the topic at hand. "Immediately?"

"As soon as I laid a finger on it. It was more disturbing than being cuffed with lead and silver. Like I didn't even have the potential for Aether anymore." He bit into his burger, brows lifting as he made an appreciative noise. "This is good. Thank you."

"Don't look so surprised," I teased.

He just arched an eyebrow at me. There was a reason he did most of the cooking. And the grocery shopping, for that matter. Comforted by the return of our usual dynamic, I hooked my foot around his leg under the table and dug into my own meal. We'd be okay.

Callista had never brooked any argument. It was her way or, worse than nothing, pain. The djinn would either shout at or slap me, or disappear. I hadn't really realized how much of my fear and anxiety on the drive home was from those patterns: harm or abandonment.

"Love you," I said around a mouthful of salad.

"Love you too." He relaxed, settling more into his chair as his shoulders came down a notch.

Right. Keithia had been at least as bad with him.

Which meant that beyond Troy's healing process and righting the wrongs committed to both him and his father, we needed to figure out what the hell she'd been trying to hide from him with Cyrus's exile.

I gathered our empty plates when we'd finished and took them to the sink to wash up. "How quickly can we finalize negotiations with Samarre?"

The change in subjects didn't throw him. "Maybe a day. Maybe two."

"You need me for it?"

"Not if you authorize me to do whatever I think best in your name as High Queen."

"Done. Do it. If we couldn't fight wars with Santiago and Matthias while fending off the mundanes, it'll be worse with the elves and whatever the tricksters are up to."

Another knot of tension slipped out of the bond. "Thank you. What are you planning?"

"I need to do some more research on the tricksters and test a theory about the gem."

His expression tightened as alarm flared in the bond, but all he said was, "Be careful."

△▽△▽

The next two days passed in a blur. While Troy bargained hard with Samarre and then scrambled to get everything needed arranged in time to take advantage of the next three-day window for extracting his father, I did my research.

I had Iaret test the gem again, just to be double sure. She still couldn't read it. Djinn were known for their ability to craft and modify magical objects—they had to be good, given it was the only way they could impact others with their magic and they'd had millennia to learn—but she was unable to even figure out what it did beyond negate magic.

Elves weren't quite as proficient with objects, but aside from Troy, I had Allegra and Iago try anyway. Iago in particular I was hoping would figure something out, given his skill with auratic magic. No joy. It ate up their Aether as easily as it had the djinn half and pissed off Allegra something awful. Even-tempered Iago got grouchy as hell.

Janae didn't let me in her house with it. She was that unsettled by its existence and the way she felt it warping her witch sense of life magic from the front yard.

Vikki nearly threw it when it blocked her from her wolf.

Zanna was so furious with the "trick" she thought I was playing that she turned every drink in the bar to piss when I took it back.

One of Maria's ranking vampires, Oscar, had been stripped of glamour and seriously weakened. If he hadn't recovered as soon as I took the gem back, Maria probably would have tried her best to beat my ass. Noah definitely would have tried when Doc Mike yelped at the sensation of his necromantic senses being stripped away, but Doc told him to act his age and sit down—after hurriedly handing the gem back. He'd taken the revelation of his magic a little hard, but apparently he'd rather have it than not now.

When I ran out of factions to test on, I tucked it back into the lead-lined neutrality box hidden in my closet behind a wall of Air, alongside my other dangerous treasures. Interestingly—to me, anyway—it did negate the blood magic in the ring Janae had gifted me, to see the unseen, but it didn't eat the crackling lightning on Mixcoatl's arrow when I touched the two together on a whim.

The only commonality between the god's arrow and my magic was that both were elemental.

There was another odd thing: the gem never quite stayed the same color, size, or shape. It morphed smoothly from one form to another, depending on who'd touched it last, but never when I held it. The only thing consistent about it was that it ate magic.

Everyone's except mine.

Before now, I'd always assumed elemental magic was just what happened when the two halves of Aether, elf and djinn, were mixed, with Chaos as a side effect of blended or mishandled magic.

Now? I had to question everything I thought I knew about myself, my magic, and its source at the worst possible time.

I wasn't sure if it was better or worse that my dreams had fallen silent.

Chapter 22

S ilent dreams or not, I kept up my research into the tricksters in between catching up on the reports of Matthias's infiltration of Jacksonville, Florida, and waiting for Acting Director Sinclaire to call again with more bullshit. I heard nothing from the Charleston Conclave, which did nothing for my nerves. Sonia sent a gift basket though. Flowers and charcuterie, which Troy checked ten different ways both magical and mundane but couldn't find a trap in.

"Tribute," was all he said when I asked what it was for.

I still didn't want anything to do with any of it though. Not the Sight or any real reason. I just didn't like the reminder of the summit or the feeling like I was getting gifts for being someone entirely too close to Callista.

Then I didn't have time to worry about it because Samarre got lucky on the first day of the window to extract Cyrus and a whirlwind of plans were set in motion. Troy stayed camped at Ebon Guard HQ, supervising all of it personally. I just stayed out of the way until it was time to go to one of the private fixed-base operators at RDU for pickup.

Then I definitely stayed quiet and out of the way because I'd never seen Troy so agitated yet trying so hard to hide it.

Allegra met us there, to my relief. I hadn't been sure Troy would say anything to her, but I was glad he had. We waited outside near our cars, parked close to the private hangar. I did my best to ignore the spring storm blowing through to the south of us and caught up on goings on in Raleigh while Troy stood off by himself, arms crossed, glaring at the horizon.

Finally, a man in coveralls jogged over to Troy. "They'll touch down in five minutes, sir."

Troy thanked him and moved a little closer to the tarmac. A few minutes later, a small jet descended toward us then landed with almost no bumps. I'd never flown before, let alone been so close to a plane, and the shifting air patterns caught my entire attention.

So that was what my power signature felt like. I smirked. The vibrating roar couldn't be comfortable to most people, but to me, it just felt like an old friend. I dropped my shields to get a better sense of the comparison, shivering with pleasure at the way the evening wind moved over the aerodynamic shape. It was like riding in the car with Troy but better.

"Show off," Allegra muttered.

I just grinned at her. "Don't hate. Appreciate."

"Oh believe me, I do. I appreciate that you're on our fucking side, sister."

The warm-and-fuzzies it gave me to be acknowledged as family—especially when I hadn't married Troy yet—distracted me from the air currents. I flushed with embarrassment both for how much it meant to me after last week's summit clusterfuck and because I'd allowed myself to be so completely distracted by the wind and air that Troy had slammed the walls all the way up in the bond. I refocused and poked him with Chaos so he'd let them down a crack.

The plane taxied down the runway slowly enough that I was tempted to give it a push with Air, if only to break the awful tension pulling Troy tight. The bond said he was in the kind of headspace where he ached for touch but would refuse it or would accept it with a stiff politeness that was almost worse if I tried to offer it.

On his other side, Allegra kept an eye on him as well.

"I can feel you both watching me." His voice was the flat, emotionless tone that sent my worry up another notch. "I'm fine."

I glanced at Allegra behind his back. Both our expressions confirmed to the other that no, he really wasn't, but we were gonna let him pretend he was for all our sakes.

Troy might not want physical reassurance just now, but Allegra, in true elven fashion, was practically quivering with the suppressed urge to offer it. I crossed behind Troy and extended an arm. She huffed in relief as she slid hers over my shoulder.

Thank you, Troy sent, just as Allegra's squeeze said the same.

I didn't love being touched by anyone except Troy, but they'd both needed something the other wouldn't give or accept for a while yet. I was trying this idea of family out. Trying to be better at it. Trying to figure out what it meant to be part of one, rather than an unwanted or feared ward or a bullying Arbiter or a terrifying queen. Troy was trying to do the same thing from another direction—trying to understand what it meant to be part of a family he chose and liked, rather than one that kept him shackled to an uncertain future and a duty he hadn't entirely wanted.

The arrival of his father was throwing all that off.

An awkward thought surfaced, and I blurted it out before I could stop myself. "What do we say about Evangeline?"

"Nothing," Troy said curtly. "He was gone before she was sired."

I blinked, momentarily confused. It made sense now that I actually thought about it, given the timelines, although Maria must've been off when she'd mentioned Cyrus's exile to me. Troy was thirteen years older than his now-dead sister, and his father had been exiled when he was ten, according to Omar. From other bits and pieces I'd gleaned, his mother had been killed in the same attack that'd left the long scar over his heart when he was sixteen—a wound a thirteen-year-old Allegra, as his knight, had stopped from being a killing blow. She and Darius had lost their own mother that night as well. I thought. Neither Troy nor Allegra talked about it, there was no way I was asking Omar, and Darius was still in exile.

"Siblings with the same mother are considered full, regardless of father," Allegra whispered, having spotted the point of my confusion. "Just like he and I are considered full siblings because our mothers were sisters, even if the humans would call us first cousins. Only the matrilineal line really matters."

I flushed, embarrassed not to have known what was probably a very basic bit of elven culture. "Oh. Got it. Thanks."

She just squeezed me again, making me wonder yet again if this was what it would have been like to have a sister of my own. A real one, not Grimm playing at it until I annoyed her.

Troy ignored us both as the plane rocked to a stop a short distance away.

I'd thought the tension was bad before, but as blocks were placed in front of the wheels, the engine wound down, a staircase rolled out, and the boarding door opened, it stretched even tighter. Allegra must have felt it too because her embrace tightened before loosening again.

A handful of elves, led by Samarre, descended first.

Allegra and I separated, drawing ourselves up into more formal stances as they approached and bowed their heads in lieu of kneeling. We were in public and couldn't draw attention to ourselves. People had started thinking any oddity was Otherside-related.

"My queen. My king. Princess," Samarre greeted us in turn in a low voice. "We thank you for this sanctuary, renounce all previous claims, titles, and obligations to our former Houses, and pledge ourselves to you and yours."

As had happened with Troy then Allegra and Iago when they'd sworn oaths, Aether tingled over me. I couldn't reciprocate

Aetherically, but we'd done this enough times now that I could link with Troy using Chaos and he could approximate my half of the binding ceremony.

"I accept your renunciations and your pledges," I said. Maybe a little quickly, so we could get this bit over with and get out of public. "Be welcome to my House and service."

Samarre and her people nodded their thanks with tenuous smiles, and I waved them toward the cars we'd brought to take them to their new home at the old Sequoyah mansion. "As for the other part of our deal..." She turned and whistled over her shoulder before nodding again. "By your leave, my queen, I'll give you privacy."

"Thank you," I said, inclining my head slightly.

That seemed to satisfy Samarre because she hefted her bag and trotted after the rest of her people.

I didn't even have time to think about having nine new elves in the Triangle because the next people to come off the plane were a dark-haired elfess and two elves, all clearly Darkwatch from the standard-issue black clothes and hard eyes...and a tall, mostly grey-haired elf with Troy's nose and facial structure, straight-backed and wary-eyed, who used a cane as he descended the steps. Handsome, in a silver fox kind of way that made it easy to see where Troy might go in a hundred years or more.

That had to be Cyrus Veisi.

Troy had seemed quietly anxious before. Now he stood with the perfect stillness he usually had when he was waiting in ambush on a hunt. Like everything in this moment came down to not being seen or heard or perceived in any way until he'd taken his father's measure.

The guards surrounding Cyrus—because they were clearly guards—acted like he was dangerous. Or maybe in danger? He wasn't cuffed or otherwise visibly restrained, and I didn't want to make assumptions, so I tried to watch the man even as Troy fisted his hands behind his back at a glance from Cyrus in our direction.

"Go on," I whispered to him.

With a quick look at me, Troy went, slow and nearly as stiff as his father, all his usual fluid grace gone. The elfess in the lead drew up and held up a hand to slow Troy's approach. I couldn't see what look he gave her, but she wilted.

Cyrus laughed, a rich, mischievous chuckle that I would not have imagined a man his age making. Maybe he was younger than he looked. He'd been tortured nearly to death and probably hadn't had the benefits Troy had had in being healed afterward. That'd age anybody.

Troy stopped short at that laugh, the bond wrenching with a nostalgia so deep it hurt.

The elfess stepped aside, and the sound cut off so abruptly I took a half step forward before Allegra grabbed my arm.

When I looked at her, she shook her head. "Trust me. Stay out of this until he calls you."

The bond said she was right. Troy's mood was in a hundred different places. I just couldn't help wanting to be there for him.

But sometimes that meant staying out of the way.

Father and son looked at each other for far too many heartbeats before Cyrus said, "Troy? My son?"

Troy nodded once, a sharp up and down that was probably as much emotion as he was going to allow himself to show.

"You're alive?"

"Alive." Troy's voice was thick. "And king."

The guards looked on grimly. I caught the eye of the elfess who seemed to lead the triad and summoned her over with a wave.

She came, but with lots of backward glances.

"We've got this," I said quietly. "Are you staying in the Triangle or returning to Lyon?"

"Staying, my queen." Like Samarre, Jacinthe, and Luc, her accent was heavily French. "By your leave. But if it please you to take a word of advice, be careful with that prisoner."

"Why?" I asked.

She shook her head. "I don't know. He was kept solitary but never left unguarded. Part of the difficulty in our arrival was getting a triad on his guard that wanted to come here and settle. To be honest, the Lyon Conclave will probably be glad to discover they're rid of him without having to make any concessions. They might make a noise over it, but it will be all show."

This was news to me. News I wasn't sure I liked, given the sensitivity of the situation not only with Cyrus being Troy's father but also being a political prisoner and exile we'd taken back without following the proper protocols.

"I see," I said. The Sight pushed me into an impulsive ask. "Would you indulge me in a request?"

"Of course, my queen."

"We've secured temporary lodging for him at the Durham Hotel downtown. If you would occupy yourself nearby, I would take it as a personal favor."

She nodded then glanced at Troy.

"I'll also intervene with the king, should it come to it." I would probably regret it, but the Sight was never wrong. I didn't always understand it, but it'd only grown stronger in the last couple of years—especially now that I had a ring enchanted with blood magic to help me see the unseen.

The elfess relaxed a little. "Thank you, my queen."

"What's your name?"

"Brielle, my queen. House Lavigne. Or formerly of Lavigne, I suppose."

I offered her a lopsided smile. "Ma'am is fine. I'm not huge on ceremony, Brielle."

"Yes, ma'am. Thank you."

"Great. Welcome to the Triangle. Oh, and y'all will be compensated for your time and effort, of course, and we'll cover your lodgings and expenses. If you stay with the Darkwatch, Omar Monteague will handle it. If you apply and are selected for the Ebon Guard, it'll be Etain Bossence. Regardless, you can stay as long as you don't make trouble."

Suspicion lit Brielle's eyes. "Compensated?"

Allegra snorted. "We do things differently here. The Darkwatch is a job you can take or leave. Not indentured servitude."

Brielle blinked. "Leave? The Darkwatch?"

I nodded. "I'll put you in touch with Thana. She can explain better."

"Of course." The elfess bowed her head again, still looking confused. "By your leave."

When I nodded again, she made a hand signal to the two elves still standing guard. They stared at her then glanced at Cyrus again until Brielle repeated the gesture more forcefully and snapped something in French.

As they hustled to the last car that wasn't Troy's, Allegra leaned close. "Do I want to know why you asked foreign Darkwatch elves to watch Uncle Cyrus?"

"Gut feeling."

"The Sight?"

"Yeah. Trust me, I don't like it either."

She frowned. "This is going to get messy, isn't it."

"Seems so."

Before she could say more, Troy half turned and gestured me over, curling a protective arm over my shoulders when I drew near.

"Hi," I said to Cyrus, resisting the urge to extend my hand. Queens didn't shake hands. "I'm Arden."

"My queen," Troy added. "And my affianced."

Cyrus looked at me, shock painting his features, before giving Troy a stern look. "Queen? You have the oyëoro and survived Keithia only to give yourself to another queen?"

I snorted, unable to help myself. "High Queen, actually."

Troy's lip curled in a grim smile. "And she's the one who saved me."

"Saved you?" Cyrus frowned, then paled. "What did Keithia do to you?"

"Beat me half to death a time or two. Tried to kill me. More than once. The last time, much like she did with you. Arden caught her in the act and killed her for it."

Cyrus looked fit to pass out. Then the wind shifted. His nostrils flared, and blood drained from his face. "The elemental."

Troy and I both stiffened and eased away from each other, taking ready stances as our shields dropped and our power signatures flared. This was exactly why we'd agreed to covering the expense of a private jet rather than having them come into the commercial part of RDU.

I tried to keep my voice even as my heart thudded. It'd been a long time since I'd been this afraid of someone knowing what I was. "I stayed hidden for twenty-five years, partly because nobody knew what an elemental smelled like. How come you do?"

Cyrus was staring like he'd seen a ghost. "Because I knew your parents." He paused, glancing at Troy before looking at me again. "And I was present for your birth. But you're supposed to be dead."

It was my turn to stand in cold shock.

"What?" Troy and I said together.

"Maybe we should go somewhere and sit down," Allegra said carefully. "Uncle Cyrus has had a long journey home."

"The bar," I said.

Cyrus stood very still. "Callista's place?"

"Mine now." I smiled, letting him see the teeth in it, because I didn't quite trust whatever the fuck was going on here. "I gave Callista back to Artemis. And then I killed her and stopped the Wild Hunt."

I'm not sure how I expected Cyrus to react, but he just smiled, almost small enough to miss. If I hadn't had years of experience with Troy, I would have missed it.

"I remand myself to your custody then. My queen."

Troy's eyes narrowed at the way the honorific was tacked on to the end of the statement, but I just turned to the side and swept a hand toward the car. Something very strange was going on here, and I didn't want to overreact until I knew what the hell it had to do with my parents.

Chapter 23

We went in the bar's back door. I led them all straight into my office, taking my chair behind the desk and waving Cyrus to one of the ones in front of it.

He watched Troy take a defensive position near me as he eased down with a wince, stretched his right leg out, and shrugged out of his jacket. "Some days, it's hard to decide what to damn Keithia's name for the most, but just now this knee is it."

Troy frowned. "Should we have a healer look at it?"

Cyrus waved him off. "No use. It was too badly broken and healed by mundane means. Magic can't fix everything. Nor should it."

That was an interesting sentiment for an elf to express, but I held back comment. Instead, I used my desk phone to dial the bar and ask Zanna to send back refreshments for four.

Father and son were looking at each other again when I hung up, not saying a word, as Allegra watched from the door. She'd taken up the bodyguard's position behind Cyrus and next to the only exit and nodded when I met her eyes. Whether princess of House Solari or Maria's girlfriend, she was still Troy's knight, first and foremost. Cyrus might be her uncle, but just like she'd threatened to kill me once if I got Troy hurt, she'd take Cyrus out in a heartbeat if he threatened Troy.

Reassured, I swept a look over our guest again, my gaze landing on one of the Darkwatch's standard-issue lead-and-silver cuffs. "Do you want the cuff off?"

Cyrus's grey gaze brightened. On anyone else, I'd call it amusement. "That confident of me, are you? Even with all the security they had on me on the plane?"

I gave him a flat look that said I didn't buy the charm. "You haven't done anything threatening. Yet."

"Without the 'yet,' I'd call you a fool, but maybe you're Ninlil's daughter after all. She was always good at looking harmless while she lured her prey."

Troy hissed at the hint of an insult.

"Sorry." Cyrus raised a hand. "Again, it's been years since I had to hold a civil conversation. I've had a lot of time to stew in resentment for queens." His eyes sparkled as he looked at me. "And yet, the point stands."

I sent a wave of pressure down the bond to Troy, a not-so-subtle push to calm down, before leaning back in my chair and intentionally making myself less threatening. "Is there a reason you're antagonizing us?"

"Maybe I don't quite believe my good fortune in being returned to my son and freedom. If indeed it is freedom?"

"It's what you make of it," I said. I was not about to commit to anything, Troy's father or not. Everything about him unsettled me, even as he was the epitome of charm, and I couldn't put my fucking finger on what it was. "The cuff?"

He extended his right hand over the desk toward me, his eyes on Troy. "I won't hurt your queen, Troy. Or you. Trust me that much."

The bond raged with conflicting feelings, enough that I pulled the walls up to leave a bare crack.

Troy leaned on my desk. "Would you swear an oath?"

"Already have."

Before I could ask what the hell that meant, a knock on the door interrupted us. Allegra opened it and peered out before letting Zanna in bearing a platter with glasses of iced tea and lemonade. When she put it down, Sarah handed her a second platter of sliced meats and cheeses.

Cyrus's brows lifted slightly at the sight of the kobold, but he inclined his head to her respectfully and held his tongue as she deposited the second platter on my desk, gave me the look that said we'd be talking about this later, and left.

When the door closed behind her, I glanced at Troy. "Objections?"

"No," he said gruffly.

Gingerly, I took Cyrus's hand and looked closer at the cuff. It'd been on so tight for so long the skin around it had shiny scarring from the chafing, and I couldn't help a wince at the memory of the cuff I'd taken from Troy's wrist.

"I'll need to heat it to loosen it enough to get it off," I said. "It'll hurt."

"Can't hurt more than not touching Aether for twenty years."

"I believe that." Being without the elements for a few hours hurt, on the few occasions I'd been strapped with bronze. I couldn't imagine years.

Drawing on Air and Fire, I replicated what I'd done to free Troy after getting him back from Keithia, guiding molecule-thin tendrils through the gaps in the woven metal and heating them slowly. This time my sense of Earth was good enough that I could tell when it was just hot enough to flex, rather than searing him anew.

When I pulled the ends of the cuff apart, Cyrus hissed as they tugged on skin partly healed around it. Elves healed fast. I had a feeling this was another petty part of his punishment, along with the constant low-level lead poisoning the cuff would give him.

"Sorry," I muttered, keeping my focus on my chords.

"Are you sure you're a high queen? They don't apologize," he quipped in a tight voice.

"They do when they know what it is to be hurt by one." I added more Fire, trying to get more flex without affecting his nervous system. Val had talked me through using Fire on the body, but I didn't dare try anything with it now.

With a last tug, I had the cuff off.

Cyrus shuddered as the scent of burnt marshmallow flared and died. "Goddess. Thank you."

Troy was ready with the first aid kit I kept in my desk. I'd been too focused on my work to notice what he was doing but was glad he was ready for the handoff. We sat in silence as Troy cleaned and bandaged the abraded skin.

When he was done, Cyrus looked at me, eyes narrowed, then at Troy. "You made my choice. Didn't you, boy."

I frowned at his use of the word "choice" when everyone else had called it a mistake, and at the word "boy" to a king.

But Troy lifted his chin. "I'm bonded to her. Twice."

"Twice?"

"A tracking tag warped. I didn't know she was an elemental. Or that Chaos would twist it."

Cyrus's expression darkened. "Magical trespass?"

I cleared my throat. "Unintentional, debt-paid thrice over, and forgiven."

Magical trespass was a killing offense in Otherside, and Cyrus was too hard for me to read for me to let it go quietly. Then there was the Sight, telling me something wasn't quite on the level here, even if he did claim to have sworn an oath. I wanted to tell Troy to hold something back, but I didn't know how he'd take it. He seemed to be at war with himself, and the situation was difficult enough as it was.

Again, Cyrus gave me the narrow-eyed look and a tentative sniff. Then he leaned back in his chair and crossed his arms as though a piece had fallen into place. "You've bonded to him as well."

I nodded. "Seems that way."

I found myself wanting to say more, to spill the story, and resisted it, frowning again despite my effort to mimic Troy's neutral expression. Troy's personal Aetheric talents were shieldbreaking, which he got from Keithia via his mother, but also an ability to read the truth in auras, which made me think House Veisi leaned toward auratic Aether rather than House Monteague's mental talents. I would have thought that was a no-no, given how strict Keithia's breeding program had been, but Troy's linking with my auratic points to bring me back from the Crossroads backed that up as well. He also had a minor passive ability to make people feel at ease in his presence, but what I was getting from Cyrus was stronger. *Much* stronger.

That made the elder elf dangerous, even if just now Cyrus was looking at Troy and me like we were wonders. Or maybe wondrous fools.

Before I could get more agitated, Cyrus said, "Well, at least you understand now why the queens never wanted us to bond to them or anyone else under their control. They tell everyone it only goes one way, but there are two steps to the process and they refuse to be restricted by anything. Especially a mate." An unsettling smile curled the corners of his lips. "But that's not what you want to talk about, is it?"

I shook my head slowly, still trying to read him while resisting whatever the fuck passive power he had going on and ignoring Allegra's look of shock.

"Quinlan came to me," Cyrus said. "About your mother."

Chills ran over me. "My father. Came to you. About my djinni mother."

He nodded. "Ninlil sent him. He and I were old friends from the same Darkwatch cohort, but Keithia would see her dead before allowing her to step foot on Monteague land. He told me

Ninlil had had a vision, something to do with the Sight. I'd have to make a choice to show my son the way forward seven years hence, and the Wild Hunt would be only the first trial of my choice twenty years later."

As I sat there boggling at the fact that my mother had been gifted enough to be that specific, Cyrus glanced at Troy then back at me as the silence in the room grew thick enough to cut.

"Troy was three, going on four. The oyëoro hadn't come in yet. It seemed a long time away, and I thought I'd be sent to stud elsewhere before it happened, even if I wanted to stay with Sareena. Easy enough to humor Quinlan." Cyrus's gaze searched his son's face as Troy gave him nothing. "Apparently, I did well with my first because Keithia kept me in hopes I'd sire a girl on Sareena."

My stomach turned. All of the high elven Houses—the three that created a conclave at any given time in any given demesne—carried out breeding programs. I found it ten different kinds of sick and twisted, but the elves seemed to accept it as just another thing the queens did to secure the species and the faction.

Most of them did anyway. Troy had rejected the very idea to the point of remaining celibate until he'd met me. His training had ensured he was no virgin, but he'd been very careful about how he might be used and abused afterward.

"In any case," Cyrus continued, "Quinlan and Ninlil were dead within less than a year." He grimaced and bowed his head when I stiffened at the blunt words. "Sorry. It's been years since I spoke any of this aloud, and they kept me solitary for a long time. Part of the terms of my exile, along with being cut off from Aether."

Terms that had to have been intended to continue torturing him. Solitary elves, even half-elves, didn't do well. It threw their body chemistry off, usually with painful and tragic results. Troy had spent a little time living with Allegra before moving in with me but had still had a rough time re-acclimating to being in constant company. That Cyrus was still here said he was incredibly strong, he'd had allies, or both.

Or maybe that he wasn't quite as solid as he appeared to be.

My throat thickened, and I swallowed hard, trying to stay focused. "I never knew them."

"I know. I found out what Keithia was planning too late."

At the implication that he might have done something—maybe not stopped Keithia but thrown some kind of wrench in her plans to destroy all of House Solari, culminating with my parents and nearly me—I nearly lost my composure. It took everything I had to close my eyes and breathe rather than standing up and pacing or grabbing Air to swirl a zephyr through the room.

"I'm sorry," Cyrus said. "Quinlan was a friend. Ninlil was a kindred spirit, of sorts."

That brought my head up and my eyes open. "What the fuck does that mean, exactly?"

Again, the barest hint of a smile that might not be one. "I wouldn't swear an oath to just any djinni, even if we did have common cause."

For all that the elves were supposed to be aligned with the hunter gods, I couldn't help but feel like Cyrus was one of the trickster gods' children. Maybe that was what'd been setting me on edge.

I stared at him, leaning into the ring Janae had given me. It warmed on my finger, which hadn't happened before. And with a nudge of the Sight, I had my answer.

Cyrus was one of the tricksters' agents. Not just aligned with them on a spiritual level. An agent, one of their hands in the mortal world.

Fuck.

All the elves swore generically to or by the Goddess. I'd never heard of one actually choosing or having a patron. I'd also assumed that, like Troy, they would all be heavily aligned with the hunters. With me being the Eternal Huntress, Troy was my Hunter, capital H. He was supposed to have ridden the Wild Hunt at my side the way he ran—or ran me down—in the woods at the new moon.

Cyrus smiled for real this time. "You have the same look she used to get when she saw something. What—"

"No," I said. "We're not playing games."

But from my phrasing, I'd given away what I'd figured out. Because in my research, I'd found that the tricksters loved games.

And Cyrus, damn him, knew it, if his widening grin said anything.

What the hell had I agreed to in securing his release? And how would it impact my already shaky relations with the djinn?

As though the question was a summoning, a burst of power pulled my attention. I looped a chord of Air around the being manifesting in the corner, only half-surprised when my magic melted away from Harqil.

The messenger took in the room, eyes widening in the first uncontrived expression I'd seen from them. "Damn you, Veisi. You were supposed to stay gone."

"Harqil." Cyrus's grin had a malicious edge to it. "It's been a while."

I didn't have time to comment on that or the answer it delivered to my question because another tug on my awareness resolved in a burst of lemon zest.

Duke.

He flickered between human and true djinni forms as his attention darted between Cyrus and Harqil. "Ishtar fuck me with a pike, when did you get back?"

The sound of metal against leather was too loud as both Troy and Allegra drew blades.

Into the sudden deathly silence, I said, "Will somebody please tell me what the *fuck* is going on right now?"

Chapter 24

Nobody answered me. Duke, Harqil, and Cyrus were far too busy keeping their attention on each other, which was frankly insulting.

I drew on elemental magic and made a ball of primordial energy big enough that it'd warp reality for a mile if it collapsed. "I have zero patience for whatever the hell this is. One of you needs to start explaining yourselves. Right fucking now."

Of course, in a room full of djinn, elves, and celestial trickster messengers, nobody answered.

"You." I pointed at Duke. "Talk. Or I use the blood tie and compel it."

He glared at me. "*I* was just bringing a warning that House Ead is self-destructing and your so-called Sinners are well aware of it. I wasn't expecting you to be in conference with *these* two."

"Frankly, Duke, I wasn't expecting to be in conference at all. How do you know them?" I asked.

With a frustrated look at Harqil, he replied, "I'll let the celestial answer that one."

Which implied that he couldn't but didn't want to admit it.

I looked at Harqil. "If you say, 'don't shoot the messenger,' I might just let this ball go."

"Then you'd lose your one assured ally for this next trial," they said. "Which was all I stepped in to say. That the tricksters are pleased with your performance thus far. Very good trick, severing the High Queen of the Richmond Conclave. And a little hint from myself, you're on the right track."

"Severing?" Cyrus paled. "That's—"

"Not a myth," Duke said with a malicious grin. "I can personally assure you of that. If you don't keep the oath you swore to Ninlil, I'll take great pleasure in assisting Arden in carrying it out on *you*."

"Hey!" Troy barked. "That's—"

"Oh, I know exactly who Cyrus Veisi is," Duke said. "The question is, do you?"

Before I could stop him, Duke twisted reality and shifted planes.

Harqil grinned. "It's been fun, but he had the right idea."

Then they were gone too, leaving me fuming, Troy on the edge of violence, and Allegra with the serious look she got when someone was about to get their ass handed to them if they didn't start acting grown.

I fixed Cyrus with an icy look. "Explain. Now."

He got the stubborn look I was well familiar with from Troy, but it was a shadow of his son's, melting away in the face of our combined glares. "Fine." He spun his chair to face Allegra. "Do you remember finding a book mixed in with your home study materials?"

She stiffened. "You?"

"What book?" Troy snapped. "Alli. What. Book?"

"A history. Incomplete. The first two-thirds of it had been torn out. But it covered the elementals. The reality, not what we were taught in homeschool. Or a fraction of it at least. Enough that I could figure out what the Ebon Guard was and who else might be one. I gave you the summary when Iago and I told you we were Ebon Guard." Her grip tightened on her blade as shock rippled through the bond to me from Troy. Allegra took a step closer without seeming to realize. "*You* left it?"

Cyrus nodded. "Keithia was already too wary of Troy. Pushing me and Sareena to deliver her another granddaughter, as though either of us had any control over it. I was running out of time to find Arden." He glanced at me. "Duke wasn't exactly forthcoming back then. Blamed us—elves in general but Monteagues in particular—for Iaret's loss."

The two younger elves looked at each other with the blank expressions that said they were both hiding feelings.

I just wanted to know what fucking book talked about elementals, why Troy's dad had it, and why he'd been trying to find me. Hearing him talk about the djinn like they were old acquaintances was making my mind spin. What the hell was all this?

"I burned it," Allegra said before I could ask. "Keithia would have beaten me as bad as she was beating Troy if she knew I had anything like it. But I read it all first. And I told Dari."

"But not me." The low growl of Troy's voice made Allegra wince.

"I couldn't, T. Keithia had everything you did—everything *we* did—watched. If it involved you, she wanted to know every detail. And for the most part, she got it."

Troy stared at his sister for so long I almost reached for him in the bond. But I was busy keeping my attention on Cyrus. Genuine pain tightened his face. Whatever this path was, he hadn't wanted it to fall on his son the way it had.

Which reminded me of my original Sight-driven question.

"Cyrus, why did Keithia—"

"Torture me before exiling me?"

I nodded. "That struck us as overdoing it, even for her. When I suggested you were a political prisoner, the Lyon elves implied I was correct."

He sighed and slumped in his chair. "Because she guessed that I was Ebon Guard. Or someone betrayed me. Twenty years in solitary and I haven't figured out which."

"What might have given her the idea?" I asked. "If I was gone, there shouldn't have been any reason."

"When Callista finally gave her the go-ahead to destroy House Solari, you were never found. Only the death certificate. It looked very real. Probably was—I imagine Callista was playing both sides and had Duke do it. But with no baby corpse... " He shrugged. "I'd sworn an oath, a very compelling one. I had to keep looking."

A handful of puzzle pieces about the past slotted into place. Callista had stopped kidnapping elementals because she had me. I knew she wanted me because of her vendetta with the goddess Artemis. But I hadn't been able to figure out why Keithia, who would have known my father, at least, hadn't recognized me as his daughter. I'd assumed it was because I took after my mother, but with Cyrus here, I had a new theory.

"What did you do to Keithia for her not to realize who I was the minute I walked into her parlor?" I asked.

With that question, a dangerous look flickered in Cyrus's eyes. "You're frighteningly perceptive. Or was that the Sight?"

I just gave him the same almost-smile he'd been giving us.

Cyrus glanced again at Troy—who'd tightened his grip on his longknife—sighed, and ate some of the half-forgotten sliced meats from Zanna's platter, closing his eyes in pleasure and sitting back with a groan. "Real meat. Most of what they fed me was protein paste. If nothing else, I'd bless you for this."

My patience was fraying with each word. But Troy didn't seem to know how he should handle the situation or what to think of his long-lost father, so I needed to keep it together. I sank into a hunter's patience and waited.

"You've noticed my passive power by now," Cyrus finally said after a few more bites. "You're shielding too hard not to."

I grimaced. "I want to tell you everything. It's almost a compulsion, but more...convivial. Like we're all old friends picking up where we left off and I can't wait to catch you up with enormous enthusiasm." I hadn't wanted to admit that, but I wanted Troy and Allegra to hear it in case they hadn't figured it out.

From the startled feeling in the bond and Allegra's look of consternation, they hadn't.

Cyrus toasted me with his glass of iced tea. "The Monteagues are known for their shieldbreaking and mindmazing. Keithia could be quite subtle with it. Sareena was better, especially with a maze. But House Veisi...we're more subtle still. Because used actively, an Aetheric suggestion layered over your aura will work its way in gradually and sink so deeply you'll think it was inspired by your own soul. Not that we told anyone about it of course. It was a House secret." He gave me a look that bordered on threatening. "I'm telling you because one, I'd like you to trust me, if only so I don't have to go back to solitary. And two, because I don't know how much Troy ended up taking after me or his mother. Crossing Aetheric foci in House lines has always been chancy, but Keithia was determined to have Monteague rule supreme. Even if that meant using unconventional or excessive methods."

When I looked at Troy to get his take, he was staring at his father with the hard expression and clenched jaw that said the man would need to offer far more of an explanation than that.

Elven family dynamics gave me a headache on the best of days. This was not one of those. I needed to wrap this up so we could send Cyrus to rest or whatever the hell he wanted to do with his freedom and I could check in with Troy and see where his head was at.

"What's your endgame, Cyrus?" I asked. "You want trust. What for?"

The flash of his fatherly smile didn't fool me. "I can't simply hope to stick around and get to know my son?" When I arched my eyebrow, he said, "Fine. I've been Ebon Guard for longer than you've been alive. Quinlan filled me in on the pieces our oral histories missed when he gave me the book from Ninlil. If the Wild Hunt was only the first trial, I would rather not die in an apocalypse, especially now that I'm free again."

Troy's voice was rougher than usual when he asked, "First trial of how many?"

"According to Quinlan, she didn't say. There was a lot she didn't say. To me or to Duke or Iaret or Grimm or even Quinlan himself."

The frustration in Cyrus's tone made me believe him. But his alignment with the tricksters meant there'd be layers, even when he was telling the truth. Looked like the ring Janae had gifted me would be getting a lot of use. Or maybe it already was, if I'd noted Cyrus's influence and neither Troy nor Allegra had.

Not a topic for right now though.

"Why not just say that?" I asked.

He gave me a tired look, finally dropping the charming mask to show the man who'd been locked up for twenty years. "I slipped once. *Once*. And I don't even know what gave me away. Keithia did everything possible to take me to the edge of death without pushing me over it while making my son watch. Your parents might have warned me, but I still find it hard to spill all my secrets to another high queen, elemental or not. I've already given everything to being an Ebon Guardsman. Forgive me for wanting something for myself. Even if it's information."

I grimaced before I could stop myself then pulled the key card and information for his hotel room from my backpack, where Troy had put them earlier. "Okay. You're free to go. We've got temporary lodgings secured for you locally, plus the necessary IDs, a funded bank account, and so on. Thanks for taking the time to speak with us after your long journey."

As I slid everything across the desk, Cyrus looked at it then at me. "Free to go, just like that?"

I nodded.

"A question to you first. My queen."

Again, the honorific as an afterthought, completely against my usual experience with elves. Then again, I suppose Cyrus had his reasons, even if the research I'd done on the way to the summit suggested the Ebon Guard had indeed looked to elemental queens. Was it really just that he was tired of giving everything up?

Rather than comment on it though, I waved a hand.

"Why?" he asked.

"Why..."

"Help me."

I leaned back in my chair and reached for Troy in the bond. *How much are you comfortable with me sharing?*

As little as possible. Something strange is going on.

"It's the right thing to do," I said.

Cyrus's lips curled in a little smile that was nothing like Troy's. "I see." He glanced at his son. "It has nothing to do with my boy?"

"Whatever has to do with me and Troy is between us."

At my side, Troy sheathed his longknife but crossed his arms. "No offense."

Cyrus nodded. "Funny thing, bonding. Well. In that case, I accept the gift of my new life with thanks. I'm sure we'll see each other around."

He rose and swept a bow that actually looked genuine rather than the mockery I'd expected.

Go with him if you want, I sent to Troy. *I'll wait with Allegra.*

"Let's go," Troy said. When the door was closing behind them, he sent, *Wait for me. Keep Alli here. We need to debrief. Start without me and fill me in later if you want.*

Got it.

I gestured for Allegra to take the chair Cyrus had vacated. "Thoughts?"

She shook her head as she sat and helped herself to what remained of the charcuterie platter. "He's not what I remember.

At all. I mean granted, I was seven years old when shit hit the fan, but Mom and Dad raised me to pay attention. Especially Dad—Mom was the second daughter. It's dangerous being the spare royal heir to the spare princess. If Troy had married and had a daughter..." She shrugged. "That might be grounds for assassination in some Houses, if she married in rather than him marrying out."

"He wouldn't."

"No, I don't think *he* would. But it wouldn't have been his say. It would have been his wife's. That's the nature of life in the Houses. Or it was anyway. I'm gonna need more detail on what the fuck happened at the summit though, while we're waiting for T to get back. He mentioned severing but refused to talk about much else."

"He's been preoccupied." I smiled at Allegra's snort—that was an understatement—then filled her in on what'd happened.

Her expression was grim when I finished. "So, almost a complete and total disaster. I can't tell if you snatched victory from the jaws of defeat or the other way around. Goddess, Arden."

I scowled. "I'm *trying* to do things fairly."

"That's your problem right there." She rolled a piece of cheese in a slice of ham and bit off half of it. "You keep thinking you can do this fairly."

"I won't be Callista. And I won't be Keithia."

"Oh, I know. You've made that clear. I'm just praying you can get away with it. There's a reason all the major territory heads are assholes."

I sighed, but before I could argue further, I sensed Troy's presence. "Incoming."

He swept in then leaned against the closed door, arms crossed and head bowed.

Allegra glanced at me, concern pinching her brow. When I didn't move, she started to go to him.

"Sit," I murmured.

She got the stubborn look that said she was thinking about ignoring me, until I tapped the side of my head to remind her of the bond. The snarl I was getting from him was the sort that usually wanted distance to figure something out, not soothing or distraction.

Troy's gaze flicked to me. "I don't know what to think. I don't know what I expected. Definitely not all of that. When you threw 'political prisoner' at Samarre, I was expecting House espionage. Maybe an assassination plot. Something normal. Not a secret member of the Ebon Guard who knew your parents, kept an oath to your mother, and got himself tortured and exiled as part of a djinn prophecy. What the fuck, Arden?"

I barely stopped myself from wincing at his assessment of espionage and assassination as normal. It'd been his full-time job once upon a time—normal was a question of experience. I also couldn't help the twisting in my gut at the way the family histories of House Monteague and House Solari were even more entangled, and more bizarre, than either of us had ever imagined.

"I don't know." I lifted my right hand and waggled the finger with the blood-magic ring. "This was barely keeping me ahead of him. I got nothing with the Sight. Too thrown by everything he said and then Duke and Harqil knowing him on top of it."

Allegra frowned. "What did Duke mean when he said we didn't know who Uncle Cyrus was?"

"I caught that too," I said. "I'm wondering if it's tied up with what Harqil said about him supposed to be staying gone. And with whatever mistake or betrayal caused Cyrus to be caught in whatever it was exactly Keithia caught him in. Ebon Guard? Conspiring with my parents? A bad deal with the tricksters? Or something we haven't thought of yet?"

Troy shook his head. "Who knows. I should know better than to hope for anything."

That comment wrenched my heart. I was the one who'd pushed him into this.

"Don't do that," he said, catching the feeling in the bond. "I wanted it. You just gave me the permission I was looking for."

"Still," I said gently. "I wanted it to...I dunno. Be like the movies. Something happy."

Bitterness twisted his lip into a sneer. "Not my lot in life."

I tried not to be hurt all over again. We were happy together. Weren't we?

But this wasn't about me. This was about Troy trying to figure out what family meant now that he had his father back, only to learn that the man was...we didn't know what he was. Just not what anyone was expecting.

Unless there was more to it?

"Allegra, can you check us for Aetheric residue?" I asked.

Her eyes flew open, like she hadn't thought of that, then narrowed as she squinted first at me then at Troy. "Nothing."

I wasn't sure if it was better or worse that Troy's current mood didn't have a magical impetus. Better, I supposed, if only because it meant Cyrus hadn't committed magical trespass.

I'd severed quite enough elves this week as it was. Adding Troy's father to the list was something I desperately wanted to avoid.

Chapter 25

When we ran out of steam speculating on what the hell had happened, we changed gears to the fallout from the press conference. The Sons of Seth were protesting in Raleigh again, apparently enraged by our having been on TV and terrorizing downtown to get some airtime of their own. Comparing them to children throwing a temper tantrum was an insult to children—and it was a dangerous thing mundanes did to excuse grown-ass adults from taking accountability for their choices. I wouldn't be doing it, and I wouldn't be excusing them.

But I couldn't settle on what to do about them.

I rapped my fingers across my desk. "Is Maria going to need to leave downtown? Does she have a backup nest?"

"She refuses to go. I've already tried." Allegra pressed her fingers to her temples and shook her head. "I think she's negotiating reciprocal safe haven with Renaud in Charlotte, but she won't leave what she worked so long to claim. And, between us, she doesn't honestly believe anywhere else will be safer. She's going to dig in and fight. Already carried out extensive works to secure and fireproof Claret and the coterie's other properties downtown. But, Arden, I don't know how much longer the coterie can hold out."

"What do you mean?" I asked.

"The Modernists are acting up again. Talking about going to war with the mundanes if they keep attacking Claret. Maria's doing what you asked of her, but her refusal to launch a blatant attack is starting whispers about her suitability."

Troy shook his head. "She needs to put them down."

"She knows that, T. Everyone knows that. If nothing else, they might need to start feeding on others of the coterie soon because it's not safe to go out. We're reaching a tipping point."

Everything was reaching a tipping point. I'd been so busy securing the borders of the demesne that I'd let this problem fester at the heart for too long.

Options. I needed options.

The Lyon elves.

"Troy, Samarre's people want to earn trust, right?" I said.

He nodded. "You want to task them with handling the Sons. Like the queens had Omar using the Darkwatch after the Reveals."

"Yep. No sensitive intel there, and they're foreign on top of being Othersiders. The Sons wouldn't collaborate with them even if the Lyonnais wanted to." As usual with those kinds of groups, their bigotry and hate didn't stop at their main target. They were perfectly happy to throw xenophobia and racism in with anti-supernatural rhetoric. Privately, I suspected me and Troy presenting as "people of color" was wrapped up in it.

Troy considered it. "That would work. Alli?"

"Yeah. Shit yeah, anything to take the pressure off." She grinned. "Hey look, I'm doing the job you sent me there to do, not just fucking the Mistress of Raleigh."

I rubbed my forehead. "You said it, not me. But yeah, let's get it done. Whatever you two think best for op parameters."

The two elves exchanged a look, and Allegra shrugged. "You're the king."

"I need Raleigh quietened down and shored up," Troy said. "The power sharing agreement in the Triangle works because the weres mind their own business while the rest of us keep our areas under control. If Duke is saying House Ead is imploding and the Supernatural Investigators are going to do something with it, I can't be worrying about a third of the power balance in the area being overrun by mundanes."

"I was hoping you'd say that." Allegra pursed her lips and tilted her head back. "Let's keep it covert for now though. Sabotage, misinformation, counterintelligence."

"I want the leaders dead," Troy said coldly. He looked at me, the gold flecks in his eyes sparking, when something in my scent or the bond told him I didn't feel good about that. "We need to show Otherside we've had enough from them and set an example in how we handle it."

"Murder is a hell of an example," I said bluntly.

"We can demonstrate quietly assassinating people we have proof directly harmed Othersiders. Or we can demonstrate blood in the streets when this inevitably boils over again, after a year of patience and waiting for the mundane courts to do something. Your choice, Arbiter."

I hated when he did that.

It wasn't unreasonable. This fell under my job description. And I had said whatever they needed. I just hated having it thrown in my face and somehow hadn't thought murder was back on the table.

Who was I kidding? My fiancé was a trained assassin with more deaths to his name than I knew about. Being a doting househusband didn't change the relative ease with which he turned to very permanent measures to deal with threats—especially threats to *my* safety.

I bit my tongue to stop from throwing the word diplomacy at him. I might not want to kill mundanes or order them killed, but there was no negotiating with people who wanted us dead. And they'd said they did. It was in their damn manifesto: that Otherside needed to be exterminated as a threat to humanity, no matter what we said about consent or laws. The feds were still holding out on speaking to me after my last refusal to limit my powers. But if we did this and they found out, I had a feeling I'd be hearing from them real damn quick, and it'd be with accusations of terrorism.

There was no winning here. One way or another, someone was going to turn up dead.

I sank deeper into my chair, crossing my arms and staring at one of my whiteboards without seeing anything on it. Resentment burrowed into my bones that we had to even discuss this.

The Reveals were supposed to have been our safety cord. Something to pull to get out ahead of a discovery. Proof that we wanted to work with humanity and didn't need to be forced out with tests like Verve's—tests I still needed to figure out how to deal with, on top of everything else.

All it had done was instigate chaos. And as the lead instigator, it was my job to fix it.

I wouldn't lay down and let Othersiders be killed. I couldn't. It went against what I'd done all this for and who I was trying to be, even as it took me further from how I'd hoped I could do it.

I'd wanted the strength to stand alone. Now I had it and had to find the strength to live with hard choices.

"Fine." I hated the word as soon as it left me. "But Troy? This *cannot* be traced back to us. All of them need to be believable. Not funny coinkydinks. Not conspiracy fodder. And only those who have made attempts on Othersiders or have solid plans to do so. This has to be arguable as self-defense, backed up by evidence, means, motive, and opportunity, if it does come out."

From his tight look, I was tying his hands a bit more than he was happy with, but I met his gaze and didn't back down. I would not start World War Three: Supernatural Edition because we were sloppy, overenthusiastic, indiscriminate, or acting out of fear or victimhood. Even this was treading into a grey area I was seriously uncomfortable with.

But Santiago's attacks on Raleigh showed me I was running out of rope with Otherside. And with the elves in freefall, the djinn making noise about getting me under control, and the tricksters circling, that rope was even shorter and fraying by the day.

Allegra fiddled with a gold cuff on one of her locs. "Question. Can we turn them? Add to our numbers while we reduce theirs?"

Troy was already shaking his head. "And have baby vampires alive to talk about what happened to them after they get caught on a blood rampage?"

"I agree with Troy. Sorry, Allegra." I grimaced. "It was bad enough when the vamp-witch went after Doc Mike. If Maria is too busy fortifying and such to keep the Modernists under control, I won't sign off on adding more vampires."

"Especially when our numbers are down as well," Troy added. "The Raleigh coterie still solidly outnumbers the local elven population now. I'll fight any addition to vampire numbers on that alone until we get enough transplants to rebuild a conclave."

Her mouth twisted. "I was thinking the shame of it could keep them in line, but I see your point."

I gave her an apologetic smile. "Thinking outside the box is good though. We just need—"

My phone buzzed with a text from an unknown number.

"What area code is 843?" I asked.

"Charleston," Troy said. "What is it?"

I read the message aloud, my brows lifting with each word until I thought they might take flight. "We request a video call this evening at nine to discuss the future of the demesne." My heart thudded as I looked at Troy and Allegra. "The fuck does that mean?"

Troy was already swiping a text on his own phone. "I don't know. But I'm tasking Etain with finding out."

My fingers rapped an uneven cadence on the desk as I thought it through. "It came through on my private number, not the Voice account. That has to be the Charleston Conclave, but they're talking about the demesne. That means they're coming to me as Arbiter, not High Queen." I frowned. "Unless we have any other populations in that part of South Carolina?"

"A couple of scattered wereclans," Allegra said. "Nobody with the resources to find your private number other than the Charleston Conclave."

A sour twist in my stomach had Troy wincing from what he caught in the bond.

"Sorry," I said.

He waved it off, still focused on his phone.

"So almost definitely the Charleston Conclave," I said. "And making a point to show me they can find my personal info. Either of you recognize the number?"

They leaned to look and compare what was there with what they had in their phone contacts. Both shook their heads.

"Probably a burner then." I sighed. "Fuck it. Let's do this." Silence met me, and I looked up from the text I was swiping out. "No?"

Troy glanced at Allegra, who shrugged, then back at me. "They invoked the demesne, not the Houses," he said. "I've got nothing. It's a slight either way, if we're looking only at the Houses. Not messaging me—because I know Ava Quet has my contact information—means they don't consider me legitimate. Messaging you as Arbiter rather than High Queen says they don't see you in that role."

Frustration boiled up in me, making my tone sharp. "Or they are following the script I set at the summit, where I arbitrated and led the severing of three royals to carry out punishment." At Troy's nearly invisible flinch, I sent a remorseful coil through the bond and quickly squeezed his arm before letting him go. "I'm sorry. I didn't mean to snap at you. I just...I'm trying, really trying, to see the bright side. For once. Because if I don't, I'm going to lose my shit."

Allegra looked between us with solemn amber eyes, scarcely seeming to breathe. She'd taken the brunt of a couple of my kneejerk rejections of good intentions from elves as she tried to bring me around, most recently with letting the Lyon elves come and observe.

"Okay." Troy inhaled deeply, held it, and let it go. Allegra relaxed as he did, apparently seeing, as I had, that my reaction on top of the stress of his father and the summit had pushed Troy too close to locking himself down.

"I'm sorry," I said again. "Really."

He reached across the desk and squeezed my hand. "Forgiven. We're both stressed. And both being pushed a little too far into our personal hells."

Allegra slumped and blew out a breath. "Thank fuck y'all are bonded because Goddess knows we don't have time for therapy." When both of us glared at her, she winced and rose. "I'm just gonna head back to Raleigh now. T, let me know what Etain and Dad say about recent developments."

I frowned. "Hang on. I thought you two were talking again?"

"We are. And we're not." She shrugged. "If it's about strictly elven duties, he's approving. If it's anything to do with Maria or the vampires, all I get is his disappointed face. You know the one."

Tory and I both grimaced. We did indeed.

"He's wise enough not to disagree with me outright, but I know he wants me to break up with Maria and secure a marriage with an elven House. Preferably the one Charleston offered. Never mind that I have no interest in what all that would entail in terms of, um, kids and that."

"Fuck," I said. "Uh, that reminds me."

From Troy's guilty expression, he'd forgotten as well.

Allegra looked between the two of us. "What."

"Sonia wants to marry Darius." The words rushed out of me as I held up a hand to forestall the words fixing to rush out of her. "Don't worry! I told her that was Darius's choice and that if she couldn't be on board with our new agenda, we'd have nothing to do with any of it."

"Good," Allegra snapped. Then she grew thoughtful. "Although a marriage alliance with House Bedoe would be incredibly useful for shoring up the northern border. And she's not bad, as princesses go."

Troy leveled her a thunderously disapproving glare as I gave her the grimace that said, *did you really want to go there?*

Raising her hands, Allegra moved toward the door. "Fine! Just keep me posted if you hear anything from Dari. He's taking this whole exile thing more seriously than I'd thought he would. I miss him."

"Will do," I said. "Give my best to Maria."

She waved and headed out, pulling the door shut with a quiet click.

I needed to be out of this room, but first things first. The lines of Troy's shoulders were high and tight, his expression was blank except for the occasional twitch of his cheek, and the bond was in turmoil.

"Hey." I stretched a hand halfway across the desk, not touching him, just being open to it. "Talk to me?"

When his gaze snapped to mine, sandstone-and-moss had shifted to shadowed labradorite. I shivered at the coldness in it, doubly so given how close we were to the new moon, and he squeezed his eyes shut for another deep breath.

"I think I need to go home," he said. "I need to be where it smells like the two of us. And where I feel more secure. There's too much shifting right now."

That went a long way to ameliorating the hurt I'd felt earlier at his statement that happiness wasn't his lot in life, especially when he engulfed my hand in his and dragged my wrist to his nose. As my scent filtered through his senses, he shuddered and calmed.

"I shouldn't need you like this. I'm a Goddess-damned king. It's been over a year, and I spent time with Alli before moving in with you. The hormonal impacts of isolation should have started reversing by now."

"The road to the nine hells is paved with shoulds," I said, as gently as I could. He kept trying to rush healing, but clearly, it was gonna go on its own time. "You've spent long enough down there. We can work together to go somewhere else in life."

He took another few breaths. "I didn't mean that I wasn't happy with you."

Of course he'd caught my reaction to that.

There was no denying how I'd reacted to it earlier, so I just said, "It's okay. I'm not going anywhere. Unless you need out, I mean."

That drew him tight so fast I froze. When the intensity in his gaze landed full on me and his grip on my wrist tightened, I forgot to breathe.

"Never," he said. "Never, Arden."

"Okay," I whispered. Relief had stolen my voice. Despite the rocky start to our acquaintance, I couldn't imagine being with anyone else. "Good. Let's go home."

Chapter 26

I texted the unknown number back in the car on the way home, confirming my availability for a 9PM call. Then since we had a few hours, and Troy could use the pressure release, I goaded him into a hunt.

Not a real one. We didn't have the time for it.

But we did have time for an explosively quick scramble through my woods.

A challenging, up-and-down look was all it took to prime him. My hot-footed run away from him at full speed was all he needed to know the game. He held himself back as long as he could. Almost made it to the front door before *fuck it* rolled through the bond and rational thought was lost to the clarity of action.

I skidded down the rocky slope toward the river then pivoted in the opposite direction of his usual running trail. Novelty combined with live prey would definitely get his mind back on track. My acceptance of him as a hunter would help too.

As always, he was completely silent.

Only the bond told me where he was, until he remembered himself enough to shut it down and leave me in the dark. I walled up my side of the bond but dropped my shields, trying to get a sense of where he was using shifting air currents.

Fuck. Too close. Nearly on top of me already.

I leaped and planted a foot on a tree trunk to change direction. Troy wasn't thrown. The scuff of a shoe on wood suggested he'd mimicked the move, although if I could hear him, it'd nearly worked.

The last vestiges of the setting sun tinted the forest gold as I hauled myself over the high curve of a fallen oak. For some reason, I looked back when I landed.

Never look back. Something—or someone—might be gaining.

Troy vaulted the deadfall, landed, and launched toward me in a single smooth motion. Grasping fingers caught my hips and threw me off balance. I staggered and went down hard, tasted rich earth and dead leaves as I hit the ground then struggled to push up and away.

He pinned me—or tried to. I wriggled halfway free before he flipped me onto my back and pinned my arms over my head with a snarl that showed the sharp teeth. Normally I wouldn't use magic for this, but I needed him to remember I loved him for his full self by pushing him into embracing his own. I reached for Air.

"No you don't," he snarled at the flash of gold in my eyes.

Before I could shape Air into a fist to knock him back, Aether flooded the bond and then every single nerve with unbearable pleasure. When a cry tried to escape me, one of the hands pinning my wrists clapped over my mouth.

When I was about to climax, he withdrew. A darkly satisfied smile played at the corners of his mouth. He had his prey right where he wanted, just how he wanted.

I wanted him so bad I could scream. He was the only one I felt safe enough to play with like this. All the fear dogging me was channeled to a safe outlet. It was safe to be afraid, to run, to fight without worrying about the repercussions.

Roman and I might have played keep away, but with Troy, it was winner takes all.

We stayed as we were, both of us breathing hard as he waited to see what I'd try next.

Then his patience snapped. He kissed me.

Kiss was too light a word, too easy, too tame. It was frustration and lust personified, transmitted in physical form. Magic sparked between us, sharp enough that we broke apart. The break lasted half a second before he was on me again, his grip shifting from my wrists to my jaw. I wrapped my arms over his back to pull him closer.

When he drew away, I gasped from the sudden absence of his mouth claiming mine.

"Do you want to stop?" I asked.

His eyes searched my face, looking for any trace of fear or doubt after literally chasing me and dragging me down in the woods. "I want you."

"Then take me. If you can." Again I wrestled to break free.

We fought for dominance, rough and snarling, rolling across the ground until I ended up on top. He was too much an elf and too well-bred for it to start otherwise. The implications of his surrender raised goosebumps along my arms as I pinned him with Air long enough to get my sneakers and jeans off. When he didn't fight me, I opened his pants, reached for his cock, and guided him into me.

Troy fit to me like it was his purpose.

My first rock against him was slow, making sure he wanted this, given the day he'd had and the shit we'd learned.

His hands clasped my hips, the pressure of his fingers urging me to go faster.

I sped up and rode him hard, and he bit his bottom lip, tilting his head back with a groan as he pumped up into me.

I met him at every thrust. My head fell back, and my body took over. Everything about him was what I'd been craving all week while he worked on negotiations, and here he was, hard and willing between my thighs.

His magic reached for me as his embrace did, and mine answered. I gasped as the two intertwined. The overlay in my third eye was a virulent purple created by the blend of cool Aether and hot Air. I leaned forward to rest my forehead against his, and he cupped the back of my head with one hand.

Troy sent the smallest curl of Aether through me, but the sensation hit me hard enough that I came, throwing my head back and grinding hard against him. He winced with the effort of holding back until I was finished.

"Is that what you needed?" His voice was thick, twisting the words into a growl.

I nodded, unable to answer, and he pushed up. We traded places, me on my back as he drove into my core. Our magic reached again, twisting, sparking, and he swore in elvish before pulling out, pushing my shirt up, and finishing on my belly.

When he was done, he propped himself over me and cupped my jaw, running a thumb over my cheekbone. "I will never figure out how you know exactly what I need."

"I don't always know. But you're a fascinating subject for investigation. I don't mind taking the time to find out."

He snorted and shook his head, then kissed me. "Once a PI, always a PI."

"You better remember it."

After another long look at me, Troy pressed up, stripped his shirt off then cleaned my belly. "Let's go get a shower and then prep for this damn call."

I eyed him as he pulled me to my feet then stooped for my jeans and pulled them back on, leaning on his shoulder as I shook dirt free of my socks before getting my shoes back on. "I dunno, if you're getting naked I might insist we make a night of it out here."

He gave me a smoldering look and tucked me under his arm, not answering except for the threads of pleasure and amusement in the bond. The awful tension driving him these last few days had been cut, and he was...if not all good, at least refocused.

We made our way back up to my house leaning on each other. I picked as many of the leaves and sticks out of my hair as I could, momentarily jealous of the looser wave to Troy's hair that let him give it a light ruffle to shake everything loose. A whiff of sulfur said the gytrash might have seen at least part of our hunt, and I flushed. They stayed out of sight though, giving us at least the illusion of privacy, for which I was grateful.

. Once inside, we had just enough time to shower and eat some leftovers before the scheduled call. There was no update from Etain other than to say Charleston had gone dark. No news in. No news out. Which left us speculating about what the hell was going on.

We decided that, since they'd only texted me, it'd be only me on the call. Troy was present of course, sitting behind my laptop on the other side of my dining table. But if they didn't ask for him, they wouldn't see him.

As we'd guessed, it was the three Charleston Houses.

But not the queens.

I frowned. "We're to discuss the future of the demesne, without your queens?"

The three women crowded into a single screen had varying reactions. Ava Quet seemed sad. Imani Tossavi was resolute. Savannah Averill, almost savagely pleased.

Imani said, "There's been a development. We're the queens now."

It took all of my willpower not to look at Troy opposite me, out of camera, especially when shock rippled through from his side.

I frowned. "Excuse me?"

Savannah shrugged. "Our mothers and grandmothers were unwilling or unable to see the needs of the future, and you were pretty damn convincing at the summit. They wanted war, but they've been driving this conclave into the ground. So we claimed our future for ourselves. They've been on their thrones longer than we've been alive. If we left them there, they'd fight you and King Troy until we all died. Not openly, given how badly you scared them at the summit. But with sabotage and misinformation."

"I see," I said, although I only partially saw it. I mean, I agreed. The older queens had all been completely against everything I was and was trying to do. Against Troy as well. I just hadn't thought their daughters would believe strongly enough in a new future, or in an elemental and a king leading it, that they'd actually do anything, despite my telling Troy I was trying to hope for the best.

This was too fucking weird.

I didn't bother hiding my skepticism, crossing my arms as I leaned back in my chair. "Where are the queens now then?"

"Dead," Imani said grimly.

Another lash of shock hit me through the bond, and I didn't bother trying to stop my blink. "You killed your mothers or grandmothers?"

Savannah sneered. "Don't sound so surprised, Arbiter. Given what we've heard about your king and Keithia, you know exactly what the older queens do with their heirs." When I kept giving her a flat look, she added, "We tried imprisoning them. It didn't work."

More victims of the elven death cult. I tried telling myself the silver lining was that Queen Merle couldn't try pushing for her son to marry Allegra and all of this saved me from eventually having to clear the queens out myself.

I'd seen them at the summit. I would have had to take action eventually.

Holding back a sigh, I focused on the action I had to take now. "What exactly are you proposing then?"

The three of them looked at each other. Expressions flickered then firmed.

Imani shifted to sit taller in her chair. "You…weren't what we were expecting for an—an *elemental*."

I barely managed to keep my expression even. Once again, being the only one in the room was coming back to slap me in the face, even if it was as a backhanded compliment this time rather than an outright microaggression. Didn't people realize saying shit like that wasn't the praise they thought it was, for either party?

She continued. "We started thinking maybe we were wrong about all the stories we'd heard, and if those were wrong, maybe the ones about males with the oyëoro were too."

"I see," I said. Definitely not the first time I'd heard this from an elf, and it was just as tiresome this time.

My lack of enthusiasm must have been clear because Imani blushed and shifted again. "It's not personal, Arbiter."

I thought I needed will before. This called for more. Because it was very fucking personal when someone had to meet me to understand they'd been lied to about a whole people or care about what happened to us.

Something about that must have shown in my expression because Troy sent a swirl of calm.

"Anyway," Savannah said. "We'll be cleaning house. Those who refuse to accept the Carolinas as a unified demesne with you as Arbiter will be exiled."

I tamped down a burst of impatient frustration as Troy sent a note of caution through the bond. It wasn't that fucking simple. Yes, the work of removing the queens was a big, difficult step. But there was more.

"And King Troy?" I said. "I would have thought you'd go through House Solari rather than me as Arbiter for this. He's closer to the impacts."

They looked at each other. If I didn't know better, they were embarrassed.

"Of course," Imani said. "We'll be in touch to complete formalities."

I tried to tell myself that they probably thought they were being polite or proper by talking to me first. Still, we weren't done. "What about those of your people who don't want to stay in the Charleston territory?"

This time, they were definitely confused.

Imani frowned, playing with a lock of her long, dark hair in a surprisingly unpolished display of nerves. "Why wouldn't they want to stay?"

"I don't know. There are any number of reasons why people would want to leave home. I'm sure King Troy would agree with me when I say any who wished to do so would be welcome to settle in the Triangle territory."

Imani's frown deepened. "That would mean freeing them from House oaths."

"Yes," I said. "It would. As well as allowing them to take their families and to choose who they started a family with."

Savannah stiffened. "That's a bit much, Arbiter."

"That's how we do things in my demesne. People have choices. I don't stand in the way of justified territory battles, coups, or traditional rites. But treating people like prize horses will end. The Raleigh coterie is under the same edict, if that makes you feel any better."

From their faces, it didn't. Much. Ava's expression smoothed a little. I had a feeling she'd be the easiest of the three to deal with and made a mental note to cultivate that relationship. I owed it to Troy—and myself, I guess—to lead the way I was demanding faction heads lead.

When they didn't answer, I tried a smile and some damn diplomacy. "Of course, I don't make empty demands like my predecessor did. Climate change is a bitch on those coastal regions. Wouldn't it be worthwhile to protect your investments in the area?"

Troy sent a pulse of approval. *Very good. Remind them of your power, as both benediction and threat.*

Apparently, the three women heard the same thing Troy had. Ava boggled, Imani grimaced, and Savannah's lips pressed together in a thin line.

"You're that strong?" Savannah asked.

"I was telling the truth at the mundane press conference. I dissipated a storm that would have dropped at least an F0, maybe an F1 tornado on parts of the area. I could handle a Category 3 hurricane or downgrade a stronger one, and hurricanes give much more time to work."

Eyes bulged, and faces paled.

"Understood, Arbiter," Savannah said. "In that case, we accept your terms and will be in touch with King Troy to further discuss anything House-related."

I smiled, trying to make it real. "Welcome home."

Troy shook his head as I ended the call and shut the laptop. "I honestly did not see that one coming. Well done, cariñamí."

A weight eased from my shoulders, and I slumped in my chair, eyes closed. A smile spread until I was trying not to laugh, I felt so good.

Something was actually going right. People were coming to my side—a whole conclave!—and I hadn't had to kill anyone or threaten them beyond what I'd already done at the summit. They'd seen my power and wanted to be on my side, rather than wanting to cut me down.

The validation was dizzying. I was *finally* getting somewhere.

Now if we could pull in Sonia Bedoe and the Richmond Conclave, we might be able to find our footing with the mundanes—and give me the breathing room I needed to secure the rest of North Carolina and then deal with whatever the hell the tricksters were after.

Chapter 27

*Y*ou're doing well. But you're not moving fast enough.

My eyes snapped open at the voice echoing in my head. Endless black surrounded me, shot with stars that were too big.

The In-Between. I wasn't awake. I was dreaming.

Words. Someone had spoken to me.

Have you figured out what our gift was yet, little trickster?

Trickster? I was the Eternal Huntress.

You are that too. But when as many threads of Fate wrap one as they do you, you can never be only this or that. Like us, you contain multitudes.

This was the third time in the last few weeks someone had mentioned Fate. Or was it the fourth? The elves might do things in threes, but four was the gods' number of completion. What did it mean?

That's for us to know and you to find out. Sharp-edged laughter echoed. *Best not take too long.*

Something was wrong.

I woke gasping, with Troy's grip on my throat tightening with each breath.

My brain scrambled to change gears from the gods to my fiancé.

I reached through the bond, trying to figure out—oh.

This wasn't intentional. It was a nightmare. He had this particular one occasionally, the result of Keithia throwing a mundane woman's head at his feet while mindmazing him to think it was me. The one time he'd explained the dream, he was trying to keep my head on my shoulders while I bled out.

The effect was the same though: I couldn't breathe.

I reached through the bond, a sting of Chaos. "Troy!"

He woke immediately. Sprang away so quickly it seemed he'd teleported out of bed even as he was still blinking awake and orienting himself. "Arden?"

I coughed and rubbed my throat. "I'm okay."

His gaze swept over me, resting on my neck. "Fuck. It happened again. I—"

"It's okay. Come here." I dropped my hand and repeated it when he hesitated, looking guilty. "Come on. I'm not counting you responsible for a dream about what *she* did."

Regardless of my opinion, he clearly held himself accountable.

I grabbed his arm when he was close enough and pulled until he toppled onto me, reluctantly at first, then with a tight grip as I wrapped my arms around him and started rubbing his back.

"I'm okay. You're okay," I said.

Before he could answer, my phone rang. I ignored it.

"Answer it," Troy said gruffly. "I'm—I'll be fine."

I considered letting it go to voicemail, but there was too much going on right now that could take everything straight to hell. With a curse, I snagged it from the nightstand. "I don't recognize the number."

Wariness slithered through the bond as Troy rolled away and dug in the nightstand on his side of the bed for one of the Darkwatch devices that made it hard to trace my location from my phone. I swear he had the damn things in every room of the house.

"Make it quick," he said.

I swiped to accept the call. "Finch."

"Ms. Finch. Acting Director Sinclaire here. I hope this is a good time for us to circle back on our last conversation."

With an annoyed glance at the angle of the morning light slanting through the blinds, I shifted to sit up and prop myself against the headboard. "Y'all get your days started early at the Bureau. And on a Sunday?"

"Some days, we do, yes. Even Sundays, when there's an ongoing crisis. I was hoping to discuss a serious matter with you. In person."

My attention sharpened, and my chest tightened. A serious matter? In person? No way that was good news. "Of course. Assuming you're in town."

"Excellent. Would you meet me at the Durham Hotel? Say, about noon?"

I glanced at Troy. He nodded and got out of bed, swiping texts with one hand while fishing clean underwear out of the dresser with the other.

"I'll be there."

"Excellent. Thank you, Ms. Finch. Until later."

I hung up and flopped back against the pillows. "Is this a mistake?"

"I don't like it," Troy said. "But I'll take the opportunity to put a face and a scent to the name."

"Do we think it's a coincidence that she's asking to meet at the same place your dad is staying?"

"Hmm. We covered our tracks well. And I would have thought they were too busy with undoing whatever chaos the djinn were sowing to discover anything about his arrival."

"We should be so lucky." I scrubbed my hands over my face, wishing I'd kept Duke and Iaret at the Bureau rather than letting them both head back to the Djinn Council. Maybe I would have had a damn heads up about this. "Shit. And with the tricksters—"

Troy's attention snapped to me. "Did you have another dream?"

I nodded, grimacing. "I'm wondering if it's what triggered your nightmare. Me registering as gone to your subconscious if you were already in REM sleep."

He scowled. "What did they want?"

"Apparently, I'm not moving fast enough."

Shaking his head, he got clothes out of the closet, all in Darkwatch black, and started dressing in quick, efficient movements. "It would damn well help if they told you what you're supposed to be doing."

"Agreed." My mind wandered back to the immediate problem, slow given the early hour and my general tiredness. "I need to warn the alliance. If the Sinners are in town, they'll be looking for Othersiders and probably hauling people in for shit as small as a parking ticket just to have the excuse to question them."

"You sort that. I'll get the Ebon Guard and the Darkwatch in place."

We got everything in order by noon, barely.

I warned the witches, weres, and elementals to be elsewhere for the day and the vamps and elves to be on their best behavior. Ruprecht, the gremlin lodging at the bar, was delighted to get orders to sabotage any listening devices, bugs, trackers, or whatever the hell else the feds might be prepping in or around the Durham Hotel. When I tried Duke via the callstone, I got a distracted acknowledgment and a lot of background noise. Still with the Council, then.

We arrived at the Durham Hotel at five minutes to twelve, with Troy back in his role as bodyguard.

A white woman with sharp features, wearing a pantsuit with her brown hair pulled up in a no-nonsense ponytail, flagged us down from a window seat. Nice and public—and in view of the rooftops across the street. Behind me, Troy muttered something in elvish, probably into his wrist mic. There was no way he'd let the setup slide without coverage.

When I reached the little seating arrangement, the woman stood. "Lara Sinclaire. Good to finally meet in person, Ms. Finch."

I kept my hands in my pockets when she extended hers.

Flustered, she dropped it and glanced at Troy. "I was hoping we could speak privately."

"I'm sure you can understand why that's not gonna happen," I said. "My security team only agreed to this if I promised to keep someone close by."

She eyed Troy as he gave her a vaguely hostile flat look back in return. The thought that I might keep him *very* close flickered across her face clear as day.

"Is that going to be a problem?" I said.

With another evaluating look at Troy, she pursed her lips unhappily but shook her head. "I suppose we can accommodate that request."

As Troy gave the armchair a quick check for needles or whatever the fuck he would do to trap or incapacitate a target in this situation, I said, "Frankly, I'm surprised you're here in person. Aren't Acting Directors a little too important to send on field work?"

"We took your title and status under advisement and wanted you to understand how seriously we're taking this."

Flattery. It might have worked on an elven queen or a vampire city master, but it just made me suspicious.

"Clear," Troy murmured before taking up a station between me and the window. He must have had someone else covering the rest of the room or the main door.

I steeled myself against the idea of him taking a bullet for me and sat, giving Sinclaire a bland look at the sharp one she was giving me, like she was noting everything about this situation for whatever report she'd be drafting later.

She took her seat as well. "Thank you for meeting me, Ms. Finch. Now, in our last conversation, we were discussing your powers."

Red flag. Big fucking red flag.

I forced a smile, sweetening it to Callista's poisoned curve when it unsettled Sinclaire. I didn't want to act like my murderous former guardian, but that lesson I'd taken in well. "As I recall, we were discussing the attempted kidnapping of me by your agents and having the Sons of Seth formally listed as a terrorist organization."

That threw her momentarily, but she pounced. "Speaking of that alleged attempt, Ms. Finch, would you happen to know anything about a vehicle exploding on I-85 in Virginia?"

I exchanged a look with Troy. His expression was as grim as mine probably was.

Keeping my tone mild, I said, "I was drugged, hooded, and handcuffed during the kidnapping." The truth, just not the whole truth. "Are you accusing me of something related to an event you're implying didn't happen?"

"I suppose not," she said reluctantly after a long pause.

So that was how we were playing it. They'd fucked up badly enough that they wanted to pretend nothing had happened—and badly enough that they'd write off all the resources they'd expended attempting it, as well as suppressing or misdirecting the media. I hadn't had a single question about it, despite the incident taking place in downtown Durham in broad daylight. Something about it should have come up at the press conference in Raleigh, but they'd wanted to know about the weather. Something that could be directly pinned on me without a messy involvement with them. That took resources, and all of mine were focused on making sure we didn't have any more incidents like we'd seen in Raleigh last month.

"And the Sons of Seth?" I asked.

"Not what I wanted to talk about. We're talking about you, Ms. Finch."

"Given I've already made it clear that discussion of my powers is off the table, I don't think we are. I told you, Sinclaire, I don't tolerate threats. If that's what's about to come out of your mouth next—some threat if I refuse to talk about my powers—then we're gonna find ourselves in a pickle."

"Where were you six nights ago?"

It was my turn to be thrown. "What do my whereabouts have to do with anything?"

"Are you refusing to answer?"

"I'm saying that sounds like the opening to an accusation. I came in good faith to have a dialogue, but I have shit to do and a whole damn territory to run. If you don't stop playing games, I'm gonna go do my job and refer you to my lawyer." Iago would have a field day with this.

"I see." She studied me, brown eyes hard. Funny how quickly she'd gone from congenial to hard-ass. "A contact of ours made some startling allegations about what you are able to do with your—your *magic*."

The Eads. This had to be their revenge play. Damn Sonia for not keeping them in line.

"Get to the point, Sinclaire," I said coldly. I didn't like where this was going.

"Some of the Bureau want you brought in and held on terrorism charges."

"On what fucking grounds?" Rage and adrenaline flooded me with heat, amplified by Troy's leashed desire for violence in the bond, and I kept my expression neutral and my voice low with an effort.

"We won't discuss an ongoing investigation. But the reason I'm here having a conversation rather than having a team prepped is because I thought we could make another arrangement."

Bullshit. The reason they weren't prepping a team was because I'd destroyed the last one.

I fumed silently, waiting for her to pull out what she thought was gonna be her carrot.

"We know who your associates are. So either you come in and help us, or we target them. Your friends go nowhere and do nothing without scrutiny. Jail time for jaywalking. That sort of thing."

Not a carrot at all then, just a different stick. I should have known everything was going too smoothly last night.

My initial instinct was to jump outta the chair and do something about the threat she'd just leveled. That was what I did: hid until I couldn't then met threats with overwhelming force. Blew everything and everyone in my path down until they were so flat they could never hurt me again.

That was also a trauma response.

So, I did the opposite.

With an effort, I leaned back in my chair, steepling my fingers and peering at Sinclaire over them. As my focus tightened, so did Troy's, although he was likely paying more attention to the surroundings and keeping half an ear on us.

The longer I sat and did nothing, said nothing, the more Sinclaire stiffened.

Not what she expected, Troy sent. *Good. Be the hunter.*

Hunters had patience. I could find patience. I sank into the headspace I'd felt from Troy when he was hunting. A burst of fear scent from Sinclaire almost made me pounce verbally, but I held my tongue and eased down on the shields keeping my power signature unobtrusive.

She shuddered, apparently enough of a sensitive to notice the signature, then snapped. "Well?"

"Well what? I haven't heard anything worth responding to. Since I made clear how I'd feel about threats, I'm sure that can't be what you were doing."

A flush swept up her neck, muted somewhat by her makeup. "You have nothing to say for yourself?"

Troy nudged me in the bond. *Reporter found us. Pull your sig in and tread carefully. Directional mic.*

I sent an acknowledging caress back and tamped down on the reach of my power signature, letting it pool in the immediate area but not so far out that it might influence the journalist. "Acting Director Sinclaire, I've done nothing wrong. Nor have my associates. Certainly nothing to merit this treatment by the Bureau for Supernatural Investigation. I'd hoped to have a collaborative relationship as we navigate these early days in the shift of human-supernatural relations, but first Senator Wright and now you have trespassed on my rights and my territory with unprovoked violence, accusations, and threats against myself and other law-abiding supernatural citizens."

Wordy as hell for me, but let the media get all that on tape.

Sinclaire's hands tightened. "I can neither confirm nor deny the circumstances of any of your previous engagements with the Bureau, but you *will* work for us, Finch. Or your people will answer for it."

Perfect. So unsettled by me that she wasn't thinking about her surroundings.

Someone else thought so too because her hand drifted to her ear and a frustrated expression pinched her face before she smoothed it again. "I'm afraid that's all I have time for today, Ms. Finch. We'll be speaking again soon. I expect our conversation to remain confidential."

I was tempted to play some queenly shit and let her know she had my leave to get the fuck outta my territory, but I had to play this one for the public. "Director Sinclaire, if you'd like me to play by your rules, you've got to abide by them yourself. Fair's fair. So yes, I look forward to further dialogue about the Sons of Seth and their acts of terrorism against domestic targets both supernatural and mundane at your earliest convenience."

The fury in her gaze matched the rage in my heart. With a tight smile, she gathered her designer purse and stalked off, low-heeled black pumps clacking.

I watched her go and noted a smaller Latina woman with a DSLR trying to move in, only to be brushed off with a terse "no comment" from Sinclaire. The journalist made a frustrated look at her back and took a step to pursue then glanced over to where I was still sitting with Troy standing at my side. I smiled, genuine this time, and raised my shields completely as I waved to offer her the seat Sinclaire had vacated.

This might not be the way I wanted to play the game, but I had to step up and take the opportunities coming my way. There was more than one way to be diplomatic, and I kept forgetting Otherside wasn't my only audience.

If Sinclaire was going to try to use my people against me, I'd do the same. And if plans fell through in the court of public opinion, I could always fall back to my preferred method of doing things.

Nobody threatened me or my friends and got away with it.

Chapter 28

As the interview wrapped up, Troy's attention zeroed in.

Trusting him to deal with whatever it was, I handed my new journalist friend, Josefina-but-call-me-Jo, one of the cards with my direct number on it. "I can't promise I'll always answer or have a comment for you, but I'm happy to do what I can to support a local indie paper and keep the community informed. As I've said, stability and productive relations within the Triangle and beyond are important to me."

"Can I quote you on that?"

"Sure," I said. "It's what we've been aiming for these last couple of years. But for better or worse, I'm used to keeping a much lower profile. All of us are on new ground though and need to adapt."

"Good stuff. Right, I think that's all I needed." She clicked her voice recorder off. "Thank you for your candor, Ms. Finch."

"Sure thing, Jo. Take care."

I dug around in my purse until she was out of earshot before looking up and around to see what had Troy's attention.

Cyrus was leaning against a nearby wall, both hands on the cane in front of him, watching us.

You wanna talk to him? I sent to Troy.

Yes.

Alone?

Not especially. Lunch?

Sure. I gathered my things and rose, staying close to Troy as he muttered a "don't hear me" spell in elvish. I had no idea what that'd do about tech, but the irritating little jangle of electricity centered in his pocket was probably a jammer.

Cyrus grinned and straightened as we made our way over. "Arbiter. Son."

"Dad." The word sounded odd, like Troy wasn't sure if it fit anymore.

"Hi, Cyrus. Before we continue, you good with being known to the mundanes? They made threats against our associates, so they'll be watching anyone we speak to."

His grin turned sly as he rubbed the shiny scar where the lead-and-silver cuff had been on his wrist. "They'll try. I have my little tricks now that I'm free. Speaking of, you should bring me along to your next meeting. That hostile mundane you were speaking to first looked like she could be charmed."

Troy frowned, and the bond went scattery in a way I couldn't recall happening before. "I'll take that under advisement."

"How are you settling in?" I asked, determined for this not to be awkward, while trying to give Troy the space to deal with whatever was bothering him.

"Comfortably, given the lodgings and the generous stipend you've allotted."

I smiled. "Good to hear."

Troy shuffled. The man was nervous, bless him. "You want to get lunch?"

"Great minds," Cyrus said. "I called Allegra and invited her and Omar up for lunch when I saw you two. I hope that's okay, Arbiter."

"Sure, Durham is mostly neutral territory."

A jolt of something very near panic flashed through the bond, quickly smothered.

You okay? I asked Troy.

He answered aloud. "Been a while since we had a family gathering."

"My thoughts exactly," Cyrus said. "I was hoping we could discuss a few things."

Which meant we needed somewhere relatively private, since we didn't want to overplay our hand with misdirection and soundproofing spells in public. Ordering up to his room would probably be more secure, if cramped, but it'd be hard to have five of us even in the superior room we'd booked until Cyrus could find a place of his own. The bar was the other option, but all of us heading in that direction would lead the Sinners straight to it.

Then again, they probably knew about it already. We'd been using both tech and magic to obscure our whereabouts, but it was probably just the threat of *my* magic that was keeping them from making a move. That fireball I'd made out of the kidnapper's van on 85 had been quite the sight, and admitting that I'd manipulated the storm would have been a bombshell.

The other option was my house. I owned it and the land it sat on outright in the mundane legal system and had done for a decade, so they knew where I lived. Troy's name was on the deed now as well, come to think of it, which did more to explain Sinclaire's earlier look. That made me shiver. I'd been trying to make Troy feel safe and secure—like he really had a home—but I might have exposed him to more danger in doing that.

Cyrus was watching me with sharp eyes that saw far too much. "Everything all right?"

"Just trying to figure out a location where we could minimize any damage." I looked up at Troy. "Ideas?"

"Other than home?" His face blanked as he thought. "Keithia's mansion is still getting finishing touches on the rebuild, so that's out. The old Sequoyah mansion is an option. Or the House owns a few restaurants in Chapel Hill and Carrboro. But that'll mean burning those as information exchanges if they get shut down for a bogus health inspection or whatever. I wouldn't put it past Sinclaire to be difficult any way she can."

"Agreed. Home it is."

Something flickered in Cyrus's expression, like he'd been hoping for that outcome, but it was gone before I could figure out what I'd seen.

It put me on my guard. Bringing Cyrus back might have been the right thing to do, but now that he was here I couldn't help wondering who exactly we'd brought to the heart of my territory. I'd been more worried about the Lyon elves, because surely things would be fine with my fiancé's dad, right?

I should have remembered that I knew fuck all about being part of a family and was much less schooled to subtlety than most elves. Troy had said so once—that I completely lacked it—and I didn't disagree with him at all. I saw it as a strength.

Usually.

"Let's get going then." I led the way, Troy falling into bodyguard position behind one shoulder and Cyrus, oddly, taking the mirroring position behind the other.

We'd taken my car today. I was tired of being chauffeured around, and my car's plates had already been switched a few times. Switching them once more wouldn't make any difference if the Sinners tracked my car. Troy called Allegra on the way over and had her redirect to meet at my place. She grumbled about the extra distance, but it was sibling grumbling. Almost cute.

I glanced in the rearview mirror to catch Cyrus watching Troy with an expression of wistfulness before he sighed and looked out the window—maybe the second real reaction we'd seen from him.

As Troy ended the call, Cyrus said, "I missed so much. Allegra always was a fierce little thing."

"Now she's a fierce pain in my royal ass," Troy grumbled. There was affection under it though.

I snorted a laugh. Another me-ism he'd adopted.

"You let him talk like that?" Cyrus asked.

"Like what?" I glanced in the rearview mirror again, to find him looking at me with as much confusion as I must've been directing at him.

Troy smirked, reached over the center console, and rested a hand on my thigh.

Cyrus noted that as well. "Hmm."

The car was silent the rest of the way home.

When Troy jumped out to get the gate, Cyrus said, "You may call yourself a queen, but you're not one."

I stiffened. "Excuse me?"

"Don't worry. It's not a bad thing."

Before I could ask what the fuck kind of thing it was, Troy was waving me through. I decided Cyrus was still playing whatever odd game had started with his reluctance to address me as queen in the first place and that I wanted no part in it.

I would own what I'd claimed.

As I pulled through and waited for Troy to shut the gate behind us, I said, "Frankly, Cyrus, I don't give a damn what you think. Your role in your son's life is your choice and his. You don't get a say in mine."

That sent his brows rocketing sky high.

Troy slid back into the passenger seat. His nostrils flared, and he frowned. "What?"

"Nothing, cariñomí."

"What she said." Cyrus met my eyes in the rearview mirror, not looking the slightest bit intimidated.

He wouldn't, if he had a god's backing.

Shit.

I couldn't forget that. Whatever Duke had implied, it was tied up in the tricksters somehow.

I frowned. The tricksters and my parents. Which meant the djinn and the elves as peoples.

"Cyrus," I started, "I hope this thing you need to talk about sheds some light on the arrangement with my mother. The djinn will have questions."

Rather than putting him on edge, that made Cyrus grin. "I like her, Troy. She's sharp. Sees the unseen."

At the familiar phrase, my gaze snapped to the rearview mirror again.

The bastard just smiled, like I'd given him confirmation of a suspicion.

Double shit.

I pulled up and parked next to Troy's black MDX. We kept both vehicles tucked under the trees ringing my house, just in case a drone or a helicopter did a flyover.

Cyrus climbed out and tipped his head to the shadows under the trees, breathing deep and closing his eyes with a smile. "Now *this* is a slice of paradise."

The sentiment mollified me despite myself. I was proud of my home. The djinn might have magicked it into being on the parcel of land they'd secured with funds from who knew where in the Aether, but I'd maintained it for the last decade.

Well, me and Troy, since he'd moved in. He handled the yard work when Zanna was too busy, losing himself in the soil and plants when his thoughts and memories intruded.

But it was something that was truly mine, past to present.

"Come on inside," I said. "Might be a minute before Allegra gets here. She doesn't drive like Troy."

Troy rolled his eyes. "I have places to be."

"Oh, I know," I said. "You always have. Not that I'm complaining." His ridiculous driving had put him in position to help or save me more than once.

He slung an arm over my shoulders and pulled me in to kiss the crown of my head. I got the feeling that he was putting on a show for his father, but so be it. I could not figure out what the fuck was going on with Cyrus, and I refused to withhold affection from Troy because his dad was watching.

I wrapped an arm around his waist and matched his pace even as we went up the stairs, both of us skipping the second step in perfect sync, and kept it there as I unlocked the door and let us all in.

Troy pulled away to do his usual thing: disarm the security alarm he'd installed and sweep the house for anyone good enough to evade it or my wards.

All of which Cyrus noted as he came slowly up the stairs and inside.

It made me realize I'd need to get a ramp or something. The djinn didn't consider things like accessibility for those who couldn't shapeshift or teleport. I should have thought of it before now, given how much I worked with mundanes.

"Don't worry about it," Cyrus said as he paused in the doorway to take in the space.

"I see where your son gets his mindreading talent," I muttered.

Cyrus didn't answer, too busy looking at things. His gaze rested longest on the framed photo of me and Troy at the vampire Reveal. We'd been faking a relationship then as cover for our being there, but there was something real in the selfie. An echo of the kiss he'd pressed on me in my flushed cheeks and shaky smile, and his eyes slanted toward me rather than the camera as his body pressed seamlessly against my side where I was tucked under his arm. It was a cute picture. I'd stolen his phone and had it printed for his birthday last year, and he'd stood there staring at it for a good minute before hanging it on the wall facing the kitchen with far more solemnity than I'd expected.

Other things caught Cyrus's attention in turn. Our two laptops on the dining table. Two pairs of socks forgotten under the sofa in a moment of passion. The way Troy visibly relaxed as he completed his checks then rummaged around in the fridge.

I smiled at that last. Couldn't help it, and fuck appearances.

It'd taken Troy months to feel safe enough here to dig in there if he wasn't serving me at my express need or request, and now he was doing it with witnesses. Elven witnesses who were blood relatives.

Cyrus inhaled and grunted in surprise. "You really love him."

"Yes, she does," Troy said, his head still in the fridge. "And I'd know even if she didn't tell me, which she does, because there's a piece of her auratically lodged in my head. Stop picking at her, Dad. She's not Keithia. Or Mom, whatever was going on there."

"Touché," Cyrus murmured.

I waved him in and toward the dining table on the other side of the half wall. "Be welcome in my home. My table is yours, my hearth is yours, and my roof is yours, while you are here."

As he stepped all the way inside, Cyrus bowed slightly, leaning on his cane.

"I honor my hostess. While your home is mine, my strength is yours." His eyes twinkled as I relaxed a notch—guest right and hospitality were sacred in Otherside—but he moved to sit at the table. "I told you. I swore to your mother I'd help keep you safe. This is the first time in twenty-eight years I've had the opportunity."

I cleared the table of our laptops and then sat opposite him. "Forgive me if the involvement of the tricksters makes me wary."

"More than just Harqil then?"

I studied him as Troy puttered in the kitchen, doing something about lunch. I'd planned on ordering for delivery, but we had a fridge full of food and cooking was both one of his love languages and a source of peace—something he could control. He still had an ear turned our way, but he'd picked up on the clash in the car and was giving me space to navigate it.

Before answering Cyrus, I sent a curl of appreciation and love in the bond. That settled Troy yet another notch, and I swear Cyrus saw that too.

"Which of the tricksters are you aligned with?" I asked bluntly.

Cyrus threw back his head and laughed. "Goddess, but you are still one of the hunters' children. Brutally direct when you have a target."

"It's worked so far."

"As have misdirection, discretion, and obfuscation on my part. My patron is my own," Cyrus said.

I didn't want that to be fair, but it was. At least he'd confirmed he did indeed have a patron.

He took it as a joke. "Not going to push?"

"Somehow, I get the feeling you answer to no authority I can call upon."

"See, Troy? She's clever," he said.

Ire flashed through the bond as Troy turned and glared. "She's also the better half of the two of us. You were gone, Dad. Whatever the reason. So Keithia took everything she hated about you out on me. Arden saved me from her. Literally came to Keithia's estate and carried me out when I was minutes from giving up and dying. Do not fuck with my queen."

A long, uncomfortable pause stretched taut between the three of us.

"Noted," Cyrus said gravely. "With apologies. To her and for leaving you unprotected. Believe me, I do grieve that."

Wine. We were going to need some kind of booze to deal with this afternoon because, try as I might, I did not handle awkwardness well. But that would risk the maenad powers we'd already seen I couldn't quite manage yet.

I was gonna have to muscle through this.

Fortunately, the wards pinged just then, saving me.

"Car," I said.

The sound of an engine came closer.

Troy listened then relaxed. "Alli's MDX."

His son might have relaxed, but Cyrus tensed. He leaned back in his chair when he caught me watching, with a faint nod of acknowledgment.

"Good," he said. "Then it's finally time to get everything out in the open."

Chapter 29

Watching Cyrus and Omar meet soothed something in my heart, however conflicted I felt about each man individually. It eased something in Troy as well, to see his birth father and the uncle who'd taken over fatherhood on the former's behalf embrace.

"Look at you," Omar said. They exchanged cheek kisses, and he clapped Cyrus on the shoulders. "Still a devil."

"Ever and always." Cyrus's grin melted away to give him a serious look. "You stayed close to your children by making them blades for my son."

Omar nodded, the blankness of his expression suggesting sudden caution.

"You always were the smart one."

The Captain relaxed. "And you had the courage to set your son an example that changed the world. No small thing."

Cyrus sighed. "As I'm reminded by the weight of it all. But thank you for looking after Troy when I couldn't. I worried for the boy he was, but the man he is seems to have turned out all right."

The bond heated, and I did my best not to squirm with Troy's embarrassed pleasure at the sideways praise as everybody turned to me for formal greetings.

Because it was Omar, and this was the first time he'd been to my house, I repeated the hospitality ritual and waved him and

Allegra to the table, fetching them water and iced tea before running out to the deck to grab another chair. I kept thinking I was going to need a bigger house for all the meetings and guests I kept hosting now—which was still strange to me, even after a couple years.

But I liked my little house and the privacy of it. I liked my haven.

While our guests chatted, I helped Troy get food plated and on the table. Pork chops with apple compote, Lexington-style red slaw, diced roast potatoes with rosemary, and a salad of arugula and dried figs had my mouth watering. Troy snagged a Chenin Blanc out of the fridge and four glasses when I shook my head at his glance. No way was I taking risks at this particular gathering, even if I agreed with his assessment that a little social lubrication would help us all out as well as being in line with what the elves apparently expected from elven gatherings. Which made me wonder all over again where Troy's one-drink rule came from, but that was neither here nor there.

I managed to wait until we were all seated to ask the burning question. "So, Cyrus. What's this all about?"

He swirled his wine, avoiding all our eyes by peering into it. "I've spoken of the oath to Ninlil, Arden."

Omar grunted, eyebrows flashing up. "Excuse me? You swore an oath to Quinlan's djinni wife?"

Cyrus grimaced. "Long story, old friend. The short of it is, she had one request."

I stabbed my pork chop a little too hard as I ground my teeth to stop myself from pushing. The tricksters enjoyed their stories. He'd get through this one in his own way and on his own time. His gaze flicked to mine, as though he sensed my impatience and yet appreciated my waiting.

"Ever the huntress," he murmured. "Your mother's request wasn't just about keeping you alive. It was to help you overthrow the matriarchy. Completely."

Omar set his fork and knife down a little too carefully as Allegra's eyes widened, darting back and forth between the two older men. Troy just looked grim, even as he topped up everyone else's wine.

Cyrus held up a hand. "I know, Omar. I know. But I hope that doesn't put us in opposition just yet. You found your way to serving an elemental queen, no? Hear me out on this."

Omar leaned back in his chair and crossed his arms, saying nothing.

"The way things have been from Atlantis to now cannot continue," Cyrus said. "Not if we're to see our way through the next challenge."

This answer, I knew. "The tricksters. And whatever task they're evaluating me for."

Both Allegra and Omar snapped around to look at me so fast I grabbed Air for half a second.

"Excuse the fuck me?" Allegra said, ignoring the disapproving looks of her father and uncle. "What *evaluation* is that?"

Uneasily, I shrugged. "If I knew, I'd have said something. All I have is the gem I showed you, some fucked-up dreams, and Harqil."

Cyrus grimaced. "Try not to summon them, maybe. They're like the djinn in that. Speaking their name pulls their attention this way."

"And you wouldn't like that at all, would you?" I asked in the soft tone that had Troy sitting up.

His father noted the reaction before answering me. "We have similar objectives at the end of the day."

Not an answer. But with the tension in the room rising with each heartbeat, I wasn't willing to push and risk Troy's first family reunion in twenty years turning violent.

Diplomacy. I focused on where we were on the same page.

"I agree things can't continue as they have since Atlantis," I said. "But if 'toppling the matriarchy' involves murder, I'm not here for it."

"Arden—" Cyrus started.

I cut him off. "No. I am High Queen and Arbiter, and I *will* find a better way to achieve my parents' vision."

Calculation flashed behind Cyrus's gaze. "I would have thought an elemental would want revenge. You can't tell me the queens didn't hurt you. Like they hurt me."

Troy shifted.

"And like they hurt him," Cyrus added.

Dirty fucking play to use the son he'd just reconnected with against me.

"I killed everyone who hurt me *and* him," I said in a low, even tone. "I tore down Keithia's fucking house and burnt the pieces. Then I burnt her alive, killed Catrionne Sequoyah with a lightning strike, put a godblade through Mireia Luna's heart, and severed all of their people who wouldn't swear to me from Aether. The people who hurt him, and me, have been dealt with."

That set Cyrus aback as Omar pressed his lips together. Allegra looked at Troy, trying to hide her sympathetic look as he nodded his agreement with me.

"It's done, Cyrus." I held his gaze with a determined one of my own. "Otherside justice calls for eye for an eye and blood for blood. I have a heap of eyes and am drowning in blood. I have my king, safe with me. It ends there until and unless someone tries to start it again. I *will* change the matriarchy. *My* way."

Cyrus dropped his gaze from mine, covering it by turning to Troy. "And you?"

"What she said." He sipped his wine. "I have enough to manage as king without going out of my way to make trouble. Securing the territory takes priority. Not vengeance. Not when there's no one left to take it from fairly."

"Life isn't fair," Cyrus said.

The gold flecks in Troy's eyes flashed as he leaned forward.

"Believe me. I know." He pointed at me without looking away from his father. "But *she* is trying to change that. And I'm behind her. One hundred percent."

"I am too," Allegra said quietly. When everyone looked at her, she sat up straighter and lifted her chin. "I've watched Troy's back my whole life. I'm oathsworn to his life. I want him safe. Not just his life but *him*." She glared at her father and uncle, pointing at each in turn. "Neither of you saw everything he was subjected to or the fallout. *I* did. *I* made sure Keithia never heard about it. *I* kept him safe. I don't always agree with Arden, but she's helping. Not just herself. Not just her king. All of us."

Both older elves looked away, Omar at his almost empty plate and Cyrus out the window.

Troy sighed as frustration snapped though the bond. "I'm not as fragile or unstable as you'd all like to think, goldeneye king or not." His expression and tone hardened. "And speaking as King of House Solari, all of you will mind your roles in this House and territory. That includes showing proper respect to its leader, Dad. She's been nothing but courteous to you on top of killing the person responsible for everything that happened to you. If you have an accusation, you make it clearly and you bring evidence. If you want a say in how *we*—Arden and me—do things, you submit a report and a proposal. One that doesn't solely rely on an oath to a djinni who's been dead for twenty-eight years. Have I made myself clear?"

I nodded, as much out of apology for talking about him like he wasn't there as to set the example. Everyone else bowed their heads.

"As our king commands, so do we obey," they said in unison. Stiffly on Cyrus's part, but he said it.

Troy took my hand and kissed the knuckles. "Good. Who wants dessert?"

We managed to get through the rest of the visit on small talk. With Cyrus's bombshell out of the way, the Solari-Monteague-Veisi family had a lot of catching up to do.

I was on the periphery of it all, present in person but not in memory. Where once I'd been a little jealous of the family ties Troy had, I found myself satisfied with my place among them now. They took the time to fill me in on any references I didn't get, and not just Troy and Allegra. Maybe for the first time, I felt like Omar was a father-in-law rather than just someone who thought I was a bullying queen or a barely competent agent.

Sinclaire had threatened me, the djinn and the elementals were pissed with me, and we hadn't heard shit from Sonia Bedoe about what was going on in Richmond.

But for the moment, something felt like it was healing.

The sun was skating toward late afternoon by the time they left, with Cyrus casting a last confused look at me washing my own dishes while Troy walked them out. I couldn't work out where he was coming from. One minute, he was telling me I wasn't a queen and never would be. The next, he was confused because I wasn't acting like one. I supposed it made it harder to manipulate me when I wouldn't consistently play the part he wanted or expected me to fit.

His problem. I refused to make it mine. Especially when Troy had stood up for me.

Troy shut the door and leaned against it with a heavy sigh as Allegra's car pulled away.

"You wanna talk about it?" I asked.

He shrugged then dragged his shirt over his head. "It's weird. All of it. But especially hearing him talk about charming Sinclaire earlier. He *loved* my mom. I know he did. He bonded to her, for fuck's sake. But he hadn't known she was gone until I told him when he landed, and now he's...I don't know. Ready to jump into bed with a mundane? Or pretend to for a mission we haven't asked him to take? It's just weird, Arden."

Right. That would do it. Thirty-one-year-old Troy was trying to piece together memories of his ten-year-old self and match them to the man we'd brought home from prison in exile. A man who was trying to prod me into...what exactly, I didn't know, but sounded a lot like the war I was trying to avoid.

I took a step closer to Troy then another, trying my damnedest to focus on his face and what he'd said rather than falling into his body and scent.

When I was within reach, he snagged me and pulled me closer, propping his chin on my head as he wrapped his arms around me. "I can't help but feel like something's not right. Or like he won't keep his word to mind his own business. I'm almost tempted to put one of the Darkwatch on him."

I couldn't help stiffening.

He loosened his hold on me, looking down with a hard expression. "You've already ordered it done."

Wincing, I nodded. "We did promise the Lyon elves employment. Samarre and co are handling the Sons, but we weren't expecting them to send guards with your dad, right?"

For a moment, he looked like he wanted to argue. Then he shook his head. "I don't know why I'm annoyed. I should have thought of it myself. I just...he's my *father.*"

"He's very influential," I said neutrally.

Troy snorted. "Understatement. I'd been wondering how he and Mom managed to stay together so long without a second child. I have a feeling he might have been influencing Keithia on more than fuddling her memory of what you might look like." He scrubbed his hands over his face then cupped my jaw and tipped my head up. "Keep me level with him, please. I don't trust myself. You seem to have some resistance though. Even Omar seemed ready to agree with him by the end of lunch. Which is weird, because he agrees with nobody."

Relieved, I pressed the rest of the way up for a kiss. "Will do. And hey, the gytrash will have his scent now. They've been wanting more work. I spoke to them about being Watchers."

"Perfect. The fae tend to be resistant to auratic Aether."

I hadn't known that, but it explained why Zanna never seemed to be as easy around Troy as most non-elves were, even when he wasn't throwing his power signature around. She wasn't susceptible to his passive magic.

With that settled, we spent the rest of the afternoon napping. I hadn't gotten nearly enough rest in the last few days, and the day had started far too early.

This time, when the dream started, it wasn't like any I could remember.

The djinn had taught me lucid dreaming as a child when I kept weaving Air in my sleep. I knew the shape of my dreams. I knew which ones were mine and which were the tricksters pulling me into the In-Between.

This one hit with a vividness and intensity that took me so deep I wasn't aware I was dreaming at first.

I stood in a lush, green land that suddenly turned to desert, except for a small patch around me. When I moved, so did it. But as far as I walked, there was nobody to be found. The twisted husks of trees clawed for the sky, dry and long dead. Brittle, yellow-brown grass showed where lawns had been, leading to houses taken down to their foundations. The newly open horizon showed the Durham skyline, broken and smoking, much like parts of it had after the Wild Hunt. Jagged chunks had been taken out of buildings.

Whatever had happened, it was an unmitigated disaster.

I came to a road lined with rusted cars. Dry, white bones sat inside or short distances away.

And still, where I stepped, everything was revitalized.

I crossed a bridge, and the Eno roared to life beneath me, only to fall silent again, a dry, dusty riverbed, when I reached the other side.

"No. No, no, no, I stopped the Wild Hunt, what's happening?" I asked.

Did you really think the Wild Hunt was all there was?

Before I could even begin to formulate a reply, Aether stabbed through my mind and wrenched me awake.

Chapter 30

"Arden! For the love of the—"

I clutched Troy's arm, searching the room for signs of the destruction I'd been so deeply immersed in, panting too hard to speak.

He peered down at me, bright-eyed and ready to kill something, even as he gently steadied my head and checked my pupil reflex with the light from his phone. "What the hell happened?"

"A dream."

"I guessed that when you started talking. Narrating something. A wasteland?"

I shuddered. "I was talking? I don't talk in my sleep."

"You never did before, no. Here. Sit up a little and drink this."

I took the glass of water from him and gulped it down with swallows so big they hurt.

He took the glass from my shaking hand when I was done. "Do we need to call Duke?"

Pain lanced through me as I thought about it, searing through my head and down into my gut.

"No," I gasped. The Sight had never felt like that before, but the pain eased as I said the word. "Not yet. This was a warning."

"The pain just now? Or the dream?"

"Both. What exactly did I say?"

"At first, it was this rushed description of some fucked-up landscape. Then it was a riddle of some kind. Hang on." He shifted to sit back against the head of the bed, curving an arm over me to tuck me in close as he pulled my legs over his and leaned his head back to think. When I settled my head on his chest, his heart was racing. "It was something like, 'Comes and goes, goes and comes. That which is given, is taken and riven. Fire goes out, crow goes home. All that's left is dust and bone.'"

I shuddered.

"Honestly, it was the creepiest damn thing I've ever heard anyone say. And the words themselves were only part of it. It was your voice but not. And you kept saying it over and over again, until you started screaming no."

"Fuck," I muttered. "Did I repeat the voice at the end?"

"Not unless it was saying what I just repeated back to you."

"Someone—whatever voice has been speaking to me in the In-Between—asked if I thought the Wild Hunt was all there was. Troy, I was walking around Durham. It was destroyed. A wasteland as far as I could see. But..." I snapped my mouth shut. It sounded like the height of arrogance to say the part about things coming back to life when I passed.

Troy didn't push. He rubbed my arm with one hand and stroked his thumb over my thigh with the other, waiting with a hunter's patience.

I sighed. He'd get the full answer out of me eventually. I didn't dare hide anything from him. Especially not something like this.

"Everywhere I walked," I continued, "everything was normal. The river ran. The cars were like new. The plants came back to life. But beyond that? Death. Destruction. Ruin. There was nothing left. Just me."

He grunted. "That's...interesting."

With a shrug, I burrowed closer against him. "It wasn't like any dream I'd ever had. I can control my dreams. Duke and Grimm beat the hell outta me until I managed it so I'd stop sending tornadoes through the house when I was asleep as a kid."

Troy's grip on me tightened in outrage, but he waited for me to continue, no stranger himself to brutal upbringings.

"The only other dream I didn't quite control after that was a couple of years ago, in the middle of the Redcap case. But it was nothing like this. That was just a dream. This felt *real*. I was *there*, Troy. In a dead future full of nothing but bones and dust."

"Except where you stepped."

I nodded.

He stayed quiet for a few heartbeats. "Duke said you're a Dreamwalker?"

"Yes. Not that I have any idea what that means."

"But my father might. If your parents talked to him. And if your mother was one too, like Duke said."

It was my turn to bite my tongue. I really, really did not want to go to Cyrus about my dreams, but Duke had already indicated going to him would be dangerous.

"Arden, what if it's not one of your dreams?"

"Huh?"

"I don't know what exactly Dreamwalking entails. But you've never talked in your sleep, let alone chanted Goddess-damned riddles. You just said you control your dreams, except for the ones the gods pull you into. And this one was unusually vivid. What if it wasn't yours? Or not a dream?"

I started to ask what else it could be and then went cold all over. "A prophecy."

"Something like that."

"But I'm an *elemental*. I'm not a djinni. I can't do any of the djinn's tricks except for a dash of the Sight that usually doesn't tell me shit!"

"Okay, but two years ago, the only element you had was Air. Now, you're a primordial who can wield Chaos well enough to counter Aether. And Aetherically bonded to an elf with low-level auratic magic. Look, all I'm saying is the gods want you for something. Again, but also in general. They might not be able to control the making and unmaking of things anymore. But they can work through agents on this plane. We saw it with Dari and Orion, and Orion was—"

"An elemental who became a celestial after the gods took notice. Shit." I huffed an annoyed sigh but stopped myself from saying I didn't want to be an agent of the gods or a celestial.

I hadn't wanted to be Arbiter or High Queen either, but all my protests had only meant it was that much more painful when I was forced into taking up the mantle anyway. Graceful acceptance might help here as well.

"Okay," I said. "I'm sorry I woke you up with it all."

"I just want you to be safe." He gave me another squeeze. "Right now, that means we have to figure out what they want. And what Harqil's gift means. Sinclaire's petty power play means nothing if you've just prophesied a second apocalypse event."

My skin prickled. It'd certainly seemed apocalyptic. But these were the tricksters. Why would they try to destroy the world? They'd have only themselves left to play tricks on and far less amusement in it.

With a shudder and a frustrated, uncomfortable squirm, I shifted my head against his shoulder. "They keep talking about a gift. In every mythological record I can find, the tricksters did indeed offer gifts. Fire, food, tools, knowledge, whatever."

"With you so far."

"Harqil said the gem was a clue and a gift. Here's what I think is the clue: nobody's magic works with it."

Troy was quick as ever. "Magic. You think magic was the gift?"

I nodded. "But there's a piece I can't make fit. Or couldn't, until what happened in the dream, the whole thing of everything dead except where I stood."

He waited.

I took a deep breath. I hadn't told this part to anyone yet because I'd wanted to test the rest of the factions first and then we'd been so damn busy with everything else going on. "Troy, you remember when I said it ate Iaret's magic? And then it ate yours?"

"Yes."

"I took it around to every faction. It eats everyone's magic. Not just suppresses but outright negates. Like they're nulls. But it doesn't affect elemental magic."

"Define affect."

"It's not just that it doesn't eat it or block it like bronze does for me, where I can sense it but not touch it. It's that it has absolutely zero effect whatsoever."

"What?" The flat tone of his voice echoed the sudden blankness of the bond for the brief moment before the gears started turning as he sought strategic possibilities.

When I pulled away, he let me.

I turned to face him, arms wrapped around my upraised knees. "Here's the other thing. I can still touch my magic when I hold the gem. But it also doesn't affect Mixcoatl's arrow."

"Show me."

It wasn't that he didn't trust me. It was that Troy was grounded in what he could see or touch or do something about. Theory was a strategic consideration, and all plans fell apart the minute they stopped being plans and started being action. It didn't stop him from mapping out a dozen possible outcomes for any given situation, but it did mean he liked having evidence as a foundation.

I went to the closet and took down my Air wall, fetching both the arrow and the box with the gem in it. The arrow sparked in my grip. Once upon a time, it'd overwhelmed my burgeoning power, leaving the knotty scar and Lichtenberg lines under my right collarbone.

Now it was as easy to hold as the lightning I called for myself.

The gem was less comfortable when I set the box on the bed and popped it open to withdraw the stone, which was a sphere of blue and amber pietersite now. It buzzed in my hand, a vibration that almost felt like a sharp edge. Fitting for a storm stone but not comfortable.

Troy frowned. "Is that the same stone?"

"Yep."

"It was a ruby before. Princess cut."

"I know. And a sapphire nugget and a cushion-cut diamond and so on."

"It's taken different forms?"

"Yes. Almost like it was responding to the magic or aura of whoever I showed it to." I set the arrow on the bed. It went quiet as soon as I wasn't touching it.

Troy reached out to tap it and hissed when it zapped him. "Okay, the arrow is live."

I set Harqil's clue on the obsidian point.

Again, Troy tapped the shaft—and again, he snarled as it sparked, shaking his hand.

To make the point, I picked up the stone, embraced Fire and Air, and made lightning crackle over my other hand. Troy's gaze darted between the gem and the spark, and I saw when he reached the same conclusion I just had.

"Goddess burn me," he said. "If we don't figure out what the tricksters want, they take all magic. Except yours. No, except for any elemental's."

I nodded. "Janae's magic either warped or didn't work, so I have to assume it means life magic is sourced from this plane. Which makes sense. It's tied to the life here. But elemental magic, which is only accessible when you blend the two halves of Aether—"

"Comes from any plane where Aether exists. And it's what the gods use, if at a higher level. Hence, why you were able to pull

Mixcoatl's arrow from your shoulder when it zapped the hell out of me and Roman. And why the gem does nothing to it now."

"That's my guess. I keep thinking about what Neith said—that they lost the primordial powers of creation after creating the world, which was why they needed me as Huntress. So that they could use the power through me on this plane. But on some level, their magic might still draw on the same source, even if they're not quite up to creating whole worlds and peoples anymore. Any one individual celestial or god is stronger than any one individual Othersider, which is why I needed you as my Hunter and Iaret as an amplifier to beat the hunters as a group. They're not what they used to be, but the tricksters aren't going to come at us like that. They're...well, trickier."

Troy frowned, eyes distant. "So what that means for us is, if magic is gone, we have a grand total of four known elementals to defend the House and the territory. You're a primordial, but you're just one woman. You can't be everywhere, and you have to sleep sometime. Especially if we don't want warped reality. But I can't ask Laurel, Val, or Sofia to fight for House Solari. Their people won't even talk to you, so they flat-out won't help, even if we asked them. They have to protect their own. From my people."

I hadn't gotten quite that far in my considerations. "Shit."

The muscle in Troy's cheek twitched, a clear sign that he was getting agitated, even if I didn't have the bond telling me. "Arden, we need magic. We—Otherside—don't have the numbers to stand against the mundanes without it. Especially not with Sinclaire's threats. And we, the elves, are almost entirely reliant on magic to maintain our position on top at this point. It's why we haven't tried a full-scale overthrow of the mundanes to begin with." His expression darkened. "It's also why Keithia broke protocol and risked breeding someone as powerful as I am. If we don't stop this, we're looking at the complete collapse and destruction of Otherside."

I tucked the gem back in its box and put it and the arrow away to give Troy a minute. Talk of his fucked-up, abusive grandmother always set him off, with good reason.

When I came back to the bed, the bond and his expression were both set in brittle neutrality. I sat a small distance away, sensitive to his occasional preference not to be touched when he was in a bad headspace. I was pretty sure it was a form of self-punishment, given that most elves were intensely social and needed regular physical contact to feel their best, especially when stressed.

This time, though, he reached for me.

Relieved, I crawled closer until he leaned forward to grab me and pull me against him, my back to his front this time.

"I don't like this," he said. "At all."

"I don't either. But even with this hypothesis, we're still lacking the information we need to do anything about it." With a sigh, I tipped my head back against his shoulder. I was going to have to involve Cyrus.

I wanted to try Duke, but even as I thought of it, my stomach cramped.

Was I being steered? Manipulated? Or was the onyx ring on my finger working on overdrive, pointing me to the better of two unseen paths? Why was Cyrus of all people the better path?

Duke knew I was a Dreamwalker. He'd repeatedly dodged my question of what it was or what it meant. And the Djinn Council was unhappy with me. Wouldn't be the first time a power player was unhappy with me. Wouldn't be the last.

But I had to *do something*. This dream, whatever it was, couldn't come to pass.

"You're thinking so hard it's giving *me* a headache," Troy grumbled. "Scoot down a bit and relax."

I did as he said, sensing he had a plan, and wasn't at all surprised when he started massaging my temples as soon as I was settled against his belly with my arms over his thighs. I allowed myself to be lulled by the movement of his fingers.

"Can I try something with Aether?" he asked.

"'Kay."

A spark of joy in the bond made me smile. He loved trying out new little tricks on me. More than that, he loved the trust I put in him.

Coils of Aether snaked through my brain, like the Thread of Thorns interrogation he'd done but just vines, no thorns. And this time, instead of sinking in with a sharp pain, Aether caressed. Stimulated rather than forced.

"Oh fuck that's good." The words didn't quite come out clearly, but I thought I'd said them.

"Relax into it," he murmured. "Let your thoughts drift as you do."

I did as he said. Sleep started rolling in with darkness at the edges of my mind.

"Too far. Come back."

As Aether eased, I came back just enough to hover between waking and sleeping.

"Good," Troy said. "Talk to me. Whatever comes to mind. Let the words flow."

It took me a minute to find them. "Can't talk to Duke, it hurts. Someone wants me to talk to Cyrus. Charleston's mine, but Sinners are mad, Djinn Council are mad, elementals are mad, Sonia not talking to us. Too many fronts again. Cyrus said we can't continue like this. We have to..."

I trailed off, frowning despite the ease of the thoughts slipping through me.

"Follow that thread, cariñamí. What do we have to do?"

"Atlantis."

Troy stiffened, and the tendrils of Aether jolted, pulling me painfully out of the half-waking state.

I gasped and sat bolt upright. "We have to go back to Atlantis."

Chapter 31

It took some doing, but I finally convinced Troy that I didn't literally mean going to find the city or re-enacting the events that occurred there here in the Triangle. I hadn't realized how badly the fallout of the Wild Hunt had triggered some deeply instilled fear in him, something I suspected he'd been raised with and kept buried or compartmentalized around me.

It hurt, but I was just getting a taste of how he felt with my elf hangup.

"I mean it," I said for the third time. "All I want to do is reorganize how the Houses are set up. Not destroy them. I promise I will try not to repeat...what I already did here."

Troy sighed. "I know. I'm sorry. The whole idea just hits hard. I was thinking reform, but this? Making the Houses headed by a djinn-elf pair again?" He grimaced. "It was going to be hard enough to get them to accept kings. Or even just not murdering us."

I gave him the same too-patient look he usually leveled at me. "I have the same problem with getting the elves to quit hunting the elementals. If they can't play nice—"

"Yeah." He sighed again. "Let's sleep on it and see what comes up."

I froze, suddenly afraid of what might be waiting if I went back to sleep. "I'm, um, gonna do a little work. Don't let me keep you up though."

He snorted. "I'm naturally nocturnal, and you know it. If you want to flip our schedule, I'm all for it."

"Maybe we could push it a few hours, at least. Neither of us are getting enough sleep on a human schedule these days. Not with so many Othersiders running on night shift."

"We'll try it then. Gradually. But do not stay up all night, Arden." The firmness in his face and voice softened. "I know what it is to be afraid to dream. I learned the hard way that it's better not to wait until I collapse to sleep."

I grimaced. He had a point. And I was busted.

He didn't scold me though, just kissed my forehead before getting out of bed and heading for the kitchen.

After a minute, I followed. Something itched at me, but I couldn't figure out what. The ring? The Sight? The remnants of the anxiety over my dream? I set it aside. The more I tried to force it, the harder it would be to find the answer.

And after napping all afternoon, I really did have territory reports to read.

Terrence and Ximena were as timely as usual with theirs. They were quietly making inroads with smaller wereleopard and werejaguar populations across the Southeast and West, little campaigns to put out feelers and see how those factions were feeling about my ascendancy. Fortunately, as with Black mundane women after the press conference in Raleigh, my "polling" was up with wereleopards and werejaguars. They saw how I could help them—in both their skins, since I was in a similar situation, presenting as a minority to the mundanes while existing as one twice over.

I'd never seen my liminality as being so beneficial before. But I'd always been catering to the majority demographic before. Those of us between worlds and straddling lines always ran the risk of being rejected to some extent by all our people, as I was by most djinn, elves, and now elementals. Too much of one thing or not enough of another. But others looked beyond heritage and into experience. Saw where proximity could be leveraged and held me accountable for doing so.

Heavy burden. But improving the situation for those of us who were worst off was what would support all of us, and I happened to have the power to do it.

In the middle of answering those reports—personalized responses to each wereclan—Samarre checked in from Raleigh. Something was up with the Sons of Seth. The leadership was where they were supposed to be, but there was a lot of chatter and a lot of other people not where they usually were.

Samarre sounded quietly alarmed. "It doesn't feel right, my queen. It feels like…"

I let her think it through, conscious of how pushy elven queens could be and aware of Troy half-listening as he caught up on Darkwatch reports.

"It feels like misdirection," she finally said. "Like what I'd do if I wanted the queen of a House looking at my queen and not at a play she was making elsewhere."

That couldn't be good. "Any idea what the play might be?"

"No, my queen. Only that there's definitely something going on."

"Got it. Thank you, Samarre. This is helpful. I'll put the word out for everyone to be watchful. It's probably another push on the vampires at Claret or Nightshade, but we can't be too careful with the threats we've been getting."

"As you say, my queen. Thank you."

I ended the call.

Across the table, Troy grimaced. "I don't like it."

"Call Terrence and Allegra, and if she's not already in Raleigh call Maria or Noah as well. I'll take Val, Janae, and Zanna."

He nodded, already dialing.

I moved outside to make my calls, needing the comfort of fresh air all around me and not just in trickles through cracked windows. That itch was still bothering me. A warning I didn't know the meaning of. Or maybe just the fucked-up dream still bothering me. I made my calls, keeping them short and to the point to avoid taking my irritation out on my people, then headed back inside.

Troy eyed me. "Back to bed."

I didn't argue. Sleep broken by the dreams I'd had earlier wasn't real sleep, and while I might be afraid to return to them, I was dragging. I snagged Troy's T-shirt from the floor and pulled it over my head, not caring that it was dirty as long as I could get the double comfort of his scent on me from both clothes and his body wrapped around mine as we slid closer to each other in bed.

"I love that you take comfort in this," he murmured, plucking at the fabric.

"You've always smelled good. Even when I didn't like you. Or when I lost my memory."

He grunted, a sound I couldn't translate beyond the bond's depth of affection and desire to keep me close. I snuggled closer, closed my eyes, and opened them to the In-Between.

You saw our vision of the future.

I had, and I hadn't liked it one fucking bit.

We know Harqil gave you a clue. And that you found Cyrus.

I had, but it wasn't like I knew for sure who was on my side. As always.

Laughter echoed in the stars. And then they exploded.

Everything flashed white.

I woke with a gasp so hard it was painful, falling out of bed. Hitting the hardwood floor nearly knocked the wind from me. Troy's training had me pushing back up almost before I registered I'd fallen.

The bed was empty.

"Troy!" I screamed it Aetherically as well.

Just as he reached through the bond and *pulled* on my magic hard enough for my mind to join his and for me to see the scene where he was with my third eye.

Front yard. At the gate.

Facing men masked with orange bandanas, carrying guns and Tiki torches.

The Sons of Seth that Samarre couldn't find earlier. They hadn't gone to harass the vampires again. They'd come here. That was what the itch earlier had been trying to tell me and why my mind was screaming now. The wards must have been triggered while I was stuck in the In-Between. Troy must have gone out to face them when he couldn't wake me, while they were still held at bay by the turn-back spells and tangled by the now semi-sentient plants bordering the property.

My heart stopped.

They had guns. Guns meant lead. Lead would kill Troy outright.

In the live vision playing through my mind, the gytrash howled and snarled like the dogs they appeared to be, darting in to hamstring targets, but Troy's only sound was a whispered spell that made my skin crawl.

Fighting the double vision, I opened the bond as much as I could while grabbing my elf-killer from the nightstand. I staggered into the doorframe, overcompensating for the scene playing out in my head, then hauled ass for the front door, snagging my shotgun from atop the fridge on the way.

Wait.

Smart. I needed to be smart.

Troy was in danger, but if anyone had slipped past him, if the attackers had come in strength or had some kind of magic to counter my wards, I might run straight out into an ambush.

Troy completed his spell, putting extra impetus behind it with a slash of his longknife.

The attackers started screaming. Another word from Troy, and the noise was suddenly silenced.

With his magic no longer overwhelming me, I was free to use mine. Bloody red rage enveloped me. I stepped outside and *reached*—Air and Fire, Earth and Water—and asked the land and trees to tell me who dared trespass.

To attack me *at my home*, the place that'd been my sanctuary for so long. Who was on my land?

Two dozen strangers total, tangled in vines and brambles that screamed as the intruders tried to cut their way free with hunting knives. Troy. Bás and Marú. And overhead, a silent drone, hovering maliciously.

A nasty smile curled my lips as I located the other three teams stuck on the sides where Troy wasn't.

Twenty-four hostiles, I whispered to Troy. *Every direction. Air support.*

These six will die slowly and painfully without a counterspell. Where are the rest?

I showed him my sense of them then added, *Stay put.*

While he reluctantly relayed that to the gytrash, I knocked the drone out of the sky with a wind gust, sending it to shatter against the old oak in my front yard. It hit every branch as it tumbled to the ground, but I zapped it with lightning just for good measure when it fell at my feet and then jumped down from the porch to stomp on it for no other reason than that I was pissed.

Some of the forces in the woods had cut free and were trying to force themselves through the wards stinging them. They didn't taste of Otherside, and the breeze blowing in my direction from the west brought me the scent of humans.

But I had to be sure.

Couldn't hurt to play a little trick on this hunt.

Amplifying my voice with Air, I modified it with a passive power to sound like Assistant Director Sinclaire's. "We got the demon, boys! Change of plans. Go on home so we've got some plausible deniability."

Be careful, Arden. The bond was taut with Troy's desire to come to the rescue.

He could also sense the elements building in me and was smarter than the average white knight.

With confused grumbles, men stopped trying to advance out of the woods.

"I thought that bitch was leaving the fun to us?" a man's voice complained in an undertone.

Just as I'd feared.

Sinclaire hadn't bothered with my friends. It was misdirection. She went for the head.

For me.

And the cowardly bitch used these human terrorists to do it. That was why they'd been ignoring my demand to list them as terrorists. Because they were *useful* to the state.

Time to take away Sinclaire's toys.

I almost wished I could see the looks on their faces as I reached for my magic again. The air around them thinned too much for them to draw breath to scream before the earth swallowed some of them whole where they stood, still trapped at the boundary lines.

Screams and shouts rang out in my woods.

They ran. Or tried to.

I gave myself over to my magic, wanting to make it quick. I wasn't a sadist. I didn't enjoy this. But I'd tried and tried and *tried* to be diplomatic. I'd tried to let mundane law enforcement do its job after forcing my people to play nice. I'd tried to work with the system we all lived within.

None of them wanted to work with me. And they couldn't live and let live.

They'd attacked me. *At home.*

That would not—could not, for my own safety among both the mundanes and Otherside—stand.

So their bones and blood, souls and auras, all of it would feed the magic keeping my land, my king, and myself safe.

All magic had a price. To all parties involved. They paid with everything they were.

And I'd have to live with the guilt and whatever fallout this brought down on my head.

So I reached. And found. And in the various ways a primordial elemental could kill when pushed to it, I ended them. Air cut off from lungs and pulled from blood cells. Bodies falling as nerves were fused and neckbones snapped. Blood frozen in veins or turned to acid.

As they fell, they were dragged under the ground. Disintegrated into their elemental parts. Them, their clothing, everything but the plastic and synthetic materials, which I buried too deeply to find conveniently.

Ashes to ashes, dust to dust.

Because, yes, the elements were wind and flame, river and soil.

But those same elements were in every living thing. And while I might not be a god or even a celestial, I still had the powers of creation at my disposal.

They fucked around. Now they'd find out.

There would be nothing to recover. No trace they'd ever been here, except for the stories of the ones Troy had allowed to live.

If we let them leave *my land*.

When the torrent of primordial magic rushing through me could find no other targets than the ones Troy still guarded at the front, I let it go and slumped against the oak, breathing hard. Thunder rolled in the near distance, and the humidity had spiked. Grimacing, I pushed through the beginnings of a power hangover to correct it and soothe the light tremor deep in the ground.

Balance. We needed balance.

"Well. That was certainly a choice."

I jumped at Harqil's voice, spinning as I raised the shotgun to find the messenger leaning against the outside of the fence.

What's wrong? Troy demanded.

Harqil. Hold tight.

"Everyone busting my wards tonight," I said, unable to help my frustration even as I lowered the gun. "What can I do for you, Harqil?"

They studied me, looking much more serious than usual. "You would do this much to protect what's yours?"

I started to answer then gave it a minute of measured thought. "I protect my people. But to protect them, I have to protect myself."

"And you'll use tricks to do it." Their grin flashed in the dark. "I always did appreciate a sylph's skill with vocal mimicry. You're even better at it than most because you remember the words themselves matter, not just how they sound."

"Thank you?" I didn't know if their approval was a good thing.

They nodded, back to looking thoughtful. "Anansi will be pleased with this, at least. He's been wanting to see colonizers properly brought to justice for years. Laverna as well. She'd like the whole Underworld touch at the end. But be mindful of how you build your power, Arden. Regulus's stamp is upon you, and revenge will be your downfall."

With a twist of magic, they were gone, leaving me with far more questions.

Chapter 32

I made it to the porch before the power hangover overwhelmed me.

Blood trickled over my lip as I dropped into a crouch then twisted to fall all the way onto my ass and lean against the porch rail with my head tilted back, taking desperately shallow breaths. It'd been a while since I'd had to push that hard, and I was new to wholesale destruction of living, sentient beings.

So much for telling Troy to deal with the Sons without anything funny that could be traced back to Otherside.

Cold flashed over me, made colder by the sweat abruptly soaking my body, and my stomach twisted. I tried to keep it down, but between the rapidly growing power hangover and the self-loathing at what I'd done, I couldn't.

The rosemary below got doused in what came up as I hauled myself upright, leaned over the railing, and let go.

Troy's worried presence hovered in the back of my mind, but I pushed him out and walled up the bond. We were safe. There was nobody else on my land except who I wanted here and who was under our control. I wanted to wallow in peace.

I spat a few more times to get rid of the taste before dragging myself back to sit in the corner next to the door and huddling, knees up, head down, just trying to breathe.

All magic had a price. Sometimes, it was more than emotional or auratic.

I don't know how long I sat there telling myself I'd only done what I had to do before Troy made his way back to the house.

"Arden."

I jumped then flinched at the sympathy in his tone.

"Let me in, cariñamí."

Trembling, I pushed harder to keep him out. I didn't want to be this person. This terrifyingly thorough murderer, self-defense or not. And I didn't want him to perceive me as her.

I was shutting myself off from Air as hard as I was from him, and as usual, the silence of elven movement gave me no clues that he was so close without the warning of shifting air molecules. I choked on a scream as his hand rested on my foot, practically climbing the wall as I tried to get up and away. Everything spun as I pushed through the power hangover to wrench Air into my control.

"Easy, my love." He backed up, hands held out wide to his sides, unarmed even as my knife and shotgun were within reach on the porch. "Easy. It's just me."

I squeezed my eyes shut, swallowing past another lump in my throat that might be fear or might be more vomit.

"Etain and Thana are with the gytrash," Troy said in the impossibly soothing tones he used with an unreasonable queen. His passive power lapped at the edges of my aura, and his voice twined between my ears like magic itself, insisting on calming me. After a brief resistance, I allowed it. He scuffed a foot as he came closer, intentionally letting me hear him this time. "There's a contingent of the Ebon Guard with them. Do you want me to sort out the remaining six humans?"

I nodded tightly. I really would hurl again if I had to see or smell a mundane right now. If only because I'd have to fight the urge growing deep inside me to finish the job and make sure what was mine was completely safe and protected.

"Okay. Stay there." He got his phone out and made a quick, terse call in elvish. The gentleness he was using with me was nowhere in evidence as he spoke to Etain on the other end, and I shivered. He finished the call with a command to report when they had information and turned his attention back to me. "Are you hurt? I smell blood."

"Nosebleed." I had to force the word out, but I couldn't stay like this. We didn't have time or space for me to be a wreck. I had to be better than this. Because I was a high queen. An arbiter. An elemental. Because I was fucking *me*. And I was the only one like me.

No excuses to be less than the best. No *space* for it. None. Never.

With an effort, I wrenched my mind back under my control and shoved all my guilt, all my fear and feelings of violation, into the tiny box I reserved for anything that didn't serve me in the moment. "I'm fine."

Troy tilted his head and narrowed his eyes at the coldness in my voice. "Okay."

Translation: he knew I wasn't, but he knew better than to fight me on it. For now.

Any other time, my natural contrariness would have kicked in and I'd have fought *him* on that. Just now though, I had shit that needed doing.

"I want the Houses in both demesnes and the djinn at the bar tomorrow. Today, whatever. Next sunset. No bullshit. No excuses," I said. "We get what comes next done. Right fucking now."

"Yes, my queen," Troy said. The cautious, formal words brought me down to earth like a slap.

I dropped the walls. "I'm sorry. I didn't—"

He took the cue offered by the dropping walls to close the distance between us slowly and gently tilt my chin up. He swiped under my nose with his thumb, wiping the blood on his pants rather than licking it like the hunger he was hiding demanded. "You defended your home and those of us on your land. You overcame a force vastly superior in numbers in less than five minutes with no casualties to allies and no evidence to pin on us. And because you're not a heartless bitch, it hurts you. I don't like it. I don't like anything that hurts you. But I can live with it for the sake of the greater good. If you can."

Could I live with that?

I'd have to. It was the kind of ruthless practicality I'd always found convenient in the ugliest way in the old queens.

But I hadn't struck first here. I'd defended.

I had to hold onto that.

I *would* hold onto that.

△▽△▽

Noon the next day found me at the bar.

After the previous night's events, I no longer gave a damn if they followed me here. My heart had hardened against people who thought they could keep kicking me. I'd simply do the same again. And again. And again, if need be. And hell, maybe drawing them out would get me a measure of fucking peace when they were too beaten to keep coming against me.

Maybe for fucking once, people would take me seriously when I made a polite request.

Zanna gave me a grim look when I told her the plan for the rest of the day. "Djinn. And elves. Out-of-territory elves. Coming here."

"Yep. Think you can help me keep order?"

She gave me a squinty look, dark eyes flashing. "I know what you're doing."

I grinned in spite of myself. "Is it working?"

Her mouth twisted, and she glared as she turned to refill a witch's beer. "Yes."

"Great. Thank you. We need a reliable third party."

She might have figured out that I was flattering her, but flattery always worked at least a little on Zanna. "I suppose I can help."

"Look at it this way: you can curse the booze, bloodline, or balls of whoever steps outta line."

That got the grin I was looking for. "Promise?"

"Hell yeah. Because I don't want a repeat of last night."

Like all fae, Zanna loved a good story. Whatever I felt about last night, it was a good story. If I ignored that I still felt like the villain.

Troy shot me a look from where he was speaking to Terrence, Ximena, Vikki, and Ana in their usual booth on the other side of the bar. *Quit with the villain shit. They'd still be alive if they'd stayed the fuck at home and minded their own business.*

I ducked behind the bar to grab a lemon and hide the grimace I couldn't quite stop, popping up again when I had my face under control to slice out a wedge and drop it in a glass. He was keeping his emotions on their leash, but the swearing was a cue that his patience was wearing thin on my personal guilt trip-slash-pity party.

Zanna sighed when she saw what I'd done.

"Sorry," I said. She liked the lemons sliced into neat rounds, not my sloppy wedges, and I'd effectively ruined one for her. Not many people could get an apology out of me these days, but no matter how powerful I got, I had enough sense not to cross a kobold. Certainly not *this* kobold, anyway.

She just rolled her eyes and hopped on her stepladder to ring the last call bell. "Bar's closing early today! You have an hour to finish your business and head out."

Consternation rippled through the room, and everyone looked at me.

"I've got business to conduct, y'all," I said. "Anybody here now can come back later and get a round on the house for the inconvenience."

That got me a cheer from the patrons and another eye roll from Zanna.

"You're too soft on them," she said.

Rather than argue with her, I simply launched into the story of last night in a quiet undertone, sat on a crate behind the bar. By the end, her light brown skin was a sickly yellow, and her dark eyes were as big as a new moon.

I shoved down a wave of something I didn't have time to feel just now. "Yeah. So if I wanna treat the people who aren't fucking with me, I'ma do it."

"Fair." Zanna pulled out a stack of thick, round cardstock and the stamp with the stylized eclipse symbol for Otherside. As she stamped a few cards to use as drink tokens, she said, "It's good to hear. Our king will be pleased. Might even get him out of the Summerlands again."

Getting Rí, the fae king, out of the Summerlands hadn't been anywhere in my consideration, but I'd have to deal with that sea fae in the Outer Banks sooner or later. Maybe it'd help to have her king on board with my plans.

I wrestled with that over the next few hours as I sat in my office, going over what I was going to say to end the cold Atlantis War for good. I'd spent more time among the mundanes than most Othersiders, passing as a human null for twenty-five years. I was still trying to move within Otherside like I was a mundane.

But I wasn't one. It was a damn wall I kept running into. And after how hard I'd worked to break out of the box Callista had kept me in, it was infuriating that I kept putting myself right back into it.

A safe zone that would get me killed...and keep me separate from the other elementals.

Another angry message from the Elemental Collective via Val and my own swirling thoughts kept me occupied until evening.

Sooner than I'd feared, I was out of time.

A knock on the door barely preceded Zanna sticking her head in. "Charleston Conclave are here. Troy has them. I'm getting platters."

"Appreciated."

She nodded and shut the door.

I rose, bowing my head to gather my spinning thoughts. The other end of the bond sharpened to a figurative point, which told me the Charleston elves had come inside and Troy was greeting them.

Showtime.

I grasped my callstone and reached for a connection with Duke. "Hey. You're gonna want to be here for this."

"For what?" he snapped back in my head. "I'm busy trying to convince the Council you're not worth killing."

"Tell them I'm about to end the Atlantis War. For real this time."

Shocked silence made a blank in the part of my head connected to Duke via the callstone. I'd worked with Troy to make arrangements with the elves last night, given they needed to drive in from a few hundred miles away, but djinn could be here in an instant.

If they were properly motivated.

I was willing to bet a last-minute meeting with elves and invoking Atlantis would be extremely motivating.

The mental background noise quietened before Duke said, "You're going to need to say that again, Arden. Very fucking carefully."

"I said what I said. I have the Charleston Conclave at the bar right now. They've sworn to me as Arbiter. The remnants of the Richmond Conclave will be here by sunset. Plus, I have an offer that will get the djinn a foothold on this plane again." I paused to let that sink in. "*If*, of course, you can convince the Council I'm not worth killing."

"You little wretch. You've been planning this."

"The Sons of Seth and the Supernatural Investigators forced my hand twelve hours ago. They attacked my home. This is the fallout."

Alarm flickered in the callstone. "The Sons attacked your home?"

"They tried. The wards and Troy held them off until I could get free of the In-Between. Eighteen attackers no longer exist as anything recognizably human. Six are captive and with elven interrogators. They'll be lucky to remember their own names tomorrow. Maybe tell the Council not to push me. I haven't had the best night's sleep in a while."

"Understood," he said neutrally. "And well-played. I hadn't thought you had it in you, little bird. Stay where I can find you, hmm?"

Before I could answer, he closed the connection.

I leaned on my desk and conjured a zephyr to center myself. My last fight with a djinni—with Grimm—hadn't gone so well. Their ethereal natures made them harder to kill than most beings on the earthly plane. I had the godblade in a sheath at my back, very much against Troy's wishes, but really hoped tonight wouldn't come to anything close to needing it.

No. No more stalling. Fighting djinn wasn't what today was about. I hoped.

Straightening, I patted my pocket to double check Harqil's gift, made a few adjustments to the designer T-shirt and blazer I'd worn over jeans that cost more than my car payment, and settled the gold-and-onyx coronet on my curls before stepping out of my office. I hadn't needed Troy to tell me to dress according to my station today.

"Good luck, my queen," Haroun said from his station opposite my office door. "And thank you."

"For what?"

"Doing what you can to break down barriers. Every time you chip away at elven supremacy and superiority, you make it a little easier for us half-elves. Even when you're not directly working for us. It's the elven power structure that limits our opportunities. You open them."

My mask cracked, just for a minute. "You don't know how much I appreciate hearing that, Haroun."

He blushed and ducked his head. "Of course, ma'am. Sorry to speak out of turn."

I squeezed his shoulder to reassure him at his bow to the power structure he just said he wanted to break free of. "Don't be."

When I pushed through the door to the main bar, two elfesses and an elf I thought I recognized from the summit stood talking to Troy. Their body language shifted as they sighted or scented me, going on even higher alert than they were around Troy.

As I approached and rested a hand on the arm Troy formally offered, they knelt and spoke in unison.

"My queen and Arbiter. We come at your command."

"Thank you," I said. "Rise and be welcome."

We weren't playing host for long before the Richmond elves arrived, led by the orange-haired Bedoe House Guard captain. Keeya? We went through a similar greeting before everyone was seated at the table.

I remained standing at the head, Troy on my right. "We're waiting for a few more guests—"

A jolt of Aether pulled my attention right before the scent of lemon zest cut through the room.

"And there they are." I turned to find Duke, Iaret, and two more djinn I didn't recognize shimmering onto this plane near the door to the hallway leading to my office, the storage area, and the downstairs sparring room, behind the elves. "Glad you could make it."

Duke shifted to his favorite human shape and stalked forward, ahead of the other three djinn. "You dropped bloody Atlantis into it. What in the nine hells did you expect?"

The visiting elves shot to their feet and spun, probably remembering my severing the royals of House Ead. Maybe at the mention of Atlantis though. Even Troy stiffened.

"Everybody calm down and sit down," I snapped. "I didn't call anyone here for punishment or games."

The unfamiliar djinn bristled, their true forms flickering with lightning and flame. Iaret shifted to her preferred humanoid form and grinned dangerously.

Drawing on all four elements to amplify my power signature, I lowered my voice. "Sit. Down. And behave like grown-ass people who can control their magic and themselves. I won't ask again."

Troy's power signature spilled out to add pressure alongside mine, and the elves sat.

After a long hesitation, the djinn did as well, to make six elves on one side and four djinn plus Troy on the other. The two unknown djinn shifted as they did, one wearing the form of a heavyset West Asian man, the other a tall East Asian woman.

And just like that, I had my peace council. My parents' dream was finally in reach. The goal behind the reason I'd nudged Troy into asking Duke for help to begin with. I might actually pull this off.

If we survived the next few hours without warping reality so bad we and everyone in a few miles' radius ceased to exist.

Chapter 33

I remained standing after introductions were finished. Partly to make the point that I was in charge, regardless of how petty the move felt. Partly because I was simply too agitated to sit.

Duke opened his mouth, and I gave him a look so hard he blinked and shut it.

"Thank you all for joining me on such short notice," I said. Regardless of what'd happened, *I* controlled how I dealt with people. I'd be grown enough to be polite until someone tried playing the jackass. "I suspect your first question is why I'm dropping Atlantis into it when the Atlantis Accords are already in place."

Keeya Bedoe nodded sharply, but she was the only one who reacted. Troy was too busy watching for betrayal with hard eyes, the rest of the elves looked like they were trying to hide that they were shit scared, and the djinn were covering their uncertainty with insulting masks of amusement.

I mentally gave Keeya points for courage before continuing. "The animosity between the djinn and the elves might not end in full today, but the cold war does. I've decided to establish two new Houses in the Triangle to form a full conclave alongside Solari. Leadership of one House will be offered to an elf selected from House Bedoe in acknowledgement of their early support.

Leadership of the other will go to an elf selected from Charleston to reward smart choices."

That got their attention. I barely managed not to wrinkle my nose as the scents of both herbs and lemon zest spiked, with threads of outrage under the latter. Allegra would have been the anticipated selection for one of the Houses, but she was still heir to Solari in the absence of a child between me and Troy. That, and my personal entanglements between the elves and my office as Arbiter were already raising too many hackles in Otherside.

I held up a hand as the djinn stirred angrily and the elves shifted in their seats as opportunity beckoned and cockiness returned. "There will be a condition. The leading royal—queen *or* king, or sovereign, since we're being inclusive—will accept a djinni as their partner. What the word 'partner' means in practice will be up to each pair. So long as there is equality and balance in the relationship, whether y'all sleep together or not is up to you and is to be negotiated in advance. No games, politics, plots, whatever, to undercut the other, from either side. Or you get my wrath. And so help me, if I can utterly destroy eighteen humans so thoroughly nothing of them will ever be found, then please believe I can do it with any of you. If not with primordial magic, then with this."

I unsheathed the godblade at my back in a swift motion and slammed it on the table. The room sat in shocked silence. Troy glared at the thing—understandable, given I'd nearly killed him with it twice. The other elves recoiled at the magic leaking from it. The new djinn flinched then looked at it with hungry gazes before Yoshi, the one appearing as a woman, looked up at me with narrowed eyes.

"There's more to this than mundane trash attacking your home," she said.

"Yes. There is. Part of it is that I can see our initial offer to the djinn wasn't strong enough to gain your attention. Part of it is this." I pulled Harqil's clue from my pocket and held it up. The gem was still pietersite, oddly. Maybe unlocking its meaning had locked its form. "A celestial messenger left me this. Touch it."

I set it in the middle of the table.

Iaret's lip twisted. She already knew what it would do. Duke pointedly crossed his arms and leaned away. But Yoshi, her eyes on me, reached out and touched it. In a heartbeat, she was out of her seat and halfway across the bar in alarm.

"What trick is this?" she hissed, reverting to her true form as the elves on the other side of the table reached for weapons.

Rather than answer, I looked at the elves.

Swallowing hard, Keeya reached out to touch the gem, hissing and shaking her hand as her magic was stripped as well. "It steals magic? Why would a celestial messenger give you an artifact that can do that?"

I reached to gather it again, holding it visible in my palm, then drew on Air and Fire and made lightning crackle over my fingers.

Keeya's jaw dropped. Duke and Iaret's expressions blanked. Yoshi grew to a massive cloud, crackling with lightning to rival mine, until I arched an eyebrow at her. She pulled herself together and returned to her human form and her seat with a stiff expression that was probably hiding embarrassment. The scent of surprise and fear rose heavily enough that I did wrinkle my nose this time, and Troy shifted his shoulders the way he did when he was getting ready to draw the longknife from its back sheath.

I set the gem back in the middle of the table, partly in case someone else wanted to try it, but mostly so that it would serve as a reminder. "This was given to me as a clue."

"Of what?" Aakesh, the other new djinni, asked.

"Of what will happen if we don't figure out what Otherside promised the trickster gods in exchange for the gift of magic."

I'd thought the room had been silent before, but this was worse.

Troy spoke in the emotionless voice of the Darkwatch agent he used to be. "We have a theory. If the tricksters take their gift back, elementals will be the only beings who can wield magic on this plane."

Duke frowned. "Not the witches?"

"No," I said. "I took it to each faction. Elf, djinn, witch, were, fae, vampire, even a human necromancer. All of them lost their magic completely. Not blocked, like with bronze or lead and silver or star iron. Lost."

It didn't take either side long to get the picture, but Troy made it plain anyway. "My queen is the most powerful elemental, certainly locally, likely anywhere. But she's one person. We know of other elementals. But they will not come out of the shadows. And rightfully so, with a bounty remaining on their heads, even if we've ended it locally. So if you will not take the first step to ending the hunts because it's the right thing to do, you *will* do it knowing that, should the worst happen, we will need them. And that means demonstrating, with unambiguous action, that the bloody chapters of the past are closed."

I couldn't help my mouth twisting at that—our having to bet on self-preservation driving the djinn and the elves to revisit the Atlantis Accords and end the elemental bounty hunts. Like Troy said, they should be doing it because we were people and it was the right thing to do.

Not everyone had his capacity for introspection, growth, and change.

Poppy Averill, Savannah's daughter and now heir-apparent, proved it. "We don't need the elementals."

I tilted my head and raised my eyebrows, halting Troy's rise with a gentle hand on his arm. Outrage rippled through the bond, even as he sank back down.

Poppy blushed, blue eyes widening as she realized what she'd said. "I— Excuse me, my queen. I misspoke."

"No," I said, dangerously softly, despite Troy's rage reverberating in me to send my own higher. "I don't think you did. You—many of you, probably—were prepared to see me as an exception. Because I'm exceptional. No?" I tilted my chin up and glared at them. "The only primordial elemental. The only one who could sever Queen Onora and stop the gods. So it's okay if there's one. Uppity. Elemental bitch. Right?"

Blood drained from all of the elves' faces as I spoke the ugly truths they were hiding in their hearts even as they sat in my bar, drinking my beer and eating my food. Enjoying the safe passage *I'd* granted them. The protection *I* offered from mundane attack.

I squeezed Troy's shoulder, as much to soothe him as to calm myself. Under his fury at the sentiment behind the words was the tiniest measure of shock that what I'd said upon leaving the summit—and all the times I'd said I had to be better because I was the only one in the room like me—was true. I didn't hold it against him.

But I did feel horribly vindicated that the feeling hadn't been all in my head.

Opposite the elves, the djinn were wisely keeping their mouths shut. Calculating glances flicked between all four of them and then to me, my hand on Troy's shoulder, and the frightened elves.

Poppy cleared her throat and squeezed shaking hands together on the table. "I'm sorry, my queen."

"Don't be sorry," I said. "I can't do shit with sorry. Do better next time. Better still, avail yourself of the archives while you're in town and educate yourself so there won't be a next time."

"Yes, my queen," Poppy said in an even smaller voice.

"Fine." I turned to the djinn. "What do y'all have to say for yourselves?"

The two new djinn looked to Duke and Iaret. Iaret's lips thinned as she pressed them together, but she nodded, her fiery opaline gaze seeming to spark.

Duke rose slowly. "As one of your advisors, I accept this solution has merit. On a trial basis, at least. The djinn have spent millennia on the ethereal plane, prevented from coming to this one in any great numbers due to the Atlantis Accords. Opportunities have dwindled, and the Djinn Council will likely welcome the new ones offered here." He paused and smiled to show sharp black teeth. "*If*, of course, any new djinni House royal was permitted a retinue befitting their station."

"Of course," I said. "Equal to the number of elves sworn to the House and present in the House's territory. I did say equality and balance, didn't I?"

Duke looked at Troy. "And you?"

"Djinn retinues equal to the number of elves," he confirmed. "As long as they're all equally as willing to pitch in with supporting the defense of the Triangle. Because if the vampires are bringing their wars here and the mundanes are attacking my queen's home, someone else will attack the territory sooner or later."

Iaret grinned, like she'd caught us in something. "There's the trick."

I grinned right back, both of us probably looking mad as Cheshire Cats, but it was how the djinn did business. "No catch. You live here, you have the same opportunities as everyone else, but you carry equal responsibility. That's what *community* is, even if all of Otherside has apparently forgotten. We're not just accumulating power in the face of the world changing or ending. We're building a community. People who can rely on each other, no matter what happens, and especially if the worst happens."

Keeya looked down at the table, frowning thoughtfully. Poppy still hadn't raised her eyes, and the other elves looked almost as subdued.

Duke crossed his arms. "Iaret and I remain your personal advisors. On top of any further djinn presence."

"That's a given," I said. "I have Troy and Etain for daily advice. The other factions have the option to send up to two people to catch my ear in the parliament. It's only fair to have two djinn as well."

All of the djinn looked confounded. They wanted to bargain and haggle, but I wasn't holding anything back or picking sides or punishing anyone for being an asshole.

I sighed, unable to hide my annoyance. "I keep saying this. Everything doesn't have to be so fucking difficult. It really does not. Let. This shit. Go." I pointed at the elves then the djinn. "Y'all will live for a good two hundred years or more, if you manage to stop killing each other. Y'all could be ageless as long as you don't piss me or the celestials off. What is the problem with taking *one* fucking year to try something new that gains all of us more? Not just more power. More peace. More hope. More children, maybe. Goddess knows we have to do something about the population decline in Otherside, and it can't just be relocating people here from elsewhere."

That last set everyone's back up.

"Elemental children," Aakesh said with a sneer.

Troy's temper snapped, and I let my hand slip from his shoulder as he rose to loom over Aakesh.

"Yes, elemental children." Troy's voice was cold with fury. "Like mine will be. If the only living elven king can be overjoyed at the prospect of having elemental children *because they would be mine*, and doubly so because they'd be sired on a woman of *my* choosing, then the rest of you can see what a fucking gift *both* factions are being handed and stop getting in the way."

I had to blink fast to stop the sudden tears and swallow hard to clear the lump in my throat. He could have reiterated the point about needing elementals if the gods took magic back. But he'd made it personal.

We'd never really talked about kids. Not beyond the abstract concept of heirs, which made it feel like another burden, even if I'd started thinking it might be one I might want. This whole negotiation had escalated very quickly into a realm I hadn't deeply considered before.

But Troy had.

He'd already thought through the fact that any kids we might have would be elementals, strong ones even if probably not primordials like me.

But he still wanted them. Wanted a family. With me.

Us. As parents. It was mind-boggling, beyond the implications for succession and the continuation of my House.

I had a lot to think about.

For now, I wrenched my brain back on track while everyone was busy arguing among themselves and between factions.

Troy was still standing, scowling at the room at large as Zanna set another round of drinks on the table, her eyes wider than usual. When she'd swapped empty mugs and glasses for full with swift efficiency and a touch of fae illusion to keep from being noticed, she disappeared behind the bar again. Probably taking notes to report back to Rí, not that I minded.

A light tap in the bond brought my attention back to Troy.

I'm sorry, he sent. *I should have spoken to you first.*

I...I'll be honest, I don't know how to feel. But it means a lot that you made that argument.

He forgot himself enough to look at me then, and for an eyeblink, his heart was in his face. All of it—the depth of what he felt for me, even as he freed a little ray of hope and deep want he'd been trying to hide.

Oh, Troy. We'll talk later, okay?

Okay, cariñamí.

Keeya and Aakesh were both looking at us rather than at their arguing factions when I returned my attention to the table. Aakesh's expression hardened even as something shifted in Keeya's.

Keeya rose. "Enough."

Nobody listened.

Slamming her hands on the table, she raised her voice to a shout. "Enough!"

The elves subsided first, both the Richmond and the Charleston reps. Keeya wasn't as strong magically as Troy or Allegra or even Iago, but she was the strongest of our guests. I was surprised Sonia had let her come, given the current risk to the Richmond Conclave. But maybe there were politics there I was unaware of.

She turned to me. "My queen, may I speak on this?"

"Be my guest." I sat and sipped the sparkling water with lemon Zanna had left for me when she cleared the mead we'd started with.

"Facts first."

"Facts and truths are always welcome." If sometimes regretted.

With a tight smile, Keeya said, "We're arguing about an event none of the elves here, or our grandmothers or their grandmothers, were alive to see. Now the Old Ones are walking again. First the hunters. Now the tricksters." She looked at everyone around the table. "Whatever it is they claim as their due, we don't know, and we might not have it." She paused, considering. "We also have the former royals of House Ead colluding with mundanes, with a federal agency who seeks to be like a Darkwatch pointed at *us*. All of us. Lastly, we have human terrorists attacking the nests and homes of the strongest of us. Does that cover it?"

I thought for a minute. "The parts relevant for our current conversation."

"Then the offer made is territory, titles, incomes, properties, and influence in exchange for allying directly with the djinn, as we once did, and in exchange for offering support, we would ourselves be able to call upon support from this local alliance. Also correct?"

I nodded, wondering where she was going with this. "Correct, as Arbiter."

Troy said, "And as King of House Solari."

Keeya looked at the table, studying it so hard she might burn a hole in it. "Okay. In that case...what the fuck are we all fighting over?"

Chapter 34

Aakesh scoffed. "It can't be that fucking easy."

"It *can*," Keeya shot back. She pointed at me. "She is *making* it that easy. But we're fighting ourselves and each other because we can't find the loophole or the trap. What if there just isn't one?"

I kept quiet, willing to let her talk herself into this.

Keeya looked around the table. "She isn't worrying about saving face. She didn't try to save face at the first summit either. I was there when Gerard tried the play Onora ordered of him. That whole mess should have ended in blood and fire and death. It would have under Keithia. Or under Onora. Hell, she tried dragging it there."

I held my breath. Was someone finally getting it?

"I want this new future," Keeya said. "I talked to her people at the summit. I thought this new elemental queen was full of shit. A liar and a murderous betrayer, like we were taught all elementals are. And all the other queens are liars, so why not her too, twice over?"

A few of the Charleston elves gasped. Some looked at me, and I gave them a blank look back. I wouldn't give them my pain at hearing what was said about elementals. I even walled up the bond to keep it from Troy so we could both focus.

Keeya glared at the Charleston and Richmond elves even as the djinn smirked. "What? You all know it's true. I'm tired of it. I want out. Queen Esi gave me leave to explore my options while I was here, rather than have a House Captain with shaky loyalties." Keeya's chin went up as she turned back to me. "I want *this*. This future. This *opportunity*. Even if it means partnership with the djinn. And acknowledging an elemental as High Queen, not just as Arbiter."

I was feeling too conflicted to summon a response, so I glanced at Troy. *It's your call.*

Troy leaned forward on the table. "You'd take the offer. Right now."

"Yes."

"All of it. Not just ignoring the elementals in the territory but actively supporting and sheltering them."

Her expression firmed. "Yes. I was as ready as anyone to believe the stories about Atlantis. Your queen made me start asking questions. We all know there are low-level wildlings scattered in the backwoods and small towns across the country. So why haven't we seen any of them? Why haven't they attacked? We've been so busy with infighting they could have taken any damn House at any time. Your people said Queen Arden only took down the Chapel Hill Conclave *after* they kidnapped her then stole and tortured her legally claimed consort. *Multiple* of your people, all with slightly different details but the same common threads. Common enough that they feel like truth rather than practiced lies. That *feeling* is more than I've gotten from any of our queens. Ever."

I choked down bitterness at hearing, once again, that the elves didn't consider elementals as people until they met one. At the burden added to my shoulders by being the character in all these elves' personal stories where they met an elemental and had an awakening to our personhood.

But I was getting what I wanted, wasn't I? I should be happy about that.

Should, should, should. With the cost being the constant weight of perfection and exceptionalism. One day, I was going to crack. I knew it.

But today could not be that day, nor tomorrow, nor anytime soon.

Aakesh idly shifted his fingernails to long black talons, tapping one on the table. "You should have told us the Houses were in such disarray, Duke."

"Oh, enough," Duke said. "The Accords hold all of us, so don't act like you would have done anything if you had known."

"They didn't hold her mother," Yoshi said slyly.

Iaret rolled her eyes. "Don't be jealous that you're not as good at finding loopholes."

Aakesh frowned. "You side with them?"

"I side with common sense," Iaret said. "Duke raised the Arbiter. She freed me from an elven soul-crystal prison. With *his* help."

Troy returned the nod of acknowledgment she tilted toward him.

Yoshi crossed her arms and leaned back in her chair. "You're her advisor. Of course you agree."

I couldn't help my snort. "You must not be very well acquainted with Iaret. She disagrees with me all the Goddess-damned time."

Iaret beamed, as though being disagreeable was a great compliment.

Maybe it was, because Yoshi nodded. "Very well. Arbiter, I request a week to take my recommendations to my party of the Djinn Council."

"Likewise," Aakesh said.

I blinked, not having realized they were both actual Council members and not just negotiators or errand-runners.

"Three days," I countered. "For both the djinn and the elves. I need to outrun the mundanes and the gods. You have your answer in three days, or the offer is rescinded and I elevate another faction to rebalance the territory." I'd rather give the Houses to the elementals, but the situation had remained blocked every time I checked in. Literally blocked, aside from today's message. My call wouldn't go through to anyone, not even Val, Laurel, or Sofia.

Whatever was going on, I was effectively shut out.

Theo, from House Quet, hissed between his teeth. "The Charleston queens won't like that."

I shrugged, trying to pretend I didn't give a shit. "Then I guess you better sell this to them because I already know who else I can sell it to." The Lyon elves would jump at the chance for those leadership positions they'd wanted, and it'd be nobody's business if I decided to put Allegra in charge of a House instead of someone at this table or bring Darius back from exile for it. "Now. Seems like we've said all that can be said or needs saying right now. If you plan to stay in town for the duration of the three days, my Chancellor has reserved a block of rooms at a hotel in elven territory over in Chapel Hill. You're more than welcome to avail yourselves of my hospitality, as long as you accept the risk of attention from the Bureau for Supernatural Investigation."

"Understood. We'll accept," Keeya said. "If there's an extra room, we brought Gerard and his family with us."

I nodded, relieved that at least that promise could be kept. "That can definitely be arranged."

"We'll stay too," Poppy said. "We were planning to turn around and drive home tonight, but if we can get at least a few hours of rest first, that's our preference."

"Great. Troy, would you see to it, please?"

"Of course, my queen," he said.

"Then that's everything. Good night, everyone." I leaned over and kissed Troy's cheek as I rose, both to ground myself in the scent of him and to show him I really wasn't upset with anything he'd said. Bonus points that any public show of affection toward him confounded every other visiting elf in the room.

The djinn shimmered and changed planes without a word, even Duke and Iaret, leaving only the scent of lemon zest and half-empty glasses behind.

Keeya lingered as the other two Richmond elves leaned to speak to Troy and get their lodging arrangements. "My queen? May I have a word in private?"

A word in private was the last fucking thing I wanted just now, but I had to get this done. "Certainly. This way."

I squeezed Troy's arm and led Keeya to the back as he responded with a reassuring curl of affection in the bond.

She handed two knives and a gun to Haroun without having to be asked and submitted to a pat-down without protest, which earned her some points despite her earlier comments.

"Thanks, Haroun," I said. "No interruptions unless it's Troy, please."

"Yes, my queen."

I hoped he was only upgrading from the usual "ma'am" to "my queen" to make a point to our guests. It got awkward after a while.

Ushering Keeya in, I shut the door and took my seat before gesturing for her to take one of those opposite. "What can I do for you, Keeya?"

She sat. Fidgeted. "I— My queen, I'm afraid I said something to insult you earlier. I'm not sure what. But I wanted to apologize."

That surprised me enough that I blinked a few times before I could stop myself. I was half tempted to drag it out for her, but that was petty revenge for my hurt feelings. Harqil's words about revenge being my downfall echoed through my head as I composed a response.

"You did, to be honest," I said. "Not just me but all elementals, in needing to meet me before being willing to consider our personhood to be as legitimate as yours and my intentions to be as honest as yours."

"Oh." She grimaced. "I didn't see it that way. You're just so..." She shrugged, clearly uncomfortable and at a loss for words.

I sighed at the further microaggression.

Again, I didn't want to help her out. But I had to make this territory shift work. "Look. It's a trope, you know? Sheltered, ignorant, or propagandized person meets demonized minority, discovers that minority's personhood and that they're 'just like us,' has change of heart. Person becomes the hero in their own story and community, a paragon of goodness as they take the story back to other folks like them."

This time Keeya's face fell, and she crossed her arms and legs. "Oh, Goddess. Oh, I'm so sorry. I didn't— I really—"

I held up a hand as I thumbed the onyx-and-gold ring on my right middle finger, willing it to show me a way out of this before I died of awkwardness by proximity.

Trust her, it seemed to whisper.

Annoyed, I decided to listen to it. "I get it. I really do. Here's the thing: while it's tiresome, there's an opportunity to do better."

She stared at me with rapt, dark eyes.

"Don't just stop at taking the word back to your people and patting yourself on the back for your enlightened views. *Do something.* You say you'd accept this deal. What would you do for the elementals in my demesnes?"

"I'd—" Her mouth snapped shut, and she frowned. Then in a shaky voice, she said, "I—I'm sorry, my queen. I honestly couldn't say. Because I've just realized I don't know what elementals need. I mean, an end to bounty hunts, of course. But I guess I've just realized I don't really know anything about...y'all."

Despite my earlier hurt, that did a measure to reassure me. "I appreciate that answer."

Her frown deepened. "You do? You won't—won't punish me for it?"

I shook my head. "That answer was honest and thoughtful. It focused on *us*, elementals, and what we might need rather than your embarrassment or status. *That's* what I demand in my territory. That's how we build community. Thinking of others. Not ourselves. Not that we're losing face or power by doing better for those around us and asking what *they* need, rather than assuming we can save them by knowing what's best."

Keeya looked down at her lap. "I feel like you shouldn't have had to tell me all that."

"Nope. I shouldn't have. But frankly, it's not the first time, and it won't be the last."

She nodded, still avoiding my eyes. "I'm sorry. I'll do better."

"That's all I ask."

Keeya nodded again, still looking solemn and a little down.

With an effort, I held in a sigh. This could have been a much harder conversation, which gave me the insight that I wasn't bad at diplomacy. I navigated diplomatic situations every day of my life surviving as an elemental in Otherside. I was unfamiliar with politics and the rules of those already in power, which was only on me to the extent that I'd run away from learning them for a year. That was a thing I could learn, but it didn't mean I was bad at diplomacy. It was time to shake that off and recognize the skills I already had.

Awkward silence stretched until I asked, "Anything else, Keeya?"

"No, my queen. I'll discuss your offer with Richmond and let you know our answer."

"Good luck."

She excused herself and left.

Haroun caught the door and stuck his head in. "Somebody named Harqil here to see you. Can't place the faction."

My stomach dropped. "Send them in."

The celestial slipped into the room and gave Haroun a playful smile before the door shut. "Good, no Cyrus or djinn this time. Gotta say, you have such pretty bodyguards."

"If you ask them nicely, maybe they'll agree to a little dalliance." I had a suspicion Haroun was sleeping with Etain, but I didn't know if it was happening, official, open, or anything else, nor did I consider it my business.

Harqil cocked an eyebrow at me. "You'd allow it?"

I shrugged. "What my people do in their off hours is none of my business as long as they don't bring harm to me, my House, or my demesne." I fixed them with a steady look. "Do you mean to bring us harm, Harqil?"

"Would you believe me if I said I was on your side?"

"Depends what you mean by that and what you're here for. Especially after your last appearance with Cyrus." I gestured to the chair opposite me across the desk. "Drink?"

"That'd be lovely, actually. Mead, if you have it."

I used the desk phone to ring to the front and asked Sarah, who'd just come on for the night shift, to bring back two glasses of mead and a small snack platter. I didn't know what this visit was about, and if there were deals to be made, we'd need the ritual of salt and booze.

While we waited, I figured I'd get ahead of things. "That's a good trick. The gem."

Harqil's look switched from boredom to mischief. "Have you figured it out then?"

"Magic. The trickster's gift was magic."

"You see? I knew you were clever enough to get it."

A quick knock on the door was Sarah with our food and drink.

"Thanks, Sarah," I said. "Need me for anything?"

"No, ma'am."

"Good. If Harqil here visits in future, they're to be treated as an honored guest, please."

Sarah's gaze swept the celestial as though she was doing her best to memorize them. Then she nodded. "Got it. Welcome in."

Harqil toasted her then me as the door closed behind her. "Refreshing to deal with someone who shows proper respect."

I snorted. "You might be one of the few people who thinks that. And I'm not always this friendly," I said. "But given everything going on, I'd like to try and avoid letting things go as far as they did at the Wild Hunt."

"Excellent. Then you won't mind doing me a favor in exchange for the clue?"

"I don't suppose I have much of a choice."

Harqil snagged a pickle and wrapped a slice of ham around it, popping the whole into their mouth. "No. I mean you do, but like I said, I'm on your side. That means I'll advise you don't try finding out what would happen if you decline."

That grated. I hated feeling like I didn't have a choice. But realistically, until and unless I became a celestial myself, I had to play their games—or try thrashing them like I had Callista and then the gods of the hunt.

Nope. Didn't have the time or resources for it just now.

"Let's hear the favor then," I said.

They smiled. "I need you to tell me what Cyrus is after."

I stiffened.

"Already that far under his influence? That might be problematic," Harqil said.

"It's not that," I snapped. "If anything, I'm one of the few people who can resist him."

"Ah. Good. You are aware that he's positively magnetic."

"I was, yes, but he told us as much."

That caught them off guard. "He did?"

"Yes. And shortly thereafter, he told us what he wanted. But Harqil, you haven't told me what *you* want."

"A little of this, a little of that. But if it's not Cyrus's passive magic that has you alarmed, what is it?"

I weighed how much I wanted to answer this question with how much I wanted answers of my own. "He's effectively my father-in-law."

"And you don't want to cross that delicious son of his."

Jealousy sparked hot, and I smashed the hormonal reaction down. "Quit toying with me, Harqil. You might be a celestial, but so was Callista."

"Is that a threat?"

"Simply a reminder." I was too tired for this after the high-tension meeting earlier. I needed my woods. Fresh air. Trees. The river. "I don't need more enemies. Or more secrets. It's obvious you and Cyrus and the djinn have some kind of history."

Harqil nodded and made a little sandwich from two crackers, two cubes of cheese, and two slices of pastrami, shoving the whole of it into their mouth. "This is a lovely little spread. My compliments to your bartender."

"I'll let her know. But Harqil, between the djinn and the elves and the dreams—"

"Dreams? You've had more?"

I shuddered.

Their attention sharpened, and all joviality dropped. "Tell me."

Unlike before, I didn't get stomach cramps at the idea of telling them. "Why does it feel okay to tell you or Cyrus but not Duke?"

I'd thought their attention was sharp before. Now it was absolutely cutting.

"Tell. Me. And I'll count it as the favor. What did you dream, Arden?"

Chapter 35

I wanted to hold back simply out of principle. I'd survived this long by keeping my secrets. But telling Duke would have repercussions I couldn't see, and I didn't want to get any more entangled with Cyrus than I already was, if it could be helped. From my research, tricksters didn't really lie, per se. They bent the truth. Harqil had said outright they were on my side. That had to count for something.

"A wasteland," I said. "Except where I walked. Everything was normal again. And—"

Harqil leaned forward as I snapped my mouth shut.

"What else, Arden?" they said. "It would be the most delightful trick if you saw something you weren't supposed to."

"I wouldn't say I saw it so much as spoke it."

This time, it was them who froze. "Go on."

I shrugged, uncomfortable and suddenly terribly uncertain. "Apparently, I was talking in my sleep. Troy says it was something like, 'Comes and goes, goes and comes. That which is given, is taken and riven. Fire goes out, crow goes home. All that's left is dust and bone.' And that it was in a voice that wasn't quite mine."

All of whatever passed for blood drained from Harqil's face. "Oh, now that is a terrible, terrible trick, Arden. I might actually be in your debt now. Damn you for saying so much."

My heart stopped. "What? What does that mean?"

"It means that one of the tricksters has been very naughty or that we aren't the only ones interested in you and someone else is being very naughty."

Dizziness hit me, and my heart started racing.

Arden? What's wrong? Troy sent.

Harqil's here. I'm getting answers. And I don't think I like them.

Resolve came through the bond.

No, I sent. *I'll handle this.*

"Good choice," Harqil said.

"Mind your business," I snapped. How the fuck could they hear telepathy between me and my bondmate?

"Hard not to hear when you're projecting that loudly. Might want to do something about that before someone else picks up on it. Now. Ask me something else. I hate owing favors."

The fuck did they mean someone else could pick up on it? I wanted to ask about that. But I'd just spoken to Keeya about the importance of community, and there was a bigger issue that affected all of us. "May I ask something further about the gem?"

They smiled slyly. "By all means."

"First, I noticed it doesn't take my magic."

"Funny how that works, hey? But that wasn't a question."

"How long do we have until the tricksters want their gift back? And what were we supposed to have paid for it?"

Harqil made another sandwich with two of everything. "That's two questions. Pick one."

I thought fast. Time was relative on the gods' plane. The one time I'd been foolish enough to go, three days had passed in what felt like an hour. "The price."

"Balance. You—Otherside—were meant to keep balance with the mundanes. Both between yourselves and them and between all of you and the Earth. It was all going well enough, until the elves got greedy and the djinn abdicated their responsibilities to balance them in favor of warring with them. Then the fae retreated to the Summerlands, and some of the weres started following the colonizing humans in their destructive patterns. So many carefully constructed checks and balances ruined. Artemis's fuckup with Orion set back their initial plans to rebalance it, and you quashed the next attempt. So now, it's our turn."

I scrubbed my hands over my face. Balance. And the elves and the djinn. Again. Apparently, we needed this new House system—and the elementals—more than ever.

Another lightning bolt of thought hit me. "That's why I'm the only one whose magic it doesn't affect. It's meant to be a reminder. When the djinn and the elves stopped making babies—"

"No more trueborn elementals." Harqil was solemn for once.

"Which meant stewardship of the Earth declined, and since humans were always more numerous, the balance just kept tipping in the wrong direction on multiple axes. Then when the fae left and the djinn were cast out, the magical balance tipped as well, as magic left this plane."

"I'm proud of you, Arden. We might actually come through this. Might." Their eyes twinkled. "The bar out front smelled like djinn and elves and a bouquet of emotions. You have your work cut out for you."

"Let me guess. If we break the Détente and openly attack humans—"

"I strongly advise against that." They swirled their mead then took a deep drink. "The gods might be more distant than they used to be, but they're still fond of their creations. All of them. You in particular need to remember what I said about revenge. On that note, I should go before Anansi or somebody notices I'm gone. Thanks for the refreshments."

Before I could say anything else, Harqil was up and out of the room.

I darted around the desk to follow, but the back door was already slamming shut by the time I made it to the hall.

Haroun was looking after them, wide-eyed. "I've never seen anyone move that fast."

"Perks of being a celestial messenger, I guess." I frowned, wondering if that was Harqil showing off for Haroun's benefit. Usually, they simply changed planes and interrupted whatever I was doing.

"Celestial messenger? Was the news good?" Haroun asked. When I didn't answer, he winced. "Oh. Well then. Do I need to call Etain?"

"Isn't she off tonight?"

He gave me the long-suffering look of boyfriends everywhere. "Ma'am, I don't even want to imagine what she'd do to me if I didn't tell her something was going on involving a celestial messenger, off day or not."

I winced. "I want her to rest. But I won't punish you if you happened to mention it in, let's say, a personal capacity."

Haroun blushed. "You know?"

"Pretty sure everyone has at least assumed."

"We tried to keep it professional."

"Don't worry. You have. But y'all are inseparable in the same way me and Troy are." I shrugged. "Harqil will be disappointed, but it's not my business what people do on their own time as long as everyone does their jobs and treats everyone else equitably and professionally, got it? And yes, that includes going to Raleigh and spending time at Claret or Nightshade."

He blushed an even deeper red, difficult as it was with his tawny skin. "Understood. Thank you, ma'am."

"Don't thank me. Just don't be a dick. I'ma go find Troy."

Haroun was already reaching for his phone when I pushed through to the main bar, heading to Sarah first.

"Go on and reopen," I said. "Assuming anyone has stopped by or does later. We gave out tokens earlier."

"Got it," she said. "Thanks, boss. Anything I need to know for this shift?"

I filled her in, high-level, knowing she'd text Janae as soon as I was back in my office. I needed to send a text to the group, but I'd get to it.

My phone buzzed. I pulled it out and looked at it, finding Troy two steps ahead of me with a quick note to the group chat including all the faction heads that made up the alliance parliament. I looked up to find him leaning against one of the now-separated tables, watching me with the small smile that said he knew he'd anticipated me.

"Thanks," I said when I reached him. The bar was empty except for Sarah, and I didn't care what she saw. I pressed myself against Troy and kissed him. "One less thing to do. Etain's on her way in, I think. I need to update you both on what Harqil just told me."

Neither of them were happy when I did.

Troy was positively thunderous. "What do they mean, 'someone else is interested'? A trickster other than Harqil and their patron? Or another group of gods entirely?"

I shrugged. "They left before I could get an answer."

Etain's grey eyes were hard as pewter. "I don't even know how to begin planning to defend against the gods."

"Don't worry about it," Troy said before I could. "Keep your focus on the mundanes. I want intimate details on each of the Sons of Seth. Things their mothers don't even know. Arden tentatively tied them to the Bureau for Supernatural Investigation. I want *everything* we might use for offense or defense. Anything we could use to make an assassination look like an accident or self-motivated."

"Yes, sir. They were completing the first round of interrogation on the last of them when I called it a day a few hours ago."

"Good." Troy scrubbed his hands over his face, clearing his grim fury to his usual flat neutrality. "Go home and get some rest. We all need to catch some when we can. Take Haroun with you. I doubt anybody will make a second attack so soon after so many people disappeared in the last attempt."

"Thank you, sir. Ma'am. Good night." Etain rose and left.

Troy and I sat in a companionably exhausted silence, slumped in our chairs.

"I'm driving," he said. "You have the peaky feeling you get when you're in the mood to run stop signs."

"That happened *once*," I said. "And it's perfectly acceptable to take the damn things as *suggestions* when we both know there's nobody else coming. Ishtar save me, it's not like *you* stop for them, not at this time of night."

He grinned and held out a hand. "First time is rarely the last for anything. Keys."

"I really hope that's not a prophecy," I grumbled as I dug in my purse and handed them over.

"Don't worry. I'll leave the prophesying to you, cariñamí. Nobody's coming for us tonight. The humans are scared by lack of contact from the people they sent against you. The djinn and elves have jobs to do and power to grab. The vampires are busy with their territory squabbles to the south. And everybody else either loves you or has enough sense not to try you."

"They better not."

On the way home, I filled him in on my conversation with Keeya.

"She's angling for queen," he said as we pulled up to the house. "Has to be."

"Obviously. I just wish I liked her better."

"Since when have you had to like someone to let them do their job?"

"Fair. I'm annoyed. But that's still fair."

He slung an arm over my shoulder as we climbed the porch steps together. The first spring frogs were calling from the wetter land closer to the river, and the smell of green things waking was dramatically stronger—especially from the specific directions where I'd decomposed multiple humans into dust.

Troy's momentum kept me moving when my body tried to lock at the memory of last night's magic.

"Don't think about that." His voice sank lower into soothing, modulated tones. "You remember what I said about it being hot when you defend yourself?"

That startled me enough to switch the track my brain was trying to run down. "Yes…"

"You've been doing a lot of defending the last twenty hours or so."

Brain was definitely on a different track now, helped along by a subtle push of Troy's passive magic, the promise in his touch, and the combination of determination and arousal I was getting from the bond. Amusement joined all that as I tripped over my own feet in my distraction, like they were the block of Air I no longer left in front of my door.

He was plotting. Something that would have me begging before dawn and sleep—or I—came.

My heart sped up, and I dropped the walls in the bond entirely. I wanted this. Needed it. And I wanted him to know because I didn't want to spend the next few hours feeling guilty for doing what I'd had to do to protect myself, my love, and my land. I didn't want to think about Cyrus's commitment to toppling the elven matriarchy or Harqil's worries or what I was going to have to do to bring Asheville and the Outer Banks solidly under my control, or what answer the elves and the djinn would have for me about my proposal to build new Houses.

I wanted the love of my life to make me forget my own name in the throes of passion.

Troy caught the edge of that thought and chuckled as he unlocked the door, the richly satisfied sound sending chills over me. He'd said recently that seducing me was a hunt that never ended, so the pure delight snaking through the bond didn't surprise me in the least. Even if it wasn't the first time I'd felt it from him, it still lit desire in me.

We'd barely gotten inside before he tossed my keys over the half wall to the dining table and whirled me to press me against the wall, pausing just long enough in his seduction to turn off the security alarm. Then he claimed me with a kiss.

When he pulled away, I traced a finger along his bottom lip. "Are we gonna talk about earlier?"

He knew exactly what I was referring to. "Not tonight. I want to. We need to. *I* need to. Having kids is more than just getting heirs for me. But between last night's attack and today's negotiations, my brain is shot."

"Just your brain?"

Heat flashed through the bond. "Yes. My stamina is fine. Which means every time I catch your mind wandering away from what we're doing, it's a punishment."

My sound of protest was cut off by the combination of his tongue dipping into my mouth and his hand tightening around my throat before dragging down my body to unbutton my jeans.

"Test me, Arden. I dare you. I love to hear you beg."

I played along. When my mind did inevitably try to shift to one of the many pieces of unfinished business, Troy followed through on his threat.

I let him. Over and over again, until I forgot everything except him.

Because amidst the clutter of my titles and responsibilities and goals, there was a truth when I was stripped down to the bare essentials of my soul: none of it really mattered. Certainly not in this moment. All my burdens, all the weight of perfection and excellence could be laid down for a time.

Right here, right now, with him.

One day, I'd learn to do that on my own. For now, I could accept his help and the pleasure that came with it.

If the gods were walking yet again, they knew better than anyone how much I'd be glad of this respite later.

So I'd take it. Lose myself in Troy as he lost himself in me. Leave the past where it lay and the future where it waited for a few blessed hours, to stand in the present and add another memory of what the hell I was fighting for.

Acknowledgments

For various reasons, this book was a little more self-indulgent than most. If you enjoyed it, you get the first thank you for coming along for the ride.

Editor Jeni Chappelle gets an enormous thank you for striking the perfect balance between encouragement, tough love, and expert advice. 2022 has been a difficult year in terms of writing and publishing, and when I found myself questioning the journey, Jeni reminded me of my true north in all of this.

My beta readers Stephanie and Callan continue to provide the early perspectives necessary to wrangle a book and a series with this many plot threads and this much worldbuilding. Never underestimate the value of early readers who can read critically while remaining engaged!

As ever, I'm grateful for the support of family and friends who want to see me succeed, and the Patreon subscribers who continue to support an indie author in these wild times.

All of y'all make all of this possible.

Also by Whitney Hill

The Shadows of Otherside series
Elemental
Eldritch Sparks
Ethereal Secrets
Ebon Rebellion
Eternal Huntress
Tempered Illusions
Talion Rule

The Otherside Heat series
Secrets and Truths
Curses and Faith
Menace and Memory

The Flesh and Blood series (as Remy Harmon)
Bluebloods

About the Author

Whitney Hill is an author and speaker. The bestselling first book in her Shadows of Otherside series, Elemental, was the grand prize winner of the 8th Annual Writer's Digest Self-Published E-Book Awards and a Finalist in the Next Generation Indie Book Awards. Her second book, Eldritch Sparks, was named one of the Top 100 Indie Books of 2021 by Kirkus Reviews.

When she's not writing, Whitney enjoys hiking in North Carolina's beautiful state parks and playing video games.

Learn more or get in touch: whitneyhillwrites.com
Get email updates: whwrites.com/newsletter
Read bonus content on Patreon: whwrites.com/patreon
Twitter: twitter.com/write_wherever
Instagram: instagram.com/write_wherever

www.ingramcontent.com/pod-product-compliance
Lightning Source LLC
Chambersburg PA
CBHW021212310726
48971CB00006B/1541